CHERYL HOLT

USA Today Bestselling Author

DREAMS of DESIRE

A Novel
of Sensual
Destiny

B
BERKLEY
SENSATION

$7.99 U.S.
$9.99 CAN

ISBN 978-0-425-23918-6

5 0 7 9 9

Berkley Sensation Titles by Cheryl Holt

PROMISE OF PLEASURE
TASTE OF TEMPTATION
DREAMS OF DESIRE

Dreams of Desire

CHERYL HOLT

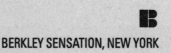

BERKLEY SENSATION, NEW YORK

THE BERKLEY PUBLISHING GROUP
Published by the Penguin Group
Penguin Group (USA) Inc.
375 Hudson Street, New York, New York 10014, USA

Penguin Group (Canada), 90 Eglinton Avenue East, Suite 700, Toronto, Ontario M4P 2Y3, Canada
(a division of Pearson Penguin Canada Inc.)
Penguin Books Ltd., 80 Strand, London WC2R 0RL, England
Penguin Group Ireland, 25 St. Stephen's Green, Dublin 2, Ireland (a division of Penguin Books Ltd.)
Penguin Group (Australia), 250 Camberwell Road, Camberwell, Victoria 3124, Australia
(a division of Pearson Australia Group Pty. Ltd.)
Penguin Books India Pvt. Ltd., 11 Community Centre, Panchsheel Park, New Delhi—110 017, India
Penguin Group (NZ), 67 Apollo Drive, Rosedale, North Shore 0632, New Zealand
(a division of Pearson New Zealand Ltd.)
Penguin Books (South Africa) (Pty.) Ltd., 24 Sturdee Avenue, Rosebank, Johannesburg 2196,
South Africa

Penguin Books Ltd., Registered Offices: 80 Strand, London WC2R 0RL, England

This is a work of fiction. Names, characters, places, and incidents either are the product of the author's imagination or are used fictitiously, and any resemblance to actual persons, living or dead, business establishments, events, or locales is entirely coincidental. The publisher does not have any control over and does not assume any responsibility for author or third-party websites or their content.

DREAMS OF DESIRE

A Berkley Sensation Book / published by arrangement with the author

PRINTING HISTORY
Berkley Sensation mass-market edition / December 2010

Copyright © 2010 by Cheryl Holt.
Cover art by Phil Heffernan.
Cover design by George Long.
Cover hand lettering by Ron Zinn.
Interior text design by Kristin del Rosario.

ISBN: 978-0-425-23918-6

BERKLEY® SENSATION
Berkley Sensation Books are published by The Berkley Publishing Group,
a division of Penguin Group (USA) Inc.,
375 Hudson Street, New York, New York 10014.
BERKLEY® SENSATION and the "B" design are trademarks of Penguin Group (USA) Inc.

PRINTED IN THE UNITED STATES OF AMERICA

10 9 8 7 6 5 4 3 2 1

Dreams of Desire

Chapter 1

"I might deign to hire you, Miss Lambert."

"I hope you will, Lord Penworth."

"But you would be expected to exhibit the utmost decorum at all times."

"Oh, absolutely. I wouldn't have it any other way."

Lily Lambert sat in her chair, staring across the massive oak desk at the arrogant, officious aristocrat John Middleton, Earl of Penworth.

He was extremely handsome, with dark hair and piercing blue eyes, broad shoulders, and excessive height. But good looks couldn't mask the fact that he was an overbearing boor.

She'd been eager to serve as companion to his two wards and his fiancée, but now, she wasn't so sure.

When she'd agreed to come for the interview, Mrs. Ford—owner of the Ford Employment Agency—had warned her that Penworth could be fussy and domineering, but no amount of notice could have prepared Lily for how unpleasant he truly was.

She'd been in his presence for all of five minutes, and he'd done nothing but chastise and complain. What an onerous boss he would be! He didn't appear to like servants very much. Or females. Perhaps it was simply *female* servants whom he detested.

She kept her expression blank, not by so much as the quiver of a brow providing any evidence of her own level of aversion to his rank and status.

For the prior decade, she'd been nanny, governess, and companion to the spoiled offspring of nobles just like him, and she'd endured plenty of nonsense. Because of her dismal history, her opinion of him was very low—even though she scarcely knew him.

She wondered if he was the sort to seduce his maids, but she thought he wouldn't be. He was too conceited, too set on being marvelous. He'd never stoop to fraternization.

"I'm a hard taskmaster," he said, intoning it like a threat.

"And I'm a dedicated worker."

"If I issue orders, they must be instantly obeyed."

"I would be yours to command."

"I'll brook no sloth or insubordination."

"I wouldn't dream of idleness or rebellion."

He snorted at that. "I won't have you down in the kitchen, criticizing me over your supper—a supper I have supplied in my own house."

"I am loyalty personified."

"I demand fidelity and constancy."

"I'm constant as the day is long."

"But are you devoted? Can you be trusted?"

"Of course I can be trusted."

He meticulously studied her, as if she was an agitator bent on causing trouble. Then he held up the thick file Mrs. Ford had sent. It was filled with glowing letters of recommendation, but all of them were forged. Lily had written them herself.

She was petite and pretty, and she had labored in grand mansions occupied by top-lofty husbands who were used to taking whatever they wanted, so she'd fended off many advances. With mischief exposed, the wife of the miscreant was never inclined to be rational.

Lily had been fired—through no fault of her own—more times than she could count, and she refused to starve merely because an oblivious noblewoman couldn't make her spouse behave.

Being all alone in the world, Lily had no family to lean on for support, so she had to do what was necessary to get by. If financial security meant drafting a few fake letters, so be it, and the positive reports weren't really false.

She *was* a dedicated worker. She *was* reliable and steady. She *was* kind and courteous, so she suffered no qualms about furthering her claims of proficiency, and she'd never been caught out.

In her experience, the person hiring was always in a hurry, needing someone to start immediately, so references were never checked. Lily acted competent, thrifty, and educated, so people were easily convinced that she was precisely who—and what—she said she was.

"You have an impressive resumé," Penworth remarked.

"I try."

"Yet I must admit that I'm wary."

"Of what?" she snapped before she could stop herself.

He'd flustered her, and her composure slipped. She hastened to shield any reaction.

"How old are you, Miss Lambert?"

"Twenty-five, milord."

"You've had numerous positions. Why so many? Are you prone to quitting? Will you pack your bags after a few weeks? Will you leave me in the lurch? I would hate to find myself trapped in Scotland with my wards unattended."

He was guardian to eighteen-year-old twins, Miss Miranda and Miss Melanie Newton. They were daughters of a friend who'd perished from fast living.

They were accompanying Penworth on his annual hunting excursion to his castle in Scotland, as was his fiancée, Lady Violet Howard. She was the same age as the twins.

Of all the dreadful situations for which Lily was remotely qualified, having to spend the autumn traipsing after a trio of rich, indolent adolescents had to be the worst available option. She viewed the coming ordeal with a nauseating resignation, but while she didn't particularly want the job, she couldn't afford to decline it.

After the disaster at her last post—what she referred to as the *incident* with her employer's husband—she was anxious to flee London for a bit. In case any gossip leaked out, she had to be far from Town so stories could fade before she returned.

Her ability to obtain work was dependent on a stellar reputation, and she was determined to hide until the storm had passed.

"Your questions are understandable, Lord Penworth, but if you look closely, you'll see that I have perfectly logical reasons for my frequent moves."

"Those being?"

"I was companion to several elderly ladies who died, so the jobs ended."

"I suppose," he allowed, as if she should have been so accursedly loyal as to have stayed on after her employer was deceased.

The man was an idiot.

"I was also governess," she said, "to various girls who went on to marry. Once they were wed, my services were no longer required."

At this news, he harrumphed as if her charges had done something shocking by marrying, and she could barely contain her exasperation.

What sort of woman was he seeking, a saint?

He opened the file and began to read, poring over every detail as she fidgeted and fumed in her seat.

Ultimately, he exhaled a heavy sigh. "Fine. You're hired."

The remark was the exact opposite of what she'd expected, and she gaped at him. "What did you say?"

"You're hired."

"Oh." She'd been so sure of rejection that acceptance was almost a letdown.

"You don't seem very excited," he mentioned.

She flashed a tight smile. "I'm positively ecstatic."

He barked out a laugh, the sound rusty, as if it didn't happen often.

"Is this you in *ecstasy*, Miss Lambert?"

She couldn't abide his condescending tone and answered more sarcastically than she should have. "Would you like me to leap up and twirl in circles?"

"I doubt my poor heart could stand the sight. A simple *thank-you* will suffice."

"Thank you."

His chin balanced on his hand, he leaned back and assessed her. She scrutinized him in return.

He was thirty, so there was only five years difference in their ages. But he was so urbane, so patronizing and sophisticated, that he seemed decades older. Wealth, station, and life experience separated them as clearly as if a line had been drawn.

His long legs were stretched out, one foot crossed over the other. Even though he slouched in his chair, he appeared to be uncomfortable, and she wondered if he ever relaxed.

"You're very interesting, Miss Lambert."

"Why do you say so?"

"I've given you a place in my household, but you're not gushing. Most females—when I take the time to personally interview them—are a tad more obsequious."

"I offered to rejoice, but you said you'd rather I didn't."

"So I did."

"Have you changed your mind? Would you like me to flatter and compliment? I certainly can, if it will make you happy."

"Don't you dare go all sycophantic on me. We're merely completing a business transaction." He tapped a pensive finger against his lips and scowled. "There's just one problem."

"What is it?"

"You're very pretty. It worries me."

On hearing the comment, she felt as if they'd stepped into a murky bog. She didn't consider it vanity when she admitted to being pretty. There was nothing wrong with her vision, and she could see her reflection in a mirror. She was blond and blue-eyed, with a heart-shaped face and pouting lips. Her high cheekbones and dimples had driven several aristocratic sons to write absurd, unwanted poetry about her.

In addition to her comely features, she was pleasingly plump, rounded in the right spots, with a bosom that was fuller than it should be, a small waist, and curvaceous hips. Her shapely figure attracted male attention that she didn't solicit or condone, and she occasionally received risqué proposals that involved her posing in the nude.

"My looks are . . . *worrying* to you?" she tentatively ventured.

"Yes, so I'm afraid I have to set some ground rules."

"Ground rules?"

"Yes."

"Such as?"

"There will be no flirting with the footmen."

"Definitely not."

"Nor can I permit drinking or cavorting. No frolicking with boys in the village. No late-night dips in the pond in your undergarments."

She was so insulted she couldn't think straight. "Anything else?"

"No gambling. I absolutely draw the line at wagering."

"I'll do my best to avoid it."

He raised an imperious brow. "Are you mocking me, Miss Lambert?"

"I wouldn't dream of it."

"Recently, we've had a rash of untoward behavior, and it's my opinion that much unpleasantness could have been averted if I'd been clearer from the start as to the conduct required."

"Your housemaids have been disruptive? They've been swimming in the pond and dallying with the footmen?"

"Not my maids. The companions I've hired for my wards."

"How many have you hired?"

"In the past year? Seven."

His cheeks flushed as she gawked at him, trying to make sense of the information. Why would so many have come and gone over such a short period? Was he just particularly bad at choosing capable people? Or was he an impossible brute?

Lily was acquainted with many of the women from Mrs. Ford's agency, and there was no more boring, humdrum group in existence. She couldn't imagine any of them instigating the type of trouble he'd described.

Suddenly, she was swamped with misgivings, and an alarm bell began to chime. "You've had *seven* companions?"

"Yes, and none of them has had the fortitude to stick it out."

"May I inquire as to why?"

"No, you may not. Suffice it to say that it was a lack of character on their parts."

"On *all* their parts?"

"Yes," he haughtily insisted. "I asked of them what I ask of myself. I maintain the highest standards of decency and decorum. I would never cause a scandal, initiate gossip, or involve myself in an immoral situation. I demand the same of my servants."

What a dreadfully dull household it must be, she mused. Then again, it had to be better than being groped in a dark hallway or having your employer's husband sneak into your bed in the middle of the night.

"I don't suppose any of this was due to mischief by your wards?"

"My wards? Why would you even suggest such a thing? Their reputations are beyond reproach."

"So . . . it was simply a scourge of amorous, flighty lady's companions?"

That imperious brow was raised again. "You doubt me?"

It would be completely impolitic to answer *yes*, so instead, she stood.

"I had said *thank you*," she told him, "but I must change my reply to *no* thank you."

"What do you mean?"

"This job sounds to be quite above my level of competency. I'm sorry, but I wouldn't be right for it."

Cursing herself for a fool, she started out. They were at his country manor, Penworth Hall, a two-day journey from the city. Mrs. Ford had loaned her coach fare to attend the interview, with the understanding that Lily would pay her back from her first month's wages.

If she walked out, how would she square the debt? And if she snubbed the earl, why would Mrs. Ford place her at another post? Lily had lost many of the positions Mrs. Ford had found for her. Why would she keep Lily on?

She'd almost made it to the door, when Penworth barked, "Miss Lambert, sit down."

"I can't. I really must—"

"Miss Lambert!" he stated more fiercely. "I haven't given you permission to leave."

"I didn't realize I needed it. I believe our appointment is concluded."

"It's not concluded until I say it is. Sit down!"

Brooking no argument, he gestured to her chair, and she vacillated, then slinked to her seat. He grinned malevolently, delighted to have his authority so blatantly demonstrated.

"You've been hired," he declared, "and you will not refuse me."

"As you wish," she tersely retorted.

"We depart for Scotland on Saturday, and I don't have time to interview anyone else."

"Lucky me."

"Your ungrateful attitude will not help matters, Miss Lambert."

"I apologize for my discourtesy," she insincerely muttered.

"Mrs. Ford assures me that you're ready to commence your duties."

"I am."

"We're sailing from London. I trust that mode of travel won't be a problem for you?"

She'd never been on a ship and had no idea how she'd weather the voyage, but when he was such an ass, she felt justified in being contrary.

"I get seasick," she lied.

"I don't care," he rudely responded. "It's a minor distance, so your discomfort will be brief."

"I'll try not to be ill in your presence."

He ignored her snide remark and continued. "I've been informed that you booked lodging at the inn in the village."

"Yes, milord."

"I will send for your bags. A chamber will be prepared for you, and you'll join us for supper so you can be introduced to the twins. Tomorrow, you'll assist them in their packing so that the three of you can become acquainted."

"I can't wait," she lied again, and she couldn't shield her distaste.

"You have a sharp tongue, Miss Lambert. I don't like it."

"Then perhaps you should reassess your decision."

"No. I enjoy getting my way, and the more you protest, the more insistent I shall be that you do as I bid you. Might I suggest that—in our future dealings—you keep that fact in mind?"

"I will."

"You may proceed to the foyer. The butler will meet you there and have a maid show you to your bedroom. We have drinks at seven and supper at eight. Be prompt and dress appropriately."

There were a thousand replies she could have made, but what was the point? He hated to be denied, and she was no better. Nothing galled her more than having an arrogant male ordering her about, which certainly had her questioning her choice of career.

She imagined thwarting him, watching until he was off the property, then running away. Would he chase her down as if she was a feudal serf? Would he call out the hounds? Would she be dragged back in chains?

He was such a conceited beast that he just might, so she'd bite the bullet and obey, but she would loathe her job—and him—every second.

Why couldn't she have had a different type of life?

Her parents had died when she was a baby, and she didn't remember them. She'd had no relatives to take her in, so she'd been shuffled among the neighbors until there was no one left.

Since she was twelve, she'd supported herself. She struggled and toiled, but she couldn't find a place where she belonged. It was her greatest dream to marry, to have a kind husband and a home of her own.

Instead, she had to rely on the whims of a man like Penworth.

They stared and stared at each other, his snooty expression letting her know how futile her spurt of rebellion had been. Her wishes were trivial compared to his, and she sighed and nodded, reluctantly acknowledging his power.

Without further disagreement or complaint, she stood and went to locate the butler so she could learn where her bedchamber would be.

Chapter 2

❧

LILY was stomping toward the foyer when a door opened down the hall. Two young ladies stepped out to block her path. Since they were identical in appearance, it wasn't difficult to deduce that they were the earl's wards, Miranda and Melanie Newton.

Their hair was a silvery blond, their eyes an icy blue. In their matching white gowns, blue sash at the waist, they were lithe and willowy, sophisticated in a fashion Lily couldn't have managed in a thousand years.

They watched Lily approach, as Lily watched them in return. It was an odd encounter, almost a confrontation, and she couldn't figure out why it was occurring. Already, she sensed disaster.

They hadn't moved, and at noting their heightened scrutiny, she was extremely uncomfortable. She stopped and smiled, but they didn't smile back.

"Miss Lambert, I presume?" one of them said. Her voice was breathy and seductive, like honey on a spoon.

"Yes."

"I am Melanie Newton."

"And I am Miranda Newton," the other chimed in. "John must have hired you. He told us he planned on it."

It took a moment for Lily to realize that in speaking of *John*, they were referring to Lord Penworth.

"Yes, he hired me," Lily confirmed.

"He's so anxious to depart for Scotland," Melanie mentioned.

"He just loves his dreary old castle," Miranda added, "and his horses and hounds. What about you, Miss Lambert? Do you love horses and hounds?"

"I can probably take them or leave them."

"You don't ride? You don't hunt?"

"No."

"How will you entertain yourself in all that wild heather?"

They cocked their heads at exactly the same angle, as they studied Lily's plain gray dress, the conservative collar and cuffs. Miranda peered at her sister, and a silent communication was exchanged. They both smirked.

"This is going to be so amusing," Miranda crooned.

They circled Lily, assessing her as if inspecting a horse they might purchase. Then, at the same instant, they halted and leaned in, so Lily was wedged between them.

Their perfect faces were mere inches from her own, so she could see their creamy skin, their plucked brows, their ruby lips and dark lashes. They were very beautiful, but in a brittle manner that Lily found disturbing.

"Did John inform you of how many companions we've had?" Miranda inquired.

"Seven?"

"Can you guess why?"

"I'm supposing you don't want a companion," Lily said.

"Touché, Miss Lambert."

The wicked pair talked rapidly, finishing each other's sentences, as if they were completely attuned. Lily glanced from one to the other as if a ball was being batted back and forth.

"Our father never required us to have a nanny."

"We were always free to behave however we pleased."

"I'll bet you were," Lily mumbled.

"It's tremendously annoying to have John smothering us."

"He means well, but—"

"—we *are* eighteen."

"He should trust us—"

"—but he's so accursedly set in his ways."

"He certainly is," Lily agreed. For his being only thirty, he seemed fussy and demanding and downright ancient.

"Can you also guess," Miranda went on, "why the others fled or were fired?"

"Was it because you made their lives miserable?" Lily asked. "Or was it because you got them into trouble with Lord Penworth?"

"The latter. We worked to convince them to go on their own—"

"—and when they wouldn't, it was so easy to persuade John of their incompetence."

"He's quite gullible, and he doesn't like women very much. You can accuse a female of any wretched conduct, and he'll believe you. Can you imagine what we might tell him about you, Miss Lambert?"

"Oh yes," Lily replied, "I definitely can."

Penworth had alluded to transgressions by the prior companions, and it all made sense now. The twins had tricked or deceived the poor women, then lied to Penworth about what had transpired.

Being an oblivious male, he'd accepted the twins' version of events, and the companions were left to twist in the wind.

"Do you really think you should stay, Miss Lambert?"

"I'd rather not," Lily asserted. "I tried to explain to Lord Penworth that I didn't want the position, but he wouldn't listen."

"He can be stubborn. Perhaps you should try a bit . . . harder."

Miranda pinched Lily's arm, firmly enough to bruise, and Lily yelped with outrage.

"Ouch!" She flashed her severest frown. "Desist at once. Both of you! You're not the first miscreants to cross my path, and I don't graciously tolerate spite."

"Don't you? You'd be surprised what we can do—when we put our minds to it."

"No, I wouldn't."

Lily thought they were the most vicious, most despicable duo she'd ever encountered, and over the years, she'd seen plenty.

They didn't wish to endure her presence any more than she wished to endure theirs. It was a lose-lose situation, and if she could induce Penworth to discharge her, everyone would be happy. Most especially herself.

"We expect," Miranda said, "that you'll speak with John immediately."

"I will," Lily concurred.

"If he won't release you, you'll simply have to vanish."

They began finishing each other's sentences again. "If you went missing, what could he do, hmm? We're leaving for Scotland on Saturday."

"It's not as if he'd have time to search."

"You'll be gone, and we'll be free."

"That's all we ask."

"It's nothing personal—"

"—but we just don't like you."

"Good-bye," they simpered in unison.

They sauntered away, and Lily dawdled in the quiet hall, watching the swish of their retreating backsides. As they disappeared, she blew out a heavy sigh.

"Well," she muttered to herself, "that was pleasant."

She whipped around and proceeded to the library to notify Penworth that she quit—whether he wanted her to or not. His wards were monsters, and he needed to be apprised that they were. Hopefully, her fortitude would save their *next* companion an enormous amount of grief.

It took some meandering through deserted corridors

before she found the correct room. She'd raised her hand to knock, to announce herself, when she realized the door was ajar and that she could peek inside.

Penworth was still there, but he'd been joined by a woman. They were a few feet away from Lily, standing very close together. And they were alone.

Lily should have tiptoed away, but curiosity had often been her downfall. She presumed his associate to be his fiancée, Violet Howard, and Lily was dying to learn what type of individual would betroth herself to him. However, after a quick perusal, it was evident that—whoever she was—she couldn't possibly be Lady Violet.

Violet was eighteen, and she was a duke's daughter, a sheltered debutante who'd just had her first Season and had snagged Penworth, the biggest catch to flounder onto the Marriage Market in a decade.

The woman sequestered with him looked to be his same age, and she was very bold, very brazen.

She had luxurious auburn hair, and a shockingly curvaceous figure, so she was particularly striking. Her breasts were most noticeable, which Lily could plainly discern because her dress was cut so low in the front.

Penworth was riveted, his concentration completely captured by so much bosom being displayed for his prurient enjoyment.

To Lily's astonishment, the woman placed her palm on Penworth's chest and massaged in slow circles. While Lily had had experience with licentious males trying to grope and fondle her, she'd never seen the opposite—a woman being so amorously forward. She was enthralled by the sight.

Penworth's demeanor had been altered, his handsome features softening. His gaze was warm and appealing, his body loose and relaxed. He seemed younger, approachable, and not anything like the pompous aristocrat who'd interviewed her.

She sucked in a deep breath but couldn't let it out. A frantic warning sounded inside her head—that she should sneak away, that Penworth need only glance over and she'd be discovered—but she couldn't go. The slightest motion would reveal her presence. How would she explain it?

"I was in the neighborhood," the woman murmured. "Aren't you glad I stopped by?"

"It's a tad inconvenient, Lauretta," Penworth said.

"Is it?" she pouted. "Are you sure?"

She stepped in so their torsos were connected; Penworth obviously didn't mind. He gripped her hips and pulled her even nearer.

"What are you really doing here?" he asked.

"Can't an old friend visit without there being an ulterior motive?"

Their lips were barely separated. Would they kiss?

Lily was agog with anticipation, as her brain roiled with conflicted thoughts: Was this the same straitlaced Penworth who'd lectured her on vice? Who'd bragged about his high moral standards? His ridiculous principles?

What a hypocrite!

"You didn't attend my grand opening party." Lauretta twined her arms around his neck. "Didn't you receive my invitation?"

"Yes, but you know I'm not much for brothels—even a fancy one like yours."

"I realize that, so I came to you instead. I wouldn't want us to lose . . . *touch*."

Lily stifled a gasp.

The woman, Lauretta, was a prostitute? Penworth had welcomed her into his home? With his wards just down the hall?

The tedious man—for all his posturing and sermons—was a fraud. A pretentious, conceited fraud, and Lily could scarcely keep from marching in and telling him so.

Lauretta's hand dropped between their bodies, and she shamelessly stroked his private parts, a daring maneuver that he clearly relished. He rippled with pleasure; a charming smile quirked his stern mouth.

"Lord Redvers split with me," Lauretta said. "He dumped me over like a bag of rubbish."

"I'd heard that he had."

"So I'm at liberty to consort with whomever I choose"—she licked her lips—"and I choose you."

"Do you?"

"It's been ages since we dallied."

"Yes, it has."

Penworth's voice had descended to an entirely new range. It was low and smooth, and the timbre did something interesting to Lily's innards. She felt hot and tingly all over. Butterflies careened through her stomach.

Penworth dipped down and nibbled on the bare skin at Lauretta's nape. She moaned with delight as his fingers settled on her breast and squeezed the large mound. At viewing the naughty spectacle, Lily's own breasts swelled and ached, the nipples growing firm so they rubbed against her corset in an irritating fashion.

It had never occurred to her that a man might caress a woman in such an intimate manner, that a woman might enjoy it. She was literally frozen with shock.

Penworth drew away, and Lauretta rose on tiptoe and kissed him.

"I have a few hours," she said, "before I must proceed on to London. How about a tumble for old time's sake?"

"I don't know," he grumbled, but his resolve was weakening.

"Won't it be cold and lonely at your castle in Scotland?"

"Yes."

"Those rural villages are awfully conservative. It's not as if you can chase after any of the widows."

"No, I wouldn't be able to."

"Who will entertain you?"

Penworth studied Lauretta, assessing her beautiful hair, her eloquent green eyes, her shapely figure. He grinned. "Why not?" he gushed. "I'm not busy. Let's take the rear stairs up to my room."

He clasped her hand and spun so quickly that Lily had

no opportunity to flee. In a thrice, they were face-to-face, with Penworth gaping. His expression was perplexed, as if he couldn't remember who she was.

Recognition dawned, and he barked, "Miss Lambert? Why are you still here?"

"I don't have any idea."

"Are you spying on me?"

"No!" she insisted, though she absolutely was.

"Then what in the bloody hell do you think you're doing?"

"Nothing?" She turned and ran.

Chapter 3

❦

"She's a lovely girl."

"Who is?"

John was staring across the crowded parlor at Miss Lambert, and he yanked his distracted gaze away from her and struggled to focus it on his stepmother, Esther.

"I'm talking about Violet, John," Esther said. "She's lovely. I'm delighted with your engagement to her."

"Oh yes, Violet. Of course."

For a moment, he'd thought she referred to nosy, meddlesome Miss Lambert, who was very pert and very sassy and too pretty for her own good.

While Violet was demure and shy, she couldn't hold a candle to Miss Lambert. Lambert exuded a maturity and sagacity that separated her from other young women. Her composure rattled him, made him want to march over and demand answers.

He simply couldn't decide what the questions should be.

"I hope," Esther grouched, "that Edward has a chance at someone as perfect as Violet."

Edward was John's half brother, Esther's only child. A more slothful, worthless soul, John couldn't imagine.

"Don't worry about him," John said. "He's hardly ready to settle down, so his marriage is a long way off."

"When he *is* ready, promise me that you'll find him a bride as marvelous as Violet. It's only fair."

It was her constant complaint that Edward was the second son, and thus not afforded the advantages he deserved.

In reality, Edward was a spendthrift who frittered away his money, but in Esther's eyes, he was wonderful. In John's eyes, he was a negligent wastrel, and if Edward had been left in charge after their father's death, he'd have swiftly beggared them. They'd be starving on the streets, dressed in rags.

Edward's profligacy was an exhausting source of familial discord, and as John peered around the cheery room, filled with neighbors who were chatting, drinking, and playing cards, he was overcome by the worst wave of melancholy.

What he wouldn't give to walk away, to shuck off his responsibilities and leave the entire mess behind. But he never would. His strict, unyielding father, Charles Middleton, had trained him too well.

"Edward will make a fine marriage," he insisted.

"Not on the pittance he inherited from Charles."

"He was bequeathed plenty, Esther."

"Easy for you to say—when you have it all."

He sighed. It was an argument he couldn't win with her.

"Edward gambles it away, which you know to be true, and I won't debate his conduct in the middle of a party."

"If you would—"

"Esther!" he sharply but quietly seethed. "You forget yourself. Stop nagging me."

He hated scenes and wouldn't tolerate hysterics. It was another lesson drilled into him by his father, who'd loathed gossip and scandal. John's disgraced mother, Barbara, had reveled in ignominy, had loved to frolic and offend and draw attention to herself.

As a result, John never did anything out of the ordinary, being determined to act appropriately in all circumstances so he would never be compared to her. Quarreling with his stepmother, while others watched, was beyond the pale.

Esther was aware that she'd overstepped her bounds, and she pursed her lips and stomped off. He was relieved to see her go. His day had been sufficiently awful—due to Miss Lambert and her interfering ways—and he didn't need Esther adding to his aggravation.

Barbara, his mother, was living in Italy, having run off with a paramour when John was two. He'd never seen her again, and his father had promptly divorced her and wed Esther, instead. She'd assumed Barbara's role, both as parent and countess, but it had been cold comfort.

Esther was dour and unpleasant, forever whining over the smallest detail. John was respectful to her because she'd been his father's wife, because she was Dowager Countess of Penworth, because she'd tried to be a mother to him. She'd failed miserably, but still, she'd tried, and he owed her his esteem.

He just wished she didn't make it so difficult to like her.

Edward was over by the hearth with the twins and various other girls. He was telling one of his pointless stories, and they were all laughing. He could be charming—when he wanted to be—and John couldn't bear to observe as he flirted. Not when John was cognizant of Edward's other, less flattering traits.

Out of the corner of his eye, he noticed Miss Lambert furtively sneaking out onto the terrace, and he whipped around, like a falcon spotting a rabbit. Since she'd stumbled onto his aborted tryst with Lauretta Bainbridge, she hadn't had a chance to discuss the situation with her.

What might she say about the imbroglio she'd witnessed? To whom might she tattle? If rumors spread, the damage to his reputation would be incalculable.

Why, oh, why had he allowed Lauretta in the house? Her prior protector, Lord Redvers, was an old friend who'd kept her as his mistress, and John had always been partial to her sexual habits.

When the butler had announced her, John should have refused to see her, but sometimes he grew weary of behaving. His world was all drudgery and restraint. Wasn't he entitled to a bit of fun? He had bodily cravings like everyone else, but how was he to explain such a thing to a spinsterish scold like Miss Lambert?

Would he have to buy her silence? She'd learned his deepest, darkest secret—he had hidden vices—and he was terrified that she might use her knowledge to his detriment.

Feigning nonchalance, he slipped outside, prepared to chase after her like an idiot. It took a moment to locate her; she was far down a pathway, slinking in the servant's entrance.

He followed, positive she was bound for her bedchamber, so she'd be alone and away from curious eavesdroppers. They'd be able to have a private conversation. He had to make her view the assignation from his perspective. As he hurried after her, he dithered over how to portray the event so it sounded less despicable.

He halted at her door, but before he could knock, she yanked it open from the inside. She was wrapped in a dowdy traveling cloak, and on seeing him, she appeared startled and guilty.

"Hello Miss Lambert," he said.

"What do you want?"

"We need to talk."

"This is a bad time for me," she had the temerity to protest. "I'll have to catch up with you later."

He ignored her and continued on. "About this afternoon, when I was . . . was . . ."

"Dabbling with a whore in your library?"

". . . chatting with an acquaintance—"

"Ha! There's nothing wrong with my ears. I heard every word you uttered."

Damn it! "She merely stopped by on her way to London."

"Is that how you've decided to play it? It seems to me

that you were a staircase away from romping with her on your bed."

A muscle ticked in his cheek. "I can see that I've left you with a completely erroneous impression, and I must counter any misconception."

She shook her head with disgust. "You're a fraud, Penworth. You're quick with your lectures, but when it comes right down to it, you're no better than you have to be."

She was correct, so how was he to reply? Still, he couldn't have her blathering the story hither and yon.

"It's clear," he stated, "that we disagree on what transpired, so I must demand that you not mention the episode to others."

"Trust me, milord, I don't intend to talk about you ever again. Your name will never cross my lips."

"Well . . . good. I'm glad we understand one another."

"Now then, if you'll excuse me? I'm busy."

Busy? It was ten o'clock on a Wednesday night at a country estate. What could possibly be occupying her?

She started to shut the door, and he frowned as he realized that she was clutching a portmanteau in her hand.

Was she running away? The prospect was so unbelievable that he couldn't accept it, but what else was he to presume?

Sanity returned, and he snapped, "What in the bloody hell do you think you're doing?"

Hadn't he asked her the exact same question earlier in the day? Would it become a constant query with her? What type of troublemaker had he hired? Would there be no end to the chaos she would bring to his staid, dull life?

"Nothing," she said, giving the answer she'd previously supplied.

"It certainly doesn't look like *nothing*. If I didn't know better, I'd suppose you were quitting your job before it had begun."

"Ah . . . no, I wasn't."

"Really?"

"Yes, really."

She was peering up at him with those big blue eyes—and lying to his face!

If it hadn't been so indescribably bizarre, he'd have laughed aloud.

"Are you claiming," he probed, "that you're eager to commence your duties?"

"Yes."

"You're elated that I picked you?"

"Of course."

"You can't wait to serve me."

"I couldn't find a boss more considerate or generous."

The little minx kept her gaze locked on his as the falsehoods rolled off her tongue. If there had been a chair directly behind him, he'd have sunk down into it in a stunned heap.

No one defied him. No one deceived him. In light of his superior status, no one would dare. Especially not a lowly, common lady's companion. He told people to jump, and they asked, *how high?* Every person in the kingdom was aware of this fact. It was like an implicit rule of nature. He spoke, and he was obeyed.

Yet Miss Lambert felt it perfectly permissible to pack her bag and leave without so much as a good-bye. She either had an enormous amount of gall, or she was insane.

"Would you like to know what has occurred to me, Miss Lambert?"

"No, but I imagine you're about to tell me."

"It has occurred to me that you're running away."

"Don't be silly." She chuckled halfheartedly. "I wouldn't dream of it."

"Wouldn't you?"

He took a step into the room, and she took one back. He took another, and she retreated until he was fully inside. He kicked the door closed with his heel.

In an instant, they were sequestered in a fashion that was totally improper, but thrilling to him in ways he didn't comprehend. He was famous for his cool aplomb, but he was so furious at her snubbing his offer of employment that red circles had formed on the edge of his vision.

He wanted to shout at her, to shake her, to bend her over his knee and paddle her shapely bottom until she couldn't sit down for a week. He couldn't remember when he'd last felt so alive.

"Miss Lambert?"

"Yes?"

"Insubordination enrages me."

She looked indignant. "Who said I was being insubordinate?"

"I did, and what I say is the law."

He reached out and—quick as a snake—grabbed her satchel and tossed it away. Feeling omnipotent and invincible, he loomed in, as she squealed with alarm and lurched back.

Suddenly, and without warning, he had her trapped against the bedpost. His torso was pressed to hers so that he was touching her all the way down. The sensation was so stirring that he was surprised his knees didn't buckle.

With a body made for sinning, she was a delectable combination of mounds and curves and valleys. He was reminded of a painting of a nude that hung in his gentlemen's club in London, and he couldn't help but wonder how she'd appear undressed.

There was a flow of energy passing from him to her, the air energized as if a huge magnet held them together. Had he wanted to move away—which he didn't—he couldn't have.

If he didn't escape at once, he just might kiss her. All he had to do was lean down, and the deed would be done. An invisible force was drawing him closer and closer . . .

"Are you going to ravish me?" she asked.

"You should be so lucky." Her anxious question jolted him out of his stupor. He stumbled away, breaking the link between them as powerfully as if he'd cut it with a knife.

They stood, glaring, breathing hard, as if they'd been quarreling, and he supposed they were.

"I hired you this morning, Miss Lambert, to aid me in a very important capacity, yet I come upon you this evening sneaking out like a thief."

"I wasn't—"

"Don't lie to me!" he roared, surprised anew by how she'd disconcerted him. "Isn't that exactly what's happening? Should I check your bag to see if it contains silverware or candlesticks?"

"How dare you accuse me of larceny!"

"With what I've just witnessed, what should I think?"

"Not that, you oaf."

"Oaf! Is that how you address your betters?"

"Yes, if they're acting crazy. I can't have you leveling such a dangerous charge. What are you trying to do? Get me hanged?"

She'd stunned him again. She had a barbed tongue, and she wasn't afraid to stab him with it. Her audacity was annoying and oddly refreshing. He was surrounded by sycophants and flatterers who told him precisely what he wanted to hear, while she felt free to share her opinions—despite how they might aggravate or offend.

"Tell me what you're doing," he commanded in his most haughty earl's tone, "and don't waste my time with more of your nonsense."

She studied him, taking his measure. Devious thoughts careened through her head as she decided on the best yarn to spin.

"I *might* have been leaving," she ultimately admitted.

"Now we're getting somewhere."

"Are you always this smug?"

"Yes."

"I don't like it."

"As I've previously mentioned, I don't care."

"You are the most vain man I've ever met."

"And you are the most infuriating woman. What misbegotten notion has convinced you to flee the safety of my home in the middle of the night?"

"You're not going to like it."

"Try me."

"You're not going to believe me, either."

"Miss Lambert, I am giving you a chance to explain yourself. Please take it!"

"Don't say I didn't warn you." She dithered and debated, then blurted out, "I hate your wards."

"You *hate* Melanie and Miranda? How could you have generated an abhorrence so rapidly?"

"After you and I concluded our interview, they accosted me in the hall."

"And?"

"They threatened me with bodily harm if I took the job."

"They did not."

"They did!"

"Ridiculous."

"See? I told you you wouldn't believe me."

At her umbrage, he snorted. "Pardon my skepticism, but why would they terrorize you? It's not as if you'll have any great authority over them."

"They don't want a chaperone. Their father let them do whatever they liked, and they're irritated by your coddling."

He scowled, irked that—after a purportedly brief encounter in a deserted corridor—she knew more about the twins than he did after over a year of acquaintance.

Their father had been a school chum with whom John had occasionally gamboled. They'd been cordial, but hardly close, and he'd only met the twins twice and that was when they were children.

Their father had died—in a messy, hushed suicide— and John had been shocked to learn that he'd been named as their guardian. There had been no way to refuse the obligation.

He'd offered to find them husbands, but they'd claimed they weren't ready to wed, so he'd brought them to reside with the family. He'd done what he could to accommodate them, but they were an onerous burden, and he didn't wish to be further encumbered.

He simply wanted them to have a chaperone so that *he* didn't have to fuss with them. Was that too much to ask?

"They're eighteen," he said, "but to me, they're still girls. They require watching."

"They're *girls*, all right. Cruel, vicious ones."

"They are not."

"They are!"

"They need a companion, and it will be you."

"Don't tell me. Tell them."

"I have."

"It doesn't appear that they listened."

Could it be true? How was it that he—a man who was heeded, no matter how grand or insignificant his remarks— was suddenly being vexed by females who ignored everything he said?

First Miss Lambert, now Melanie and Miranda. If he wasn't careful, he'd have a full-blown feminine rebellion on his hands.

"Don't make me do it," she pleaded. "Don't make me stay."

"I don't have time to search for anyone else."

"They informed me that they'll involve me in all sorts of mischief. They plan to trick and deceive you until you fire me."

Could she be correct? Had the twins harassed the others whom he'd terminated? The possibility was too outrageous, and he couldn't credit it.

He scoffed at her. "You have the most vivid imagination."

"I'm not imagining it."

She looked so forlorn, and her melancholy was exasperating.

Women *loved* him. They begged for opportunities to enjoy his company—even though he shared it sparingly. Yet she couldn't wait to be shed of him and the security he would provide.

She was still leaned against the bedpost, and he stepped in again, tickled by how the area around them was instantly enlivened. A thrilling intimacy was growing, and there was the most marvelous sense of expectation, as if any wonderful thing might happen.

"I want you to remain," he insisted. "I want you in my home."

"It will be a nightmare for me."

"No, it won't. I'll protect you."

The words sounded strange, as if they'd been spoken by another man, one who was considerate and sympathetic to the needs of others as he never was.

"Promise me you won't leave," he said.

She sighed. "I won't."

"If you sneak off in the dark, I'll be very worried. Promise me you'll be here in the morning. Swear it to me."

"I swear I'll be here."

There were a dozen other, more personal comments he wanted to utter, but he didn't dare, and he was alarmed by the odd sentiments that kept flaring when she was near.

He seemed to . . . to . . . *like* her more than he should, but it would be entirely inappropriate for any relationship to develop.

"You'll be fine," he vowed. "I'll see to it."

Though he knew it was wrong, he couldn't resist reaching out and tracing a finger across her lips. Then he turned and ran as if the hounds of Hell were nipping at his heels.

Chapter 4

༄

"I'm beggared."

"After your shenanigans in Town last month, I'm not surprised."

"I could use an infusion of cash."

"I bet you could."

Edward Middleton glared at John, and he struggled to keep his fury in check. He'd provided John with a dozen openings to cough up some money, but John was being maddeningly tight-fisted. As usual.

With John being thirty and Edward twenty-seven, Edward had dealt with John's temperament for nearly three decades. It was pointless to quarrel with him. He was stoic and unflappable and couldn't be swayed by emotional argument. Any request had to be posed with levity, as if the matter was unimportant.

They were sequestered in John's library, with John seated behind his desk and wallowing in the pomp of his position like a blasted king. He looked cool and composed, while Edward had been up all night, drinking and carousing at the village tavern.

Rumpled and unshaven, his head throbbed with a hangover. He was dying to stagger over to the sideboard and pour himself a whiskey, needing to imbibe a little hair of the dog to quell his shaking hands, but it was just what John would expect him to do. Edward wouldn't grant him the satisfaction of being right.

"I don't suppose," Edward casually pressed, "you could lower yourself to extend an advance. The next quarterly payment from my trust fund isn't due for six weeks."

"I know, but I don't see how your fiscal difficulties are my problem."

"Give a bloke the benefit of the doubt, would you? I've had a run of bad luck. It wouldn't kill you to relinquish a few pounds. You have plenty. Why not share?"

Edward grinned, but John didn't grin back.

"I'd rather not," John said.

"Listen, old fellow—"

"Don't call me *old*. I'm your brother, not your father."

"Yes, well, you act like a decrepit penny-pincher. It's hard to remember that we're only three years apart in age."

"Three years older, but a lifetime wiser."

John's sanctimonious attitude was beginning to grate, and even though Edward had planned to stay calm, he was in it up to his neck financially.

"Damn it all, John, must you be such a miser?"

"Yes, I must."

"You're so bloody smug, with your title and your properties and your overflowing bank accounts."

"I can't help it that I was born before you, and I can't change the British laws of inheritance."

"If it hadn't been for your whore of a mother marrying Father first, I'd be earl now instead of you."

"Yes, you would be."

The remark about his mother, Barbara, was despicable, and Edward shouldn't have uttered it, but true to form, John evinced no reaction. The man was carved from stone. He had nerves of steel. Nothing moved him; nothing upset him.

"How am I to carry on while you're out of the country?" Edward inquired. "You'll be cavorting in Scotland, and I'll be stuck on this accursed farm without a farthing in my pocket."

"If this tale of woe has been offered to elicit sympathy—or get me to empty my purse—it hasn't."

"I can't remain here without any funds. If that's what you have in mind, then I'll have to tag along to Scotland with you."

John didn't want Edward in Scotland any more than Edward wanted to be there, but what choice did Edward have?

They'd been at John's rural estate for several weeks, and Edward was chomping at the bit to leave, but he couldn't return to London.

Creditors hounded him wherever he went, yet there was naught to do in Scotland but shiver in the cold and breathe the fresh air, the notion of which had him sick to his stomach.

"By all means," John said, "come to Scotland with us. We'll be happy to have you, and you can keep the twins entertained."

John's expression was unruffled, giving no hint as to his opinion over Edward's abrupt decision to make the trip, and with Edward having thrown down the gauntlet, he felt as if he had to follow through. He'd be heading for Scotland with the rest of the family—his irritating mother nagging the entire time—when it had never been his intention to travel with them.

How was it that John barely spoke a word but won every argument?

"I'd better pack my bags," Edward grumbled.

"Yes, you'd better. We'll be on our way at dawn. If you oversleep, you'll miss the carriage."

Edward smiled tightly and sauntered out, fighting to appear relaxed and unaffected, but he was thoroughly steamed. The moment he was down the hall, he stomped off, eager to vent his rage.

It was the very devil being the second son. While his father had provided for him, Charles had known Edward's proclivities and had tied up all his money. Edward had enough to survive, but he couldn't withdraw the amounts necessary to live as he *deserved*. And John was the trustee—the bastard!

Edward had to plead and cajole to have the tiniest bill paid.

He loomed into the foyer, but Violet was coming down the stairs, so he reined in his temper. A classic beauty, she was blond and blue-eyed, with a serene, aristocratic face and thin, willowy figure. She seemed to float rather than walk.

She'd been groomed to marry a pompous ass like John, and she'd be the perfect, boring wife for the perfect, boring husband. She would never cause a scandal, would never exhibit an ounce of inappropriate conduct, and she'd be dry as dust in bed.

How John could shackle himself to her was a mystery, but then, John sought out the dullest people on earth and cultivated relationships with them. Violet was the obvious choice to be his fiancée. She was vapid and shy and naïve as a post, but she was also a duke's daughter and rich as Croesus.

If Edward had been the earl, he could have wed someone like her, someone who was stupid enough to ignore his failings but attractive enough to look good on his arm at social functions. As it was, he'd be lucky to snag a poverty-stricken hag for his bride.

"Hello, my dearest, Violet," he said, turning on the charm.

"Hello, Edward." At using his Christian name, she blushed a fetching shade of pink.

She reached the bottom stair, and he clasped her hand, bowed over it, and kissed the back.

"How is it," he asked, "that you're always pretty so early in the morning?"

She giggled annoyingly. "You're such a flatterer."

"I simply point out the truth."

She preened under his male scrutiny, expecting it as her due.

"I have the most wonderful news," he murmured. He stepped in, his boots brushing the hem of her skirt, suggesting an intimacy to which he wasn't entitled.

"What is it?"

"I'm coming to Scotland, after all."

"Really?"

"Yes. I couldn't bear to be away from you for two whole months."

She shook a slender, scolding finger at him. "You shouldn't say such things to me."

"But you love it when I do."

He leaned even closer, so that his leg touched hers through all the petticoats and fabric. He was taking an outrageous liberty, but he reveled in it. In his most wretched hours, when he was broke and alone, he fantasized about seducing her, about their eloping before John realized what had happened.

Edward could easily convince her. She was an adolescent fool, a prime candidate for a furtive flirtation. If Edward ended up with her fortune, and John ended up jilted, it would serve him right.

"Edward . . ." she breathed, overwhelmed by his proximity.

"I can't help myself when I'm around you."

"You're so wicked."

"I'm just what you want in a husband, just what you need. Don't deny it. John will never be man enough for you. You're all fire and sparkle, while he's—"

"Hush! You mustn't speak ill of him. Not in his own home."

"You're correct." He forced a pained grimace, as if torn by emotion. "Pardon me."

He seized her hand and kissed it again, then—thank God!—footsteps sounded down the hall so he had an excuse to lurch away.

"*Adieu*, Violet," he whispered.

He acted as if the words had been wrenched from his very soul, and he circled her and started up the stairs, knowing she couldn't see him smiling as he climbed.

Like taking candy from a baby, he mused. When it came to men, she was gullible as a nun.

He reached the landing, and he was delighted to find one of the twins beckoning him to follow her. From a distance, it was difficult to tell them apart, but he assumed it was Melanie.

Without discussion, they proceeded to the next floor where her and her sister's adjoining bedchambers were located.

They arrived at her door, and he hesitated, aware that he shouldn't go in, but as was typical of many decisions in his life, curiosity overrode prudence.

If he was caught, there would be hell to pay. John would brook no indecent behavior toward two orphaned girls living under his protection.

Any infraction would spur John to extract punishment, but what kind? The options were all unsettling, but Edward discounted them and forged on. He marched into her room, and as the door was shut and locked behind them, he reeled with anticipation.

What could she want? Whatever it was, it would be thrilling, the precise cure for the tedium he loathed.

"Did you need something, Melanie?"

"I'm Miranda."

"Oh, of course you are," he blithely agreed. "My mistake."

"Melanie is taking a bath."

Ho-ho! "Is she?"

"She sent me to ask if you'd like to wash her back. Father used to all the time."

The lucky, incestuous bastard! "You don't say."

"She's missed his . . . assistance. She thought you might like to aid her in his stead."

"I've never been one to refuse a lady." He grinned like a lunatic. "Lead on, lead on."

Though he knew it was insane, he'd participated in their mischief in the past and was eager to do so again.

They often plied him with liquor, then engaged in ribald conversation. Once, they'd procured some opium, and he'd smoked it with them. On another occasion, they'd had him flirt with their companion. He'd lured her out for a swim in the pond in the middle of the night, but John stumbled on her—drinking and in her drawers—and he'd fired her on the spot.

Edward's successful involvement in the companion's removal had earned him a second evening of opiates, but that was as far as their interactions had progressed. They'd never previously proposed anything remotely sexual, but if they were inclined to take their relationship to a new level, he was happy to oblige.

Miranda escorted him to the dressing room, which was situated between the two bedchambers. The hip bath was filled to the rim. Melanie was in it, submerged in the water, her head balanced on the edge. Her dazzling silvery hair was piled in loose disarray, a few ringlets dangling down.

As he entered, she glanced over, then came up on her knees. She was wearing a black ribbon around her neck, an ivory cameo in the center, but other than that, she was naked. Water dripped off her arms and lapped at her thighs.

Holding her pose, she encouraged him to ogle her, and he definitely did.

She was thin, her skin quite pale. He could see her ribs, her flat stomach, her protruding hip bones. Her breasts were small, like a girl who had just begun to develop her woman's body, and her privates had no hair on them, or perhaps it was such a light color that he couldn't discern it.

She looked young and supple and nubile, and in an instant, his cock was hard as a rock.

"Hello, Edward."

"Hello, Melanie. Miranda tells me you need a bit of help with your bath."

"If you wouldn't mind?"

She spun, showing him her narrow shoulders, her tiny waist, and the greatest ass he'd ever observed. It was tight and smooth as an adolescent boy's.

Miranda guided him to the side of the tub, urging him to kneel. She placed a cloth in his hand, and he dipped it and stroked it across Melanie's back. He yearned to attempt more, to touch her breasts or rub it between her legs, but he was afraid he'd break the carnal spell they'd created.

Melanie turned toward him and asked, "Do you think I'm pretty?"

"Yes, very pretty."

"Do you ever wish you could . . . *fuck* me?"

The crude word was casually voiced, and spewing as it had from her cupid's mouth, it sounded extremely coarse. His cheeks actually flushed with embarrassment.

"I've thought of it. I won't deny that I have."

Melanie leaned forward and almost kissed him, but she didn't. Her lips were a hair's breadth from his own.

"That's enough for now," she whispered. "Will you visit me again?"

"Yes, yes!"

"I'll have another surprise for you."

"I can't wait to discover what it will be."

"You'll like it; I promise."

She sank down in the water, her intimate parts disappearing, as Miranda tugged him to his feet and ushered him away.

"When may I come back?" he inquired.

"I'll let you know."

"But . . . but . . . how long will it be?"

"It could be a few days. It could be . . . never."

He was desperate for another meeting and already pondering how dreary the hours would be until they summoned him. They'd commenced a dangerous game, and he was anxious to learn the rules, to spar at the next match. What might they permit? He was agog over the possibilities.

Miranda peeked into the hall, then shoved him out. The door was closed and locked. For a moment, he dawdled, hoping he might hear what they were saying. He pressed his ear to the wood, but all was silent.

Finally, he yanked away and hurried to his room to tend an erection that was painful in its intensity.

LILY stomped down the road, proceeding to Penworth Hall and cursing under her breath with every stride.

The twins had demanded she accompany them into the village, which she had, but they'd passed through the nearest town and traveled to the next one. They'd insisted on buying a certain color of ribbon before they could sail for Scotland.

Lily was sent into a shop, then they'd driven off, leaving her stranded. She'd had coins in her reticule, so she could have purchased fare on a public conveyance, but there'd been no coach going toward Penworth Hall and no way to return except to walk the six miles.

Normally, she would have enjoyed a stroll in the countryside, but she was furious at being duped and angrily speculating over how she'd get even. And she *would* get even. She just hadn't figured out how. She wasn't a novice at dealing with tomfoolery, and she had some tricks of her own she could play.

How she yearned to change her life! To marry and have a home of her own! She was sick of being alone, and it was exhausting having to rely on the likes of Lord Penworth to keep a roof over her head. She would glean enormous satisfaction from telling him she'd wed, and thus could no longer work for him.

"My husband won't allow it," she said aloud, testing how the word *husband* rolled off her tongue, but she snorted with disgust.

As if some man would ever marry *her*. She was fetching

enough, but without a dowry, she couldn't entice anyone worth having. A kindly, competent fellow who was gainfully employed would expect a wife to add wealth to the family coffers.

Lily had nothing, so the sorts who noticed her were cads like Penworth who didn't need riches from her, but were happy to take what she wasn't inclined to give. She couldn't believe he'd already sneaked into her bedchamber. On her first night in the house!

He hadn't exhibited any dastardly conduct, but it was only a matter of time before he would. If he grew amorous, what would she do? Especially once they were in Scotland?

With how her luck was running, she'd deflect an advance, then be tossed out without her wages being paid. She'd be marooned in the foreign country and unable to get back to London.

Why couldn't she alter her fate? It was so unfair that she struggled so hard but none of her plans came to fruition.

She rounded a corner and stumbled on a colorfully painted peddler's wagon. The rear doors were open, the bottles and jars artfully arranged.

She stopped to read the placard on the side, chuckling to see that he claimed to sell everything: medicines, love potions, invigorating tonics. She wouldn't mind being *invigorated* for the remainder of the galling trek to Penworth Hall.

The peddler approached, and he wasn't at all what she'd anticipated. Tall and handsome, he had long, dark hair tied with a strip of leather. His delicious brown eyes drew her in and made her want to dawdle and chat.

His skin was bronzed, whether from the sun or ancestry she couldn't decide, but it had her supposing he was a Gypsy or an Italian.

"Bonjour, bonjour, Mademoiselle," he greeted in perfect French, and she was captivated as he swept up her hand and gallantly kissed it.

"Hello," she replied. She smiled and he smiled, too.

"I am Philippe Dubois. Your name, *chérie*?"

"Miss Lily Lambert."

"Welcome to my humble wagon, Miss Lambert."

"I'm delighted to be here."

"Why are you alone? It is not safe for you to be walking by yourself."

"Let's just say I had a ride, but my carriage driver forgot me."

"*Mais non! C'est terrible!* You are too pretty. Who could forget you?"

"Just about anyone," she grumbled, feeling surly and ill-used by the twins.

"Perhaps it is time to hire a new driver, *oui*?"

If only it were that simple. "Yes, perhaps."

He gazed at her, his expression compassionate and concerned. He had an interesting way of looking at a woman—as if she was unique and exotic. She felt more at ease, her troubles less vital and imposing.

"You are having a very bad day," he correctly deduced. "How can I make it better?"

"You can't."

"Ha! I am Philippe Dubois. I can see your problem as clear as the nose on your face. You need a love potion."

"No, I don't."

"But every woman should be loved. Why not you?"

Yes, why not me? she fumed.

Why was she so unlovable? Why did she attract men like flies, but always the wrong kind with the wrong motives?

Should she buy a potion? She didn't believe in superstition or charms, but so far, she hadn't had any luck in her personal affairs. It would take a miracle for her to find a husband, and a bit of magic might be just the ticket.

She explored his rows of merchandise, handling the odd-shaped bottles, pausing to sniff the contents. He stood off to the side, letting her survey his wares, and he was quiet, seeming distracted, but it was a companionable silence.

"What is this?" she asked.

"It is my famous elixir, Woman's Daily Remedy. It calms body and soul, being especially beneficial when you are distressed."

"May I have a little taste?"

He urged her to try it, and she removed the cork and took a huge gulp. The elixir slid down her throat, and her eyes watered. She coughed and coughed. There was no mystery to the brew. It was laced with alcohol.

No wonder he could tout a calming effect. If she drank too much of it, she'd be passed out on the floor!

"Oh my," she sputtered. "It's quite potent."

"It definitely is."

"With where I'm going, though, it might be just what I need."

"Are you off on a journey, *chérie*?"

"To Scotland—as companion to the two most horrid twins you've ever met."

He commiserated, being very supportive of her complaints, which she appreciated. No one ever listened to her; no one ever sympathized or consoled, and he was so understanding that—before she knew it—she had not one, but two bottles of the Daily Remedy in her reticule.

She held up a vial. "What's this?"

"Ah . . . it is my biggest seller, my Spinster's Cure."

"It *cures* spinsters? Of what?"

"If you swallow it while staring at the man you hope to marry, you will be wed within the month."

It was an absurd declaration, and she laughed as he bragged about a successful customer he'd had, an ordinary commoner who had ingested the potion and wound up wed to a viscount.

Though his story was nonsense, it intrigued her against her will, niggling at a feminine part of her character that yearned for love and romance. She wanted there to be magic in the world, and she thought life would be marvelous if she could solve all her problems simply by consuming a peddler's elixir.

"My Spinster's Cure," he boasted, "will aid you in fulfilling your wish to be married. You crave a husband, yes?"

She gaped at him, stunned by his comment. "Of course. How did you know?"

"It is my job to know. You would like to have a home of your own, a cozy cottage in the country, with dogs and cats and three"—he halted and studied her—"no, *four* children."

She gaped again. How could he have guessed? She'd dreamed about the family she wanted—so often and in such detail—that she had already picked the names of her four babies: Michael, Marcus, Margaret, and Mary.

Late at night, when she was alone in her bed, she would envision herself with a handsome husband. She'd be puttering about in her own kitchen, her children seated at the table, immersed in their lessons. They'd chatter away, asking her questions, and she'd be so happy, surrounded by people she cherished.

Suddenly, Mr. Dubois didn't seem so farcical. Nor did his stories seem so false or contrived.

Perhaps he really knew something about amour. Perhaps he really had a tonic that could help. If she bought his Spinster's Cure, where was the harm?

If it was fake, it would be no great loss. Naught would happen. She'd have a fond memory of Dubois, and she'd chuckle over her gullibility in making a silly purchase.

But if his potion worked, if it actually altered her destiny . . .

She wasn't prone to fantasy or flights of fancy, but wouldn't it be splendid if his claims turned out to be true?

"You are absolutely amazing," she murmured.

"Aren't I, though?"

"I'll take two vials."

"A prudent choice. A double dose can never hurt."

Chapter 5

❦

"Miss Lambert, the sea air is giving me a chill."

"You poor dear."

John was seated at the head of the intimate dining table in Captain Bramwell's cabin, and he furtively watched the exchange between Miss Lambert and Miranda. He pretended he wasn't paying attention, but it was impossible not to notice the tension.

Bramwell's vessel was a merchant ship, so the group surrounding him was a small one, comprised of John's family and two of Bramwell's officers. Bramwell himself was on deck, directing them through the busy shipping lanes leading out of the city.

John had grown up sailing in the summers, and it was a diversion he relished. He was an investor in Bramwell's company, and he traveled with the man whenever he could, seizing any excuse to be out on the water.

While most people would have endured a long, bumpy carriage ride to Scotland, he chose an exhilarating alternative, and he wouldn't have others spoiling it.

Miss Lambert had informed him of the twins' intent to harass her. At the time, he'd discounted her complaint, but it was becoming patently clear that her description of the relationship was accurate, which he found problematic.

He hated discord and quarreling, and he planned on a quiet eight weeks in Scotland before he settled in London for the winter. He wouldn't tolerate any friction among the female members of his party.

"Would you run and fetch my shawl?" Miranda requested of Miss Lambert.

"I'd be happy to," Miss Lambert said.

It was a task a servant should have completed, and with supper having just been served, it was churlish of Miranda to make Miss Lambert go below. Plus, they had left the calmer currents of the Thames, and the turbulence was increasing as they moved from the protected river and out into the ocean.

Miss Lambert wasn't accustomed to the pitching of the ship, so it would be difficult for her to manage the ladder down into the hold.

"We've just sat down," John was surprised to hear himself say, "and Miss Lambert hasn't even picked up her spoon. Perhaps, Miranda, you could wait until she's finished her meal."

"I'm cold now, John," Miranda claimed, even though the room was hot as Hades with eight other bodies crammed into it. "When I'm so uncomfortable, I won't enjoy my food."

"You'll survive," he curtly retorted.

"I don't see why Miss Lambert can't get it," Melanie chimed in, defending her sister. "She's a servant, after all. Where's the harm in having her perform a servant's chore?"

"Her supper will still be here when she returns," Miranda added.

They were being extremely discourteous, and John was about to scold them, but Miss Lambert glanced up, her furious gaze cutting into him like a knife.

"I don't mind getting it," she insisted. "The air is stuffy

in here. I could benefit from the cooler temperature out-side."

She flashed a severe scowl, warning him to be silent. Then, with smiles all around, she pushed back her chair and hurried out.

An awkward moment passed, but John smoothed it over by beginning to eat. The others joined in, muffled table chatter resuming. Concealing his aggravation, John studied his plate, and the twins smirked when they thought he wasn't looking.

The little beasts! What scheme were they hatching? How would it work to Miss Lambert's detriment?

Oddly, he was concerned as to the answer. He kept thinking about her more than he should, but he shouldn't have been thinking about her at all, and he wouldn't make it a habit.

She was gone for an eternity, and he was wondering if he shouldn't send someone to check on her, when she strolled in, carrying a blue shawl.

She sat, and as she handed it to Miranda, Melanie whined, "I'm cold, too. Would you get mine for me?"

"I suspected you might want yours," Miss Lambert replied, "so I brought it as well. That way, I don't have to go back down right away."

"Aren't you considerate?" Melanie cooed, venom in her tone.

"Yes, aren't I?"

Miss Lambert stared at the twins, her expression noti-fying them that she was aware of their malicious game and determined to beat them at it.

Brava, Miss Lambert! he mused. She was no shrinking violet, and if the twins meant to trick her with their bully-ing tactics, they'd have a hard time besting her.

To emphasize the point that they hadn't really needed the shawls, the twins laid them on their chairs, and John was incensed anew on Miss Lambert's behalf.

"Melanie, Miranda," he snapped, "aren't you forgetting something?"

"What?" they asked in unison.

"First, you will say thank you to Miss Lambert, then you will cover your shoulders to shield yourselves from the chill that has you both so discomfited."

They fumed, then muttered an insolent, "Thank you, Miss Lambert."

Grudgingly, they tugged on the shawls as he'd demanded.

As for Miss Lambert, if he'd been expecting gratitude, he was grossly mistaken. She glowered at him, irked by his intervention, but he'd merely tried to help her deal with the pair. Apparently, she'd rather fight her battles on her own. Fine. She could spend the next two months wallowing in misery. He'd be damned if he'd stick his neck out a second time.

He spun toward Violet and inquired, "Are you enjoying the trip, Violet?"

"It's been . . . interesting."

It was a tepid response and not anywhere close to what he'd been hoping to hear.

She'd never sailed before, and he'd been anxious for her to thrive during the voyage. He didn't know much about her, their courtship having been one of the fussy, stilted ordeals typical of an aristocratic match.

The engagement had been finalized after extensive discussions with lawyers, bankers, and land agents. The process had taken more than a year to complete.

Prior to his proposing, he and Violet been allowed a few brief, highly structured conversations, with her chaperones hanging on their every word. They'd danced at several balls and had sat together at three suppers, but that was the sum total of their betrothal interaction.

The reason he'd had Esther invite Violet to Scotland was so he could become acquainted with her. It didn't seem as if they had much in common. She was so much younger, and she was very timid. He couldn't abide nerves or shyness in a female.

He wanted her to love his Scottish castle, to revel in the history of the place as he did. He wanted her to love his horses and dogs, and he absolutely insisted that she love sailing. If she didn't, he would . . . would . . .

He suffered a moment of panic, terrified that he was planning to wed a stranger, someone who might not value what he valued. The thought of it—of entering an empty marriage devoid of camaraderie—filled him with dread, but as fast as the ridiculous notion swamped him, he shook it away.

He wasn't like his mother, Barbara, who'd pined for excitement, who'd been ruled by her emotions. His pending union with Violet had naught to do with romance or affection or any such folderol. It was a business arrangement, initiated for the financial benefit of the parties.

Nothing more. Nothing less.

He peered over at her. "The moon is out this evening, so it will be very beautiful on deck."

"How nice," she mumbled, looking green around the gills.

"Will you walk with me later?"

She sucked in a deep breath, held it, let it out. Inhaled again. Exhaled.

"I'm not feeling very well," she said.

"I'm sorry to hear it."

"I don't think the ocean agrees with me."

His heart sank. "It can take some getting used to."

"Would you excuse me?" She stood abruptly. "I must return to my cabin."

With one hand clutching her stomach and the other covering her mouth, she ran out. He watched her go, struggling not to show any upset.

If she didn't care for sailing, they'd just have to find other similar hobbies. It wasn't the end of the world, but as he pondered their lack of common ground, it certainly seemed like it was.

His despondent rumination was interrupted by Miss Lambert rising to her feet. She was the only person sensible enough—or kind enough—to chase after Violet.

"I'll check on her," Miss Lambert said to no one in particular.

"Aren't you feeling sick?" Melanie asked, appearing hopeful.

"It's your first sea voyage, too," Miranda stated. "You can't be faring much better than she."

"I'm fine." Miss Lambert threw it out like a challenge. "I'm healthy as a horse."

She marched out, and the twins exchanged another significant look, as if they were already plotting how to next test Miss Lambert's patience. He sighed, hating all the drama.

The meal dragged on for two more hours, and he endured it with as much grace as he could muster. To his surprise, after Miss Lambert departed, he lost the energy for socializing. It became a trial, and he observed—bored out of his mind—as the twins flirted with Edward, as Esther quipped and complained.

By the time he was able to slip away to his cabin, he was brimming with annoyance and eager to be alone. Vaguely, he wondered about Violet, but worry over her condition produced scant concern because Miss Lambert was front and center in any musings.

Was Miss Lambert attending Violet? How was she herself weathering the rougher seas?

Miss Lambert . . . Lambert . . . Lambert . . .

She'd infested his head, like a malignant brain disease. Why was he so captivated? Why couldn't he focus on anything but her?

He paced like a lion in a cage. Though his cabin was second in size to Bramwell's, it was small and austere, with a bunk, a chair, and chest of drawers. The ceiling was so low that he had to stoop when he entered, and the cramped space was driving him mad.

He opened the door and tiptoed into the hall, excited to climb up on the deck and stand under the starry sky.

As he reached the ladder, Miss Lambert emerged out of the darkness from the other end of the corridor, where she was sharing a cabin with Violet. In an instant, they were very close, a hint of her perfume tickling his male senses.

Moonbeams wafted through the hatch, lightening her blond hair so it seemed silvery white. Her skin glowed with the same shimmering hue, her big blue eyes sparkling like diamonds.

She'd let her hair down, the luxurious locks curling to her waist, and she had to have dressed hastily. The top few buttons of her gown hadn't been buttoned, and bare toes peeked out from under the hem of her skirt.

"Hello," he whispered.

"Hello, milord." She whispered, too.

The encounter was very shocking, very intimate.

"How is Violet?" he remembered to ask.

"Not well. The odor in our cabin is a tad . . . ripe."

"You sneaked out?"

She frowned, deeming his comment a chastisement.

"Her maid is with her."

"Then you're free for a bit."

"As free as I can be while trapped on board a ship in the middle of the night."

He chuckled, as he noticed she was holding a vial in her hand. He took it from her, and she released it with reluctance. He lifted it toward the hatch, assessing the contents. It contained what appeared to be red wine.

Was she a drinker? Why hide it? He wasn't a teetotaler, and he didn't demand abstinence from others. Wine had been served with supper; she could have had plenty.

"What's this?" he queried, as she snatched it from him and tucked it into the folds of her skirt.

"It's a . . . tonic a peddler gave me. To ward off seasickness."

"You seem unaffected. Have you needed it?"

"No, but I thought I should keep it with me—just in case."

"How are you enjoying the trip so far?"

"I'm enjoying it immensely. I believe I'm meant for sailing. I wish I could sail off to the ends of the earth and never stop."

"Ah, a kindred spirit. I often feel the same way."

He studied her, seeing her in a whole new light. How was it that he'd known, deep in his heart, that she would love to sail? What else might they have in common?

"You're having some trouble with the twins," he mentioned.

"Not really. I've caught on to their games. They think they can scare me off, but they have no idea who they're up against."

"You're a pistol, Miss Lambert."

"I can be—as they're about to learn."

"Would you walk on the deck with me?"

"No, I would not."

"Why?"

"We shouldn't be seen together. It wouldn't be appropriate."

It was the sort of remark he normally would have made himself, and if he hadn't been working so hard to be quiet, he'd have laughed aloud. Imagine it: his servant lecturing him on morals and behavior!

"Everyone is asleep," he said. "No one will see."

"Some of the sailors are awake."

"I don't care about them," he bizarrely insisted.

"I do."

"Coward."

"I won't deny it."

Vividly, he recalled the evening in her bedchamber at Penworth Hall, when he'd improperly entered. His body still tingled at the memory of how he'd pressed himself to her, how her private areas had touched his own.

He loomed in as he had that night and trapped her against the ladder. Their torsos were wedged into the narrow space, and he was agog to discover that—in her haste to flee Violet's nausea—she hadn't donned a corset. Her full, round breasts were unencumbered.

He couldn't recollect ever being in a woman's presence when her bosom was so blatantly unfettered. The realization nearly brought him to his knees.

To steady himself, he rested a hand on her waist. She

inhaled sharply and leaned away, but he wouldn't let her escape.

She peered up at him, her concern evident.

"Are you afraid of me?" he murmured.

"Yes."

"Why? I'm harmless."

"In your dreams maybe—but not in mine."

He riffled his fingers through her hair, riveted by the soft, lengthy tresses.

"You're very beautiful."

"You shouldn't say that to me."

"Why not? It's true."

He felt as if he'd been inhabited by an alien being that was driving him to attempt conduct he'd never previously considered. He wasn't the type who harassed his maids, who tumbled his servants or demanded sexual favors, so she'd pricked at a reckless facet of his personality that he hadn't known he possessed.

Without pausing, where he might have arrived at a different decision, he bent down and kissed her. She didn't pull away, and he was thrilled.

In the history of kisses, it wasn't much about which to brag. He didn't grope or fondle. He simply stood very still, breathing in the warm, lush scent of her.

She was the one to break away, and if she hadn't, he couldn't guess how long he'd have tarried. Perhaps till morning. Perhaps the family would have stumbled from their cabins, hungry for their breakfast, only to find them frozen in the naughty embrace.

The prospect didn't bear contemplating, and usually, he'd have been aghast at such a lack of decorum. But he wasn't sorry and didn't regret his bold act.

"You shouldn't have done that," she charged.

"Why?"

"It's wrong." When he might have argued the point, she asserted, "It *is* wrong. Don't pretend it's not."

"Then let me be damned for it. I enjoyed it, and I won't apologize."

"What do you want from me?"

"Everything. Nothing."

"You can't keep forcing your attentions on me."

"I know."

"I haven't sought them."

"I know that, too."

"If I've misled you, if you think I'm loose or brazen or . . . or . . ."

"I don't think any of those things about you."

They stared and stared, then she spun away, but he grabbed her wrist, stopping her.

"Come up on the deck with me."

"No."

She yanked away and stepped around the ladder to be swallowed up by the darkness.

"Lily . . ." he said, seizing the chance to speak her name.

"Go away," she hissed from down the hall. "Go away and leave me be."

A cabin door opened and closed as she went back into Violet's sickroom.

At recalling Violet, he shook his head, astonished by his shamelessness. His fiancée—the one he'd waited years to pick, the one he'd selected with the concerted strategy of a war general—was lying in her bunk, twenty feet away, while he was dawdling outside and kissing her companion.

It was a hideous betrayal, yet he didn't feel an ounce of remorse! What was happening to him?

He whipped away and clambered up to the deck, before Miss Lambert returned and he made an even bigger fool of himself.

LILY climbed the ladder and peeked out the hatch. Moonlight rained down, so objects were clearly visible. It was very late, very peaceful, and though she knew there were always sailors on duty, she didn't see any of them. Nor did she see Penworth. Enough time had passed that he had to have gone back to bed.

She crept onto the deck and sneaked her way past ropes and boxes, lifeboats and masts, until she was by the raised section at the rear where the helm was located, where Captain Bramwell and his officers steered the ship.

As she'd hoped, Bramwell was there. He was gazing out at the stars, lost in contemplation, so he didn't notice her lurking in the shadows directly below him.

He was very handsome, very proper in his dress and demeanor. He exuded confidence and courtesy, and she thought he might be an excellent husband.

The Spinster's Cure potion, given to her by Mr. Dubois, was clutched in her hand. He'd instructed her to drink it while staring at the man she wished to wed and that was precisely what she intended to do.

She pulled the cork from the vial and lifted it to her lips. Poised like a statue, she whispered a prayer—that Dubois's claims be true, that Bramwell be smitten by Cupid's arrow. She gaped at him till the entire area surrounding him faded away, and he was a single, solitary soul in the center of her universe.

Her eyes never leaving him, she poured the elixir into her mouth and swallowed. The liquid had just started its path to her belly, when suddenly, she was seized by the arm and yanked around.

She came face-to-face with Penworth.

"What are you doing out here, you little minx?" he asked.

"Ah!" she shrieked.

She fought to jerk away, to wrench her focus to Bramwell where it belonged, but she couldn't.

A magnet might have been holding her in place, because she could only look at Penworth. It was the strangest thing, but there was an odd, audible *click*, as if her destiny had been realigned.

The sensation was eerie and profound in a fashion that scared her to death. Time slowed. The world ceased its spinning while the new configuration took shape, then gradually, the interval waned. The perception of unreality dwindled until it might never have occurred.

Their connection was severed; his hand dropped, and she stumbled away.

"Are you mad?" she fumed.

"Me? You're the one standing in the dark, with your hair down and your shoes off."

Coughing and sputtering, she pounded on her stomach in an attempt to reverse the ghastly error, but it was impossible to *un*swallow the elixir.

She tried valiantly anyway, sticking two fingers down her throat, desperate to make herself wretch, but it was no use. The blasted brew had journeyed down, and she couldn't convince it to travel the other way.

Penworth watched it all, gawking at her machinations as if she was a lunatic escaped from an asylum.

"Miss Lambert," he finally inquired, "what on earth is wrong with you?"

"Nothing."

"What were you drinking?"

"I told you: a medicine given to me by a peddler. For seasickness."

"So you were trying to vomit it up? Isn't the whole point to keep it down?"

"Oh, do be silent!"

To her horror, she was unaccountably distraught. She'd imbued Dubois's potion with a significance all out of proportion to what she could have achieved with it. Her dreams had been dashed, and she was heartbroken.

Bramwell had been someone she could actually have married, someone closer to her own ancestry and status, yet she'd imbibed the liquid while staring at Penworth. His situation was so far removed from hers that she might have been trying to reach out and touch an angel in Heaven.

If Dubois's potion had had any magical effect, it would never be in an amount sufficient to overcome the gulf separating her from Penworth. The effort had been completely wasted. She felt as if her future was overly bleak, and there was no reason to hope or pine. The empty decades stretched before her.

Captain Bramwell had heard her commotion, and he came over to the railing and frowned down at them.

"Is there a problem, Penworth?" he asked.

"It's just Miss Lambert, strolling the deck in her nightclothes."

"I'm *not* in my nightclothes," she protested, but the two men ignored her.

"What brought this on?" Bramwell queried. "Is she intoxicated?"

"Not that I can tell."

"Why is she ambling about?"

"I haven't a clue."

"Miss Lambert," Bramwell scolded, "it's not a good idea to flaunt yourself. My crew is generally well-behaved, but they are men. I'd hate to have you precipitate an incident where one of them would have to be punished."

"Yes, Miss Lambert," Penworth agreed, a wicked gleam in his eye, "you shouldn't be *flaunting* yourself. You never know who might see you."

Lily glanced from Bramwell to Penworth. She was angry and forlorn and so weary of her life that her teeth ached with it.

"You ruined everything!" she hurled at Penworth.

At her vehement accusation, he scowled. "What did I do?"

On the verge of tears, she pushed by him and hurried to her cabin, where Violet Howard proceeded to void her stomach till dawn.

Chapter 6

❦

"COME in, come in. I thought you'd never arrive."

His heart pounding, John gaped in confusion at the voluptuous, striking woman who was welcoming him inside. She was in her late forties, though her glorious brunette hair gave no indication of her age. Not a single strand of gray showed through.

Her green eyes were merry, her cheeks flushed, and she was dressed in a fashionable red gown that was cut too low in the front. She appeared lively and vibrant and happy, a brightly plumed exotic bird in a room of dull sparrows.

He blinked and blinked, wondering if, after the draining journey from England, he wasn't hallucinating.

They were in the entryway of his Scottish hunting lodge, which was a misnomer. It was literally a castle from the days of knights and jousts and damsels in distress. Though it had been remodeled with modern conveniences, it was chock-full of secret passageways and ancient dungeons. Ghostly apparitions abounded, and it was John's favorite spot in the whole world.

What was *she* doing in it?

"Mother?" he wheezed.

"Yes, darling, it's me."

"Mother!" he gasped again, truly feeling that he might faint.

She'd been gone for twenty-eight years, since the evening she'd tucked him in bed, read him a story, then walked out and never returned.

How was it that he still remembered that smile? That face? That sultry voice?

"Look at you!" She hurried forward and took his hands. "You can barely stand. You must be exhausted."

"I'm fine." He eased away.

"There's a toasty fire burning in the parlor, and Angus"—the butler—"is waiting to pour you a whiskey."

"I hate whiskey."

"You do not," she said as if she'd spent the past three decades with him and knew his likes and dislikes. "I had your best keg hauled up from the cellar."

"You've certainly made yourself at home."

"I've enjoyed every minute of it, too."

She was trying to guide him toward the parlor and the fire and the whiskey. He pulled away, like an uncooperative horse refusing to be led.

"Mother . . ." He stopped. The affectionate term seemed wrong.

"Barbara," he started again, "why are you here?"

She grinned, a dimple creasing her cheek, but before she could speak, Edward traipsed in.

"Really, John, the servants in this place are . . ." He saw Barbara and trailed off. "Hello there, lovely lady. Please tell me that I may introduce myself."

"No, you may not," John replied for her.

Edward was overtly shocked by John's rudeness. "Why?"

"She's no one important—and she was just leaving." John glowered at her, but it had no effect.

"Honestly, John," she scolded, "when you talk like that, you sound as tedious as your father used to be." She sashayed over to Edward. "I am Barbara Middleton."

As she casually mentioned Charles, John's father, John was so angry that he yearned to shake her till her teeth rattled.

"Her surname is *not* Middleton," he insisted to Edward.

"It is, too," she blithely retorted. "Charles may have divorced me, but I never gave up the name. I went through plenty to get it, and I wasn't about to relinquish it simply because he was an ass."

Edward was staring from John to Barbara to John again.

"Are you . . . are you . . ." Edward couldn't finish his question. There was no polite way to ask it.

"Yes, I'm John's mother. You must be Edward. You look just like Charles. Much more than John ever did." She leaned in and whispered, but loudly, "Charles spread rumors that John wasn't his. Can you imagine a father saying such a hideous thing about his wife or his child? It boggles the mind."

"Barbara!" John snapped. "Be silent."

"It's old news," she breezily claimed, "so don't have an apoplexy. There's no reason to pretend he didn't say it, and I'm sure Edward has heard it all before."

For once, Edward was too stunned to remark. Others entered behind Edward, and he flashed a visual warning, but John was so flustered that he couldn't decipher it.

The twins came in, then several servants with armloads of luggage. Esther followed them, and Edward's message was clearly received.

John's mother was the disgraced, disreputable doxy who'd previously been Countess of Penworth. But the current Dowager Countess, Esther Middleton, had just arrived. All of John's plans for a serene, relaxing autumn holiday flew out the window.

Esther scowled at Barbara, and as recognition dawned, she gasped.

"You! What are *you* doing here?"

"Oh, my Lord," Barbara complained to John. "Don't tell me you brought *her* along. How could you?"

"Get out of my house!" Esther demanded.

"Your house!" Barbara scoffed. "Don't make me laugh, you pathetic interloper. This property belongs to John. Not you."

Esther stormed over to Barbara, and John would have liked to say that they stood toe-to-toe, but Barbara towered over Esther, and the differences between them were extremely stark.

Barbara was buxom and statuesque, with a perfect face, lush hair, and a vivacious personality that filled the room to overflowing. Esther was short and frumpy, a gray-haired, dour mouse who was prone to whining and grim bouts of melancholy.

"You never had the sense God gave a gnat," Esther sneered at Barbara.

"I was always smarter than you," Barbara taunted. "That was enough for me."

"You harlot! How dare you show up among decent people."

"Decent!" Barbara fired back. "Who would these paragons be? Your son, Edward, with his gambling and womanizing and—"

Esther whipped around to John. "Get her out of here! Get her out! Get her out!"

"You were always such a jealous little shrew." Barbara smirked. "Edward, your mother chased after Charles her entire life. She grew up thinking he would marry her, but he met me and the rest—as they say—is history."

"Liar!" Esther shrieked.

"Charles fell in love with me instantly," Barbara continued, "and he proposed a week later. I'm afraid it left her . . . bitter."

"Shut up!" Esther bleated.

"After I fled, she was like a vulture, ready to swoop in and take my place. How did she do in my absence, John? Has she earned any medals for mothering?"

Esther was about to attack. The twins were agog. Edward was aghast. Violet was horrified. The servants were hiding grins. Only Miss Lambert was unaffected. She watched dispassionately, as if viewing a melodrama on the stage. John envied her detachment.

As for himself, he was reeling with emotion. His head was spinning, his ears ringing, and his heart ached, as if he'd been punched in the chest.

What was he to do? He had to seize control before his mother and stepmother were brawling on the floor.

"Barbara"—he stepped between the two women—"in my library. Now."

He gripped her arm and led her away, and as she passed the butler, she said, "Angus, please be a dear and deliver John's whiskey to us. I'll have one, too."

"Yes, Lady Barbara." Angus appeared smitten. "I'll bring it right away."

"Angus," John admonished, "remember yourself. You are not to call her *Lady* anything."

Barbara winked—she *winked!*—at the elderly gentleman, and he winked back.

John's temper boiled. How long had Barbara been living in the castle? Why had no one told him? Was his whole staff involved in an insurrection?

John had never specifically ordered them to keep her out, but why should that have been necessary? Who could have predicted such an abrupt return?

He entered the library and marched to the desk, practically throwing her into a chair in the process. Angus tottered in after them, but as he set down his tray, John waved him away.

"Go to the foyer," John commanded. "Straighten out the mess Barbara's presence has created."

"Very good, sir."

The obsequious man bowed his way out, and John dawdled, rigid with fury, until the butler's strides faded.

Barbara poured them each a whiskey, but when she tried to push his across to him, he refused it, which was ridiculous. He'd never needed a shot of liquor more.

At his declining, she rolled her eyes in exasperation, took his glass, and downed the contents in a single swallow. Then she took hers and downed it, too.

"Are you a drunkard?" John inquired.

"I enjoy a nip now and again. I won't deny it."

"Lucky me. I finally meet my mother, and she's a sot."

"It was unnerving, seeing Esther. The old harridan! I think I'm entitled, don't you?"

John shrugged, but didn't respond.

"And it definitely wasn't easy seeing you." She refilled their glasses and shoved another toward him. "It can't have been easy on you, either. Drink the blasted whiskey. Quit being such a boor."

He didn't reach for it—merely to spite her—and she sighed.

"Gad, you're so much like him. How sad."

"What do you mean?" he asked through clenched teeth.

"When you were little, you were so much like me, so alive and full of mischief, but your father has managed to drum out all my best traits. Did he beat them out of you? Or did he grind you down until you don't remember me or what you used to be like?"

His thoughts churned with anguish. He wanted to rail at her, wanted to demand she never speak of Charles, but any remark would simply encourage her in further denigration of the man.

"How did you know I would be here?" he queried.

"You always come for the autumn hunting." He gawked at her, and she chuckled. "Are you surprised that I'm aware of your habits?"

"Very surprised."

"Were you imagining no one ever wrote to me? That I had no acquaintances in London?"

"I never pondered it."

"Of course you didn't. You were a child. Why would you have? But I knew all about you—from friends and enemies alike."

The news was terribly disturbing. He didn't want to be apprised of how she'd kept track of him, how people all over London had been spying and reporting to her. If he accepted her story as true, it might indicate that she'd cared enough to collect information.

"Why didn't you write to me yourself?" he pressed. "You could have asked for details rather than relying on secondhand accounts."

"I wrote for years. Charles wouldn't let you read my letters."

"I don't believe you," he said, more vehemently than he'd intended.

"I stopped when you turned sixteen because you finally wrote back and insisted I not bother you again. Don't you recall? It's certainly vivid in my mind."

He'd never written to her, so she had to be lying or else Charles had . . . had . . .

"What do you want from me?" he inquired.

"I want to stay with you for a while."

"Why?"

"I've missed you."

"No, you haven't. Tell me the real reason."

"I don't have another one. Should I invent something?"

"Do you need money? Is that it? How much will it take to make you go away?"

"No, I don't need any money. How awful of you to suggest it."

He studied her, a thousand questions on the tip of his tongue, and he hated that he was so curious.

She'd traveled to Italy with a lover, a dashing young army captain with no funds and no prospects. After she'd vanished, a lawyer had contacted Charles about sending her an allowance, and his answer had been to immediately file for divorce.

Over the intervening years, there had been occasional tales of her wretched condition, of her surviving in dire poverty and begging for scraps in various European cities, but now, he had to doubt what he'd been told. She was hale and beautiful and well-fed and . . . and . . . quite magnificent.

There! He'd admitted it. She was stunning.

"I want you out of here by morning," he advised her.

"Don't be silly."

"I can't have you annoying Esther and causing a ruckus."

"Who cares about Esther?"

"I do."

"You didn't when you were a baby. She used to visit all the time, and you'd burst into tears whenever she entered the room."

She'd flustered him again, with her talk of his childhood. It was too alarming to be in her presence.

"I want you to go," he declared.

"I won't." He glared, unaccustomed to blatant insubordination, and at his scowl, she laughed. "What if I refuse to leave? Will you toss me out on the road?"

"I might."

"No, you won't. You were such a sweet boy, and I hear that you still are. A tad stuffy and cold, but you have a good heart."

"I have *no* heart. Not where you're concerned."

"You're being a bully. The behavior doesn't suit you."

"You don't deserve a shred of kindness from me."

"While I'm here," she said, ignoring his cruel comment, "we'll work to bring you 'round to my way of thinking. Before you know it, you'll forget you were ever Charles's son."

Her calm assurance infuriated him. It seemed they were playing cards, that she had all the aces. He wasn't a brute. He wouldn't throw a woman out on the road, no matter how much he loathed her, and she'd gambled that he wouldn't. Apparently, she'd won.

"All right, you can stay," he grumbled. "But only for a week, and you'll retire to the west wing, so the family doesn't have to be constantly bumping into you."

"I'm already settled in the countess's suite. I don't wish to move."

It was where Esther would expect to sleep. She would have a fit.

A muscle ticked in his cheek. "No, you'll move. I'm afraid I have to insist."

"And I'm afraid *I* have to insist."

She stood and came 'round the desk, and she laid a hand on his shoulder. He flinched, shocked that she would touch him. With her standing and him sitting, he felt very young, out of his element. Her striking green eyes were expressive and troubled.

"Let me stay longer than a week," she begged. "Please?"

"Why should I?"

"I don't have anywhere to go."

"It never bothered you before."

"My dearest, Giorgio, died last winter," she informed him.

"So?" He wouldn't ask who Giorgio had been, why he was *dear*, why she was grieving.

"I need to be surrounded by people who love me, and I'm so lonely."

He fumed and fretted, then was enormously astounded to hear himself say, "Two weeks, and that's it. During that time, I'll make arrangements for you."

"Thank you."

"You'll keep to yourself, and you'll instigate no discord. You'll avoid Esther, and you'll refrain from insulting or offending her."

"If I can't harass Esther, you'll take all the fun out of my visit."

"I mean it, Barbara. You'll behave, or you'll leave."

She smiled a slow, seductive smile. "I'll be as good as I can be. You won't even know I'm here."

"Now *that* I doubt."

She leaned down and placed a tender kiss on his cheek, then she sauntered out, and he was all alone in the austere, somber room. His heart was beating so hard that he wondered if it might simply burst from his chest.

His hands shaking, he grabbed the decanter, filled a glass to the rim, and finally had the drink he so desperately needed.

"WILL that be all, Lady Barbara?"

"Yes, Peg, but I'd like you to come back in an hour to dress my hair. Since my son has arrived, I want to look especially grand when I join him for supper."

"Yes, milady."

The girl curtsied and tiptoed out, being so deferential and polite that Barbara might never have been away a single day.

The door shut behind her, and Barbara slumped in her chair, weak with relief that she'd bluffed her way into staying, that John hadn't sent her packing as she'd absolutely feared he might.

She'd been in Italy, flat broke and suffering through Giorgio's lengthy demise, and she'd assumed she would continue on in the foreign country after his death. But once he'd passed away, his villa had been so quiet, and creditors had begun circling, so she couldn't remain.

Yet where was she to go? She'd burned all her bridges.

She'd been married at fifteen and had been much too immature to deal with the very demanding and much older Charles Middleton. When she'd foolishly fled, she'd been suffocating on his rules and criticisms. She shouldn't have run off, but she had, and that fact couldn't be changed.

If John ever learned the truth of how she'd struggled, perhaps he wouldn't be so smugly derisive. Her life had been horrendously difficult, romance and security fleeting.

She'd let her army captain convince her that Charles would forgive their impulsive flight, that funds would be provided to tide them over, but they hadn't been. Six months of poverty and bickering had doomed the amour.

After he'd abandoned her, she'd engaged in a series of

torrid affairs with Europe's most eligible bachelors, but at age forty-six, she was destitute and exhausted. England had called to her in a manner she hadn't supposed possible.

She'd been notified that Charles was dead, that John was the earl, but she hadn't been able to predict how he would react to her return. A brazen appearance had seemed best, and she'd chosen to make it at Penworth Castle. It was far from London, so if he'd spurned her, gossip would have been minimized, but mostly, she'd come because she'd always cherished the wild spot.

In her short tenure as countess, she'd visited many times. She'd curried favor with the servants, and they still adored her. Nary a one had suggested she wasn't welcome, and all of them were happy to complain about Esther and how the family had never been the same after she had taken Barbara's place.

It was a small solace, but comfort nonetheless.

She sat at her dressing table and gazed in the mirror. Her hair and face were still beautiful, but there were tiny wrinkles around her eyes and mouth. Where had the years gone? Could she get some of them back?

She had to try.

John was the only person on earth who might ultimately exhibit the least amount of concern for her. She *had* to make him love her again, and she was determined to wear him down until he relented and she earned his pardon.

Footsteps marched up the stairs, heralding the encounter for which she'd been waiting. She poured a glass of wine and went to relax on the sofa in front of the fire. The door was flung open, a bevy of servants hustling in. Esther followed behind.

"Put my trunks in the . . ."

Esther stumbled to a halt and gaped at Barbara, not understanding what she was seeing. It was the countess's suite, and clearly, Barbara was ensconced in it.

"What are you doing in here?" Esther huffed.

"This is my room. What are *you* doing in here?"

Barbara pointed toward the hall, indicating that Esther should depart, but Esther regrouped, pulling herself up, straightening her spine.

"Get out. At once!" Esther commanded.

"I don't take orders from you, Esther."

Barbara gestured to the servants, and like ants in a line, they spun and left with Esther's trunks.

"Bring those back!" Esther bellowed, but no one heeded her. At having her authority so blatantly flaunted, she was aghast. "You won't get away with this," Esther warned.

"I believe I already have."

"I'll speak to John. He'll have you out of here like that!"

Esther snapped her fingers, but the *click* didn't sound, so the drama of the moment was foiled.

"You'll *speak* to John?" Barbara was disdainful, condescending. "Why would you? He gave me the suite himself."

"But it's . . . it's the countess's! He wouldn't have! He didn't!"

"He did. Good luck with changing his mind. You're aware of how stubborn he can be."

Esther was so furious that her entire body was shaking, but she didn't know what to do with all her rage. She'd never been the sharpest tack in the shed, and obviously, she'd gained no intellect in the intervening decades.

"I . . . I *hate* you," Esther hurled. "I've always hated you!"

"Sticks and stones, Esther. Sticks and stones." Barbara made a shooing motion with her hand, urging Esther out. "Now please go. I'm needed downstairs to greet John's guests, and I'm not dressed."

Esther hovered for a few seconds, then she whirled away and raced out.

"John! John!" she screeched, her voice echoing to the rafters.

Barbara grinned.

John would never intervene on Esther's behalf. In that regard, he was too much like his father, who had loathed discord and wouldn't tolerate it. Especially from a hysterical female.

The boudoir was hers. The first battle was won. Supper—and playing hostess to John's company—would be next. She would keep ingratiating herself until he realized he couldn't manage without her.

"One day at a time, Barbara," she murmured to herself. "One day at a time."

Chapter 7

LILY tiptoed down the dark corridor, the flame from her candle flickering on the walls, making the shadows large and menacing. It was very late, everyone asleep, but in the parlor up ahead, a lamp burned. Anxious for company, she rushed toward it.

While she wasn't usually timid, the nocturnal sounds of the old castle were disconcerting. She'd awakened with a start, convinced that someone was in her bedchamber. Not a person, specifically, but there'd been a definite *presence*, accompanied by groaning noises and a chain rattling.

Her heart pounding, she'd actually whispered, "Who is it? Who's there?"

Of course, there'd been no answer, but she'd been spooked beyond all reason. She'd grabbed her robe and fled to the lower floors.

With no small amount of relief, she entered a cozy salon. A fire crackled in the grate, a comfortable couch positioned in front of it, but the room appeared to be empty. She took a hesitant step inside, then another.

"Is anybody here?" she tentatively murmured.

There was no reply, and she stopped, listening and hearing heavy breathing, which scared her out of her wits.

Suddenly, the door slammed with a bang, and a male voice shouted, "Boo!"

"Ah!" she shrieked, and she whipped around to find Lord Penworth lurking behind her.

He laughed and laughed until he was bent over with jollity.

"What is so funny?" she snapped.

"You. Oh, if you could have seen the look on your face. It was priceless."

He swiped a hand across his eyes, wiping away tears of merriment as he collapsed into a chair.

Apparently he'd been sitting in the corner, drinking, and watching her as she'd sneaked in. He seemed to expect that she would stay and chat, but she wasn't in the mood to spar.

After their kiss on Bramwell's ship, she'd studiously avoided him. She'd liked the intimate embrace much more than she should have—so much so, in fact, that she often caught herself daydreaming about it.

She'd obsessed so frequently and in such detail that she wondered if Dubois's potion hadn't had a reverse effect, if it hadn't caused *her* to grow infatuated rather than Penworth.

"Why are you walking the halls?" he asked once his amusement had eased.

"I . . . couldn't sleep."

"Are the ghosts keeping you up?"

She scoffed with false bravado, "There's no such thing as ghosts."

"Isn't there?"

"No."

"It's a castle, Miss Lambert, with centuries of history. Ghosts abound. It's what I love about the place. Just admit you're terrified and be done with it."

"Well . . . now that you mention it . . . I might have witnessed a sight that was a bit . . . peculiar. It unnerved me."

"The initial encounter can be unsettling."

"I thought I heard groaning, too."

"Apparitions and groaning! On your first night! My goodness. You're certainly receiving a warm welcome."

"I didn't care for it."

"You'll get used to it."

"I doubt it."

Her surly retort ignited another bout of hilarity, and as she stared at him, she couldn't help noticing how mirth made him look younger, how it made him look handsome and charming and approachable.

It occurred to her that she was viewing a side of him he rarely showed to others. If she'd been more brazen, she might have tarried, might have drawn him into a conversation and inquired about his mother's surprising arrival.

But it was late, they were alone, and he was imbibing. It was a recipe for disaster.

She headed for the door. "I'd better get back to my room," she said.

"So soon? Aren't you afraid the goblins might be waiting?"

"I'll survive."

"Won't you feel safer by the fire?"

She peered at him, at the fire, at the sofa. She glanced down at her nightgown and robe.

"Actually, no." She reached for the knob. "I'll just be going."

"I don't think so."

Quick as lightning, he jumped up and spun the key in the lock. Then he laid it on top of the doorsill, where she couldn't retrieve it unless she climbed on a chair.

"Give me that key," she fumed.

"No."

"Give it to me!"

"No," he maddeningly repeated.

"I can't be in here with you."

"You already are."

He took a step toward her, and she took one back. He took another, and she did the same. They kept on, with him herding her across the floor as deftly as if they were waltzing at a fancy ball.

There was a gleam in his eye she'd seen before, but it had strengthened to a worrisome degree. A few knocking ghosts didn't seem quite so frightening. Not when she was confronted by a real-life knave who wasn't a figment of her imagination.

"Hold it right there, you bounder." She extended her palm as if the paltry appendage could ward him off.

"You must learn something about me, Miss Lambert."

"What is that?"

"I never do as I'm told."

"Couldn't you start? Just for me?"

"What fun would that be?"

He swooped in and scooped her off her feet. In an instant, she was on her back on the sofa. She'd intended to elude any advance, but he was on top of her so fast that she couldn't. His entire body was stretched out the length of hers.

For several delicious moments, she wallowed in the pleasure of feeling his weight pressing her down, but she swiftly recalled her moral underpinnings. She had to redirect his focus so she could distract him and race out.

The key on the sill posed a problem, but she refused to ponder it. She would find a way to divert him and escape.

"Why are you sitting in here drinking all by yourself?" she asked. "Is it a habit? Should I assume it's yet another secret vice?"

"I have no secret vices."

"Liar."

On being reminded that she knew about Lauretta, his cheeks flushed.

"You have the sharpest tongue," he charged.

"Don't I, though?"

"I never allow anyone to speak to me as you do."

"Why is that, do you suppose?"

"I believe you've driven me insane with your bizarre conduct."

"I'm a perfectly normal woman."

"There's no such thing."

"You bring out the worst in me."

"I'm sure that's true," he said.

"You didn't answer my question."

"About what?"

"About your sitting here in the dark. Why are you?"

He stared and stared, then he stunned her by saying, "If you must know, I've been thinking about my mother."

"Have you?" She struggled to keep her expression blank so he'd continue.

"Have you been apprised of her history?" he inquired.

"Some of it."

"So you're aware of how she . . . when she . . ."

"Yes," she hurriedly interjected to save him the embarrassment of explaining.

"I haven't seen her in three decades." He scowled, appearing somber and solemn. "If you were me, would you kick her out?"

Would she? Her own mother had died when Lily was tiny, and Lily couldn't picture her face or remember her voice. If she could have her mother back, she wouldn't begrudge her any foible. No matter what she might have done or how she'd acted, Lily would welcome her with open arms.

At least he *had* a mother to worry about. Lily had no one at all.

"No, I wouldn't kick her out."

He sighed. "I was afraid you'd say that."

"You won't make her leave, will you? I heard her mention that she has no money and nowhere to go."

"I wouldn't necessarily assume it's the truth."

"Why would she lie?"

"She has a penchant for drama."

"I didn't notice that about her," she fibbed.

"She wouldn't hesitate to tell a tale of woe in order to get what she wants."

"And what would that be?"

He paused and studied her. "Miss Lambert?"

"Yes?"

"I don't want to talk about my mother."

"What do you want to talk about?"

"When we are alone, you're to call me John."

"I'd rather not."

"I shall call you Lily."

"I don't give you permission."

"I don't care."

The room became very quiet. An ember cracked in the grate; the clock on the mantel ticked away. Her heart thundered in her chest.

"Have you ever wished," he said, "that you could be someone else? That you could wave a magic wand and have a different sort of life?"

"I wish it all the time."

"So do I."

He was so near, his beautiful mouth only an inch away. Would he kiss her? She hoped he both would and wouldn't. Further flirtation between them was wrong and dangerous, yet she yearned for him to proceed nonetheless.

Just once—just once!—she wanted to have an adventure. She, who'd always been boring and ordinary, wanted to do something extraordinary, and she wanted to do it with him.

He dipped down and brushed his lips to hers, then he pulled away.

"You shouldn't have done that," she said, not meaning it.

"I know, but when I'm around you, I can't help myself." He grinned from ear to ear, so that he looked young again and possessed of his mother's mischief. "Do you remember that night on board ship," he asked, "when I kissed you?"

As if she would ever forget!

"Yes."

"Since then, I've been able to concentrate on naught but you and how soon we could do it again."

"You can't be serious."

"I most certainly am. Why have you been hiding from me?"

"I haven't been!" At his dubious glare, she mumbled, "Well, maybe a little. Sometimes."

He nodded, an imperious brow raised. "I hate to tell you, Miss Lambert, but our relationship is about to change."

"It is?"

"Yes. You and I will fraternize privately wherever and whenever I can arrange it."

"I don't think that's wise."

"Who said anything about wise? My feelings for you—and what I want to do with you—have no bearing on intelligent behavior or rational choices."

"What is happening then?"

"Don't you know? It's lust, Miss Lambert. It's lust— pure and simple."

He crushed his mouth to hers, sweeping her into a maelstrom of passion, the likes of which she'd never previously imagined existed.

She'd been kissed before—against her will by men she didn't like—so she'd viewed kissing as a distasteful exercise in frustration, where she'd spent every second fighting to escape.

This was nothing like those prior experiences. It was thrilling and astonishing and exhilarating, and she couldn't decide what to do except kiss him back.

His hands were everywhere, stroking across her hair, shoulders, and arms. Her own hands were busy, too, exploring with a reckless abandon. He seemed to relish her brazen curiosity, and the more bold she became, the more intensely he participated, as if he couldn't get close enough to her.

He loosened the belt on her robe and shoved at the lapels so he could caress her breasts. They were covered only by the thin fabric of her nightgown. His questing fingers squeezed her nipples, tormenting them till they were taut and rigid, and the sensation was so arousing that she was glad she was lying down. If she hadn't been, she might have swooned.

He broke away and nibbled a trail to her bosom. He nuzzled at her cleavage, the gesture sending jolts of excitement to her womb and out to her extremities. As he drew a nipple into his mouth, she squealed with surprise.

"Hush!" he teased, chuckling, "or the entire household will hear you."

"You can't . . . can't . . ."

"Can't what? Can't touch you here?" He pinched her nipple very hard. "Or here?" He pinched the other one even harder.

"It's indecent," she tried to claim.

"Yes, it is. That's why it's so enjoyable."

He fell to her breasts again, and he suckled her nipples, going back and forth, back and forth, until she was so fraught with stimulation that she felt she might explode.

"Penworth, desist!"

"No."

"Please?"

"I might if you call me John."

"I won't."

"Then I guess I'll have to continue, won't I?"

He jumped in with a renewed vigor that had her writhing and moaning. He was lifting the hem of her nightgown. Her calves were bared, then her knees, and as her thighs were exposed, she panicked.

"What are you doing?"

"You don't know?"

"No."

"Hasn't any man ever touched you like this?"

"I'm a spinster, Penworth. Of course not."

"Lucky me to be the first."

His hand came to rest between her legs, and to her amazement, he slid a finger into her womanly sheath.

She gasped and arched up, as he smiled his wicked smile. A second finger was added, and he began stroking them in and out. They fit exactly right, as if he'd been specifically created to caress her in just such a fashion.

She flopped onto the cushion, her arms flung wide, like a virgin about to be sacrificed.

"I give up," she muttered. "Have your way with me."

"I intend to."

He laughed as he drove her up and up, until her heart was pounding so violently that she thought it might cease beating altogether.

"Almost there," he murmured.

"Good. I feel as if I'm dying. Have mercy on me."

"No. No mercy for you."

He kissed her again, as his thumb made a few seductive circles. He jabbed at a sensitive spot she hadn't previously noticed. Like magic, the most unexpected wave of pleasure shot through her.

She was blinded by bliss, and she soared to the heavens, then gradually, the agitation decreased and the moment ended. Her body was in shock, her limbs rubbery and limp. How would she stand? How would she walk to her room? Had she been crippled by amour?

He shifted, stretching out behind her along the back of the sofa, offering her the perfect chance to slip away. She tried to sit, but posture was impossible. Instead, she tumbled to the floor. Frantically, she pulled at her nightgown, covering her private parts and legs.

Their ardor quickly waned, and she wasn't quite so overwhelmed. Sanity returned, and with it, her prudence.

What was she thinking? Why was it that, when she was in his company, she couldn't behave?

It's Dubois's potion, an absurd voice whispered in her mind, and she was terrified anew that it was having a reverse effect. While Penworth seemed the same as ever, she was changing by the minute.

Why was she growing attached? She wasn't able to fight her attraction. What was causing it? What if it got worse? Would she soon be lurking outside his bedchamber, hoping to be invited in?

She glanced at him over her shoulder. He was casually lounged, his head balanced on his hand, his lazy smile mesmerizing her. He looked completely at ease, comfortable and composed, but she felt rumpled, out of her element, and thoroughly undone.

"You are so wicked," she scolded.

"Not usually. This is all your fault."

"Mine! What is it that I *do*? Please tell me so I can stop doing it."

"Why would I want you to stop?"

"We're marching down the road to perdition."

"And I'm enjoying the view."

His hot attention meandered down her torso, and she tugged at her robe and tied the sash extra tight.

"Get back up here." He patted the empty spot she'd just vacated. "We're not finished."

"Yes, we are."

He motioned her nearer with his finger. "Come here."

"No."

He reached for her and she scooted away on her bottom, out of range. They engaged in a staring match.

"Don't pretend to female umbrage," he said.

"What?"

"You love dallying with me. Admit it. Don't be coy."

"I'm not being coy. I'm just not going to do it again."

"Aren't you?"

He sat up as if he might grab her, and she leapt to her feet and stumbled away. Keeping a wary eye on him, she lugged a chair over to the door, climbed up, and snatched the key. She'd presumed he would attempt to prevent her, and when he didn't, she couldn't decide if she was relieved or not.

"Where are you off to now?" He stifled a yawn, as if—with his having debauched her—he couldn't care less about where she'd be.

"To my bedchamber."

"Aren't you afraid of the ghosts?"

"There are bigger dangers in this castle."

"Meaning *me*."

"Yes."

He chuckled. "Coward."

"To the marrow of my bones."

His chuckle became a hearty laugh. "Would you like me to escort you upstairs?"

"I'm not about to let you catch me in any dark corners. I'll take my chances with the goblins."

He unfolded his large frame from the sofa, and he sauntered over, his blue, blue eyes holding her spellbound. He took the key and stuck it in the lock.

"Has it occurred to you," he said, "that the *ghosts* you heard might be the twins trying to frighten you?"

Her jaw dropped, and she smacked her forehead with the heel of her hand.

"Oh, how stupid of me!"

"I'll be very disappointed if you let them win this battle."

She grinned. "You believe what I told you about them?"

"Yes, Lily, I believe you."

He leaned down and kissed her, then he pulled the door open.

She dawdled, gawking at him like an imbecile. There were a thousand things she yearned to tell him, but she didn't dare.

"Go," he quietly advised, "before I make you stay."

He urged her into the hall, where she promptly bumped into his mother. Barbara's curious gaze raced down Lily's body, scrutinizing her nightclothes, her disheveled state, and her bare feet.

Lily blushed from the roots of her hair to the tips of her toes.

"Well, well," Barbara said, "Miss Lambert, isn't it? Violet's *companion*?"

"Hello . . . ah . . . Mrs. Middleton." Lily was stammering, not certain what to call the imposing woman. "I was just . . . just . . . I wasn't doing anything."

"Really?" Barbara guffawed.

"Why are you sneaking about, Barbara?" Lord Penworth asked.

"I'm not *sneaking*. I couldn't sleep."

"Was there something you wanted?"

"No. I think I've found all I need and a bit more besides."

Lily glanced at Lord Penworth, her alarm clear. If Barbara blabbed about what she'd witnessed, Lily's job would be over, her reputation shredded.

The earl—to Lily's astonishment—understood her apprehension.

"She won't tattle to anyone," he calmly assured Lily. "Will you, Barbara?"

He glared at Barbara, his expression cold and hard.

"I'm a veritable fount of discretion," Barbara insisted.

He nodded at Lily and waved her away. "You go on. Don't worry about her."

Lily was frozen in place, overcome by the strongest desire to explain or defend herself.

Barbara looked at the earl, then at Lily again, and she snorted.

"Tumbling the servants, John?" she mused. "I find it completely unlike you, but I also find it absolutely fascinating."

She strolled on and disappeared down the dark corridor.

Lily spun and ran the other way.

Chapter 8

❧

"It's not so bad, is it?"

"I beg to differ. It's as awful as I imagined it would be."

"Stop fussing. Stop scowling at everyone."

Phillip Dudley—also known as Frenchman and master charlatan Philippe Dubois—studied the bejeweled horde in the drawing room of Lord Penworth's Scottish castle. He glared at his sister, Clarinda.

"I can't help scowling," he said. "My collar is so tight that I'm choking."

"I should be so lucky," Clarinda retorted. "Perhaps if I tighten it a bit more, you'll fall to the floor and stay there."

"All right, all right. I'll cease my complaints."

"Rumor has it that the punch bowl is spiked with Penworth's best whiskey. Why don't you check?"

"I am always in a better mood when I'm drinking."

"Yes, you are. And *I* will have more fun if you're not hovering and frowning at every fellow who gets within ten feet of me."

He flashed a fierce glower, simply to hear her laugh, then he sauntered away.

He wasn't used to wearing fancy coats and tailored trousers, frilly cravats and boots that pinched his toes, but he'd come to Scotland for Clarinda. If it killed him, he would act the part of a British gentleman. Just to make her happy. Just to give her some semblance of a normal life.

He was thirty and she was twenty-five, a pair of orphaned, nomadic wanderers. Ever since she was a baby, she'd tagged after him, living on the road, participating in his schemes, and keeping him out of trouble.

She was an accomplished apothecary and midwife, but he sold amulets and charms and coerced women into wasting their hard-earned money on magic and sorcery.

Clarinda was his only sister, his only family, and while he thrived on their itinerant travels, she yearned for a more traditional existence. When he'd stumbled on the chance to provide it to her, he hadn't been able to refuse.

In London, after a series of dramatic events, their acquaintance—Captain Tristan Odell—had asked them to journey to Scotland where he owned a fine property that was standing empty. He'd urged them to move in to his country house and watch over it for him.

After much fussing and fretting, Phillip had agreed. For Clarinda's sake.

They'd spent years trekking from place to place, so he didn't believe she'd take to four walls and a solid roof, but for the moment, she was content, and he wouldn't ruin it for her. Let her make friends. Let her flirt with a beau or two. It wouldn't kill Phillip to permit it.

He meandered through the crowd Penworth had amassed for his first hunting party of the season. The old castle was jam-packed with neighbors who'd come to eat, dance, and fraternize.

He hadn't met the earl yet, but he'd been introduced to the man's relatives. A sorrier bunch he couldn't have found anywhere: the grim stepmother, the slothful half brother, the haughty fiancée, and the spoiled wards. They were like characters in a bad theatrical play, and he couldn't fathom why Penworth had brought them along.

If it had been up to Phillip, he'd have told the entire crew to remain in England. How did Penworth find any peace when surrounded by the wretched group?

Phillip wondered how poor Miss Lambert was faring. He hadn't seen her. Was she still working for Penworth? Or had she swallowed Phillip's potion, married, and fled the man's employ?

Phillip certainly hoped that she had. She was too sweet to be trapped in such a miserable situation.

He located the punch bowl and was elated to note that Clarinda had been correct: The frothy concoction was laced with liquor. He downed a glass then ambled to the terrace, wanting to be away from the gowns and perfume and sweat. Leaned against the balustrade, he gazed out at the park, the trails clearly marked by hanging lanterns.

If Clarinda kept insisting she was happy, glad for the lodging Odell had offered, Phillip couldn't make her abandon it. But where would it leave them? They'd always been a pair, a team. If he left Clarinda behind, what would become of him? The notion of carrying on without her was unbearably sad.

How long would he dicker in Scotland? How long would he wait to hear Clarinda say she was ready to return to London? What if she was never ready?

"It's a lovely night, isn't it?"

Phillip spun to see that a woman had joined him.

"Yes, it is."

She was very beautiful, with vibrant brunette hair, big green eyes, and a voluptuous figure. Initially, he thought they were close to the same age, but he quickly realized that she was older, perhaps by a decade or more. She wore her maturity well, her attractiveness flowing out in a pulsating wave.

"You won't swoon if I introduce myself, will you?" she asked.

"I'll try not to," Phillip dryly responded.

"I'm renowned for doing what's completely improper."

"My favorite sort of female."

"Then I suppose we'll get on famously."

"Yes, I suppose we will."

"I'm Barbara Middleton."

She extended her slender hand, and he clasped hold. She didn't seem inclined to pull it away, so he didn't either.

"I'm Phillip Dudley."

"Hello, Mr. Dudley. Tell me that you'll rescue me from the dullards inside."

"Will you walk with me in the garden?"

"I would be delighted."

He took her arm and started for the stairs. They proceeded down the manicured paths, the noise from the party fading in the distance. The farther they strolled from the castle, the better he felt.

"You sound very English, Mr. Dudley," she said.

"I am."

"Allow me to rudely pry into what brings you to Scotland?"

"My sister, Clarinda, and I are friendly with Captain Odell, Penworth's neighbor to the west. Do you know him?"

"No."

"He'll be in London for a time—he's marrying an English girl—and he asked us to come up and look after the property for him."

"Have you had any visitors yet?"

"No."

"Then I shall be your first. How about if I call on you tomorrow?"

"I would be honored, and Clarinda will be thrilled. Now, what about you? Why are you here? If you're a Middleton, you must be related to the earl."

"I'm his mother."

"Oh," he mused, "*that* Barbara."

"Yes, *that* one."

"Everybody is whispering about you."

"Wouldn't you think they could find a more interesting topic than me?"

"Apparently not. We're in the country, after all. If you weren't here, what would they have to gossip about?"

"I aim to please."

Phillip chuckled, and they sauntered on in a companionable silence, and he had to admit that he was extremely intrigued.

No one who lived in London could have failed to hear the stories about her. She was probably the most scandalous woman in the kingdom, certainly the most notorious he'd ever met personally, and he had a thousand questions he was dying to pose.

Why was she home? What about her son? What was his opinion as to her unexpected appearance? With the whole family in residence—including Esther Middleton— Barbara had to have rattled a few cages.

"In case you're wondering," she said as if she could read his mind, "my Italian paramour recently passed away. I was lonely and alone—and dead broke—so I came back."

"How does your son feel about your arrival?"

"He's a tad grumpy, but I'm wearing him down." She laughed, and it was a sultry, sexy sound that settled low in his belly. His testicles clenched, his cock stirred, and he was stunned to catch himself assessing her in a thoroughly carnal fashion.

It had been a while since he'd tumbled into an affair. Would he have one with Barbara Middleton? The prospect was enticing, and it would definitely make the time in Scotland speed by more swiftly.

His thoughts were already awhirl, calculating the risks. Discovery was always a possibility, and it paid to be wary. He'd been run out of many villages by angry fathers or brothers. If he tangled with Barbara Middleton, who would care? Would anyone?

Her son maybe, but why would he? Barbara was no

innocent maiden with virtue to protect. Still, it was dangerous to cross a nobleman. They had a tendency to lash out and lash out viciously.

"Are you bored here in Scotland?" Barbara inquired.

"I've been going mad, struggling to keep myself busy."

"Do you hunt?"

"No."

"Do you ride?"

"Not if I don't have to."

"How will you amuse yourself when all the other fellows are off shooting guns and jumping hedges?"

"I've been trying to figure that out."

Suddenly, she stopped walking, and she pulled him around to face her. She stepped in so their torsos were pressed together. Her body was every bit as lush as he'd suspected. She wasn't shy, being perfectly happy to let him feel her full, curvaceous breasts, while she enjoyed the feel of his raging cockstand against her hip.

"You're a fine masculine specimen, Mr. Dudley," she boldly remarked.

"Well . . . thank you. I guess."

"I noticed you as soon as you arrived at the party with your sister."

"Did you now?"

"Yes."

"So our meeting wasn't an accident. You were stalking me."

She winked. "I won't deny it."

"To what end?" As if he didn't know!

"I just love a man with dark hair and eyes. I wanted to learn if you were as delicious up close as you were from across the room."

She laid her palm on his chest and rubbed in slow circles.

"And now that you've seen me," he queried, "what is your opinion?"

"I'm very pleased." She licked a tempting tongue over her bottom lip. "Are you a betting man, Mr. Dudley?"

"Absolutely."

"I presumed you were. I'm betting that you and I will become very good friends."

Her intent clear, she raised a flirtatious brow. She planned an affair! Far be it from him to dissuade her. He usually got himself into trouble because he seduced younger women, and when he was caught, family members took umbrage.

It had been ages since he'd consorted with an older woman, and when he did, *he* was the rogue who instigated the liaison. It was never the female. He couldn't remember the last time he'd had such a brazen invitation, and he was aroused merely from envisioning how naughty it could turn out to be.

"I'd say," he replied, "that you and I will be the very *best* of friends."

"Marvelous. When is your sister at home?"

"Most days."

"Let me rephrase my question: When is she likely to *not* be at home?"

"It's a huge bloody house. You can sneak through the woods and enter by the rear door. Even if she's present, she'll never know."

"I could stop by anytime?"

"Anytime at all."

"How about tomorrow at eleven? I can stay all afternoon."

Blimey! No beating around the bush with this one.

"Eleven o'clock will be perfect."

She rose on tiptoe and brushed a kiss to his mouth. "I'll see you then," she said.

She drew away and hurried back to the party. He watched her go, cursing his rampant erection and worrying over what the hell he'd set in motion. She'd be a handful, that was guaranteed, but wasn't he due for some excitement?

He grinned, his sojourn in Scotland suddenly not seeming quite so dreary.

He started toward the party, too, whistling as he went.

* * *

"MONSIEUR Dubois? It is you!"

Lily leaned over the balustrade to get a better view as he returned from a stroll in the garden with Barbara Middleton. Barbara swept up the stairs, but Dubois approached more slowly.

Lily had noticed him earlier in the card room, but she'd been sure her eyes were playing tricks. She'd seen his sister, Clarinda, as well, promenading in a line of dancers, but again, she'd told herself that she had to be mistaken.

She'd met Dubois twice previous, and both occasions had been brief and in passing: near Penworth Hall after Lord Penworth had first hired her, and later, at the harbor in London.

Dubois's wagon had been parked at the dock, and he'd been hawking his wares to departing travelers. His sister had been with him, and they'd enjoyed a cordial good-bye as Lily had boarded Bramwell's ship to sail for Scotland.

What on earth was he doing at Penworth Castle?

He stepped onto the terrace, his hands extended in greeting.

"Miss Lambert," he said, "how lovely to see you. I was wondering if you were still working for Lord Penworth."

"Hello, Mr. Dubois. I'm so glad you're here. I've been dying to ask you about—"

He cut her off. "Actually, it's Dudley. Phillip Dudley."

At the admission, she frowned. "What happened to your accent?"

Flushing—as if embarrassed—he glanced over to where Barbara was about to go inside. She halted and peered over her shoulder.

"His accent?" Barbara inquired.

Dubois looked at Barbara, then Lily, and he shrugged.

"It's a long story," he claimed.

"She called you *Dubois*."

"It's just a little joke between the two of us," he contended.

"A secret name," Barbara mulled, "and a lost accent. I'm guessing there's a fascinating tale behind it all."

"There might be," Dubois allowed.

"Oh," Barbara gushed, "this will be even more entertaining than I imagined."

She flashed a sultry smile, then continued on. Lily was alone with Dubois or Dudley or whoever he was.

"We need to talk," he said.

"We certainly do."

He guided her down the stairs and out into the garden, away from the other guests. They came to a bench and sat.

"I must ask you," he began, appearing uncomfortable, "not to mention a few things when you bump into me."

"Which things?"

"Well, my French name and my occupation—for starters."

She studied him, gazing into his beautiful brown eyes. She'd suspected he was a mysterious fellow, but apparently, she'd had no idea!

"What are you up to, Dubois?"

"It's complicated."

"Why don't you attempt to explain? Are you scheming against the earl? Should I warn him?"

"No," he scoffed, "it's nothing like that."

"Then what is it?"

"I'm here with my sister. We're living on the next property. She's trying to fit in in the neighborhood. I want people to believe she's gentry."

"She's not."

"She's close enough, and she can pull it off. It's important to her, and I won't ruin it."

"So you've become an Englishman?"

"I've always been an Englishman."

She should have been angry with him, but he gave her such a saucy grin that she couldn't be. The knave.

"You're Dudley, then. Not Dubois."

"Phillip Dudley, yes. I pretend to be French sometimes, but I'm not."

"Why pretend?"

"It helps me sell my merchandise."

To gullible women like me, she pathetically realized.

She'd been charmed by him, by his foreign accent and his flamboyant manners, and he'd coerced her masterfully. She was so desperate to be loved that she'd let him convince her he dispensed miracles.

For weeks, she'd been fretting about Lord Penworth and the Spinster's Cure she'd swallowed, but it had all been nonsense, and she was inordinately sad that no magic had been performed.

She felt like a fool. A naïve, stupid fool.

"It was all fake, wasn't it?"

"What was?"

"Your Spinster's Cure, and your Daily Remedy, and your ability to read my mind. You're a charlatan."

"I beg your pardon?" he huffed.

"You're an imposter. I should have known."

"Merely because my accent is different doesn't mean my recipes have changed."

"It's all right. You've been caught out, Mr. Dudley. You can drop the pretense."

"Pretense! My mother was a Gypsy. The mixtures I create are thousands of years old, passed down from generation to generation."

"Stop it." She scowled and punched him on the arm. "I'm embarrassed enough that I believed you. You're only making me feel worse."

"Miss Lambert—Lily—listen to me."

"I won't. Not if you're going to spew more gibberish."

"I traveled to Scotland to see my sister settled in Odell's country manor. Currently, I'm not working at my craft, but I shall return to London very soon, and when I do, I will once again be selling the very items you denigrate."

"I pity the women of London upon whom you intend to prey."

He assessed her, his astute gaze digging deep, and she squirmed under his avid scrutiny. His focus was very powerful, as if he could peer all the way to her soul. She didn't like the perception he produced, as if he were wiser than he should be, as if he could view what he shouldn't.

"Miss Lambert, what is it? You can confide in me."

"I've naught to confide."

"I must look at your hand."

"Why?"

Before she could prevent him, he clasped it and flipped it over, tipping it toward a nearby lantern. He traced the line in the center.

"Ah," he murmured, "I see."

She yanked away and scooted across the bench.

"What? What do you see?"

"You drank my potion."

"I did not," she insisted.

"You shouldn't lie to me, Miss Lambert. You're terribly bad at it." He meticulously evaluated her, then he said, "Let me guess: You drank it, and now, you're unnerved by events that seem beyond your control."

She almost answered, then shook a scolding finger at him. "Oh no you don't. I'm not playing this game with you again."

Ignoring her protest, he continued, "There is a man enamored of you. He shouldn't be; there's no reason for his interest. It's frightened you, and you're anxious to discuss the situation with me. You're afraid you might have applied the elixir incorrectly or that it is having an erroneous result."

As he waited for her reply, he was very smug, sure he was right, sure she'd relent and spill all. She dawdled, trying to decide if she should speak up or be silent.

She'd accused him of being a charlatan, but how could he know the details he'd mentioned? Unless he possessed some genuine clairvoyance, he couldn't have deduced her exact dilemma.

"Well?" he pressed.

"I might have drunk it," she groused.

"And?"

"Could it have had a reverse effect?"

"What do you mean?"

"Could it have altered my destiny, rather than his? Could it have made me . . . uh . . ."

She was too mortified to finish the sentence, and he shrewdly and instantly ascertained her predicament.

"You've fallen in love," he said.

"Nothing that dramatic. I'm just . . . just . . ."

"Smitten?"

"A tad." He raised a skeptical brow, and she admitted, "Perhaps more than a tad. I carefully followed your instructions, but there was an . . . *accident* and I wound up staring at the wrong man. Ever since, when I'm around him, I can't help myself."

"You seduced him?!"

"Mr. Dudley! I wouldn't have the faintest idea how."

Her cheeks heated with chagrin, as he sighed and patted her shoulder.

"It's like that, is it?" he muttered. "What is your biggest worry? Is it that there could be a babe?"

"No!"

"You can tell me the truth, because if that's the problem, I'll have you talk to my sister. She has remedies for every type of feminine difficulty."

"Matters haven't progressed so far."

"I'm relieved to hear it."

"I seem particularly affected. That's all."

"The gentleman in question, he is not?"

"He's lust-filled, but hardly infatuated."

Dudley pondered, then nodded pensively. "Male lust is often an early sign of amour. We're thick creatures; we don't always recognize what's occurring."

"But he can't be besotted. It's ludicrous to think he would be."

"Why is that? You're very pretty. You're smart and pleasant. Why couldn't he be besotted?"

"Because he's very much above me in station, and . . . and . . . he's engaged to be married."

He sucked in a sharp breath. "It's Lord Penworth?"

"Yes," she miserably confessed.

"It's happening again," he reflected more to himself than to her.

"What is?"

"The last batch of Spinster's Cure that I mixed has been very powerful. It's produced several matches that were completely impossible."

"Are you saying that Penworth might end up married to me?"

"Yes, that's precisely what I'm saying."

"Don't be absurd. Men like him don't wed women like me. It's a law of the universe."

"Over the past summer, it's happened twice. As the romances were blossoming, I had this same conversation with the other two young ladies."

"I need an antidote." At the request, she felt like an idiot. Why ask for an antidote for a concoction she deemed to be fake? "Is there one?"

"No."

"What should I do?"

"There's nothing *to* do."

"I have to try something. I still have the second vial you sold me. Should I take another dose? Should I find a different man—a more suitable man—and drink it while staring at him?"

"You can, but it won't help."

"Why wouldn't it?"

"I told you when you bought it: My potions are extremely potent. Your destiny has been altered. So has Penworth's. He just doesn't realize it yet."

"Stop saying that."

"Why shouldn't I? It's true. He won't be marrying Violet Howard. She might as well pack her bags and depart for London."

Lily glanced around, terrified that Dudley might have been overheard. Luckily, no one was hovering.

She stood, irked with herself for participating in the

inane chat, for giving credence to his outlandish remarks. It only encouraged him to be ridiculous. "This discussion is silly," she said, "and I'm putting an end to it."

"If you didn't want my opinion, why ask for it?"

"Temporary insanity."

He laughed. "You can pretend I'm a fraud, but it won't change anything."

"We'll see."

"Yes, we will. Drink the contents of the other vial. If it's all so much nonsense, where's the harm? If you're wrong . . ."

His voice trailed off. He looked smug again, much like the earl when he was being belligerent while making a point.

She was aghast. "Could the situation get worse?"

"It's all poppycock, so why would it?"

A frisson of fear wiggled down her spine.

"I do not believe in potions," she declared.

"You don't have to believe for the magic to work."

"I do not believe in potions!" she repeated more vehemently, the phrase running through her head like an incantation.

She stomped away, and he called, "Miss Lambert?"

She whipped around. "Yes?"

"After you swallow the second dose, inform me at once. We'll talk."

"Why?"

"Your problems will be exacerbated, so we'll have to decide on your next course of action."

"You are mad, and I am done with listening to you."

She spun and fled.

Chapter 9

❦

"HE'S quite a manly fellow."

"I've noticed that about him."

"Probably much more *masculine* than you realized."

Edward and Violet stood on the terrace, arm in arm. He smiled wanly as he pointed at John, whose horse had just jumped a fence, then thundered away over a distant hill.

The smile Violet flashed in return was troubled, which certainly boosted Edward's mood. It was humorous, making her question her choice of John as fiancé.

John was in his element, riding about the estate. His color was high, his hair tousled by the wind, and—clinging to the back of a magnificent stallion—he cut a dashing figure. Any woman worth her salt would have been riveted, but Violet was easily swayed, and it was a simple matter encouraging her to see what wasn't there.

"He's rigorous in his habits," Edward said.

"Yes, he is."

"It's indiscreet of me to mention this, but you have such

a delicate constitution. Have you thought of what it will mean for you?"

"In what way?"

Edward managed a competent blush. "In your . . . ah . . . wifely duties." He patted her hand. "You'll be fine. You'll weather it well."

"If only . . ."

He seized on her hesitation. "If only what, darling?"

"If only Father had selected someone who was a tad less . . . *robust*."

"Someone who appreciated what a slight and feminine creature you are?"

"Yes."

"Someone more like me, perhaps?"

"Yes."

Edward pulled her around to face him, so they were very close.

"My dearest, Violet!" he gushed.

"Yes, Edward?"

"I'm sickened that John will be your . . . your . . ." He bit off an oath. "Oh, it's hopeless."

"What are you saying?"

"Nothing. John is my brother, and the two of you are due all the happiness in the world. Despite my feelings, I can't wish for more."

"What feelings?"

"Don't you know, Violet?"

"No."

"It's always been you—the girl of my dreams—but with John in the picture, I never had a chance."

"I had no idea."

Neither did I! Edward crudely reflected.

He was in love with her, all right. With her dowry and her status as a duke's daughter. It was the story of his life that it would all fall to John, who'd already received so many boons that he failed to appreciate any of them.

"I wonder if I should speak to Father," she tentatively broached, but Edward was quick to quash any rash conduct.

If he perpetrated a betrayal with Violet, it would be reckless and fast, such as absconding with her on her wedding day. He would glean enormous satisfaction from leaving John standing at the altar.

"No, my sweet," he cooed. "You can't speak to the duke; he's made his decision. You shall be John's bride, and I am doomed to admire you from afar. We can't yearn for more. It would be wrong."

"I suppose it would be." She sighed.

Over her shoulder, he glanced up and saw Miranda beckoning to him. From the sultry gleam in her eye, it was clear the twins were planning decadency again, and he was eager to participate. Scotland was proving to be as boring as he'd anticipated, his only amusement being his flirtation with Violet.

He'd invited her to go riding in the gig, and she was like a clinging vine. How was he to be shed of her?

"Did you hear that?" He peered toward the front entrance of the castle.

"No."

"I think my mother is calling you. She told me she wanted you to accompany her on her afternoon visiting."

"How considerate."

"She must be searching for you. Perhaps we should check." He pretended to ponder. "Never mind. We can catch up with her when we return."

"We're in no hurry," Violet insisted, her perfect manners surging to the fore. "I'll talk to her."

"Last I knew, she was in the drawing room."

"I'll just be a minute."

"While I'm waiting, I'll dash up to my bedchamber and fetch my coat. I'll meet you out in the barn."

She hastened away, and he dawdled till she'd rounded the corner. The instant she was out of sight, he strolled over to Miranda.

"You're getting awfully friendly with Violet," she noted.

"Violet is of no consequence, and she's engaged to John. What do you want?"

"Are you busy?"

"No."

"Melanie has finished her bath. She needs you."

"Then I am hers to command."

They climbed the stairs to the twins' bedchamber, and by the time they entered, his anticipation was so great that he could hardly walk. His erection was that pronounced.

As occurred at their previous dalliance, they marched straight to the dressing room, where Melanie was immersed in the tub. She came up out of the water and stepped to the floor.

"Will you dry me?" she inquired. She whirled around, showing him her back. Her hair was piled high on her head, a few wet tendrils curling down.

Miranda handed him a towel, and he started at Melanie's neck, wiping with slow motions so he could prolong the moment.

He arrived at her waist and dropped to his knees, running the towel over and over the globes of her ass, daring once to swipe it in her crack.

Unsure as to what would happen next, he was delighted when she spun and ordered, "Do my front."

He fumbled up her calves, being particularly clumsy, but he couldn't help himself. With him still kneeling, he was staring directly at her pussy, and he was able to definitively determine that she had no hair covering the indecent mound. Her privates were bare as a baby's bottom.

How had she removed it? Did she shave herself? Did a maid? Did her sister shave her?

Gad, he could vividly picture it! The two of them nude, Melanie on her back, her thighs spread so that Miranda could work unimpeded.

If he was lucky, he might be asked to watch someday, maybe even assist. At the prospect, blood rushed down to his penis so quickly that he nearly fainted.

"Open your legs," he advised her.

"No talking!" Miranda barked, sounding like a captain of a military regiment. "Melanie, give me the whip."

Edward was agog with speculation as Melanie reached into a dresser and pulled out a riding crop. She offered the whip to Miranda, and Miranda tapped him on the shoulder. Not too hard, but with sufficient force that he knew it would hurt if she chose to play it rough.

"You missed several spots," Miranda sternly chastised.

He hesitated, not certain to which spots she referred, and she slapped his other shoulder, harder than before. He applied himself to Melanie's breasts, rubbing the towel in circles, arousing her nipples till they were taut little buds.

"That's enough for now."

Melanie shoved him away as Miranda took the towel.

"Stand up," Miranda snarled.

He obeyed as she shifted behind Melanie. Her clothed torso was snuggled to Melanie's naked one. She wrapped an arm over Melanie's waist and held her close.

"We want to look at your phallus," Miranda said. "Unbutton your trousers."

He swiftly complied.

"Let us see how big you are. Let us see if your cock is worth having."

He wasn't worried about exposing himself. His rod was impressive. He yanked it out, and it dangled toward them, a rigid, angry appendage, begging to be stroked.

"Would you like Melanie to touch it?" Miranda asked.

"Yes . . . yes . . ."

Melanie knelt down, while Miranda observed. She was in charge of events, but curiously unaffected.

Edward braced, hissing out his breath as Melanie put her tongue to the root, then traced a leisurely trail to the tip. He assumed heaven was approaching, that she would suck him between those ruby lips and take him to paradise, but as his balls clenched, she drew away and stood.

He lunged for her, and Miranda cracked the crop across his wrist, leaving a red welt.

"You may only proceed if you have my permission," Miranda explained.

"But I want to—"

"I said *no!*"

She smacked his cheek. At any other time in his life, with any other woman, he'd have wrenched the whip away and given her a taste of her own medicine, but for reasons he couldn't fathom, he didn't move.

It was thrilling, having her in control. She'd dominated him in a fashion he'd never encountered prior, and he was incredibly excited by it. Her behavior called to a deviant part of him, one that enjoyed how he'd been subjugated.

"We're finished for today," Miranda stated. "You may button up."

Without speaking, he did as she'd bid him.

"On your next visit," Miranda said, "you will fuck my sister. I will tell you how." She tapped the crop on his thigh. "You will do it *exactly* as I say, or you will be punished. Do you understand?"

"Yes, I understand."

"You may go."

She ushered him out and pushed him into the hall. She started to shut the door, and he frantically asked, "When will you send for me again?"

"We'll let you know."

He staggered to his bedchamber, trying to figure out how he could accelerate their summons and needing—once again—to rapidly ease the pressure in his loins.

"ARE you still with us, Miss Lambert?"

"Yes."

Lily carefully maneuvered the last few steps down an ancient staircase that wound into the bowels of the earth to a hot springs below the castle. She was following the twins, who were up ahead.

As they'd descended, the air had grown warm and humid, so the stones were very slippery, and it had slowed her pace. Yet she couldn't dawdle. The twins had both brought lanterns, but they hadn't instructed her to bring one. If she lagged, she would be left in the dark.

The twins had insisted she accompany them to help them bathe. She'd considered refusing, but curiosity had prodded her to tag along.

What could go wrong? she'd asked herself. She'd told a maid where she'd be, so it wasn't as if she could vanish.

She'd never been to a hot springs spa, had never tasted the medicinal waters or swum in the bubbling currents, so she'd been eager for the adventure. But when she'd agreed to attend them, she hadn't known that the walk would be so treacherous, or that she would end up such a distance from the occupied sections of the castle.

She let go of the slimy, moss-covered wall and entered a huge underground cave. Lantern light flickered off the ceiling, making it glow a silvery white. Water gurgled at the rear, trickling down in a waterfall to form a large pool. It was very clean, very clear, and she could see the bottom. It looked just the right depth for wading and floating.

The place was decadent and hedonistic, and she hoped she'd be able to come back sometime. She'd like to strip to her chemise and jump in, but with the twins present, she never would.

"How do you like it?" Melanie inquired of her.

"It's spectacular," Lily had to admit. She pointed into the pool. "Are those benches in the rocks?"

"Yes."

"Who carved them?"

"John believes it was the Romans."

"So it's very old," Lily mused.

"And very magical," Miranda added.

Lily concurred. There was an eerie, almost reverential stillness to the grotto, as if primeval spirits were observing them.

Miranda began fussing with the buttons on her gown, but she couldn't reach them.

"Miss Lambert," she said, "I need your assistance."

"Certainly."

Lily approached, prepared for any mischief, but she didn't see what trick they could play. They might shove her into the pool, but it wouldn't kill her to get wet. She'd survive a dunking.

"Do you swim?" Miranda probed.

"Yes."

"Will you swim today?"

"No."

"Shy, are you?"

"I'm not shy. I'm just not about to remove my clothes, for I'm sure that—the moment I did—you would grab them and run, leaving me to traipse upstairs in my drawers."

"My, my!" Melanie batted her lashes. "I wonder what John would say?"

"Precisely. You'd have me convicted before I could defend myself."

"You'd be fired, as our prior companions were all fired."

"Yes, I would be, so I'm not taking any chances."

"How is it that you know us so well, Miss Lambert?" Miranda queried. "The other ladies never figured out that we were trying to get rid of them. They were never suspicious—as you always are."

"You aren't my first tough assignment, and you won't be my last."

"We won't stop our attempts to be shed of you. You must realize that."

"Yes, I realize it, so I won't let down my guard."

"It seems we're at an impasse."

"It seems we are," Lily concurred.

She should have seen it coming, but she didn't.

They'd lured her into complacency with their civil conversation, and she'd turned slightly to peer out over the water.

Her initial indication of calamity was activity at the periphery of her vision. Her adrenaline surged, and she meant to spin toward them, but before she could, Miranda pushed her very hard. Lily stumbled to her knees, then was pushed a second time, her head hitting the stone floor with a muted thud.

Dazed and disoriented, she struggled to rise, but she

was pushed, once more, her head smacking rock again, so she was barely conscious.

She felt herself being rolled into the pool, but she couldn't forestall them. It was a drop of several feet, and it transpired slowly, as if she was watching it happen to someone else.

For a brief instant, she was positive their blows had blinded her. She couldn't see anything, but then, it dawned on her that they had taken their lanterns and fled. They hustled up the staircase, their giggles echoing in the vaulted chamber.

She ordered her limbs to respond, but they didn't, and it occurred to her that she might be drowning. If she perished, would anyone care? Would anyone search?

In complete darkness, in a total vacuum devoid of light or sound, she sank down, her heavy, soaked garments dragging her to the bottom.

"ANY news?" John asked.

"We've looked everywhere, Lord Penworth," the butler, Angus, said. "Miss Lambert seems to have disappeared."

"How could that be?" John mused. "She's an adult woman who weighs at least ten stone. Such a person doesn't just vanish."

John was secluded in his library, away from his supper guests and their merriment in the other wing of the castle. He was trying to maintain his composure but finding it impossible.

It was after eleven. Where could she be? Had she left him?

Though he was panicked, he couldn't show any overt alarm. As far as the world was concerned, she was merely an employee, and thus not entitled to any excessive worry.

She'd been out all afternoon, but no one could say where she'd gone. She'd missed tea, then supper, and when the dancing had commenced, he'd finally sent a maid to her bedchamber on the pretext of asking if she was ill.

The maid reported that her clothes and portmanteau were still in her room. Her reticule was there, too, her small amount of money tucked inside. He couldn't picture her leaving without her purse and the coins it contained.

So . . . where was she?

Suddenly, someone banged on the door, and it was flung open. A man stormed in.

"Mr. Dudley, isn't it?" John curtly inquired.

"Bloody right," Dudley barked in reply as he strode over to the desk.

They'd been introduced, but were scarcely acquainted, yet the fellow was mad as a hornet. Why would he presume he could accost John? The knave had gall sufficient for a dozen!

"What can I do for you?" John queried.

"I have a few questions."

"I'm sorry, but I'm in the middle of a . . . situation. Would you mind if we talk later?"

"Yes, I would bloody well mind."

John's temper sparked. He wasn't in the mood to deal with the furious oaf, but he didn't relish a tussle, either.

"Fine," John fumed. "Speak your piece, then go. I'm busy."

"I was hoping to see a member of your household this evening—your twins' companion, Miss Lambert."

John was instantly on alert. "Really? What is your connection to her?"

"She's a friend of mine."

Dudley's explanation was casually supplied, giving no hint as to the true state of his relationship with Lily. But he was tall and handsome, the sort John imagined the ladies would deem mysterious and dashing, and John suffered an odd wave of jealousy.

"A friend?" John scoffed. "You bumped into her here in Scotland?"

"Yes. Where is she?"

"Why would you assume I know?"

"Don't annoy me, Penworth. I heard a footman whispering. Apparently, she's disappeared. What have you done with her?"

"Me! Why would I have done anything with her? I have people searching. We'll locate her. Now . . . if that will be all?"

"No, that's not all." Dudley glared over at Angus, who was lurking and eavesdropping. "You! Get out, and don't slither back in until I tell you you can."

"I don't take orders from you," Angus huffed.

Dudley was ready to throttle the older man, and John intervened. "You may wait outside, Angus."

"Make yourself useful," Dudley suggested. "Go fetch those two brats."

"Which *brats* would that be?" Angus snapped.

"The earl's wards, those paragons of grace and charm. Let's see what the little monsters have to say."

"Dudley," John interrupted, "I insist that you cease your—"

"Let me guess: You haven't spoken to them yet."

No, I haven't. John flushed with chagrin and gestured to Angus. "Find them."

Angus nodded and marched out.

His strides faded, and Dudley said, "If you've harmed her, I'll make you pay."

"Mr. Dudley! I have no idea why you would walk into my library and threaten me."

"You've been trying to seduce her."

The charge was quietly leveled, and John was so stunned that he couldn't formulate a response. Why was Dudley aware of his private business?

"Shut your rude mouth," John seethed, "or I will shut it for you."

Dudley was undaunted. "Have you succeeded? Is that why she's vanished? Was she ravished? Is that why you sent her away? So she couldn't tell anyone what you did?"

John stomped around the desk, and he approached until they were toe-to-toe. They were the same height, but Dudley was stockier, broader across the shoulders and arms. If they brawled, it would be a close call as to who would be the winner.

"I won't ask," John hissed, "where you come by the temerity to insult me, but as to Miss Lambert and myself—"

"You may think she is alone and unprotected, with no father or brothers to intercede on her behalf. You may think she's easy prey, but she's not. She has me."

"I don't *think* about her at all, Dudley," John lied. "She's companion to my wards. No more. No less."

A scuffle might have transpired, but Angus knocked, preventing any fisticuffs.

"The twins are here, milord."

"Show them in."

Dudley shifted so he was standing with John—as if they were partners—and they faced the girls together. John hated giving the impression that he and Dudley were on the same side, but he didn't have time to worry about it.

"Hello, John," the twins cooed in unison, and they came forward.

"You know our neighbor Mr. Dudley?" John asked.

"Yes," they answered. "Hello, Dudley."

They grinned—as if seeing him there was a great joke. Dudley bristled.

"Angus said you wanted to talk to us," Miranda began. "What about?"

"Where were you this afternoon?"

"We were at home."

"You didn't go visiting or riding?"

"No."

"Had you required any assistance from Miss Lambert?"

"No, we had no need of her. Not all day."

"We thought about swimming in the hot springs," Melanie chimed in, "but we couldn't find her, so we didn't."

John studied them. They looked young and innocent, so surprised at being interrogated. Were they deceiving him? How was he to discover if they were? He'd never been good at reading women, and in the past few minutes, he'd gained no superior knowledge.

"Thank you," he said. "You may return to the party."

They started out, when Dudley sputtered, "That's it? You're just going to let them saunter away?"

"They claim to know nothing, Mr. Dudley. What would you have me do?"

Dudley scowled at them, having a knack for assessment that John lacked. Under his scrutiny, they flinched, as if he could see an aspect of their character that John could not.

"If I learn that you're lying," Dudley told them, "I'll take a whip to both of you, and I don't care what Penworth says. He won't be able to stop me." He nodded toward the door. "You two discuss it, and if you decide there's something you'd like to tell me, I'll be in the card room."

The twins exchanged a look that John couldn't decipher, but it seemed as if Dudley's arrow had hit its mark. Clearly, they had a secret, but how was John to pry it out of them? Or were they simply unnerved by Dudley's bluster?

They left, and John whirled around.

"Are you mad, Dudley? Offending me and threatening to abuse them. Who the hell do you think you are?"

"I *think* I'm the only person in the world who will fret if we never locate her."

"I have the situation well in hand."

"Really?" Dudley oozed sarcasm. "You could have fooled me."

"Isn't it time you departed? I don't like to be rude, but you've overstayed your welcome."

"I'll go after Miss Lambert is found and not a second before."

They were on the verge of blows again when Angus knocked.

"Beggin' your pardon, milord, but I just spoke to one of the maids. She'd been in the village, so she hadn't heard that we were searching for Miss Lambert."

"And?"

"She advises that Miss Lambert went to the hot springs with the twins."

"When?"

"About two o'clock this afternoon."

"How did she know?"

"Miss Lambert specifically mentioned it to her."

"Dammit!" John muttered.

Dudley snorted with disgust. "You're a gullible idiot, Penworth, and that's the kindest thing I can say about you."

Dudley hastened out, and John grabbed his arm.

"Where are you going?" John asked.

"Where would you imagine? Where is this hot springs? You don't suppose they drowned her, do you?"

John's heart literally skipped a beat. Were they capable of such ferocity? How badly had they wanted Lily out of their lives?

"Angus," he said, "we'll need two lanterns. We'll be out on the terrace. Hurry, please."

Angus raced out as John dashed down the hall, Dudley dogging his heels.

"How far is it?" Dudley inquired.

"It's quite a distance. Past the west tower, then down through the siege tunnels that lead by the old dungeons."

"Are you still using them as a prison? Will we see men stretched out on the rack? Maybe some thumbnails being torn out?"

"Dudley?"

"Yes?"

"Be silent."

John was wondering why he'd permitted Dudley to come along. He seemed a handy fellow to have around in a pinch, but his attitude made John's temper boil.

In a matter of minutes, Angus arrived with the lanterns.

"Wait here for us," he instructed Angus, then he and Dudley went down into the garden.

They followed the path to the west tower and were circling it when movement in the shadows caught his eye. He paused and lifted the lantern, and he nearly collapsed with relief.

Lily was stumbling toward them, toddling with some

effort. Her dress was sodden, the skirt heavy and dragging on the ground.

"Lily," he breathed.

"Sweet Jesu," Dudley mumbled at the same time.

They sprinted to her. Her face was covered with dried blood, and it had dripped down onto her gown. At first, he thought she'd been shot or stabbed, but as he drew closer, he saw that she'd simply had a terrible knock on the forehead. There was a swollen bump and a cut that had bled profusely.

"Lily, Lily," John repeated as they approached.

She stopped and stared, but she was very confused, as if she didn't recognize them.

"Oh, my Lord," he murmured, "what did they do to you?"

She didn't reply, which alarmed him.

He set the lantern on the grass, and he seized her and gave her a light shake.

"Lily, it's me. It's John. Are you all right?"

"John?" she whispered, her voice weak.

"Yes, darling, it's me." He offered the endearment without hesitation, not concerned that Dudley had overheard. "What happened?"

"They . . . they . . . pushed me into the pool, then they left with the lanterns."

He was aghast. "You were alone in the dark?"

"I was so afraid." She began to cry, and she was shivering violently. The air down in the grotto had been balmy and humid, but outside, it was a cold autumn night.

"How long have you been walking?"

"Forever." Her teeth were chattering. "I couldn't find my way out."

John swooped her into his arms, taking it as a sign of her reduced condition that she didn't utter a word of protest. She was too disoriented.

Dudley reached out and clasped her hand. "Gad, Penworth, she's frozen."

"Mr. Dudley?" she said. "What are you doing here?"

"Looking for you, you silly girl." He flashed a warning glare at John. "She must be warmed—as fast as possible."

"I know. Run back for me, will you?" John requested. "Inform Angus that I'll need a hot bath, and tea and soup and whatever else he can drum up. Dry clothes. Woolen socks. A roaring fire. Go."

"I'll tell him." Dudley took off at a jog, but called over his shoulder, "Then I'm hunting down your wards. I intend to skin them alive."

"Don't bother, Dudley. I can flay them without any help."

John stormed to the castle, Lily cradled to his chest. He was angrier than he'd ever been, raging and out of control and sick with fury. His distress was great, but he kept himself focused by envisioning the punishment he would inflict on the twins the moment he was certain Lily was safe.

Chapter 10

❦

LILY sat on a chair in her bedchamber. A blanket had been draped over her shoulders, but she was still wearing her wet clothes, and her hair was soaked, so she couldn't get warm.

There was a bustle of activity around her, but she scarcely noticed. Her wits had been addled, her limbs lethargic, and she was content to dawdle without moving or speaking.

Behind her, Lord Penworth grumbled, "What are you doing here?"

"Mr. Dudley asked me to come up," his mother responded, "to check on Miss Lambert."

"She's fine," Penworth snapped, "so you may leave."

Barbara leaned nearer to the earl, her voice lowered.

"People are gossiping, John."

"Let them."

"You're upset so you're not thinking clearly," she scolded.

"I'm cogent enough to know that she needs a hot bath immediately."

"And you will give it to her? *Think*, John. You have a castle full of guests. If you assist her, her reputation will be shredded."

"What would you have me do?"

"I'll shoo everyone out—including you—then I'll help her. Once I have her squared away, I'll let you back in. She'll be alone, and no one will see you."

A tense standoff ensued, and Lily could picture him angrily looming. She yearned to tell both of them to go away, but she hadn't the energy.

"Thirty minutes, Barbara," he tersely agreed.

"That should be plenty of time."

Barbara clapped her hands to get the servants' attention.

"If Miss Lambert could have some privacy?" she requested.

One girl piped up, "Would you like me to stay, Lady Barbara?"

"I appreciate your offering, but I have matters under control."

Footsteps clomped out, Penworth the last to depart. Before he exited, he paused.

"Thank you, Barbara," he said. "I'm grateful."

"Go," Barbara replied, urging him on his way.

The door closed, and she came over to Lily. She bent down so they were nose to nose.

"Well, Miss Lambert, you've certainly caused a stir. Let's get you in the tub so we can put an end to it."

Lily just gaped, relief flooding her. Others could say whatever they liked about Barbara Middleton, that she was selfish and vain and flighty, but at that moment, if Lily could have lifted her arms, she'd have hugged Barbara till she couldn't breathe.

"It will be all right, dear," Barbara comforted. "John and I will take care of everything."

She pulled Lily to her feet, and she chattered away as she stripped off Lily's sodden garments. Her mundane remarks made it seem as if they were having a perfectly normal discussion and a perfectly normal bath. Her aplomb alleviated much of Lily's distress.

Lily climbed into the tub of scalding water. Or perhaps she was inordinately cold. Her skin sizzling, she sank down, and she hissed with pain. It passed quickly, though, and she acclimated.

Barbara knelt beside her, gently swabbing the cut on Lily's forehead, cleaning her cheek and chest where the blood had dripped.

She ladled soup into Lily's mouth and forced her to swallow several cups of tea. Gradually, Lily's chill began to wane.

Lily dipped down and wet her hair, then Barbara soaped and rinsed it, surprising Lily when she sat behind her and combed out the lengthy tresses.

"Feeling better?" Barbara eventually asked as she laid the brush on a stool.

"Yes."

"Ah . . . she speaks!" Barbara chuckled and stood, holding out a towel. Lily stood, too, and Barbara wrapped her in it. Barbara grabbed a second towel and dried Lily's extremities, then guided her arms into a robe. Treating Lily like a tiny child, she escorted her to a chair, pushed her into it, and swathed her feet in a pair of thick woolen socks.

She poured another cup of tea, this one laced with a generous dollop of whiskey. Lily was drinking it when there was a quiet rap on the door.

"Thirty minutes," Barbara mentioned. "My son is always prompt." She scowled. "Do you wish to see him? Or should I have him come by in the morning?"

Did Lily wish it? Could she bear it?

She didn't want to be alone. Barbara was about to leave, and if Lily had her send Lord Penworth away, too, she'd be by herself with her frightening recollections.

"I'd like to see him," she murmured.

"Then I'll let him in."

Barbara went to the door and opened it. The earl slipped inside.

"How is she?" Penworth inquired of Barbara as if Lily wasn't present and listening to every word.

"Warmed and fed—and a tad rattled—but who wouldn't be, hmm?"

"Would you . . . ah . . . talk to Mr. Dudley for me? Inform him that she's all right."

"I'll locate him at once."

"Advise him to ignore the twins. If there's punishment to be meted out, I'll be the one to administer it."

"Good luck calming him. He was rather incensed."

Penworth gestured toward Lily. "He is so worried about her. Have you any idea how they are acquainted?"

Barbara smirked as if she possessed knowledge to which Penworth wasn't privy. "You'll have to ask her, I guess. Maybe she'll divulge some of her secrets."

Penworth frowned. "What do you mean?"

Barbara winked at Lily, patted Penworth on the chest, then sauntered out.

An awkward silence descended. They stared and stared, neither able to start the conversation.

Lily remained in her chair, while he dawdled by the door, balanced against it, his hands in his pockets. He looked embarrassed, but she couldn't imagine why. He'd done nothing wrong. It was his wards who were insane.

"I must know what happened," he ultimately said.

"They demanded I go to the hot springs with them."

"Why did you?"

"It's my job to attend them."

"Yes, I suppose it is."

"I didn't realize it was so far away or so isolated."

"Down in the grotto, what were they saying to you?"

"Just the usual: how they didn't want a companion, how they would persist with their attempts to be rid of me."

"They left you there?"

"Yes."

"Why didn't you chase after them? Had they restrained you in some fashion?"

The question made her furious. He seemed to intimate that the incident was her fault, that she'd *allowed* it to transpire.

"They shoved me down," she angrily explained, "and I hit my head."

"I'm not blaming you," he hastily insisted. "I'm trying to understand."

"I was very dazed. They rolled me into the water"—he inhaled sharply—"and I couldn't get out. I thought I would drown."

"They deliberately put you in the pool?" He was aghast at the notion.

"Yes, and they took the lanterns. I heard them giggling as they ran off."

"You were there in the dark."

"Yes."

"How did you find your way out?"

"Once I regained my senses, I felt along the walls."

It had been a terrifying nightmare. After dragging herself to the edge of the pool, she'd lain there for a lengthy period. Slowly, she'd crawled to the stairs and started up. Unable to see an inch in front of her face, her goal had been to keep climbing, to rise higher and higher until she'd escaped.

Through it all, she'd truly despaired, her courage flagging, her fear great that she would die and her body never be found.

They stared again, lost in miserable contemplation.

Finally, he muttered, "I'm sorry."

It was the last comment she'd expected. "Why would you be sorry?"

"You told me what they were like, and I knew they were playing pranks on you. I assumed their tricks were harmless. I'm stunned to learn that they're capable of such malice."

"I want to go back to London," she said. "I don't want to stay here with them."

"No."

"Please?"

"No."

He walked over to her, and he bent down, his hands on her chair, trapping her in her seat. "I need you with me."

"I'm afraid of them," she admitted, when she'd never previously been afraid of anything.

"I'll protect you. They'll never hurt you again. I swear it."

He studied the knot on her head, and he reached out to trace a finger over it. She flinched away, aware that it would be painful if he touched it.

"Head cuts are notoriously vexing," he stated. "They bleed and bleed. You might have to have it sewn."

"I won't."

"Nevertheless, I'll send for the apothecary in the morning. I'll have him look at it."

She might have argued that she hated doctors, that she wouldn't permit an apothecary to stitch a needle through her skin as if she was a worn sock being mended, but she knew him well enough: He had decided on an apothecary, and there would be no dissuading him.

She stifled a yawn, the whiskey she'd drunk kicking in, the weight of her ordeal bearing down. Fatigue swept over her.

"You're exhausted," he said.

"I am."

"Come."

"To where?"

"I'll tuck you into bed."

He tugged her to her feet, led her over, and pulled back the covers. After he helped her climb in, she assumed he'd leave, but he didn't. He rested a hip on the mattress, and he scrutinized her, his gaze troubled. He appeared to have much he wished to say, but he was nervous about saying it.

"I was searching for you all day," he claimed.

"You were not."

"I'm getting used to having you around. When I realized you were missing, I was so worried."

"I didn't think anybody would notice I was gone."

"Oh, Lily, you silly girl. I noticed immediately."

He brushed the sweetest kiss across her lips, then he went about the room and blew out the candles. Flames from the fire left a pleasant glow as he ambled over and sat on the mattress again.

"Can you forgive me?" he asked.

"There's nothing to forgive."

"Sleep now."

"I will."

To her horror, tears filled her eyes. So far, she'd kept her emotions in check, but with her tribulations concluded, she was sad and weary.

The trials of her life—the reduced opportunities, the need to work and work and work just to get by—were pressing down, making her melancholy in a way she never was.

"Don't cry." He swiped at her tears with his thumb. "It kills me to know that you're unhappy."

"I thought I would die down there. I thought I'd never see you again."

"Not see *me* again? Are you mad? I'm like a plague of locusts. You'll never be shed of me—no matter how hard you try."

"Lucky me," she said with a watery smile.

He stood and raised the blankets, and he motioned to her. "Scoot over."

"Why?"

"I'll watch over you—until you doze off."

She'd been anxious about being alone, about having the fire dwindle and the room grow dark. She'd never been scared of the dark, and after a few days, her fear would pass, but just then, she couldn't abide the notion of the silence and shadows.

"I'd like it if you stayed," she told him.

"I figured you might."

He stretched out, his arms wrapped around her. In two seconds flat, she was asleep.

JOHN peered out at the brightening sky. Lily was snuggled to his chest, as she had been for hours, and she'd barely stirred. He loved how her small hand lay on his stomach, how puffs of air from her exhalation tickled his nape.

Dawn was approaching, and he had to sneak out, but he couldn't drag himself away. He'd never been so reckless, had never seduced a servant or crawled into a woman's bed in his own home. Of course, he'd never previously met a woman who affected him as Lily did. He constantly strove to be a model of decorum, but—due to his fixation with her—he'd rejected all appropriate conduct.

If he kept breaking the rules and behaving badly, he wasn't sure where he'd wind up. There might come a time when he wouldn't recognize himself as the man he'd been before she'd crossed his path.

He didn't understand his obsession. Occasionally, he felt as if a magic spell had been cast over him, and he couldn't counter it.

Perhaps his mother was rubbing off on him, or perhaps her imprudent tendencies were catching. Whatever the cause, he was foolishly, dangerously besotted, and he had to dampen his attraction, but at the moment, he wouldn't fret over it.

He lifted the hair off her forehead, and as he studied her injury, his fury surged anew. They were extremely fortunate that the twins hadn't done her serious harm. She could never be in their presence where they might have further chances to hurt her. Yet if he rescinded her chores, there was no reason for her to remain in Scotland.

So what were his options?

Again, he'd fret about it later.

Out in one of the barns, the cock crowed. His window

of opportunity for a clean escape was closing, but he wasn't ready for the intimate episode to end.

He kissed her nose and her mouth, and her eyelids fluttered open.

"Hello," she murmured.

"Hello, yourself."

"I was having the most wonderful dream."

"About what?"

"I was walking in a field of flowers, and my mother was in the pasture on the other side of the fence. She was waving at me."

"Is your mother living?"

"No, you oaf." She pinched the skin over his ribs. "I'm an orphan. Why do you think I have to support myself by working for men like you?"

"How are you feeling?"

"My head is pounding as if it was whacked with a sledgehammer." She extended her legs and winced. "And I ache in every bone in my body. How are you?"

He chuckled, then sobered. "I have to get going."

"I don't want you to leave."

"Which is music to my ears, but I must slip away while I still can."

"Yes, I suppose you must."

She sighed and draped a lazy arm across his waist. There was no sign of awkwardness or embarrassment. She acted casually, as if she'd awakened next to him a hundred times prior.

"Thank you for coming to find me last night."

"It was my pleasure."

"Thank you for carrying me up here, for the hot bath and the food." Those pesky tears were back, and he couldn't bear to see them. "I can't remember when anyone has ever been so kind to me."

The comment was poignant, and it wrenched at a part of him that was deeply buried beneath layers of societal mores and ingrained habit.

He was one of the richest, most powerful men in the kingdom. He was one of the largest landowners. Tens of thousands of people were employed by him and depended on his prosperity, but he never pondered their personal situations. There was a wall between him and all of them, a wall of wealth and status and class, and he'd been trained not to care.

What must it be like to be Lily? To be young and alone and forced to rely on others to eat or have a bed to sleep in?

He'd never considered such weighty questions, and the realization that she struggled with them every day only heightened his interest in her. His feelings were moving into a perilous realm that had to be thoroughly scrutinized.

It was pointless to grow attached. No relationship was possible, and he wouldn't fantasize that one could become possible.

Men of his station didn't fall in love with women like her. They didn't make them their wives or the mothers of their children.

For another type of aristocrat, she would have been a perfect choice as mistress, but not for *him*. He'd spent too many years hearing lurid stories about his mother, about how she'd been mistress to various noblemen, and he'd sworn he'd never corrupt a female in such a despicable fashion.

If he needed physical companionship, he visited a doxy like Lauretta Bainbridge. She understood sexual dalliance to be a business transaction, and she expected naught but a quick tumble and the coins she'd be paid for participating.

So . . . where did Lily fit in to his life? What should he do with her? If he couldn't marry her and wouldn't keep her as a mistress, what was his plan?

He knew he should behave honorably, that he should tell her good-bye and walk out, but he couldn't go. Morning passion had swelled his loins, and while he usually strove to ignore it, a niggling voice was urging him to satisfy it for a change. The message was drowning out coherent thought.

Why not enjoy himself? Why not take what he wanted and damn the consequences? He was always so bloody restrained. Would it kill him to act out of character? Would the world cease to spin if he selfishly proceeded?

The front of her robe was gaping open, providing tantalizing glimpses of her bosom. His decision swiftly made, he slipped a hand under the fabric to fondle her breast.

She didn't order him to desist, so the chance to select a different course was lost. The rationalizations flew: When he desired her so vehemently, why deny himself? He was eager to have carnal knowledge of her. Shouldn't he get it over with and stop fretting?

He came over her, pushing her into the mattress, and he could feel her all the way down his torso. His rigid phallus was pressed to her belly, and he was practically giddy with elation.

What was his intent? Was he about to fornicate with her? Was that his scheme? Apparently so. For once, he would carry on without ruminating over every little detail.

He started kissing her and kissing her, and she joined in with vigor and abandon that thrilled and titillated in equal measure.

His fingers went to her breasts, then his lips, as he suckled her nipples. He kept on and on, shifting back and forth until she was writhing beneath him.

She craved the intimate contact as much as he, and he wasn't surprised. He'd heard that human beings—after experiencing a potentially fatal event—celebrated in the most elemental way.

He caressed her between her legs, and she was such a sexual creature that, with no effort at all, he sent her soaring to the heavens. As she reached her peak and floated down, she was giggling with merriment.

"You are so wicked," she said.

"I never picture myself as being depraved, but I guess I am."

"I can't believe I let you do that to me again. I've become a wanton."

"Good." He wiggled his brows. "I've hardly begun to pleasure you."

"Ooh, what have you in store for me?"

Their banter ceased, and as he gazed down at her, the most eerie impression swept over him. The space around them narrowed so that he seemed to be viewing her through the lens of a telescope.

His senses were heightened. Lights were brighter, colors more vivid, sounds louder.

He could see her so clearly. The future they were meant to have was obviously marked so that he couldn't miss a single step in their road together. They were happily married, with four children—two girls and two boys. Then Lily was older, their children grown with children of their own. He was still with her, still content that he'd chosen her as his bride.

It seemed so *real*, as if it had been his destiny without his knowing. He could bring it to fruition; he simply had to be brave enough to grab for it.

It was on the tip of his tongue to speak up, to inform her that he'd been waiting for her forever, that he was so glad she'd finally arrived, but before he could, his name echoed, as if from a far distance.

"John . . . ?"

The odd vision waned, then disappeared, his memory of it fading fast, until he could barely recollect what he'd witnessed.

"John, are you all right?"

He grinned. "You called me John. We're making progress."

"You had the strangest look on your face."

"I did?"

"You were a thousand miles away."

"I was just thinking about you—and what I plan to do to you."

"What is that?"

"I'll show you."

He gripped her thighs and spread them, and he dropped

between them so he was wedged tight. She was wet and relaxed from her orgasm, and any residual reservations vanished in an instant.

He would blithely ruin her, but he didn't care. It was horrid and wrong, and as her employer, he would be abusing her terribly, but it was the sole conclusion he could accept.

Starting in again, he drove her up and up the spiral of lust. She participated with an eagerness he relished, providing all the evidence he required to continue.

He wanted to be inside her more than he'd ever wanted anything. If he failed in his quest, he might . . . might perish! His determination was that strong. He—who was always in control, who never committed a reckless act—had to join with her or die trying.

He fussed with the buttons on his trousers. While she was mostly naked, only her arms covered by the fabric of her robe, he was still fully dressed, and he was so aroused that he couldn't pause to remove any clothing.

He pulled his cock free and lodged the tip in her sheath. She frowned, her confusion clear.

"What are you doing?" she asked.

"I'm going to make love to you—as a husband does his wife."

"I don't know what that entails."

He touched her at the spot where his phallus was primed for action.

"I'll push myself into you. Here." He flexed his hips, his need extreme. "Don't you see, Lily? This is where we've been heading since we first met."

"But it's not the ending I intended."

It was a peculiar comment, and if he'd been in a more rational state, he might have pondered it, might have asked what she was implying, but he was too agitated for lucid discussion.

"Let me do this," he implored. "I'm aching with desire for you."

"I can't bear to say *no*, but I don't know what's best."

"Trust me. It will be all right."

She studied him with eyes that seemed old and wise. "I want to make you happy," she murmured.

"You *do* make me happy." He grinned a roguish grin. "And you'll make me even happier if you let me proceed."

She chuckled, then dithered over her decision. The longer she calculated, the more her resolve weakened. He held his breath, the suspense killing him.

Ultimately, she nodded, granting permission, and he began again. He continued titillating her until she was mindless with pleasure, until another orgasm commenced.

As she tensed with ecstasy, he thrust once, twice, and just that easily, he entered her.

The feel of her maiden's blood, so slick and hot, immediately goaded him to the edge. Without warning, he emptied himself against her womb—the deed was done and couldn't be undone—but even though his seed was spilled, he shoved himself in and in.

He hated that he had to stop, hated for it to be over, but as his hips ground to a halt and he drew away, he was swamped with guilt. He should have gone slower! He should have prepared her for what was to come!

She'd been a virgin, for pity's sake, yet he'd behaved like a rutting beast with no concern for her chaste condition.

He'd opened his mouth to apologize, to counsel her on how it would get better with repetition, but a knock sounded on the door, and the words died in his throat. Out the window, he noted that morning had arrived. The servants were up and seeing to their chores.

"Miss Lambert?" a maid softly called, and he suffered a moment of alarm.

The previous night, he hadn't spun the key in the lock. What if she strolled in and caught them?

Reality returned with a vengeance.

What was he doing? What was he thinking?

He'd spent his entire life castigating his mother for her immoral lapses. If he was capable of the same sort of illicit conduct, what did it indicate about his true character?

"Tell her," he whispered in Lily's ear, "that you're not up yet, and you'd like her to come back later."

Lily appeared stunned, her expression a mix of distress and regret, and he wished he could calm or placate her, but there was no time.

She remained silent, and he urged, "Tell her! Quick! Before she turns the knob and peeks in."

"It's . . . it's . . . Miss Lambert," she stammered. "Could you come back in a half hour?"

"Yes, Miss. Are you needing anything for now?"

"No, I'm . . . fine."

The girl walked on, and as her strides faded, he slid from the bed. In a panic, he rushed about, straightening his trousers and tucking in his shirt. Lily watched, not speaking, her gaze anxious and perplexed.

He yearned to climb under the covers, to soothe and console her over the abrupt coupling and even more abrupt conclusion. But they'd already courted sufficient disaster. He didn't dare dawdle further.

Leaning over her, he braced his hands on the mattress.

"Sleep in," he said, "all day if you'd like."

"What about . . . about . . ."

He wasn't sure what she was trying to ask, but he suspected any query would involve his contemptible, abbreviated seduction. He was a disgraceful ass, but with the carnal heat of the encounter waning, he was too embarrassed to hash out his failings.

"I'll see you this afternoon," he insisted. "We'll talk then."

He went to the door and peered out. Espying no one, he tiptoed away and—like the cad he apparently was—he hurried to his room without glancing back.

Chapter 11

♥

"Lock the door," Barbara whispered. "Hurry."

Phillip sneaked in behind her and did as she asked, quickly sealing them in her boudoir.

She'd thought their initial tryst would be in *his* room, at *his* home, but she was more than happy to seduce him in her own suite. It was particularly thrilling to know how vehemently Esther would disapprove. She was still whining about how Barbara had stolen her bed, and if she had any idea of what Barbara was about to do on its mattress, she'd suffer an apoplexy.

"If your son finds out I'm in here," Dudley said, "there will be hell to pay."

"He won't find out."

"How can you be sure?"

"He's with Miss Lambert. He'll probably be with her all night."

"In her bedchamber?"

"Yes."

She walked to her dressing room, and he followed,

being a man accustomed to lingering in a woman's private quarters. From the moment she'd first noticed him, she'd suspected a lusty character. With that dark hair and those seductive brown eyes, that tall frame and muscular physique, he was a sin any female would gladly commit.

She sat on the stool and studied herself in the mirror as she drew the combs from her hair and let it tumble down her back. She was putting on a show for him, wanting him to watch, wanting him wild with desire, but would he be?

He could have had his pick of several neighborhood widows, but she'd snagged him before anyone else had a chance. But with her being so much older than he, would she keep his attention?

He was casually lounged against the doorframe, observing as she went about her simple feminine rituals.

"Miss Lambert told me," he said, "that Penworth is strangely enamored of her."

"Why would it be strange? She's very pretty and very sweet. It's not odd that he'd be enchanted."

"Will he ruin her?"

"Yes. He's a healthy, red-blooded male. What would you expect?"

"Could he fall in love with her?"

"Are you joking?" She spun around and scowled. "He's his father's son. He's not capable of that sort of strong emotion. Charles drummed it out of him when he was a boy."

"What will happen to her?"

"I suppose what happens to all girls like her when a handsome nobleman becomes interested. He'll trifle with her until he grows weary or until she winds up pregnant. Then? I can't guess what John might do."

"Would he ever marry her?"

"Stuffy, fussy John?" she scoffed. "No, he never would. Miss Lambert is so far beneath him that I'm amazed he can see her."

"If he gets her pregnant, I'll kill him."

His ferocity made her imagine that he might actually

perpetrate violence, and she reveled in that type of passion. It was a rare man who exhibited it.

He came over and hauled her to her feet, then led her to the bedchamber. He rolled onto the mattress and tugged her down with him. She stretched out atop him, and she arched like a lazy cat, relishing the feel of his body beneath hers.

"You're awfully friendly with Miss Lambert," she said, glaring down at him.

"I am," he agreed, but offered nothing more, which infuriated her.

She hated that he wouldn't confide in her, and she hoped his reticence wasn't because he and Miss Lambert were lovers. Though Barbara was loathe to admit it, she worried he might be smitten by the engaging, much younger woman.

"Why does she call you Dubois?"

"I'm a charlatan and a fraud. It's one of my false names."

"Really?"

"I speak fluent French, too, with a very sexy accent. Women drool over me."

"You're a man of many talents." She grinned, not able to discern if he was telling the truth, but fascinated that he might be. "What are you? A spy? A bandit who's wanted by the law? A traitor to the Crown? What?"

"Something much worse."

"Worse than a traitor, spy, or bandit? What could be worse than those?"

"You'd be surprised."

She sat on her haunches and grabbed the lapels of his coat.

"Spill all, you knave!" she commanded. "What are you about?"

"I'm a sorcerer."

"Would you be serious?"

"I can make a woman fall in love with the man of her dreams. I can make the man in question return her affection."

"You expect me to believe such a ridiculous tale?"

"Why wouldn't you?"

"All right, Mr. Sorcerer. If you're so powerful, can you make my son love me again?"

He smirked. "I'm a sorcerer, not a miracle worker."

She snorted with disgust. "You're impossible."

"Yes, I am."

"Why won't you divulge your background?"

"You'll like me more if I keep it a secret."

"No, I won't," she pouted.

He chuckled. "You're horridly spoiled, and I can't abide that you display it so blatantly. I'm not certain we'll get on all that well."

"Trust me: We'll *get on* just fine."

"As long as I don't provoke your temper?"

"Yes, and as long as you always let me have my way."

"Now *that* I can't promise at all."

She was tired of waiting for him to kiss her, tired of waiting to learn what it would be like, so she bent down and kissed him first. He was aggravated that she'd taken charge, and he flipped her onto her back, seizing control of the embrace. He was very adept, very thorough, so it was as delicious as she'd predicted.

She probably should have forgone an affair, should have focused her energies on reestablishing her connection to John, but she was terribly nervous as to how events would unfold. Her confidence would surely be bolstered by being involved with Phillip Dudley.

If she had a paramour, she would feel younger and stronger, better able to maintain the pretense that she knew what she was doing. Dudley—for his part—would bring intrigue and excitement to her life, and he would provide the added benefit of keeping her occupied so she didn't fret over her troubles.

Whenever she thought about John, she panicked. What if he evicted her? Where would she be?

She was desperate to block out any anxious rumination

with a bout of rough, fast sex, yet Dudley was in no rush, being perfectly happy to dawdle.

There was no hasty groping, no fumbling with her skirt, no race to the next level. He simply kissed her, then kissed her some more, until she grew impatient. Why didn't he hurry, the oaf?

Perceiving her dismay, he pulled away and peered down at her.

He had the shrewdest way of looking at a woman, as if he could see to her soul, and she didn't care for the sensation. In light of her notorious history, there was plenty she liked to conceal.

"What's wrong?" he asked.

"Nothing, why?"

"All of a sudden, you're tense as a board."

"I have a lot on my mind."

He laughed. "I haven't distracted you from it?"

"Of course you have," she gushed, worried she might have bruised his poor male ego.

"I know a thing or two about amour. If I can't entice you, you're obviously not in the mood."

"I'm absolutely in the mood!"

"There's no need to continue." He patted her on the shoulder, then slid away and sat up. "I'll come back another time."

Her panic soared. Recently, she'd been deluged by her pitiful reflections. She had too much to regret, and she wasn't eager to be by herself. Dudley had been invited to her room so she could keep her demons at bay for a while.

He couldn't leave! How would she fill the quiet hours till dawn?

"Don't be a boor," she scolded, sitting up, too. "Turn off the lamp, and we'll start in again."

"You want to have sex in the dark? Why? Do you think— if I can't see you—your upset will be hidden from me?"

"I'm not upset!"

He studied her again, those astute eyes digging deep,

and she squirmed with discomfort—as if she'd misbe-haved and had been found out.

"My beautiful, brazen Barbara," he murmured, "what is it?"

He posed the question so kindly, and with such com-passion, that she had to glance away. She stared at her lap.

"I hate to be alone," she whispered as if he'd wrenched the confession from her.

"Everyone does."

"And I'd like to pass the time with you."

"With some dispassionate sex?"

"Well . . . yes, but I hope it's at least a little passionate."

"You only want me for my magnificent body," he teased.

"I won't deny it."

"I feel so . . . *used*," he sarcastically complained, and he put a finger under her chin, forcing her to look at him.

"Just . . . stay," she begged. "Please?"

"I will on one condition."

"What is that?"

"I want to know everything."

"About what?"

"About what happened to you. I want to know how you got so lost that you can't find your way back."

"I'd have no idea where to begin."

"How about with the day you were a young wife and decided to leave your husband? Tell me all that tran-spired between then and right now." He leaned against the headboard, a pillow propped behind him, as if settling in for a long story. He watched her intently, daring her to confide in him, and the notion was tempting.

No one had ever sought to understand what occurred, why she'd left, or how awful it had been.

"You can trust me," he urged, "and I'm a great listener."

He held out his arms to her, and for a moment, she hesitated, then she fell into them. She snuggled herself to his chest, her ear over his heart so she could hear its steady beating.

"I was nineteen," she said, "and I had already been married for four years. I was so miserably unhappy . . ."

"YOU have one chance to explain yourselves. Who would like to start?"

John glared at the twins, his cold, hard gaze slithering over them.

Their eyes were wide with an expression of innocence, as if they were perplexed over why they'd been summoned to his library.

Though they'd lived with him for close to eighteen months, he didn't really know them. Their father had been a renowned ne'er-do-well with whom John had occasionally debauched.

Why the girls' guardianship had been given to John was a mystery. Perhaps, in view of their father's unsavory tendencies, he'd recognized that John would be a good influence on his daughters.

John had tried his best with them, had brought them into his home and kept them with him despite the troubles their presence caused. Yet this was how they repaid him? With treachery?

On his way to the library, he'd nearly gone to the woods and cut a switch in order to administer a sound thrashing to both. He was that enraged.

"What are you talking about, John?" Miranda inquired.

"You're pretending ignorance?"

"We're not *pretending*. We simply can't fathom why you asked us here."

"You seem angry," Melanie added. "Is something wrong?"

Their pretty heads were cocked at the exact same angle. Identical frowns marred their brows.

"Tell me what you did to Miss Lambert."

"Miss . . . Lambert?" Miranda said as if she wasn't acquainted with Lily.

"Tell me about the hot springs!" he shouted, and they jumped.

"What . . . what do you wish to know?"

"I'm curious about your version of events. I want to hear how big of a lie you'll have the gall to spew."

They gaped at him; then, as if on cue, they burst into tears.

He stoically evaluated them, completely unmoved by their waterworks. He was positive the charade had been thoroughly rehearsed.

It was now clear that they'd maliciously tormented several very nice women whom he'd hired to serve as their companions. Every time calamity had struck, the poor victims had attempted to defend themselves, but he'd accepted the twins' false tales over the true ones.

He'd fired people because of them, had tossed people out of the house with no notice or warning, had threatened arrest and refused to write letters of reference.

Seven women had had their careers destroyed. What had become of them? Had they found other employment? Or—more likely—were they scraping by on the streets, unable to support themselves because the exalted Earl of Penworth had branded them thieves or sluggards?

"Why are you crying?" he queried, merely to learn what they would say.

"We didn't intend any harm," Miranda declared.

"Didn't you?"

"No. We were just playing a trick on her."

"We weren't aware that she'd fallen," Melanie claimed, "or that she was left behind."

"We thought she chased us up the stairs," Miranda said. "We thought she could see the light from our lanterns."

"We were trying to scare her," Melanie asserted, "not hurt her."

"As soon as we arrived in our bedchamber, we asked a maid about her, and—"

"Really?" John interrupted. "Which one?"

"Becky. She told us that Miss Lambert was in her room, too."

There was no maid in the castle named Becky, but Miranda mentioned her with great certitude, giving not the slightest hint of deception. The girl had to be the most accomplished liar who'd ever lived.

"It never occurred to us," Melanie contended, "that Becky was mistaken. We assumed Miss Lambert was fine."

"If we'd had a clue," Miranda continued, "as to her actual situation, we'd have gone down to help her."

"But we didn't know," they wailed together. They slid matching kerchiefs from their sleeves and dabbed at their eyes. They gazed at him, looking candid and miserable. If Lily hadn't lifted the veil that kept him blind to their shenanigans, he might have once again swallowed their nonsense.

A lengthy silence ensued, as he stared, and they stared back, not realizing that the rules of the game had changed. Even if their behavior had started as a prank—which he didn't believe for a second—the results could have been catastrophic.

"Is that it?" he finally asked. "Is that all you have to say?"

"What else could there be?" Miranda replied.

"How about the fact that you pushed her down? That she hit her head?"

"We didn't push her! She tripped."

"Did she?"

"Yes!"

"And I suppose she simply rolled into the water all on her own."

"My goodness!" Melanie gasped, appearing shocked. "Miss Lambert fell into the pool? She could have drowned!"

John scrutinized them, waiting for some sign of regret or shame, but other than a swatch of color on their cheeks, their expressions could only be described as serene.

"Here is what I've arranged for you," he stated.

"What do you mean?" Miranda inquired.

"I'm sending you back to London. You'll leave on Friday."

It was almost a week away, but there was no suitable ship departing any earlier.

"We don't want to go to London," Miranda complained. "We're enjoying ourselves too much in Scotland."

John ignored her. "Once you debark, my clerk will meet you at the harbor, and you will be escorted to Penworth Hall. You will remain in the country—seeing no guests and engaging in no entertainment—until I return and decide what's to be done with you."

"But . . . but . . . that's cruel," Melanie whined.

"Not nearly as cruel as your assault on Miss Lambert."

"Assault!" Miranda blustered. "What has she alleged? Whatever it is, bring her in here and I shall call her a liar to her face!"

"I wouldn't force her to endure your company long enough to give you the chance."

They simultaneously sucked in insulted breaths, their anger evident.

"How is it," Miranda demanded, "that you would take a mere servant's word over ours?"

"It was rather easy. I don't like you, and I'm struggling to remember why I've been considerate to either of you."

"Well!" they huffed in unison.

"The next few days will be awkward," he informed them, "but you are not to be in the same room with Miss Lambert. Should you bump into her on the stairs or in a hallway, you are not to speak to her. You are not to molest her in any fashion. Do I make myself clear?"

He stopped, watching them again, trying to guess what was going through their devious little minds.

When they didn't respond to his question, he posed it more sharply.

"Do I make myself clear!"

"Yes, you've made yourself perfectly clear," Melanie said, but Miranda had the gall to taunt, "What if we don't obey you? What if we abuse her hideously?"

John leaned back in his chair, being a veritable master at exhibiting a cool, calm façade. If they presumed they could best him in attitude or manner, they were gravely mistaken.

"I am a major benefactor of a convent in Belgium," he told them. "Many English girls—from good families—are housed there to conceal various scandals."

"So?" Melanie snapped like a petulant toddler.

"I control your lives and money until you're twenty-five—or until you wed. During the coming week, if you so much as peek at Miss Lambert, I shall have you bound and gagged and delivered to the nuns." He raised a casual brow. "And there you shall stay for the next seven years."

"You wouldn't dare," Miranda seethed.

"Wouldn't I? If that is what you stupidly imagine, then I suggest you tread very, very cautiously, because with the mood I'm in, nothing would give me greater pleasure." He waved toward the door. "Now then, I'm sick of the sight of you. Be gone, and don't compel me to ever again suffer your presence unless I specifically request it."

Chapter 12

❦

"How are you enjoying my castle?"

"It's very . . . *rural*."

"Yes, well, castles are like that."

Violet smiled at John, wishing she had the temerity to say what she really thought.

The rooms were small and oddly shaped, the ceilings low, the chimneys poorly designed so smoke hung in the air. Being a medieval edifice at its core, the stairways wound in strange directions, and the layout of the various sections made no sense.

It was drafty and dull, and she couldn't imagine why anyone would cherish it.

"Do you visit often?" She hoped the answer was *no*, that she wouldn't be required to frequent the dreary building after she was countess.

"Usually twice a year."

"Will I accompany you on every trip?"

"Yes."

Her mask must have slipped, her distaste momentarily revealed, for he frowned.

"Unless you don't care to," he hurriedly said. "I could come alone if the journey would be too much for you."

"I'm happy to travel with you. I love it here. Truly."

He took her arm and led her across the terrace to the balustrade, and they gazed out over the park.

"The place will grow on you, Violet. Just give it some time."

"I told you: I already love it." She forced another smile. "There is one question I have, though."

"What is it?" She hesitated, and he pressed, "You can ask me anything. We're betrothed, so we should be able to discuss whatever is necessary."

"Yes, we should," she heartily concurred, but it was hard to raise the subject vexing her.

She had scant experience talking with men. Her father, the duke, was her sole example of male conversation, and he didn't believe in wasting energy on a daughter. Yet she was positive that—should he learn of Violet's situation—he wouldn't be pleased. But how was she to broach such a deplorable topic?

"It's about your . . . ah . . . mother. Will she be staying here? Will she be in residence whenever we arrive?"

"My mother? Why would you worry about her?"

"I've conferred with Esther, and she says that—"

"Pardon me, but I won't listen to what Esther said about Barbara, and I won't have you gossiping about Barbara either."

His anger was evident, and she was rattled by his sharp tone. Was she to be silent? Was she to continue with her complaint? Why didn't matrimony come with instructions? It would be helpful to have a book of rules so she could open to a certain page and locate advice on how to proceed.

"Yes, gossip is awful"—she nodded in agreement—"and I understand your feelings on the matter."

"You couldn't possibly."

"I'm sure that having your mother here is difficult."

"You don't know the half of it."

"Have you a plan for her?" His frown increased, but she forged on. "Will she remain in Scotland? Or will she return with us to England? You're not intending that she live with us, are you?"

He rested a hip on the balustrade, his arms crossed over his chest. He was being particularly cantankerous, but then, both Esther and Edward had warned her that he thrived on belligerence.

"What if I *was* thinking of bringing her with me?" he absurdly threatened. "What's it to you? She has no bearing on you or your relationship with me."

Could he really be that thick? Could he really not grasp the uproar that would ensue should Barbara reappear in London?

"People would be shocked," she insisted.

"So?"

In light of how he always shunned scandal, his reply was very peculiar. If he'd suddenly sprouted a second head, he couldn't have seemed any more odd.

"Is this your way of telling me that she'll be joining us? For if it is, I must inform you that I doubt my father will approve."

"Since you will be my wife, his opinion would be irrelevant."

At hearing what could only be construed as an insult to her father, her temper flared. She moved in the highest echelons of society, and she was aggrieved that he would discount what—to her—was a grave circumstance.

Was this how they would carry on together? Would he forever chastise and admonish? Would he forever denigrate the issues that were vital to her?

Her view of marriage was an idealistic, hazy vision of unending contentment that—she had to admit—might not have any basis in reality.

She yearned for a grand, romantic lark, and she refused to have a husband who was like her father, someone who was so much older, who ignored her and treated her as if she were a silly child.

Her greatest fear was that she would wed, but naught would change, that she would limp along just as she had under her father's roof. If she went through with the ceremony, but wound up a mute puppet, expected to vapidly grin while she tolerated John's ill moods, she didn't know how she'd survive it.

Laughter wafted by from out in the garden, and she glanced down a pathway to see Edward strolling with the twins. They were a merry trio, the twins giggling as Edward teased them, and a virulent wave of envy washed over her.

She would give anything to be down there with them. To be listening as Edward spewed his humorous stories. To watch with glee as he flirted and joked.

Though John was thirty and Edward twenty-seven, John seemed ancient by comparison. Where John was stodgy and grumpy and irascible, Edward was cheerful and quick to entertain.

Why, oh, why couldn't Edward have been the first-born son and earl? Why had Violet been left with the boring, irritable elder brother? Edward cherished her as John never could. He looked at her and actually *saw* her. But even though he possessed a heightened affection, it could never be acted upon.

Had there ever been two more star-crossed lovers? If Shakespeare had been alive, he might have composed sonnets about them!

She whipped around, too jealous to observe as Edward bantered with the twins. Annoyance rippled through her, and as she faced John again, her posture and manner were combative.

"You haven't answered my question," she fumed.

"What question was that?"

"Will Barbara—or will she not—be residing with us?"

"I'm still figuring out what to do with her," he maddeningly retorted.

"I'd appreciate it if you'd let me know the moment you decide."

"I will."

"In the interim, I'll have to write to my father so he's aware of what's happening."

She'd thought the prospect of her contacting the duke might alarm him, but he merely shrugged, unafraid of her father and the power he could wield.

"If you think," John said, "that he ought to be bothered over such a paltry concern, then by all means, write to him."

"The company here has grown unsavory. He may not want me to stay on. He may demand that I return to England at once."

"The twins are going back on Friday. If you would like to go with them, I can book an extra passage."

Awhirl with panic, she glared at him, lips pursed in a fashion that she knew was unflattering. She hated not getting her way, hated that she'd put her foot down and that her fury had had no effect.

They were on the verge of a major quarrel. She'd drawn a line in the sand as to what she would abide, but he'd called her bluff and urged her to scurry home to her father, which would be a disaster.

If she appeared in England without John, the duke would pitch a fit. He'd be certain that any fight had been Violet's fault, that she'd been sent away in disgrace.

The duke had counseled her to be accommodating and submissive to John. It was an onerous burden, having to grovel and suffer so that he was always happy, but she would die before she'd let others realize that she'd failed to please him.

Again, she pondered Edward. *He* would have heeded her complaint. *He* would have comprehended her outrage over Barbara.

She smiled tightly, her cheeks so taut that she was amazed the skin didn't crack. "I have no desire to leave for

London," she lied. "I'm eager to remain so I can learn more about you and this marvelous spot you obviously love."

"I'm glad to hear it. Tea is about to be served in the drawing room. May I escort you inside?"

"Actually, I'd like to take a walk." She had to escape him, or she might start screaming and never stop. "I could use some fresh air."

"I have guests arriving, so I can't attend you."

"Oh, that's too bad. I was hoping you could show me the lake and point out the interesting views."

"Perhaps tomorrow."

"I'm looking forward to it."

The door behind her opened, and Miss Lambert stepped out. When she saw them, she stumbled, seeming surprised to find them together. There was an awkward pause, as if she'd caught them doing what they oughtn't.

"Miss Lambert," she said, "I'm going for a walk. Would you fetch my parasol? Then you must accompany me around the park." Miss Lambert didn't move, and Violet snapped, "Miss Lambert, I must have my parasol. Now."

Still not speaking, Miss Lambert scowled at John, almost supposing he'd countermand Violet's order. She had the strangest expression on her face, as if she'd been hurt or betrayed. John was equally discomfited. Two slashes of red stained his cheeks.

The interval stretched to infinity, both of them waiting for something Violet couldn't fathom, then Miss Lambert curtsied. "As you wish, Lady Violet. I'd be delighted to retrieve your parasol."

"No, Violet," John suddenly interjected. "Miss Lambert isn't working today."

"Not working? How ridiculous. She need only amble after me. How difficult can that be?"

"She had an accident and was injured. I advised her to rest."

"She appears quite hale."

"She's not," he curtly replied.

"Next I know," Violet protested, "you'll be giving her paid holidays."

"Miss Lambert," John commanded, "go inside. Violet is eighteen years old. I'm sure she can manage to navigate the garden on her own."

Violet had been chaperoned and fussed over all her life, so his comment was hideously rude. If he'd slapped her, it couldn't have been any more bracing.

"I'm recovered enough," Miss Lambert insisted. "I am a servant here, after all. I can carry out the tasks required of me."

Miss Lambert's words were appropriate, but her tone oozed sarcasm, as if she believed she shouldn't have to complete her chores or that they were beneath her.

Her statement infuriated John—Violet could feel him tense—and he grouched, "Fine. Far be it from me to keep you from your duties. If you want to traipse after her, go ahead."

A heated visual exchange passed between them before Miss Lambert yanked her gaze from his.

"I'll get your parasol," she told Violet, "and I'll be right down."

"WHAT about the evening meal for Wednesday?"

"Beef isn't the best choice."

Esther halted and frowned. The remarks had emanated from the blue salon, where she met every morning with the housekeeper and cook.

"What would you suggest?" Cook asked, and an all-too-familiar voice answered.

"With all the men coming for the hunt, they would probably enjoy it if we served the venison they bring home."

"How silly of me to forget."

The two women chuckled, conspirators in proceeding behind Esther's back, and Esther's temper sizzled.

Over the next week, John would host the annual autumn festival. Crops would be harvested, game slain, dances held, whiskey drunk, banquets eaten. It was the highlight of their year in Scotland, the most important of all their visits as John displayed his prosperity and generosity.

Esther wasn't much for socializing, but she was nothing if not loyal. She always did her part, always pitched in as much as she was able. Guests were beginning to arrive, so she'd planned to spend the afternoon with the senior staff, reviewing their preparations. Apparently, Barbara had beaten her to it.

How dare she! How dare she! How dare she!

Esther's pulse pounded with ire. Since she'd discovered Barbara ensconced in the countess's suite, she'd been enraged. John had refused to intervene in the squabble, so Esther had been humiliated into taking smaller, less prestigious quarters.

Though she'd had no evidence to support her suspicions, she thought that Barbara continued to undermine her. Household details kept varying from what Esther had authorized, but she hadn't had any firm proof.

Were the servants plotting with Barbara to Esther's detriment? Had Esther given orders—only to have the staff run to Barbara and ask what *she* wanted instead?

Esther stormed into the room to find Barbara and Cook sitting at the table. Their chairs were pressed close, and they were sharing a pot of tea as if they were bosom buddies, as if there were no class lines separating them.

"Barbara!" Esther barked. "What are you doing?"

"I'm checking the menu for the first night of the hunt. What does it look like?"

"Where do you come by the gall to assume the countess's duties?"

"Honestly, Esther, your food selections have been atrocious."

"They have not!"

"I can't stand by and have John shamed in front of his

peers simply because you never bothered to learn which wine should be poured."

"Be silent!"

"Nor will I allow you to embarrass Cook again. Not when she's capable of excellence. You thwart her with your asinine decisions, and I won't have you ruining her reputation."

Esther started to tremble, and she pointed an irate finger at Cook.

"Get out!" she spat.

Cook glanced at Barbara, seeking Barbara's permission, and Barbara nodded. "Let me deal with this. We'll finish up later."

"You will not talk to her!" Esther shrieked to Cook. "If you need further guidance, you will come to me."

Cook strolled out without acknowledging Esther, skirting by as if she was invisible.

As her strides faded, Esther seethed at Barbara, "You won't get away with this."

"I keep telling you that I already have. When will reality lodge in your thick skull? I'm back, and *I* will be John's hostess. He's had to endure your dour attitude and prudish ways long enough."

"I am countess here!"

"You were never up to the task, Esther, and we both know it. Why not admit it and save everyone a bucket-load of trouble?"

Esther was shaking so hard that she was afraid she might fall to the floor. She felt as if she'd hated Barbara for all eternity, and it was amazing that thirty years could pass and she could still loathe her as much as she had the very first time they'd been introduced.

Esther had grown up with her husband, Charles; she'd been a ward of his father's. She'd been ten when his father had informed them that they would eventually wed, and it had seemed the most logical solution.

At least to *her*. Charles had had a different view.

From the second he'd met the beautiful, lurid Barbara, he'd been blind to Esther. She'd been forgotten in a haze of Charles's lust to have Barbara at all costs.

His disgusting passion for Barbara had destroyed Esther's life, had made her a laughingstock. Most despicably of all, it had ensured that John was the heir, rather than Edward.

After Barbara fled, Charles—a divorced, disgraced scoundrel—had come crawling back. Esther had accepted his tepid proposal, but she'd never forgiven him.

Often, when she'd stood in the nursery at Penworth Hall, staring down at John when he was napping, she'd dreamed of smothering him in his sleep—just to retaliate for the humiliation Charles had heaped on her. Only her fear of being caught, of being jailed and separated from Edward, had stopped her from harming John.

Why couldn't John perish so Edward would be earl? Why did John have to be so accursedly healthy? People died so frequently. Why couldn't John have the decency to succumb and put Esther out of her misery?

And now . . . and now . . . Barbara was back like a bad penny. Lording herself over Esther. Rubbing salt in Esther's wounds. Esther was so livid that—if she'd been clutching a pistol—she'd have shot Barbara right between the eyes.

"I'll get even with you," Esther warned, "if it's the last thing I do."

"You will not. You were always a great one for drama, Esther, but you don't have the spine to wrangle the conclusion you desire. You merely nag and whine. You have no idea how to reach out and take what you want."

"I might surprise you."

"I won't hold my breath."

Esther stomped out, and she loomed down the halls, searching until she found John out on the terrace.

He was leaned against the balustrade and sipping a glass of wine, even though it was nowhere near time for supper. He peered out across the park where, off in the distance, Violet was determinedly walking. Miss Lambert trudged along behind, looking the part of the beleaguered companion.

"Drinking, John?" Esther scolded. "Isn't it a bit early in the day?"

"It certainly is."

"What will the servants think if they see you?"

"Why is everyone suddenly so concerned about my behavior and what others will think of it?"

"It's unseemly to exhibit sensational tendencies. You know that. Your mother's blood runs in your veins, so you carry a propensity toward her worst traits. You must constantly fight them. I shouldn't have to remind you."

"Reputation matters above all?" he snidely asked.

"Yes."

He downed the contents of the glass—evidently just to spite her—and he set it on the railing hard enough to crack the stem.

"You're in a snit about something," he groused, "but the past few hours haven't exactly been a picnic for me, either. State your complaint, then go away. At the moment, I don't have the patience to listen to you."

She inhaled sharply. It was the only truly rude remark he'd ever made to her, and she couldn't understand what had come over him. Had he ingested more alcohol than she'd realized? Had he been imbibing all afternoon?

Why would he have been? What worries did he have? He'd inherited Charles's title, money, and property. His life was perfect. What could possibly trouble him?

"I'm aware that you don't wish to discuss it," she said, "but I take issue with your mother being on the premises."

"As I believe you've mentioned previously."

"She's planning the menus with Cook."

"So what? You hate the chore. You've told me so over and over again. Let her handle it."

"It is not the assumption of the task to which I object!" she stridently declared. "It is the arrogant usurpation of a rank and station she no longer possesses."

He wrenched his gaze from Violet and focused it on Esther. His rage was so blatant that she had to steel herself to keep from flinching.

"What would you have me do, Esther? Should I toss her out on the road?"

"Yes, that is precisely what you should do. What respect had she for you and your father all those years ago? What do you owe her now? Nothing! Make her leave."

"And if I don't choose to?"

"Then I can't remain in Scotland with you. I will insist on going back to England at the earliest opportunity."

"Good. The twins are going on Friday. I've needed to find someone to accompany them. It might as well be you."

His answer infuriated her to such a degree that she thought she might swoon. With Barbara in residence, Esther would never abandon her post, and she'd threatened departure as a bluff.

Now what was she supposed to do? John should have *agreed* with her. He always agreed with her; it was the tenor of their relationship. He couldn't change course in the middle of the stream. Not after they'd been interacting in the same fashion for most of three decades.

"What is wrong with you?" she demanded. "Why are you being so discourteous and insulting?"

"I'm turning over a new leaf."

"I raised you better."

"Yes, you did, but I'm sick to death of playing by the rules."

"Proper comportment is the bedrock of civilization. I suggest you remember yourself."

"Oh, I'm *remembering* myself, all right, and I don't like what I see."

"Your insolence is maddening, and I won't speak with you when you're being obnoxious. We will continue this conversation when your manners improve."

She huffed away, as he called, "Stop gossiping with Violet."

Blanching with dismay, she halted. "What?"

"You're eager to chastise me for my conduct, but you might reflect on your own. If I learn that you're whining to her about Barbara again, I'll lock you in your room."

Too shocked to respond, she whipped away and kept on.

Chapter 13

❦

"I really shouldn't."

"Why not?"

Edward smiled at Melanie. He'd once again been lured to her bedchamber, and while he'd come eagerly enough, he felt he should make at least a token protest.

The castle was full of guests, and he was the earl's brother, so it was rude to sneak off. Not that he gave two figs about John or his neighbors. His phallus was already so hard that he was surprised his pants hadn't burst at the seams.

"The men are out on their horses," he said, "running with the hounds. I'll be missed."

"No, you won't. There are too many people here. You can be gone for a bit. No one will notice."

"All right," he grumbled, pretending to be gracious. "I suppose I can spare you a few minutes. What do you need?"

"Follow me."

They went into the bedroom. The bed had been stripped

of its covers, and to his utter amazement, there were ropes attached to the headboard.

Were the little scamps planning to tie him up? Or would he be allowed to fetter Melanie before he had sex with her?

She spun, showing him her back.

"Unbutton my dress."

He jumped into the task, the buttons quickly falling away so the garment was loose. She shimmered out of it, and it slid to the floor and pooled around her ankles. She kicked it away, then turned to face him, wearing a corset, stockings, heels, and nothing else. He couldn't hide his excitement.

"Remove your coat," she said, and he shrugged it off. "Now, your trousers."

Her instructions continued until he was down to his drawers. His erection tented the front, his arousal plainly visible.

He hoped she'd reach for him, that she'd fondle or lick him as she had previously. Instead, she pointed to the bed.

"Climb up and lie down."

"Why?" As if he didn't know!

"Just do it."

He smirked, wondering where they had learned such vicious games. Who had taught them? And when?

They'd once mentioned their father, had hinted at having carnal relations with him. Edward wasn't sure if he'd believed them or not. He suspected they were pulling his leg, but what if they weren't?

He lay down and stretched out as Miranda entered.

She was also attired in corset, stockings, and spiky heels, and she held her riding crop. She approached and shoved her sister.

"Get on the bed with him."

"I don't want to," Melanie whimpered with false dread.

"It is not for you to question your orders." Miranda whacked Melanie on the ass. "Get on the bed!"

Melanie clambered up and straddled Edward's lap. Her pussy was pressed to his raging cock, and the intimate placement was so titillating that he could barely prevent an instant orgasm.

"Tie him!" Miranda commanded.

Melanie grabbed his wrist, and he suffered a moment of panic.

Did he actually wish to be restrained by them? A few slaps with the riding crop had been humorous, but the notion of having his limbs constrained was unnerving.

"Let's not be hasty," he said.

"Be silent!"

Miranda cracked the whip on his calf, distracting him so Melanie was able to bind his wrist. He frowned and tugged, but the motion simply tightened the knot. As he fussed with it, she managed to secure his other hand.

He objected and fought, which merely exacerbated his predicament. While he was diverted by his arms, the girls each seized a foot and bound his ankles, so with scant effort, he was trussed like a Christmas goose across the mattress.

"Release me," he insisted.

"No."

"Release me!" he fumed more shrilly, but they ignored him.

He was terrified of Miranda and what she might do, but at the same time, he was agog with lust. It made no sense, but the harder he struggled, the more stimulated he became. His fear of the unknown, of the salacious depth of the game they had commenced, only added to his willingness to play.

Miranda leaned over him, her beautiful face inches from his own. For a second, he thought she might kiss him, but she didn't, and he couldn't decide if he was glad or not.

"You're very wicked, Edward."

"I certainly can be."

"We bring out the worst in you."

"I'm not complaining."

"John is sending us back to London."

"So I heard. You poor dears." He feigned sympathy,

when in fact, he'd be delighted to have them leave. Once they were gone, he'd have more chances to scheme on Violet without constantly worrying that they were spying on him.

"We'd like to stay here," she said, "so you must talk to John for us."

"Of course I will," he lied. He'd do no such thing.

If John had made up his mind, there'd be no dissuading him. Edward had to pick his battles with John. The twins—and their paltry problems—were far down on his list of the wars he'd wage.

"We'd like Miss Lambert to be fired, too. We haven't settled on the type of scandalous dilemma to create for her, but you can participate in her downfall—as you have with our other companions."

He nearly rolled his eyes. Their nasty tricks annoyed him, and he felt sorry for Miss Lambert. She seemed a decent sort, and she didn't deserve the twins' brand of animosity.

Still, he said, "I'd be happy to assist."

"You love how we arouse you."

"Yes, I do." He rattled the ropes, relishing the combination of fury and helplessness.

"What if you could be with us all the time? Wouldn't that be marvelous?"

"Oh yes."

"You could marry one of us," Miranda bizarrely suggested. "We have dowries. The money could be ours very fast."

He knew about their dowries, pitiful little bank accounts that would only interest a working man or a fool.

"It's definitely worth considering," he fibbed.

"We need an answer very soon. We're eager to be free of John's influence."

"I understand."

"You'd do it for us, wouldn't you?"

He wouldn't marry one of them if they were the last females on earth. He intended to find an heiress, some pathetically rich sow from the lower classes whose father was dying to ally himself with the exalted Middleton family. Edward would pick a pretty girl, an innocent girl, a biddable girl.

Not a deviant whore like Melanie or Miranda.

Yet Miranda had a whip in her hand, his limbs fettered, and he was completely at her mercy.

"I could wed you," he claimed. "We'd have to discuss it, though, to hash out the details."

"Who would you choose? Melanie or me?"

"I'll have to reflect on it."

"You do that." The conversation apparently over, she glared at her sister, her tone all business. "Remove his drawers. I wish to inspect his privates."

Melanie seized the front of the garment and ripped it down the center so his loins were exposed. He had nothing of which to be ashamed, but still, he yearned to curl into a ball and shield himself from her prurient scrutiny.

His cock had a different view of the situation. It swelled even further, becoming so rigid that he moaned in pain.

"He's quite large," Melanie said.

"I suppose," Miranda agreed. "Larger than I anticipated anyway."

Miranda opened a dresser drawer and pulled out a small jar. She offered it to her sister, and Melanie swiped out what looked to be an ointment. She stroked it onto his skin, slathering it across his nipples, testicles, and ass. The areas she touched grew warm, the heat increasing his agitation.

She finished with his phallus, and at the feel of her slender fingers gliding over his erection, he couldn't hold back. He spewed in a hot rush, his seed gushing over his belly in jerky, embarrassing spurts.

On witnessing his humiliating conclusion, they snickered as if the adolescent display was precisely what they'd sought.

Melanie slid off him to stand by Miranda. They shook

their heads and walked away, going into the dressing room and closing the door.

For several minutes, he lay very still, not sure what would happen next. The chamber was eerily silent, and he muttered, "Melanie? Miranda?"

He frowned at the door, expecting them to pop in, to laugh and come over to release him. But they didn't.

"Melanie! Miranda!" he said more vehemently. "Get back in here!"

There was no sign of them, and his fury surged.

With all his might, he tugged on the ropes, and eventually, the headboard gave way. He untied himself, then leapt off the mattress as if he'd discovered it was crawling with ants. Frantically, he scurried about, grabbing his clothes and yanking them on.

The sadistic fiends!

Gad, if a maid had strolled in, he'd have been in a pickle!

John was a stickler for the proprieties. If he learned that Edward was dallying with the twins, he would demand a quick wedding. He'd have Edward shackled to one of the devious monsters before Edward could blink.

Had that been their scheme all along? Had they wanted him to be caught?

He hurried to the dressing room and flung open the door, figuring they'd be hiding inside, but they weren't. He kept on to the adjacent bedchamber, but they weren't there, either.

Evidently, they'd shed their erotic attire, donned their conventional gowns, and flitted off to the party, leaving Edward to fend for himself.

"I'll get even with you, my pretties," he vowed. "Just see if I don't."

He stormed out so they couldn't return and entice him again.

CLARINDA Dudley wandered down a dimly lit hallway of the castle, trying to locate the route by which she'd entered.

The structure was notorious for its winding corridors, having been constructed to confuse medieval marauders, but they were just as tricky for a modern woman who was merely hoping to rejoin the festivities in the garden.

She rounded a corner and barely avoided plowing into a pair of lovers, secluded in a dark alcove. They were locked in a torrid embrace, their lips melded, their hands roaming freely, and she blushed to the roots of her hair.

"Pardon me," she mumbled.

The duo drew apart, scowling as if *she* was in the wrong for interrupting, and as she recognized them, she groaned.

Her brother and Barbara Middleton? She had to be hallucinating.

"Phillip!" she hissed. "What are you doing?"

"What does it look like?"

"It *looks like* you're kissing the earl's mother."

"I see your vision hasn't failed you."

"I assume you have a good reason."

"Don't I always?"

"Is this your sister, Phillip?" Lady Barbara asked. "We can finally be introduced."

"Finally!" Clarinda gasped. "How long has this been going on?"

"We started in the first day you stopped by the castle," Barbara said.

"*She* seduced me," Phillip added, "in case you were wondering."

"I wasn't," Clarinda snapped.

"Yes, it was at my instigation," Barbara concurred. "I saw him, and I simply had to have him."

She grinned at Phillip as if he was a favorite pet, as if her taking responsibility for the amour would lessen Clarinda's rage. Of course it didn't.

Phillip had a knack for getting himself into trouble with the ladies. As they'd traveled across England in their peddler's wagon, dispensing potions and advice, it had been the story of their lives.

They would stumble on a scenic village, but Clarinda

never had a chance to form any friendships. He would trifle with someone's wife or daughter, and they'd end up fleeing an angry mob in the middle of the night.

He was the most arrogant man she'd ever met, so he never thought any of it was his fault. Women naïvely trusted him, so it was easy for him to land in a jam. And the consequences inevitably fell on Clarinda.

She loved the house that Captain Odell had provided for them. For once, she actually had a home, and she wouldn't relinquish it without a fight. Only catastrophe could result from his behavior with Barbara, and Clarinda wouldn't allow him to ruin the world she was building for herself.

"Would you excuse us?" she said to Barbara. She grabbed Phillip and dragged him away, and he staggered after her like a recalcitrant boy.

"When you're finished," Barbara cooed to him, "I'll be outside."

"I'll find you," Phillip called over his shoulder.

"I'll be with my future daughter-in-law, whom I plan to upset and annoy."

"I've talked to Lady Violet on several occasions," Phillip admitted. "She's dumb as a post."

"I suspected as much, which will make our chat all the more amusing."

Their intimate banter—as if they knew each other extremely well—increased Clarinda's aggravation.

"Come on!" she nagged, lugging him away so he could no longer see his inamorata.

She found a deserted parlor, hauled him into it, and slammed the door. He gazed about, located a sideboard, and helped himself to the earl's whiskey.

"Would you like one?" he asked.

"No."

"Your loss."

He downed the glass, then poured himself another and downed it, too.

"I'll give the rich credit," he said. "They know how to pamper themselves."

"Would you stop drinking and tell me what you're doing."

He scowled as if it was the stupidest comment ever. "I'm having a clandestine affair, as you deduced clearly enough. Why are you raising such a fuss?"

"You're having sex with the earl's mother!"

"Yes. So?"

She threw up her hands and marched over to join him at the sideboard so she could pour her own whiskey.

"What if you're caught?" she inquired.

"What if I am?"

"She's not some farm girl from nowhere. She's not some widow with no family to care what she does. She's Barbara Middleton."

"Do you really think Penworth gives two hoots about her? He can't abide her, and he never even speaks to her. She could race through the garden, naked and on fire, and he wouldn't notice."

"You're mistaken. It doesn't matter what occurred in the past. It's a son and his mother. If he learns of your dalliance, all hell will break loose."

"Don't be melodramatic."

"I'm not. I'm trying to get you to focus. Now tell me: If Lord Penworth catches you, what is your plan?"

He poured a third drink, and he sipped it as he pondered.

"I suppose I'd . . . I'd . . ." He paused, then muttered, "I guess I'd have to marry her, wouldn't I?"

Clarinda had just swallowed a mouthful of liquor, and at hearing the whopper of a lie, it went down the wrong way. Pounding on her chest, she sputtered and coughed.

"*You'd marry her?* For pity's sake, Phillip. I've been your sister for twenty-five years. You can fool others with your nonsense, but you can't fool me."

"Why couldn't I marry her? There are worse fates than being wed to an earl's mother."

"How about the fact that she has no income and no home? If Penworth doesn't offer to support her, she'll be living on the streets."

"There is that," he allowed.

"What would you do with her? Would you tie her to your wagon and have her lumber after you like a milk cow? Somehow, I don't see her content with that scenario."

He chuckled. "No, I don't imagine she'd take to it."

"And she's so much older than you. How many years is it? Twenty?"

"Only sixteen."

"Only!" She inhaled a deep breath, struggling for calm as she peered over at him. "You'll never wed. You're too independent, but if you ever decided to proceed, wouldn't you like to have a bride who loved you?"

"Perhaps."

"How could Barbara Middleton be that person?"

"She's just lonely—like all the rest of them. I make her feel better about herself. It's what I do. What's wrong with that?"

"What's wrong with it? There are so many things *wrong* with it that I can't tabulate them all."

"Nothing bad will happen. Trust me."

She'd known him a long, long time. When he said the words *trust me*, they were headed for catastrophe.

"Don't wreck this for me," she begged.

"I won't."

"Please. I'm happy here, and I don't want to leave."

He grinned his impudent grin, the one that made female hearts flutter whenever they saw it, and he tossed an arm over her shoulder.

"You worry too much, Clarinda." He spoke in the coaxing tone that *always* had her worrying. "Everything will be fine. I've got it all under control."

"If that's what you believe, then I'll brace myself, for calamity is about to mow me down like a runaway carriage."

* * *

Barbara strolled the grounds, pretending no destination, but in reality, she was working her way toward Violet Howard. The snotty imp was adept at scurrying away, but for once, Barbara wouldn't let her.

Violet acted as if Barbara was invisible, but what addle-brained Violet didn't understand was that Barbara was back to stay.

If John had resolved to marry, she intended he would wed someone Barbara liked, someone who would like Barbara in return. Was Violet Howard the best choice to be his bride? Though she'd never conversed with the ghastly child, Barbara was sure the answer was a resounding *no*.

John would have selected Violet for inane motives—property, dowry, ancestry—but Barbara didn't think any of those aspects were vital. As her own situation had proven, there were other, more imperative issues: compatibility, respect, and common interests, to name a few. She was enough of a romantic to add *love* into the mix.

Wouldn't it be wonderful if John married a girl he loved?

Silly, immature Violet Howard would be an appalling wife, and Barbara had to convince John of his potential mistake.

Through the crowd, Violet was approaching, and Barbara hid behind a tree until Violet had passed. Then she stepped out and took Violet's arm—as if they were bosom companions.

"Hello, Violet. You don't mind if I call you Violet, do you? After all, you're about to be my daughter-in-law. It's only natural that we be on intimate terms."

Violet's eyes widened with dismay, and she tried to yank away, but Barbara simply gripped her arm more tightly. Her spine rigid, Violet walked on, staring straight ahead.

"What do you want, Mrs. . . . Lady . . . ah . . ."

"You may call me Lady Penworth. Or you may call me Barbara. Either will suffice."

"What do you want?" Violet snapped, ignoring both appellations.

"We need to talk."

"About what?"

"You've been very rude to me, and I'm tired of it."

"There's no reason to be courteous to the likes of you."

"Isn't there? If you insist on being a shrew, how will we get on in the coming years?"

"A shrew! How dare you!"

"How else would you describe your conduct? From the moment you arrived in Scotland, you've been uncivil and vulgar. Unfortunately for you, I won't pretend that you've behaved any differently."

Violet's pert nose was thrust in the air. "My father is a very important man."

"Your father is a womanizing boor."

Outraged, Violet gasped, "I will not listen to you denigrating him."

"Too late. I already have."

"I've written to him, to inform him that you're here."

"I'm shaking in my boots."

"He'll be very upset." Mention of the duke had had no effect on Barbara, so Violet threateningly repeated, "Very upset!"

"Enough about your idiot of a father. I couldn't care less about him. I'm curious about this: If you remain so disagreeable, how will your marriage to John ever occur?"

"What do you mean?"

"Have you considered how easily I can sabotage your betrothal? If I decide to view you as an adversary, the wedding might never be held."

Barbara stopped and pulled Violet around so they were looking at each other. Barbara was taller and older and more sophisticated. In every way, she loomed over Violet.

Having survived three decades of intrigue in the palaces of Europe, Barbara had thrived by knowing who her friends were, but knowing who her enemies were, too. If pathetic Violet Howard was anxious to clash, Barbara would oblige her, but Violet would be eaten alive.

"I don't have to worry about you," Violet boldly declared.

"You don't?"

"No. I've spoken with John."

"Have you? About what?"

"He's kicking you out."

"Is he? As a favor to you?"

"Yes."

Barbara laughed. "If you want to play with the master, you should learn the rules before the game starts."

"What rules? What are you talking about?"

"You're an awful liar. John never said any such thing." Barbara dropped Violet's arm and moved away. "Last chance, Violet. What is it to be: friends or enemies?"

"I don't wish to be either. You're nothing to me."

"Is that what you imagine? That you can fight me and win? Fine, then. Let's battle. My first foray will be to tell John a terrible rumor about you. It will be a bald-faced lie, but I'll tell it anyway."

"You wouldn't!"

"I would. What should it be? How about that you're in love with Edward? I'll claim I heard your maid gossiping, and you'd rather have Edward as your husband."

"What?"

Violet was gravely alarmed, and Barbara snorted with disgust.

Barbara had occasionally seen Violet huddled with frivolous, disreputable Edward, but she hadn't speculated over it. Had their tête-à-têtes actually been illicit flirtations?

"Or maybe," Barbara jeered, "I'll pen an anonymous letter to your precious father. I'll report that you've disgraced yourself with the earl's brother, that the whole estate has watched the scandal transpire."

"But . . . but . . . that wouldn't be true."

"Who cares? I'll say it just to spite you. What sort of trouble would it cause?"

Violet gaped with revulsion, then began to tremble from head to toe. "You horrid, horrid witch!" she hurled, and she spun and ran.

Barbara walked on, pondering the encounter. She wanted John to be happy, and she was positive he wasn't. Violet Howard would never make him happy. He needed someone who was more mature and stronger of character, who could appreciate his dreary history and cherish him regardless of his failings.

Where could she find such a suitable bride?

She ambled along, not realizing how far she'd strayed from the castle. She was on a quiet, deserted path, when a familiar male voice brought her to a halt.

"I don't accept your resignation," John haughtily intoned.

"You don't own me," a woman answered, "and you can't force me to remain."

"Is that what you think?"

"It's what I know."

Barbara peeked through a nearby hedge to see him sequestered in a secluded copse of trees with Miss Lambert. As Barbara spied on them, he stunned her by grabbing and shaking Miss Lambert. "You will not quit! I will not allow it!"

"It's not up to you!"

"Isn't it? If that's what you suppose, then you don't comprehend the power I can wield."

Miss Lambert wrenched away, and she was quaking with fury. "You're a bully, and I hate you," she seethed.

"Well, at the moment, I can't say I like you any better."

"Just . . . just . . . leave me alone. Oh, please, just leave me alone!"

Miss Lambert raced off, and John shouted at her.

"Lily, get back here. At once!"

Miss Lambert, intrepid scamp that she was, kept on as

if Barbara's exalted son hadn't uttered a single word. John dawdled, looking aggrieved and at a loss.

People never defied him. They never disobeyed or argued. Because of his rank and station, it simply never occurred to others that such brazen behavior would be tolerated. Yet Miss Lambert felt perfectly comfortable with flouting him.

Ultimately, he stomped after her, and Barbara was agog. Would he chase her into the castle? Would he proceed straight to her room, unconcerned about the indiscretion? Would he dare?

She remembered the odd night when she'd caught Miss Lambert locked in a downstairs parlor with him. It was obvious she'd been debauched, but Barbara had assumed John seduced her as a lark, as a one-time venture into lust that wouldn't have been repeated.

Had Barbara been wrong? Had she misjudged the episode? Was there more to the relationship than she'd recognized?

Barbara knew passion when she saw it, knew love when she saw it. Why would a couple quarrel as John and Miss Lambert had unless a deep and abiding affection was present?

"Miss Lambert," she mused. "Who would have guessed?"

She grinned and hurried to locate Phillip.

Chapter 14

❧

LILY walked across the park, struggling to look inconspicuous. The second vial of Spinster's Cure was clutched in her hand.

Despite the fact that she didn't believe the potion contained any magical power, she was going to drink it anyway. There were hundreds of guests roaming the castle grounds, and among the large crowd, she'd noted many bachelors. One in particular had caught her eye.

Captain Bramwell was visiting, which Lily considered an omen. Had fate brought him to Lily so she could try again?

Mr. Dudley insisted it was futile to ingest another dose, that she had altered her destiny and couldn't repair the damage, but she had to do something.

She'd recklessly surrendered her virginity to Lord Penworth, but she hadn't understood that the act was so intimate. It had left her in a maudlin state, her emotions scraped raw as if she'd been flayed alive.

Her feelings for him had manifested in a dangerous

way. She loved him, but she absolutely *couldn't*. Nor could she expect any reciprocal affection. She had to buck up, had to get a grip on herself and figure out how to proceed.

Without question, she had to escape him, but where was she to go? And how was she to accomplish it?

She was in a foreign country, with very little money, and no friends except for Mr. Dudley. She could attempt to quit her job, but the earl wouldn't let her. Her other option was to sneak away, but she truly thought that he would chase after her and drag her back. He was fixated to the point of obsession, yet he was engaged to Violet Howard. He would never break his betrothal, and Lily had to accept the reality of her situation.

Penworth might fancy her, but it was in the abstract manner of all aristocrats who dallied with their servants. Lily had spent the night with him, but she couldn't continue with the precarious, fruitless liaison. There was no benefit to be gleaned. Only detriment.

She had to divert Penworth's attention—and fast! Marriage would be a foil to his interest, with a husband serving the role of vital buffer to keep him at bay.

Through the woods, she heard a horse approaching, and as it neared, she could see Bramwell in the saddle. She had a clear view of him, as clear as she'd had that evening on his ship when Penworth had wrecked her opportunity.

She stared and stared, imprinting his image into her head, then she tipped the vial to her lips and swallowed.

As the liquid flooded down her throat, she smirked, thinking she'd proved Mr. Dudley wrong. Fate could be mistakenly shifted in one direction, then shifted back in the other. But as she pondered the notion, she was suddenly wrenched away.

"There you are," Penworth said. "I've been searching everywhere."

"Ah!" she shrieked, her gaze ripped from Bramwell to settle on Penworth. Again!

She peered up into his handsome face, and strange as it sounded, time seemed to grind to a halt. The forest, the sky, the breeze, the birds in the trees all disappeared. There was John Middleton and no one—and nothing—else.

Providence unfurled a vision that only she could see: the children they would have, the places they would reside, the minor tragedies and major triumphs that would buffet their existence.

The stirring portrait depicted the future she'd always wanted, and it was hovering within her grasp. She could reach out and seize it—if she dared. Violet Howard didn't matter. Lily's humble antecedents didn't matter. John's station in the world didn't matter. It was ordained that they be united for all eternity.

Then Bramwell crashed through the foliage on his horse, shattering her dreamy reverie as cleanly as if he'd shot a gun through it.

"What is it, Penworth?" he asked, riding up. "A woman called out. She seemed to be in distress."

"It's Miss Lambert overreacting again," Penworth explained.

From his high perch, Bramwell glared down his snooty nose, gaping at the vial in Lily's hand.

"Still drinking, Miss Lambert?" he chastised.

"No, I'm not, Captain Bramwell, though if I *was*, I hardly suppose it would be any of your business."

"She's awfully flighty," Bramwell said to Penworth, "even for a female."

"She grows on you," Penworth claimed.

"It's the middle of the day. I know you're loyal to your employees, but perhaps you should reconsider. If such a drunkard worked for me, I wouldn't let her within a hundred yards of my fiancée."

He trotted off, as Lily grumbled, "Pompous ass."

Penworth chuckled. "My goodness, Miss Lambert! Such language."

He was still gripping her arm, and she jerked away and started toward the castle, but after taking a mere two steps, he grabbed her and yanked her back to him.

"We have a moment alone," he pointed out. "Don't run off."

"I'd rather be by myself."

"Why?"

"You've spoiled everything," she complained. "Just like before!"

"What have I spoiled?" he demanded. "What are you doing out here?"

The trials of the past few weeks pressed in on her, her frantic emotions simmering below the surface.

What if she was pregnant? What then?

She would be a pariah. Decent people would shun her. She'd never find another job. She'd be tossed out on the streets; she'd starve.

Had it been worth it—to throw it all away just for him?

The overwhelming answer was *no*.

He'd copulated with her, then gone on his merry way. He hadn't forsworn Lady Violet, hadn't cancelled his wedding. He was blithely walking down the road to matrimony, and the fact that he hadn't cried off from his betrothal was the most striking evidence of how foolish Lily had been.

"If you must know," she snapped, "I was drinking a love potion."

"A . . . love potion?" He laughed and laughed, deeming it the silliest comment ever, and as his mirth waned, he asked, "Why would you need a love potion?"

"To make someone fall in love with me. Why would you suppose?"

He frowned, then grinned. "You were hoping it would be Aiden Bramwell? Oh, that is too rich for words."

Another bout of hysterical laughter seemed likely, and she cut him off, unable to abide his hilarity. "Why couldn't he love me?"

"He never would."

It was a cruel remark, but he didn't notice. He wouldn't. She was a servant. An employee. An underling. Any insult was of no consequence.

"How about you?" she fumed. "Could you ever love me?"

"What?"

"You heard me: Could you ever love me?"

"No." At her sharp intake of breath, he hastily added, "It's nothing to do with you personally."

"Of course not."

"I could never love anyone. It's not in my nature."

He took the vial from her, and he held it up toward the sunlight, seeing that it was empty. "Is this the same nonsense you had on Bramwell's ship?" he inquired. "You told me it was a cure for seasickness."

"I lied."

"You expect me to believe it's a . . . a . . . magic potion?"

"I don't care what you believe." She retrieved the vial and stuck it in her pocket.

"Where did you get it?"

"From Mr. Dudley."

"My new neighbor?"

"Yes. He uses the fake name Philippe Dubois. He's a charlatan who travels around the countryside, convincing women that he can change their lives, but he can't."

Her tone was so solemn, her expression so gloomy, that he was taken aback. "What is wrong with you?" he queried.

"I'm fine."

"If it's about yesterday, and your accompanying Violet during her—"

"This isn't about Lady Violet!" she stridently insisted.

"What is it, then?"

"You and I had marital relations, but it was meaningless to you."

"That's not true."

"Really? Will you marry me now? Is that your plan? For if it is, I must have missed your proposal."

"Marry . . . you?" He shook his head. "I never could, Lily. I thought you understood."

"I *understand* all right." She swallowed down the lump in her throat, being absurdly close to tears. "What will happen to me?"

"Why would anything *happen*? We'll continue on just as we have been."

"Where does it leave me? Will you merely flirt and flatter, then occasionally sneak into my room when you can get away from your guests? Is that all there will ever be for me?"

"Well . . . yes. There could never be more."

"What about Lady Violet?"

"What about her?"

"You're engaged to her."

"She's irrelevant to you and me. The two of you occupy totally separate places in my life."

"Do we?"

Yet when it was over, Lady Violet would be his wife and countess, but what would Lily be?

"What's to become of me?"

"Why even ask the question? You'll keep working for me."

"But I'm not assisting the twins anymore, so I don't have any chores."

"You'll help Violet."

"Have you even the smallest clue of how inappropriate it is for me to tend her now that you and I have . . . had . . ."

She couldn't utter the word *intercourse*. It was beyond her, and he, too, seemed unsettled by her need to speak of what they'd done. He scowled with dismay, so at least he was capable of some amount of chagrin.

"I told you"—he appeared exasperated—"that Violet is irrelevant to us."

"How can you say that? You're going to marry her!"

"Yes, I am."

"What if she finds out about us?"

"She won't," he declared with a pompous certainty.

"You've betrayed her."

"Betrayed! You're being ridiculous. My wedding is almost a year away."

"And you're demanding that I be her companion till that date. I can't do it. I can't watch you court her. I assumed I could, but I can't."

"Why can't you?"

"Because it hurts me!" She clutched a fist over her heart, which was breaking. "It wounds me to see you with her, to know that I can never be good enough for you. I could never be your fiancée, but she can be simply because of who her father is."

"Why would you want me as a husband? You talk as if you have . . . *feelings* for me."

He pronounced *feelings* as if it were an epithet, as if she had too many of them while he had none worth mentioning. His condescension only underscored what an idiot she'd been.

Their sexual congress had changed her in ways she couldn't explain. She felt overwrought and exposed and bound to him in an abiding fashion, but he was the same as ever: haughty, aloof, detached, and ready to wed Violet Howard with nary a ripple in his conscience.

"I want to return to England," she said.

"No."

"It's insane to make me stay here."

"Then call me mad—for you will not go."

She was growing angry, but he was, too. She didn't imagine anyone ever argued with him. He gave orders, and they were instantly obeyed. Obviously, he expected her to be just as subservient, but she couldn't passively heed his edict.

She felt used and sullied, the *other* woman in a seedy affair. There was no putting a better spin on it, and she refused to persist with shaming herself.

How had she landed in such a wretched predicament? She had no idea, but she had to extricate herself as swiftly as she could.

"Fine then," she seethed, "if you won't let me go, I quit!"

"I don't accept your resignation."

"You don't own me, and you can't force me to remain."

"Is that what you think?"

"It's what I know."

His rage bubbled over, and he grabbed her and shook her. "You will not quit! I will not allow it!"

"It's not up to you!"

"Isn't it? If that's what you suppose, then you don't comprehend the power I can wield."

She pushed him away, not wanting him to touch her, for when he did, her reasoning became muddled. She was dangerously, stupidly attracted to him, and she desperately yearned for things to be different. But they never would be.

Regardless of Mr. Dudley's claims to the contrary, there was no magic in the world strong enough to make him love her.

Loathing was her best defense against him, and she hurled, "You're a bully, and I hate you."

"Well, at the moment, I can't say I like you any better."

"Just . . . just . . . leave me alone. Oh, please, just leave me alone!"

She whirled away and ran, and though he lunged for her, she was too quick. She slipped away, vanishing as neatly as if there'd been fog in the meadow to shield her from view.

"Lily," he shouted, "get back here. At once!"

She kept going, aware that he would stop bellowing before he was overheard, that he would never chase after her. He was nothing if not predictable, and with a castle full of guests, he would never make a scene.

Chapter 15

❦

"OPEN this door. Right now."

"No."

"Open it, or I will kick it down."

There was a lengthy silence as Lily debated whether or not he was serious. John himself wasn't sure what he might do.

After a long day of revelry, it was the middle of the night, the entire castle abed. All was quiet, so an abundance of noise—such as he'd just instigated—would be easily discernible.

He was risking discovery and scandal, but he didn't care. It occurred to him that he'd had too much to drink, that he was making awful decisions, but for once, he wasn't concerned over proprieties.

If it had taken an enormous quantity of alcohol to spur the conversation he intended, so be it. He had numerous cogent remarks to share with Miss Lily Lambert, and by God, she would listen to them!

He pressed his ear to the wood, and he could hear her tiptoeing nearer.

"Go away," she hissed.

"No."

He banged with his fist, then kicked the wood so hard that it bowed. She squealed with alarm and jumped away, stunned by his violence, and he had to admit that he was a tad stunned, too.

What had come over him? Why did she drive him to such extreme displays?

Another protracted silence ensued, then the key turned in the lock. She pulled the door open a crack, grabbed him by the wrist, and dragged him inside.

"Get in here," she fumed, "and cease your caterwauling!"

She spun the key again, locking them in, which suited his purposes.

Since her tantrum in the forest earlier in the afternoon, he'd been in a fine fettle. She was correct that he was behaving badly—toward her *and* Violet—and though such misconduct was out of character for him, he couldn't control himself.

Over the past few weeks, he'd become a teeming morass of discontentment and disapproval. Nothing made him happy. Nothing satisfied him. His disposition was foul, his patience at an end. He complained and criticized; he snapped and nitpicked, and it was all Lily's fault.

After she'd stormed away from him, he'd tarried at the party, pretending all was well, when in fact he was exhausted by the whole charade.

When it came right down to it, he loathed hunting, and he wasn't particularly keen on fraternizing with his neighbors. He loved the rustic solitude of the castle, which was why he traveled to Scotland every autumn. Yet he allowed himself to be pushed by convention into hosting numerous feasts and soirees.

Edward nagged, and the twins simpered. Esther begged him to mediate her quarrels with Barbara. Violet irked him with her girlish nonsense. He wished everyone would go to the devil, that he could be alone with Lily, just the two of them free to act however they pleased.

He'd spent hours in his room, pacing and drinking. Gradually, it had dawned on him that it was pointless to rage at himself. Lily was the cause of his irritation, so it was only fair that she bear the brunt of his dour mood.

"Explain yourself!" she demanded. "And since it's three o'clock in the morning, make it quick."

"I will not make it *quick*, Miss Lambert. I have many pertinent comments, and I will talk until I'm finished."

"Get on with it then."

She was tapping her foot, her annoyance obvious, and his anger soared.

Why was she annoyed? *He* was the one who'd been wronged. Not her.

"Let me be perfectly clear," he said.

"What is it? I keep waiting to hear, but you can't seem to begin. If you never begin, you'll never conclude."

Narrowing his gaze, he studied her, trying to figure out why he was enamored.

He had no idea.

"You are full of spit and sass," he mused. "I've never liked that about you."

"So what?"

"I insist that my women be mild-mannered, respectful, and good-natured."

"Well, I am not one of your *women*, so you needn't fret over my lack of suitable attributes."

He bent down till they were nose to nose. "You are mine until I say you're not."

"Ha! That's what you think." She laid her palms on his chest and shoved him away, creating space between them. "You imagine you can bully everyone, but you can't bully me."

She was so aggrieved, a pretty, petite virago who drove him wild and made him crazy. With her eyes flashing daggers, her elevated temper had left her even more beautiful. Her cheeks were rosy with color, her hair down and brushed out. She was barefoot, the tips of her toes peeking out from under her nightgown. The toenails had been painted bright red.

He'd never seen a woman's painted toes before, and the sight was exotic and arousing in a fashion he didn't understand. It confused him; he lost his train of thought.

His aggravation waned, to be replaced by lust. As he'd learned early on in their relationship, it was impossible to be in her presence and not desire her. He'd given up fighting his attraction.

He glanced around, focusing in, realizing that a candle was lit. Coals burned in the stove. The blankets on the bed hadn't been disturbed.

"Why weren't you asleep?" he asked.

"I've been remembering how much I hate you. How could I rest with so much animosity careening through my veins?"

"You do not hate me. I will not allow it."

"Why does everything always have to be about you? Why can't my feelings matter for once?"

"Your feelings are absurd. That's why."

"Ooh, I can't abide you!"

She stomped over to a table by the window, where she grabbed a half-empty bottle. It was filled with what appeared to be red wine. She tipped it to her lips and swallowed a huge gulp.

"Are you drinking?"

"Yes."

He marched over and snatched the bottle from her.

"Give me that!" she protested.

"No." He ran his thumb over the label and read, "Woman's Daily Remedy. What is it supposed to do?"

"It's meant to relieve feminine stress." She glared at him. "It's not working."

He took his own sip, and at establishing its intoxicating potency, his eyes watered.

"Where did you get it?"

"I bought it from Mr. Dudley."

Dudley, again?

One of the few blessings of recent days was that—after Lily had been rescued from the grotto—Dudley had vanished. He'd been markedly absent from castle events, so hopefully, he was gone for good. John didn't like him, and if Dudley loitered on the premises, John might have to be civil.

"Dudley sells female tonics that are laced with alcohol?" he asked.

"Yes. I told you he was a charlatan. You ought to see what else he sells. You're such an uptight boor"—she drunkenly stammered on the word *boor*—"that you'd probably have an apoplexy."

"Very funny."

He was greatly bothered by her comment. He didn't want to be a boor around her, didn't want to be cross or stuffy. He wanted to be playful and carefree, more like his . . . his . . .

Oh, hell, like his *mother*. There! He'd admitted it. But when he'd spent three decades trying to be conventional, it was so difficult to be frivolous.

Before he could stop her, she yanked the bottle away and enjoyed another swig. Like the imperious ass he could definitely be, he yanked it back. She lunged for it, and he held it over his head, out of her reach. "I believe you've had enough," he scolded.

She gazed at the bottle, at him, at the bottle again, and she sighed.

"Never mind." Her balance precarious, she flopped into a chair. "There isn't enough liquor in the world to cure what ails me."

She looked so glum, and his heart made the strangest flip-flopping motion.

"What ails you, Lily?"

"You."

At her surly tone, he chuckled. "Why?"

She peered up at him with those big blue eyes of hers, eyes that seemed to delve to the core of his being.

"Just once," she quietly said, "I want to be important to someone."

"You're important to me."

"Shut up. I can't bear it when you lie."

"I'm not lying. You *are* important to me."

"You have a peculiar way of showing it."

"I can't marry you."

"I know, I know. I'm not a dolt."

"You claim to understand"—he shrugged—"so what else would you have me say?"

"How about that you're sorry you can't? How about that you wish things could be different? How about that you'd marry me if you could?"

"I would marry you if I could."

His tepid assertion had her scoffing with disgust. "Be silent before you embarrass yourself beyond all redemption." She stared and stared, then asked, "Why am I so unlovable?"

It was on the tip of his tongue to refute the notion, to boldly shout, *You're not unlovable. I love you!* But he couldn't force out the affirmation. He'd never previously declared himself, and he hadn't a clue what the word *love* meant.

Was it what he felt for her? When he was with her, he was so content. When they were apart, he moped and pined, wondering where she was and what she was doing. She occupied his thoughts and tormented his dreams.

Was that love?

If it was, what purpose would be served by telling her?

They could never wed, because he wasn't free to choose any available girl. There were bloodlines to consider, fortunes to protect, land and people and property to enrich.

He didn't want to marry at all. Not Violet or anyone. He'd seen the damage matrimony could inflict on a man—

his father being the prime example. If it had been left up to John, he would never have become engaged, but he'd been raised to do his duty, so he would wed Violet Howard.

Lily had no role to play in that scenario. She couldn't change what would happen. It simply *was*, and only a fool would fail to grasp why she was upset.

He'd callously ruined her—without regard to the consequences. There was no compensation he could provide to make it right. There was no way to repair the damage he'd wrought, yet he'd dally again in an instant, so where did it leave them?

He walked over to her chair, and he slapped down his hands, trapping her in her seat. He leaned down and kissed her, but she turned away so he brushed her cheek instead.

"I hate you," she repeated, but with less vehemence.

"I don't hate you."

"What do you want from me?" she asked, exasperated.

"Just this. I want to spend time with you—when I can."

"Why?"

"Because you make me happy."

He kissed her again, and she participated with a bit of vigor. She wasn't immune to him, and he would exploit her attraction. He intended to wear her down, to keep on till she smiled, till she admitted she was glad he came.

"I need more than this from you," she said. "It's not fair that I have to sneak around and hide what's occurring."

"No, it's not."

"I should find a man who loves me."

"Of course you should."

"I deserve someone better than you," she grumpily insisted.

"I won't argue the point."

"Let me go back to England."

"No."

"Why not? Why are you being so obstinate?"

He had no answer for her.

His conduct was irrational, and he recognized that he

was courting disaster, but he couldn't let her go. Not quite yet. Or maybe never.

He scooped her into his arms and carried her to the bed. At the swift movement, she grappled for purchase, clutching at his shoulders, laughing as he tossed her onto the mattress and followed her down.

"I'm so dizzy," she muttered. "I must be drunk."

"Good. It will make it easier to take advantage of you."

"I don't want you to take advantage of me."

"Yes, you do."

He rolled on top of her, pinning her down in case she thought to escape, but she had no fight remaining. She gazed up at him, looking so miserable, and he couldn't bear to see that she was unhappy, to know that he was the cause of her woe.

"Don't be sad." He kissed her forehead, her nose, her mouth. "I hate it when you are."

"I'm not sad. I'm . . . I'm . . . resigned."

She pronounced the word *resigned* as if it had been wrenched from her very soul.

"Are you?"

"Yes. Mr. Dudley said I couldn't change what I'd done, and he was correct. My fate is written in stone."

"What is this horrid destiny that you can't avoid?"

"You! You're my destiny."

He grinned. "Marvelous."

He was nibbling at her nape, as his busy hands tugged her nightgown up her legs, and she didn't protest. She'd imbibed too much alcohol, and the liquor—along with her despondent condition—had rendered her relaxed and compliant.

If he'd have been any kind of gentleman, he'd have simply tucked her under the covers and departed, but where she was concerned, he'd lost his chivalrous tendencies.

He planned to make love with her again and again until he'd slaked his lust. There had to be a reason he was so obsessed, and regular sexual congress would quell the itch he needed her to constantly scratch.

"Don't take off my nightgown," she said as the hem was at her hips, but she didn't try to stop him. "I have no desire to be undressed in front of you."

"And I have *every* desire to see you naked."

With a particularly nimble flick of his wrist, he had the garment over her head. He peered down her torso, delighted with her feminine form, with her full breasts and curvaceous hips.

"I'm so glad you're mine," he murmured.

"Am I yours?"

"Yes."

"For how long?"

"For forever," he lied.

She would be his until time or scandal or indifference separated them, and for the moment, he'd act as if they would continue on into infinity. He felt they were trapped in a bubble and the outside world could never intrude. Violet was a distant memory, and as long as he could maintain the pretense, he would.

He dipped to her breasts and feasted on them. Her nipples were so lovely, so sensitive, and he pleasured her until she was writhing beneath him.

"I want you naked, too," she suddenly surprised him by saying.

"You do, do you?"

"Yes. If I have to remove my clothes, it seems only fair that you remove yours."

"So it does."

He drew onto his knees, and he let her watch, her interest keen as he stripped off his coat and shirt. She rolled them so that he was on his back, and she yanked off his boots and stockings. Ultimately, just his trousers were left.

The flap at the front was loose, and she slipped her hand inside and took hold of his cock. She was barely past her virginity, so she'd never been taught how to stroke it, but the sensation was extreme, and he nearly spilled himself like an adolescent lad of fifteen.

"Are all men the same size?"

"Some are bigger. Some are smaller."

"How would you describe yours?"

"Definitely bigger."

His answer had her squealing with laughter, and she toppled onto the mattress. They stared at the ceiling, giggling like a pair of naughty children, and he couldn't remember when he'd ever been so foolish or lighthearted.

Before he'd met her, he'd have been aghast at the notion of behaving so merrily, but she made everything seem more vital. She made him feel alive and essential and necessary.

He came over her, and he began kissing her in earnest. There was a new seriousness to the endeavor. He wanted to please her, wanted to show her how it could truly be for them so she would never forget.

When their affair ended, when circumstances coalesced to force them apart, he hoped she would always fondly recollect their time together.

He dropped to her breasts again, and he suckled her, his fingers busy down below, spurring her to a quick orgasm. As she spiraled down, he spread her thighs, pushed himself in, and started to flex.

He couldn't believe how much he needed her, how much she trusted him. They'd generated a closeness that went beyond the mere expectation of sexual gratification. There was a poignancy to it, a sweetness he hadn't ever previously encountered with a woman, and he hadn't known such an intimate joining was possible.

He kept on and on, and as her second orgasm commenced, he emptied himself deep in her womb, relishing every instant of the reckless conclusion.

Gradually, his thrusting slowed, and he pulled away. He spooned himself to her, his chest nestled to her back, his loins cradling her bottom.

"Don't leave me," he said, amazing himself. "If you did, I couldn't bear it."

She was quiet, then she sighed. "I won't leave."

"We'll figure it out," he claimed. "Just don't be angry with me."

"I'm finished with being angry." She glanced at him over her shoulder. "I'm not very good at displays of temper, and since the end result is that I wound up in bed with you, it's been a wasted effort."

He chuckled and snuggled her down. They were silent again, each lost in difficult contemplation.

Eventually, she confessed, "It will hurt me when you marry her."

"I know it will."

"I can't work as her companion. I can't fetch her parasol or ride in the carriage when she goes visiting."

"You won't have to. Not ever again."

"Then what will you do with me? How will you explain my continued presence? You already abolished my duties to the twins. If I have no duties to Lady Violet, either, what will you tell people as to why I'm still here?"

He couldn't guess what lies he'd spew in order to keep her with him, and he didn't like her mentioning Violet. Her comments rammed at the wall he'd constructed between his real life and the false one he was building with her. He couldn't ever let the two worlds collide.

"We'll figure it out," he insisted more firmly.

"Yes, I suppose we will." She hesitated, then asked, "Everything will be all right, won't it?"

"As long as you're with me, everything will be fine."

Her breathing lagged, her body relaxing as she fell asleep.

Though he was exhausted himself, he fought slumber, dawdling, cherishing the moment, wanting it to last forever.

The first ray of dawn broke on the horizon, and he beat the cock's crow. Sliding off the mattress, he tugged on his trousers and sneaked away.

Chapter 16

‡

"CAUGHT you, you wicked minx."

"Let me go."

"No." Edward wrapped his arm around Miranda and held her tight. "Let's have a chat, shall we?"

"I'm busy."

"I don't see that you have any choice."

They were in an upstairs hall, next to several unoccupied bedchambers, and he was eager to make use of one of them. He wasn't generally prone to ravishment, but what female had ever deserved it more than she?

He'd been riding, and he was dressed in boots and spurs. He'd brought his riding crop, and he tossed it into a nearby room, then he tried to pull her in after it, but she wouldn't budge from her vantage point by the window.

She was peering off across the garden, and as he yanked her away, she started to struggle in earnest.

"No." She kicked at his shins with her heel. "I have to keep watching."

"Watching what?"

"Miss Lambert. She's taking her afternoon walk, and we're tracking her route."

"Planning future attacks, are you?"

"We don't understand why she's still here. She was forbidden to help us anymore, so what's she doing?"

"She helps Violet, instead."

"No. John told the housekeeper that she wasn't available to Violet." She glared over her shoulder. "Why do you suppose that is?"

"I don't care why."

Determined to remain in her spot, she scrapped and fought, but he was bigger and stronger. He wrestled her into the bedchamber and closed the door.

"Now then," he said, "let's have that chat."

Before she could reply, Melanie knocked.

"Miranda, let me in."

"No," Miranda surprised him by retorting. "I'm with Edward. He's picked me, and we want to be alone."

"I have to talk to you," Melanie insisted.

Edward hadn't been prepared for an interruption, and he most especially didn't like how Miranda had announced that he'd *picked* her.

To what was she referring? Did she mean his lie that he'd wed her or her sister? As he fretted over the prospect, Melanie hustled in without being invited.

Fine, he thought. He'd hoped to trap them together, and they'd made it easy.

They stood side by side, staring at him.

"Is it true?" Melanie asked. "Have you chosen Miranda over me?"

"I haven't decided," he claimed.

"We should both have a chance to convince you," Melanie nagged. "Miranda always gets her way."

"And you don't?"

"No. I have to do what she wants, and she always goes first."

Miranda smirked. "It's the bane of being born second."

"You'd like me more than her," Melanie asserted to Edward.

"Would I?" Edward inquired. "How could I be sure?"

Suddenly, the most wicked notion occurred to him.

If he pretended to be interested in matrimony, he could play them off one another. He'd be able to stretch out the competition for weeks or months, and in the process, he'd be showered with decadent acts.

"I believe," he said, "that we shall have to have a contest."

"What type of contest?" Miranda queried.

"You'll have to show me how thoroughly you can satisfy me."

"In a sexual manner?"

"Yes. I won't have a bride who's a cold fish. She must be proficient at her wifely duties. My standards are very exacting. I wonder how you'd fare?"

They gazed at each other, sharing one of their odd visual exchanges. When they grinned, his balls clenched, but not in a good way. It seemed they had a secret, as if they'd set the rules without consulting him. If they had mischief in mind, he might not realize it until it was too late.

They stepped nearer, so he was boxed in between them.

"How long will the contest last?" Miranda asked.

"The length will depend on how skillfully you perform."

"Two weeks," Miranda interjected, giving him no leeway. "Then you'll have to choose. You'll have to speak with John, too, so he doesn't send us back to England before we're finished."

"Once you make your selection," Melanie added, "the wedding can be held here in Scotland—where it's so easily accomplished."

They leaned in, a bosom crushed to each of his arms, a mons to each thigh.

"Yes," he agreed, "two weeks should be plenty of time."

"You wouldn't lie to us, would you, Edward?"

"No."

"Because we don't like it when people deceive us. Just remember our father. In the end, he was very, very sorry."

Edward frowned, speculating over what the hell they were intimating. Their father had suffered a pathetic demise, an accident with a gun in his library, which was a euphemism for suicide. But they were hinting at a darker conclusion.

What had the little demons done? Had they harmed their father? Would they have stooped to . . . to . . . murder?

The moment the lurid possibility blossomed, he shook it away.

He knew the twins. They'd lived with the family for a year and a half. Their father had been quietly dead and buried all that time. There had never been a whiff of gossip regarding his early demise.

Still, the fiery gleam in their blue eyes was unnerving, and he was having second thoughts as to whether he should foster further involvement, but he was so captivated by their rough carnal treatment. He craved more of it, just as he yearned to dish out a bit of it himself.

He wanted to see *them* fettered to the bed, wanted them pulling on the ropes as they begged for mercy.

Dare he proceed? Should he?

As he debated, Miranda crouched down and grabbed his riding crop, cutting off any divergent path. In an instant, the position of power was altered, and she was in control.

He should have marched out, but he didn't. He was frozen in place, riveted by the promise of debauchery, and wild horses couldn't have dragged him away.

Miranda smacked the crop across Melanie's bottom.

"Bare your breasts to him," Miranda ordered.

"Please don't make me," Melanie cried, and his cock grew hard as a stone.

"Do it!" Miranda commanded, slapping with the crop again.

Melanie turned, and Edward started undoing the buttons on her dress, any chance of restraint lost in a fog of twisted desire.

"VIOLET and I have something to say."

"What is it?"

Esther studied John, her fury meticulously concealed. She forced a smile, even though she wasn't feeling cheery or cordial.

They were in his library, and he was seated at his desk. He waved them to the chairs across, and they sat.

She'd spied on him all afternoon, but he'd simply pretended to work, doodling or blindly gazing out the window. His stack of bills and correspondence hadn't been touched.

She'd raised him and knew him well. He wasn't given to lethargy or sloth, and he'd heeded her biblical teachings: Idleness invited trouble.

What was happening to him? Why was he so distracted?

She didn't like him to have secrets, and she had to discover what was bothering him. After he went to bed, she'd sneak down and search his desk. He kept it locked, but years earlier, she'd made a copy of the key.

It paid to be vigilant, and she couldn't be caught off guard, especially if any information pertained to Edward. She had to stay one step ahead of John, had to ensure Edward was safe.

"It appears," she began, "that Violet and I have angered you with our talk about your mother. It wasn't our intent." She paused, waiting for the stupid girl to pipe up. When she didn't, Esther pressed, "Was it, Violet?"

"No. We apologize for any hard feelings we may have caused."

"Thank you," he coolly stated, but from his steely glare, it didn't seem as if they were forgiven.

Ever since they'd foolishly badgered him about Bar-

bara, he'd rarely spoken to either of them. Nor had he
spent any time with Violet. She'd become invisible, which
was disturbing on many fronts.

She was terrified that he would call off the betrothal
and send her home, and she had solicited Esther's advice
on how to fix things with him. Esther had been skating on
her own thin ice, about to be sent home, too, so she'd
agreed to help Violet in pleading her case, thereby hoping
to improve her own.

"We realize," Esther continued, "that your mother's arrival has left you in a difficult position."

He merely stared, providing no clue as to his opinion
on the matter, and Violet filled the void.

"I'm sorry if I gave you the impression that I don't like
her. I find her to be a very interesting . . . person." She
tried to smile, but couldn't manage it. "However you elect
to deal with her, it is fine by me. I know better than to have
chastised you on any topic."

It was the perfect opening for him to graciously reply,
to display the manners that Esther had taught him, but he
remained so mute that his mouth might have been glued
shut.

An awkward silence ensued, she and Violet on tenterhooks, braced to hear their sentence.

"Will that be all?" he finally inquired.

"I was wondering," Esther requested, "if I might stay
on in Scotland. You had mentioned that I could travel to
England with the twins, but I hate to leave you without a
hostess."

He could have embarrassed her by countering with, *My
mother has assumed your role; you're not needed here,*
but he didn't, and she was exceedingly relieved.

"You may stay on," he said, "if that is your wish."

"It is; I will."

"And I was wondering," Violet ventured, "if you
would . . . would . . . walk with me in the garden after supper. It should be a lovely evening, and you've been so busy
that we've scarcely had a second to chat."

If he said *no*, that he had no desire to walk with her after supper, the engagement would be over. His coach would be readied, and Violet would be immediately dispatched to London.

Esther held her breath, while beside her, Violet was trembling.

Ultimately, he nodded. "Yes, I'm certain I will have time for you."

Esther stood and dragged Violet from the room before John could change his mind.

LILY hurried through the woods.

It was a beautiful autumn afternoon. The sky was so blue, and there was a crispness to the air, a hint of the colder weather that was just around the corner. The trees were a canopy of red and gold, and she could smell smoke as bonfires burned and the fields were cleared.

Up ahead, the forest thinned, and she glimpsed the house that belonged to Captain Odell, where Phillip Dudley and his sister, Clarinda, were living. Though Lily had never previously been inside the residence, it called to her like a beacon.

She had passed the morning in her bedchamber, hiding and plotting. As promised, John—no, she couldn't think of him as John. The familiarity confused her, made her forget her station in life. Lord Penworth had arranged that she have no chores to perform, and as every servant knew, there was only one way a female could earn such a dispensation.

Calamity was approaching. She could feel it as plainly as she could feel the breeze on her face. At the slightest whisper of gossip, the affair would be exposed. Penworth's fiancée and stepmother would learn of it. Once they were apprised, what would they do? What would happen to Lily?

The answers to those questions were all disconcerting, and she wouldn't tarry while disaster unfolded.

After much reflection, there seemed to be only one option, but she would require assistance to carry it off. Mr. Dudley was the obvious choice as conspirator. She had no idea who else to ask.

She banged the knocker, anxious to hear that he was home and would see her. A footman opened the door, and she was welcomed in and escorted to a cozy parlor. She entered, but Clarinda Dudley was present, rather than her brother.

Lily didn't know Miss Dudley that well, having mingled with her on rare occasions at Penworth's parties. Lily was sufficiently dismayed at having to seek Mr. Dudley's aid, and it would be a giant leap to presume she could discuss the mess with his sister.

"Hello, Miss Lambert." Miss Dudley came over to take Lily's hands. "How kind of you to visit. I'm so glad you stopped by."

She guided Lily to a small sofa, and they sat in front of a window and looked out across the park that led back to Penworth's castle. Lily was very uncomfortable and wanted to leave, but it would be the height of rudeness to get up and go.

"By any chance," Lily asked, "is your brother here?"

"No, I'm sorry, he's not. May I help you?"

If only she could . . .

"I probably ought to speak with him."

Lily's cheeks flushed with humiliation. Miss Dudley and her brother were very close. Would Mr. Dudley have shared Lily's foibles with her? Had she been informed of the predicament into which Lily had landed herself?

Please, Lord, she prayed, *don't let her question me about it!*

Outside, on the edge of the woods, she noticed a couple strolling along, their arms wrapped around each other. As they paused and hugged, it dawned on her that she knew the pair.

Before she realized she shouldn't comment, she said,

"There's your brother now. And isn't that . . . Barbara Middleton?"

Their affection evident, they started to kiss, and Lily sucked in a stunned breath. Miss Dudley glanced out and blanched.

"Ah, yes, I believe that is my brother."

"Oh my," Lily muttered.

Miss Dudley jumped up and yanked at the drapes, fussing with them until not a peep of the torrid scene was visible. When she turned back, she appeared flummoxed.

"Would you like a . . . tour of the house?" she asked to distract Lily.

Lily was still locked in the moment. "Your brother and Barbara? Isn't that a bit . . . tricky for all of you?"

She had selected the word *tricky* after recognizing that she couldn't utter some of the other words she'd considered—*salacious? indecent? bizarre?*—and Miss Dudley was grateful that Lily hadn't been more insulting.

"Yes, it's been tricky," she agreed, Lily's casual remark breaking the ice between them. "I warned him not to proceed, but he wouldn't listen."

"If her son finds out, I don't imagine he'll care for it."

"No, I don't imagine he will."

"I've spent some time with Barbara," Lily said. "She seems a tad ruthless to me."

"To me, too."

"What is it about her that attracted him?"

"He's always been a pushover for a pretty face and a sad story."

"She has plenty of those."

"She certainly does." Miss Dudley shrugged. "He likes her."

"Then who are we to quibble, hmm?"

Miss Dudley chuckled, and she peered at Lily and grinned.

"Would I shock you, Miss Lambert, if I asked you to enjoy a whiskey with me?"

"I'm quite sure I'd survive the invitation."

Miss Dudley went to a sideboard and poured them both a drink. She sat again and downed hers in a quick gulp as Lily sipped more slowly.

"You wanted to speak with Phillip," Miss Dudley said, "but he might be busy for a few hours."

"I can come by later. It's no problem."

"I hope you won't be offended if I mention that I know you'd swallowed one of his potions."

Drat it! "Yes, I had."

"If you have a question, I'd be happy to answer it." Lily looked as if she'd refuse the offer of assistance, and Miss Dudley rushed to add, "I understand the effects of his remedies. If you're anxious, I could put you at ease."

Lily was enormously tempted, for now that she'd settled on her plan of action, she was eager to swiftly implement it. She was saved from any mortifying disclosures by Mr. Dudley hustling into the room.

He was smug, extremely pleased with himself.

"Good heavens, Clarinda," he scolded, "it's a beautiful day outside. Why are you sitting here in the dark?"

He marched over and was tugging on the drapes when he noticed Lily.

"Miss Lambert? This is a surprise."

"Hello, Mr. Dudley."

"We had the drapes open," Miss Dudley grouched, "but we didn't care for the view."

"Not care for it? Why would you—" He glanced out and observed the park from their perspective. "Oh. It appears we've been found out."

"If you're going to carry on in plain sight," his sister complained, "how can you possibly keep the affair a secret?"

"Miss Lambert won't tattle," he insisted. "Will you?"

"No," Lily vowed. "I wouldn't have the faintest idea who to tell."

Mr. Dudley smirked at his sister as if to say, *See?*

"What brings you by?" he asked Lily. "If you were driven to visit our humble abode, it must be something horrid."

"I need your help."

"Is it Penworth?" Mr. Dudley perked up like a dog at the hunt that had scented the fox. "What's he done now?"

"Well . . ."

Lily dithered, ashamed to discuss her dilemma with Miss Dudley being present, and as usual, Mr. Dudley read Lily's mind.

"Don't worry about Clarinda," he said. "She's very discreet. We can talk in front of her. And she might have some useful suggestions."

Lily peered from one sibling to the other. They were smiling at her, friendship in their gazes, and Lily—who had always been alone, who'd never been dear to anyone—decided to take a chance.

"I must go back to England." Her heart was heavy with the pronouncement. "I'd like to depart as soon as I can, and I can't have anybody know. Not about the trip or the route."

"You think Penworth would prevent you?" Mr. Dudley queried.

"I'm sure of it. I've tried to quit my job, but he won't let me. He's revoked my responsibilities to the twins and Lady Violet, so—"

"So it's only a matter of time," Miss Dudley finished for her, "before others wonder why. With discovery of the liaison, your reputation will be shredded."

"Yes, so I must leave, but I can't ride on the public coach. I truly believe he'd chase me down and force me back. I'll have to travel in a fashion he wouldn't suspect, on a road he would never investigate."

"We have a coach," Miss Dudley stated. "Phillip could take you to London."

"That would be too much of an imposition," Lily hastened to say.

"No, it wouldn't," Miss Dudley replied. "We'd fret if you left and we didn't know your condition during the journey."

Mr. Dudley had been silent through the exchange. He went to the sideboard to pour his own whiskey, and he frowned at Lily.

"What about the second vial of Spinster's Cure?" he inquired. "We talked about your drinking it. Have you?"

"Yes."

"And?"

"I'm embarrassed to confess what happened."

"What did?"

"I attempted to entice another man, to avert the calamity I've been pursuing with Lord Penworth, but he got in the way again."

Dudley and his sister shared a long look, and Miss Dudley raised a brow in consternation.

"You shouldn't leave, *chérie*." A hint of Mr. Dudley's French accent crept into his voice. "Penworth loves you. The potion is working, and you should stay so the circle of magic can be completed."

"He doesn't love me."

"You don't know that."

"He said so. He told me he could *never* love me."

"Maybe that is what he assumes, but if we have toyed with his fate—"

She held up a hand, halting a diatribe she couldn't bear to hear.

More than ever, she wanted Dudley's potion to be real, for Lord Penworth's destiny to have been altered so he would fall madly in love with her. But she wasn't a fool, and she couldn't keep behaving like one.

Penworth might actually possess some fond feelings for her, but he would never act on them. He was a man of duty and obligation, and he would never rock a boat or break a rule.

He'd proposed to Violet Howard, and he would never go back on his word to her. Despite how vehemently Lily wished there could be a different conclusion, that he would jilt Lady Violet and pick Lily instead, he never would.

She had to stop fantasizing, and *he* had to stop courting disaster. She would save him from himself by fleeing— without his knowing that she had.

"I just need to return to England," she said to Mr. Dudley.

"What will you do there? I can't stand to imagine you alone and struggling on your own."

"I won't struggle," she claimed with more confidence than she felt. "I'll find a new job as a companion or governess, but I'll move to a rural area where he would never search for me."

"You really suppose you'll be able to get away from him?"

"Out of sight, out of mind, Mr. Dudley. At the moment, he's intrigued, but after I'm gone, he'll forget all about me."

"Perhaps," Mr. Dudley cautiously concurred.

"Can you help me plan a furtive journey south?"

Mr. Dudley stared at his sister, and another visual communication passed between them.

Mr. Dudley shrugged. "I'll take you myself in our carriage."

"What? No, I didn't mean you should go to all that trouble on my behalf. I merely want your advice as I devise a method of—"

"I'll take you, Miss Lambert. I won't have you flitting off by yourself. Let's not quarrel about it."

He spoke with a resolve that could have matched Penworth's when he was at his most obstinate. Dudley wouldn't be dissuaded, and since he'd made such a generous offer, she ought to be gracious enough to accept it.

"All right," she consented.

"When would you like to go?"

"Friday would be best." It was two days away. "The twins are heading to Edinburgh, to sail to London, themselves. Everyone at the castle will be occupied with their departure, so my own escape won't be noticed."

"Oh, I think your absence will be *noticed*, Miss Lambert."

"Not for a while, Mr. Dudley, and by the time it is, I will have vanished."

"IT's such a lovely evening."

"Yes, it is."

John scowled at Violet, assessing her beautiful blond hair and perfect face. Why had he proposed to her?

The castle was overflowing with guests, and he had slipped away with Violet for the stroll she'd requested, but it had been a debacle. Though John had tried for inane banter, he couldn't maintain any semblance of affability. Their prior cordiality had disappeared, and they'd trudged about, moping and lost in thought.

He was dying to tell her she was too young for him, that she should end his misery by going back to England and marrying some eighteen-year-old boy who'd be excited to have her.

"Thank you for walking with me," she said.

"You're welcome. I'm glad you suggested it. We've hardly spent any private time together."

"No, we haven't."

They were approaching the castle, the uncomfortable promenade nearing its end, and he could barely hide his relief. A few dozen more yards, and they'd have returned to the party. He'd be swallowed up by the crowd; he'd be shed of her.

They reached the stairs, and he was frustrated as she pulled him to a halt.

"May I ask you a question?" she inquired.

"Certainly."

"Are you still angry with me? It seems that you might be."

"I'm not."

He glanced up at the castle. A trio of fiddlers was playing a lively tune, and their music drifted out. Candlelight poked through the windows and doors. It was a magical, stirring sight.

He wondered where Lily was. He wondered what she was doing.

She hadn't attended the soiree, declaring herself weary of the festivities, and he couldn't blame her. They'd agreed to meet later, after everyone was abed, and it was the only topic he could contemplate.

He peered down at Violet, reflecting on how he'd betrayed her by carrying on with another woman right under her nose. He knew it was wrong, knew it was immoral and cruel, but he couldn't renounce his affair.

Lily was like a disease in his blood. There was no cure. There was no antidote.

His wedding to Violet was almost a year away. He hoped that—when the date rolled around—he'd have had his fill of Miss Lily Lambert, and she would be gone from his life.

But what if she wasn't? What if a year passed, and he desired her more than ever?

What then? What then?

The frantic query echoed in his head, and he shoved it away. He had to quit obsessing over Lily. Since he was standing arm in arm with Violet, it was particularly disconcerting.

"I was curious." Violet hesitated, unable to continue.

"About what?"

"I know you won't like to hear me mention your mother—"

"No, I won't."

"—but I was worried that she might have . . . have made a derogatory comment about me. Is that why you're upset?"

"I haven't discussed you with my mother. Nor would I."

"Well, then. Good. Because if she *did* say something, it wasn't true."

Like a frightened rabbit, she skittered away, climbing

up onto the terrace and hurrying inside before he could ask what the hell she'd meant.

She and Barbara must have quarreled. He couldn't imagine what Barbara might have said, and he didn't wish to be apprised. He was in no mood for trouble between Violet and Barbara, and he refused to referee any discord.

As if he'd conjured her up by thinking about her too intently, Barbara emerged from the shadows.

"John, are you really going to marry that girl?"

"Yes, Barbara, I really am."

"You don't have to."

"I realize that. She was the best candidate in an entire flock of debutantes. I selected her after a lengthy search. I *want* to marry her."

"No, you don't." She clucked her tongue like a mother hen scolding her chicks.

"Don't presume to tell me what I want or don't."

"She'll make you miserable."

"Barbara, I will not debate my pending marriage with you. It's none of your business."

"Not my business? If your future contentment isn't my business, what is?"

"Leave it be."

"You should wed Miss Lambert, instead."

"What did you say?"

"You love her. It's so patently clear."

Panic slithered through him, and he peeked about, terrified that others might be loitering and would have overheard the ridiculous remark.

"I have no idea what you're talking about," he claimed.

"Do what you want for a change," she urged. "Behave with a reckless abandon. Do the unexpected." She grabbed his coat and shook him. "You're my son. Though you deny it, some of my blood is raging in your veins."

"There's nary a drop."

"Who cares about Esther's opinion? Who cares about a bunch of stuffy sods in London? Let them all go to the devil. Make yourself happy. Pick Lily. Let her make you happy. Violet never will."

John clasped her hands and removed them.

"Good night, Barbara."

His heart pounding, dismay rocking him, he spun and escaped.

Chapter 17

❦

"YOU'RE not afraid, are you?"

"When I'm with you? Never."

Lily clasped John's hand a bit tighter, wanting to seem very brave, but she was a tad frightened—despite how fervidly she claimed otherwise.

They were descending into the cavern under the castle, headed for the ancient hot springs where she'd suffered the twins' foul play. She'd assumed she would never again visit the isolated place, but he'd begged her to accompany him, and she'd been unable to refuse.

Though he had no clue of her intentions, she was leaving in the morning. Her small assortment of clothes was folded in her portmanteau. Mr. Dudley's coach was loaded, the driver and outriders hired. The speedy journey would begin as soon as she appeared on his stoop.

She would never see John Middleton again.

While she'd promised she would stay with him, she hadn't meant it, and in light of his experiences as a boy—

when his mother had left him and never returned—he would view her act as an incredible betrayal.

If she had had any sense, she would have declined this final opportunity to dally, but she loved him too much. A night of intimacy would build fond recollections that would console her during the ensuing weeks and months without him.

She'd never met a man like him, and she would always be proud that she'd known him, that he'd fancied her. They would revel and frolic till dawn forced them back to their bedchambers. Then she would sneak away.

They arrived at the bottom of the winding staircase, John steadying her as she entered the grotto. His lantern had set the ceiling aglow, and she smiled at being reminded of how beautiful it was.

"Are you still all right?" he asked.

"Never better."

"Come."

He escorted her to a stone bench carved from the rock. They'd brought a large picnic basket, but there were several more boxes discreetly shoved out of sight.

"What's this?" he inquired as he pulled one out and glanced inside.

"After my incident, I had two footmen carry down some extra provisions. I didn't want anybody to ever be caught as I was."

"You'd have been a good soldier." He riffled through the supplies, seeing candles and blankets, dried beef and preserves. "You certainly packed enough for an army."

"I wasn't taking any chances." She frowned. "You're not angry that I took the liberty, are you?"

"Of course not. I wish I'd thought of it." He grinned. "It never occurred to me that a person could run into trouble down here. To me, it always seemed such a magical spot. I didn't think disaster preparation was necessary."

Neither had she, but the twins had taught her many valuable lessons, the main one being to be cautious, to be wary.

She sat and retrieved a bottle of wine Cook had put in the picnic basket. Lily wondered as to the woman's opinion when she'd assembled the romantic meal. She had to have understood that the earl would use the items for an assignation.

Had word spread that the paramour in question was Lily? Or would Cook presume he was enamored of a guest?

Lily stifled a sigh, realizing that the servants' attitudes no longer mattered. In a few hours, she'd be gone. Very likely, no one at the castle would ever ponder her again.

She was pouring the wine as he knelt in front of her.

"I want to swim with you"—his wicked expression had her laughing—"and I want you naked when I do it."

He was already removing her shoes, his naughty hands sweeping up her legs to her garters. Swiftly, he had her stockings off, her feet bare on the cool stones. She might have protested or refused to shed her clothes, but she wouldn't.

Whatever he asked her to try, she would try it. On this night—this *last* night—she would be the seductive vixen for whom he yearned.

He urged her to stand so he could unbutton her gown. It slid to her ankles, and she stepped out of it and draped it across the bench.

He made quick work of her corset, then her drawers, yanking them down and off so she was attired only in her chemise. She was still covered from bosom to mid-thigh, but if she'd been completely nude, she couldn't have felt more exposed.

The fabric was worn and faded, and it rubbed her nipples, enlivening them. They poked at the material, the rigid tips galvanizing his attention.

He bent down and kissed one, then the other, but as he grabbed for the hem to wrench the garment over her head, she panicked. She wasn't quite ready to be as brazen as she'd intended.

She eased away and smiled a smile as old as Eve's.

"My turn," she said. "If I have to be naked, you have to be naked, too."

"My pleasure, you minx. Have your way with me."

He flung his arms to the side, like a prisoner lashed to a crucifix, and she chuckled and began stripping him.

Coat, shoes, stockings, shirt. As each piece fell away, the excitement between them escalated. When she had him reduced to only his trousers, he pulled her to him, their bodies melded, and he instituted a stirring kiss that left her dizzy.

He backed into the pool, his trousers still on, and he guided her in after him, a stair at a time. The water rose to her calves, to her hips. He sank down and held his arms out to her. She floated into them, and he hugged her close, the kisses starting again.

Her legs were wrapped around his waist, and she was balanced on his lap. They bobbed together. He tugged off her chemise so she was nude, her bare chest pressed to his. The warm water made them both slippery, adding a sensual element to the encounter that rendered it particularly decadent.

She plucked at the waistband of his trousers, reminding him that she was undressed while he was not.

"You!" She sounded like a stern headmistress. "You are wearing entirely too many clothes."

"So I am. You must divest me of them."

He stood and she was on her knees, so he towered over her and undid the top three buttons.

She hovered like a supplicant, watching him, awestruck by his male beauty. She wanted to remember him just as he was at that moment: happy, aroused, and totally fixated on her and what they were about to do.

It seemed they were the last two people on earth, that she was the sole woman, and he could never desire anyone but her. She felt exotic and special, the only one for him, the only one who knew how to please him, how to love him.

He pointed to the remaining buttons.

"The rest are for you," he commanded, "if you dare, my innocent little maiden."

"Innocent, ha! I'll show you innocent."

In a thrice, she'd finished the task, and she grasped the trousers and drew them off. Blithely, she tossed them over her shoulder—as if she stripped men every day.

She was still on her knees, his hard torso stretched out before her, his private parts on full display. His masculine appendage was strangely shaped, red and angry-looking. It reached out to her, beckoning her nearer.

Tentatively, she touched it with her finger, a move he definitely enjoyed. He tensed, and the rod grew even harder.

She gazed up at him. "I don't know what to do with it."

"Take it in your hand and lick your tongue across the end."

"Really?"

"Yes."

It was an odd request, but it goaded a feminine craving that lurked deep inside her. She recognized that it would satisfy him on a primal level that went far beyond anything else she could ever attempt. She leaned forward and followed his instructions, flicking her tongue on the tip.

His body became so rigid that she wouldn't have been surprised if he shattered.

"Now what?" she inquired. "There must be more to it than that."

"Suck it into your mouth." His voice was strained.

"Really?" she asked again, agog at the prospect.

Did adults always behave like this? Was it common? How could she have lived to be twenty-five and not know?

No wonder young ladies had to be so strictly chaperoned. No wonder they were liable to get themselves into trouble. What female—when faced with such marvelous debauchery, offered by such a delicious scoundrel—would ever decline to proceed?

Without hesitation, she opened wide and sucked him inside.

At first, it was awkward. He was very large, and she

had some difficulty figuring out what was required of her. She clasped his thighs to steady herself, and he placed a palm on the top of her head.

He only thrust a few times, then he jerked away and fell into the water with a splash. He plunged below the surface, and he hovered there for many seconds. When he reemerged, he swiped the droplets out of his eyes, and he loomed up, advancing on her like a hawk swooping in on a rabbit.

"You, Miss Lambert, are very, very wicked."

"I try."

"Who could have guessed—when I initially interviewed you—that you would turn out to be precisely what I needed?"

"I only pretended to be a boring lady's companion. Deep down, I'm an accomplished vixen."

He was studying her so intently that she was unnerved. She licked her lips, riveting his attention again.

"Oh, gad, that mouth!" he muttered. "Have you any idea how completely you've aroused me?"

"No."

"Have you any idea how badly I want you?"

"How badly?"

"Let me show you."

Lunging, he picked her up and carried her to the edge of the pool, her bottom on one of the underwater benches. He spread her legs and penetrated her, his cock sliding in all the way. He flexed once and again and emptied himself.

As he shuddered and relaxed, he was laughing, biting her neck and nuzzling her ear.

"You. Drive. Me. Wild."

He appeared irreverent and carefree, and she couldn't help thinking how different he was from the autocratic despot he'd been when they'd first met.

She was glad she'd given him this, that he'd learned to smile and frolic, and she hoped that—after she was gone—he'd retain some of the lightheartedness she'd kindled. He'd be a better man for it. He'd have a happier life.

He dragged her off the bench and into the pool. Down below, his cock was still hard, still impaled. They floated, caressing and kissing, and gradually, he started thrusting again.

The fervor of their original joining had waned, so the pace was leisurely and luxurious. There was no reason to rush. They had all night.

"What I did to you a bit ago," she queried, "does it have a name?"

"A French kiss."

"Ooh, those French! They certainly have some naughty notions."

"They certainly do."

"You seemed to enjoy it immensely."

"With those sweet lips of yours, how could I not?"

"Will you let me try it again sometime?"

"It's a whore's trick. I shouldn't have asked it of you."

"I didn't mind. I liked it."

He groaned. "If we keep on like this, you'll be the death of me. You'll kill me with pleasure."

He dipped to her breasts, nursing at them, and the stimulation came fast and furious. She couldn't get him close enough, couldn't hold him near enough. The minutes were ticking by with alarming speed, and she was desperate to slow everything down, to make everything last.

He touched her between her legs, at that special spot where all feeling gathered. She spiraled to ecstasy, and he did, too.

It was a spectacular conclusion, so tumultuous that the earth shook with their efforts. There was a roaring in her ears, as if the world was being ripped apart, and it took several hectic moments to realize that it wasn't her imagination.

John scowled, and they glanced up to see that the walls of the cavern were swaying back and forth. Rocks were released from the ceiling, pelting them with stones.

"What the devil?" he muttered.

"What is it? What's happening?"

"Oh, my Lord. It's an earthquake. Hurry! Let's get out of the pool."

Having the strength of ten men, he leapt from the water and carried her out with him, stuffing her under a bench. He stretched out in front of her so she was shielded from falling debris.

The noise grew louder and louder, permeating bone and tissue, and she shut her eyes, praying that it would end soon, but it didn't.

The trembling went on and on, and with a thunderous crash, the tunnel through which they'd entered gave way. The lantern crashed to the floor and sputtered out. Dirt and rubble filled the grotto, burying them alive.

"ANGUS," Edward asked the butler, "what have you learned?"

"We have some damage to two of the stairways and to the main chimney, but the castle is a tough old bird. She held together well."

"I'm relieved to hear it."

It was full morning, the quake having struck hours earlier. They were in John's library, with Edward seated behind John's desk. He wondered where John was. In the middle of a crisis, it was so unlike him that he hadn't marched in and seized control.

Edward, for once, had gotten the chance to command and delegate.

"The outbuildings were hardest hit," Angus explained. "One of the barns collapsed."

"Have we lost any animals?"

"Three horses."

"Anything else?"

"The worst situation is under the west tower. There was a cave-in past the dungeon."

"Down toward the hot springs?"

"Yes."

"Drat it," Edward mumbled. "What about the staff? Have you located all the servants?"

"Everyone is accounted for except . . . except . . ."

"Except for whom?" Edward pressed.

"Your brother, Master Edward."

"You can't find John?"

Angus shook his head. "I didn't want to mention it until I was sure."

"Is he the only one who's missing?"

Angus's cheeks flushed. "I hate to stir any rumors."

"Tell me!"

"Miss Lambert appears to be gone, too. It isn't my nature to gossip, but I must report that Cook packed a picnic basket yesterday, for your brother."

"And?"

"He informed her that he would be taking a late-night swim in the grotto."

"In the grotto! But the tunnel has failed!"

"I'm aware of that fact, sir." Angus looked as if he might burst into tears.

"Did John let slip if a friend would be joining him?"

"No, but the housekeeper assumed he'd arranged . . . ah . . . an assignation."

"With Miss Lambert?"

"It wouldn't be my place to speculate."

John, you randy dog! Edward mused. Engaged to Violet, while swiving her companion! Edward hadn't thought John capable of such bad behavior.

"How about the housekeeper?" Edward inquired. "Would she speculate for us? Has she a suspicion as to who the woman might have been?"

"Miss Lambert has recently been relieved of her duties—by the earl himself. The staff found it . . . odd."

Esther was sitting in the corner, and at the news, she lurched forward in her chair. "Are you telling us," she asked, "that John and Miss Lambert are trapped down in the hot springs?"

Angus took out a kerchief and wiped at his eyes. "I believe it is a distinct possibility."

Edward's gaze locked with Esther's, a thousand comments swirling between them that couldn't be voiced while Angus was in the room.

"Shall we mount a digging expedition, Master Edward?" Angus suggested.

"Digging?"

"If you give me the word, I can muster the footmen with shovels and buckets."

Edward nearly shouted, *yes, yes, let's begin digging,* but Esther made an imperceptible motion that urged restraint.

"Yes, Angus," Edward said instead, "we'll get going shortly. Let me talk with my mother privately for a moment, would you?"

Angus glared from mother to son, and he dared to remark, "If I may say so, sir, time may be of the essence."

"It certainly is. I'll have instructions for you in a few minutes."

Edward stood and went to the door. He pulled it open and gestured for Angus to exit. The instant Angus was gone, Edward rushed to Esther and sat in the chair next to her, their heads pressed together.

"What is it?" he whispered. "What are you thinking?"

"I don't wish John ill—"

"Neither do I."

"—but if he was deceased, you would be the Earl of Penworth."

"Yes, I would be."

"The title would be yours. The money. The property. Violet, a duke's daughter, could be yours—if you wooed her the right way."

"Yes, I see what you mean."

"He's probably dead."

"I don't doubt it for a second."

They stared and stared, each knowing precisely what the other was contemplating.

"We have to dig," Esther stated. "We have to at least *try* to save him—to placate the servants."

"I suppose we have to. There will be ugly rumors if we don't."

"That said"—Esther grinned—"I just don't feel we ought to dig very deep or very fast."

BARBARA raced down the hall to her bedchamber. The morning air was chilly and she had to grab a cloak and get outside.

She'd heard that the grotto collapsed, that someone was buried, and the person might still be alive.

A group of footmen had been gossiping, complaining as to how they were anxious to ride to the neighbors, to bring back extra shovels, but no orders had been issued to commence a rescue.

Barbara had interrupted their conversation.

Who is trapped? she'd cried, but no one would say. No one would look her in the eye.

Where was John? Where was John?

Since the quaking had stopped, she'd been searching for him, but he seemed to have vanished. Her terror was mounting.

As she approached her suite, the door was open. She hastened in, but as she saw Esther, she stumbled to a halt. A thuggish fellow—who appeared to be a bodyguard— lurked behind Esther, and a bevy of maids was packing Barbara's belongings.

"What are you doing in here, Esther?" Barbara scowled at a maid who was stuffing Barbara's negligees into a trunk. "Put those down. You don't have permission to handle my things."

The maids froze, waiting to learn who would win the quarrel, who should be obeyed.

Esther came forward. She clutched a piece of paper, and she slapped it into Barbara's hand.

"What is this?" Barbara shook the document under Esther's nose. "What are you trying to tell me? If you have something to say, then say it."

"The Earl of Penworth, Edward Middleton, demands that you vacate the premises. Immediately."

Barbara gasped. "What has happened?"

"John is missing and presumed dead. Until his condition can be decisively established, Edward will act in his stead. He's written to the king regarding the tragedy."

"No . . . no . . ."

"Once the fatality is confirmed, Edward will be installed as earl. We intend a quick and easy transition."

It couldn't be. Not after she'd been away for so many years! Not after she'd come home, eager to make amends, eager to be part of his life.

She needed John to love her. She'd lost everything else or had squandered it with apathy. If she didn't have John, what good was any of it?

"Get out!" Barbara fumed, refusing to listen, refusing to believe that John could have perished.

"No," Esther retorted, "I will not get out. *You* shall go, Barbara Middleton. My son has assumed control of the castle, and we do not want you here."

"Unless I'm told differently—from someone other than you—I am the earl's mother. Edward has no authority to toss me out."

"He already has." Esther smirked, the tables having turned for both of them. "John may have been stupid enough to tolerate you, but Edward and I don't have to."

Barbara loomed up over Esther, delighted to see Esther flinch. "You witch!" Barbara bellowed. "What have you done to John?"

"I have done nothing to him. He has expired, and Edward is the new earl. Now get out of our house!"

Barbara seized Esther by the front of her dress, causing stitches to pop along the shoulder seams.

"You had better hope he's deceased," Barbara warned, "because if he's not, and he comes back to discover how you've—"

"He won't be back."

Esther's certainty was alarming, and Barbara spun and

ran out, shouting, "Angus! Angus! Where are you? They've murdered him! They've murdered John!"

Behind her, Esther calmly said, "Finish packing her possessions. Then take it all down and set it out in the drive. I'll lock the door after you."

Chapter 18

❦

"DEAREST Violet," Edward crooned, "what can I say?"

"He's dead? You're sure?"

"Yes."

"There's no hope?"

"None. We'll do our best to recover his remains"—at the harsh comment, Violet sucked in a shocked breath—"but you shouldn't harbor any illusions. He's perished."

Hidden from prying eyes, they were sequestered in what had been John's library. Edward forced a pained expression, then he lurched forward and clasped her hands, crushing them to his chest.

"It's the very worst time to speak up," he said, "but I have to ask. Now that he's gone, is there any chance for me?"

Violet smiled tremulously, and he knew he'd read her emotions correctly. He'd been secretly courting her for months. How could she not love him?

"Yes," she insisted, "of course there's a chance for you."

"I'm so glad."

"Should I . . . I write to my father and tell him about us?"

What harm could there be? Edward mused.

At his mother's urging, he'd sent several letters himself, informing the king and prince regent of the tragedy, as well as the family's bankers, lawyers, and land agents.

The news would quickly spread, and Edward was panicked that Violet's father might have already been apprised. The duke would immediately begin plotting as to who Violet's next fiancé should be. Edward had to move swiftly so the duke didn't dump her on someone else. And really, what was there to worry about?

By proposing, he was implementing the perfect solution. After all, Violet had been slated to marry the Earl of Penworth, not John Middleton. What did it matter who the groom was so long as he was the earl?

Currently, Edward was only the acting earl, but with minimal effort, he would become the earl in fact. John was buried so deep in the ground, the collapse so complete, that his body would never be found.

A coroner's inquest would be scheduled to determine John's status. Angus and Cook would be excellent witnesses as to his whereabouts: flattened under tons of rubble. The servants would try to dig him out—fruitlessly—and they would testify as to the extent of the calamity, the impossibility of rescue.

With ease, John would be declared legally deceased, and all Edward's dreams would come true.

"Yes, my sweet," Edward gushed, "write to your heart's content. Tell your father how devastated we are, but also tell him that great joy has risen from the ashes of despair. We're in love and prepared to proceed to the logical conclusion—with his blessing, which he'll be happy to bestow."

"He'll give us his blessing. Why wouldn't he?"

"Why wouldn't he, indeed?"

Out the window, he saw the twins in the garden, walking toward the castle. They'd been out at the west tower, where the entire staff was milling about, waiting for orders.

Gad! In the chaos of the moment, he'd forgotten all about them and their absurd request that he wed one of them. He was now their guardian, so his furtive sexual relationship was even more depraved, but he wouldn't reflect on it.

With Violet's capitulation so near, he'd have to put them off for a bit. Hopefully, before they demanded an answer, he'd be married to her. Then he'd find a way to be rid of them for good.

He'd heard that, after the incident with Miss Lambert, John had threatened to imprison them in a convent. It was definitely worth pondering, locking them behind thick walls. He had no doubt—once they learned how he'd tricked them, how he'd snatched up Violet the instant she was free—they'd be out for blood, and he wasn't about to shed any for them.

"Listen, darling," he said to Violet, "I just had a thought."

"What is it?"

"I'm not certain you should notify your father about our betrothal. For the time being, we should probably keep the arrangement to ourselves."

"Why?"

"Circumstances with regard to John are so recent. There might be some who would view our decision as a tad . . . precipitous."

"I hadn't considered that."

"Appearances are important."

"When will we marry then? John insisted we delay a whole year."

"Where you were concerned, John was a buffoon." Edward's eyes burned with a lover's fervor. "I'm anxious to make you mine right away."

"Oh, Edward . . ."

He leaned in and brushed a chaste kiss across her

cheek, even as he wondered what sort of cold fish she'd be in bed.

She was a trembling, timid maiden, and after his escapades with the twins, she'd be a bore. Their wedding night would be amusing, as he stripped her naked and taught her conduct she'd deem disgusting, but he'd rapidly weary of her tears and begging.

He'd be eager for degeneracy but shackled to Violet, and the notion was depressing. Then again, he'd never been partial to monogamy or fidelity.

Why couldn't he wed Violet *and* continue on with the twins? Why not? He was about to be Earl of Penworth. He could do as he liked. If the twins complained, he could whip them to shut them up, and no one could gainsay him.

"You still haven't told me when we'll marry," she nagged. "Shouldn't I give my father some hint of our plans?"

"I wouldn't," Edward asserted.

"Why not?"

Edward's reputation wasn't the best. What if the exalted ass had reservations about the match? What if he forbade Violet from marrying Edward?

"We'll forge ahead on our own and surprise him when we return to London." She didn't jump to agree, so he hurriedly added, "Won't that be fun, Violet? Just imagine: a secret wedding! Your friends will be green with envy."

"What if the duke doesn't want me to go forward?" she inquired. "I should at least ask his opinion."

"Don't you trust me?"

"Well . . . yes."

"If you're not sure, talk to my mother. She always gives you solid advice."

At his prompting, she was once more firmly in his camp. Being stupid as a post, she swayed in whatever direction the wind carried her.

"Yes," she concurred, "I'll speak to Esther, and see what she says. She'll know what my father would choose."

"She's in the solarium. Why don't you confer with her immediately?"

Violet scurried off, and he went outside to confront the twins.

"Hello girls," he said as they neared.

"Hello, Edward," they replied together.

"How are things over at the west tower?"

"Everyone is waiting for you to arrive so the digging can begin."

"I'm on my way now."

"What took you so long?" They shrewdly gazed at him, as if aware of his ploy, but they didn't seem overly concerned about John's fate. John had crossed them, and they never forgot a slight. If he was dead, they wouldn't fret.

"I've been busy," Edward claimed, puffing himself up. "What with my pending ascension to the title, I've had many matters to attend."

"You'll really be the earl?" Melanie asked.

"I really will be."

"So one of us," Miranda declared, "is about to be a countess."

"Yes," he lied.

"Will you still need two weeks to decide who is to be your bride?"

"I'm afraid I will, and with the tragedy so fresh, I may require more time besides. I'm thoroughly occupied with arranging John's final affairs."

The twins stared at him in that way they had, as if they could peer to the center of his black heart. He actually squirmed with discomfort.

"Is our contest still on?" Miranda inquired.

"Of course."

"Will you meet with us tonight?"

"I don't see why not."

"But tonight! You're not grief-stricken? You're not in mourning?"

His answer was a tad too slow in coming, and they giggled and strolled away.

Ignoring them, he continued down the drive toward the

west tower. He was eager to play lord of the manor, to order everyone about and have them obey, but after he'd taken a dozen steps, a rider barreled up the lane on horse-back.

The mount was a fine animal, the type that would be owned by a gentleman, so the fellow had to be a neighbor who'd heard of the calamity and had rushed to assist Edward in his hour of need. It would be Edward's first official visitor as earl, and he grinned, then tamped down his excitement, not wanting to look too happy, which would set tongues to wagging.

The man raced up, stirring a cloud of dust and gravel. Edward registered that it was Phillip Dudley, as Dudley leapt to the ground and marched over.

"You pathetic swine," Dudley snapped, "why haven't you started the excavation?"

The comment was so at odds with what Edward had been expecting that he stammered, "What . . . what . . . ?"

"Let me guess: You're hoping a delay will bring about the divine intervention you were too much of a coward to orchestrate yourself."

"I have no idea what you talking about."

"Don't you? If nobody digs him out, you're certainly sitting in a fancy chair."

Dudley had exactly gleaned Edward's scheme, but Edward was astute enough to react as if he was innocent of any malice.

"What are you insinuating?"

"I'm not insinuating anything. I'm flat-out saying you're deliberately dawdling so your brother dies."

"How dare you, sir!"

Before Edward realized Dudley's intent, Dudley punched Edward in the stomach as hard as he could. Edward teetered on his heels, then Dudley punched him in the face. He collapsed in a stunned heap and curled into a ball. Edward was wheezing, struggling to catch his breath.

Dudley grabbed him by the collar and explained, "That was for Barbara."

"Barbara? Who the hell is Barbara?"

"The true earl's mother, you little weasel."

Edward tried to stand, and Dudley hit him a third time and then a fourth. Edward gave up and slumped down, his mind discombobulated, his limbs not working. "You have struck the Earl of Penworth," he spat. "I'll see you hanged for your outrage."

Dudley pulled him up till they were nose to nose.

"My sister is a witch," Dudley informed him. "If you lay a hand on me, she'll poison you. You'll be dead before you have a chance to spend a single farthing of your brother's money."

Dudley dropped Edward in the dirt, jumped on his horse, and cantered toward the west tower, where he would steal Edward's thunder by assuming control of the rescue effort.

Edward leaned over and vomited up his breakfast.

"Brawling with Edward Middleton," Clarinda scolded. "Are you insane?"

"Oh, please," Phillip grumbled. "As if that pitiful mama's boy would fight me. It's only a brawl if at least two parties are exchanging blows."

"What would you call it then?"

"I beat him senseless, then trotted off. He never threw a punch."

"Well, *that* makes me feel better."

Clarinda jammed his bruised knuckles into a bowl of disinfecting whiskey, which Phillip considered to be a waste of perfectly good liquor.

He'd endured a long day directing the servants at the west tower, so he hadn't had occasion to worry about his injuries.

Clarinda, however, was a fastidious healer, and the moment he'd walked in the door—filthy and sweat-stained and exhausted—she'd dragged him to the kitchen and begun her doctoring.

The alcohol stung the cuts, and he hissed with pain as Clarinda enjoyed her petty torment. She never liked his displays of temper, had never approved of his tendency to lash out at those who deserved a sound thrashing.

"What if Penworth is never found?" she grouched. "What if Edward actually becomes earl? His threat to have you hanged wouldn't be an idle boast."

"If that sniveling coward ever has the gall to move against me, you must follow through and poison him. Give him a fatal dose, but one that works slowly so he suffers for weeks before he expires."

"What makes you think I'd avenge you?"

"If you don't, I'll haunt you from the other side."

She grunted with aggravation. "I won't have you pestering me from beyond the grave."

Clarinda lifted his hand, saw the raw spots still flecked with grime, and retrieved a brush and scrubbed across them. He yelped in agony and yanked away. "Your cure is worse than the illness," he complained.

"I'm just trying to ensure that I have your attention."

"You have it, you have it!"

"Aren't you the one who always tells me we shouldn't immerse ourselves in the troubles of the rich?"

"Yes, that's me."

"Take your own advice: Don't antagonize Edward. Don't get yourself killed for Barbara Middleton. She's not worth it."

"I'm not doing it for her."

"Who are you doing it for, then?"

He thought and thought, then snorted with disgust. "Maybe I am doing it for her, but I'm also looking out for Miss Lambert. She doesn't have anyone to speak for her. In all the uproar today, not a single person mentioned that her life is in jeopardy, too."

"Are you certain she's down there?"

"The butler and housekeeper insist she is, but no one cares about her. If they decide Penworth is dead, there'll be no reason to keep digging. They'd leave her to suffocate and starve."

"Why would she be with him? It makes no sense. Not when she was so desperate to escape."

"She loves him."

It was the simplest, most obvious explanation, but Clarinda rolled her eyes.

She'd never been bitten by the bug of amour, and most likely never would be. She counseled women on the perils of passion, deeming it all so much foolishness.

He studied her, feeling morose in a way he never was. Every bone in his body ached, his physical fatigue overwhelming his mood so he was pensive and reflective in a manner he hated.

Had he done right by Clarinda? Had he been a good brother to her?

She'd spent her girlhood tagging after him, participating in his schemes and keeping him out of jail. What sort of path was that? Why had he picked it?

And what about himself?

He was thirty years old. He'd never married, and while he'd loved many, many women, he'd never been *in love* with any of them.

He had no ties, no friends, no family but for Clarinda. Suddenly, the lack seemed unbearably sad.

Clarinda grabbed for his hand again, but he jerked it safely out of range.

"Should I stitch that cut?" she asked.

"With the temper you're in, I won't have you near me with a needle or sharp pair of scissors."

"How about a bandage?"

"I'm fine, Clarinda. Stop fussing."

"If I didn't, who would?"

She stood and patted him on the shoulder, and she was gathering up her supplies when a maid peeked in to inform him that his bath was ready.

There was a small chamber off the kitchen, where

water could be easily heated behind the stove and quickly transferred to the bathing tub. Just then, it sounded like a slice of heaven.

"Don't fall asleep and drown," Clarinda warned, tugging him to his feet and urging him on his way.

"I'll try not to."

He retrieved a bottle of whiskey from the cupboard, then went into the room and shut the door. He was dirty and grubby and grumpy, and his battered hands were stiff, so it took some doing to remove his clothes.

There was a manservant on the premises who claimed to serve as Odell's valet. Phillip could have summoned him to assist, but he'd be damned if he'd have some oaf poking around at his trousers. On his own, he flung them off, then wrestled with the remainder of his garments.

He climbed into the tub and sank down, and he pulled the cork from the bottle and downed several long gulps. His eyes closed, and he was dozing off when the door opened and someone tiptoed in.

Recognizing Barbara's stride and perfume, he smiled and gazed over at her. She was dressed in a nightgown and robe, her hair down and brushed out.

Though he'd never admit it, she looked ghastly and seemed to have aged. She was chasing fifty, after all, but usually her years were carefully concealed with cosmetics and a brazen attitude.

"Am I interrupting?" she asked.

"No."

She drew up a stool and sat, and he held out his damaged hand to her.

When Esther Middleton had tossed her out, Barbara had come straight to him, and he was glad that she had. But if her son was never found, what the hell was he to do with her?

"What happened to your hand?" she inquired.

"I beat Edward to a pulp."

"My hero!" She leaned over and kissed him. "Thank you."

"You're welcome."

Early that morning, she'd stumbled in, frantic and homeless and indescribably angry. She'd begged him to go to the castle, insisting Edward and Esther would never truly search for John, and she'd been correct. Phillip had arrived to discover that nary a shovel of earth had been turned.

He'd formed lines and bucket brigades, had sent women scurrying to bring food and ale, and they'd made enormous progress. Edward had eventually showed his sorry face, but the servants weren't stupid. They'd flashed such dangerous glares that he'd mumbled a few words of faint praise before skedaddling back to his mother.

If Edward was ever installed as the earl, how would he overcome the day's debacle? The servants' disdain would spread from Scotland to his properties in England. His dearth of endeavor on John's behalf would never be forgiven or forgotten.

Barbara clasped his bruised hand and kissed each of his sore knuckles.

"Better?" she asked, to which he replied, "Yes," even though the gesture hadn't helped.

He was miserable, and he swallowed a swig of whiskey. He offered her the bottle, and she did the same.

"What is the news?" she queried.

"It's more optimistic than I'd imagined. Angus tells me it's only the bottom section of stairs that collapsed."

"The last one? After you pass the dungeon?"

"Yes."

"So it's not a huge amount of dirt."

"No, and one of the men swears he heard tapping on the other side."

"He thought it was John, signaling him?"

"He wouldn't go that far. He just heard tapping. That's all. It could have been anything or nothing."

"John could be all right."

"He could be," Phillip cautiously agreed, "if the roof in the grotto hasn't caved in."

She shuddered, and he squeezed her hand; it was his turn to kiss her knuckles.

"I can't bear to think," she said, "that he was buried alive."

"Don't give up hope. Not till we're sure. Esther can't have the satisfaction of killing him. I won't let her."

Chuckling morbidly, she stood and shed her robe. Her nightgown went next, and she was naked. She was very beautiful, a gracious and generous lover who was comfortable in her body and utilized it to bestow maximum pleasure.

"I believe you could use some company," she said.

"No, I believe *you* could use some."

"Perhaps."

She joined him in the tub, water sloshing over the rim, dampening the floor, but they didn't notice.

Their torsos were melded together—she was slippery and wet—and if he hadn't been so exhausted, he'd have spread her thighs and impaled himself. But he was in no mood to fornicate, and she needed something other than sexual gratification.

She rested against his chest, her ear over his heart, as he stroked her hair and back. He was growing accustomed to her presence, enjoying the fact that she was with him.

Was she his future? If so, he hadn't seen it coming. Nor had Clarinda. Wouldn't it be the wildest conclusion, after so many flings in so many towns and villages, to wind up with her?

"What will become of me?" she ultimately asked. "If we can't save him, what will I do?"

"We don't have to worry about it now," he gently advised. "Trouble will hunt us down without our chasing after it."

"Yes, I suppose it will."

He snuggled her down, content to smile and nap with her in his arms.

* * *

Lily was sleeping, John spooned to her back, when she awakened with a start. Pulse racing, her eyes flew open, but it was pitch-black.

They'd survived the quake unharmed, and due to her stock of emergency supplies, as well as John's picnic basket, they were fine. For the moment.

They didn't know how deep the collapse was, how much rubble lay between them and escape, but they were digging and digging. John was positive there'd been comparable thumping and banging on the other side, which was encouraging.

It was difficult to calculate how much time had passed, but their cache of food and candles was quickly dwindling. Something had to occur—and soon. They had to find their way out, or people had to find their way in.

Behind the grotto, there were four tunnels that meandered farther into the earth. John had never explored them and couldn't guess where they led.

There were portentous decisions to be made. Should they continue to wait for rescue? Or should they venture into the tunnels? What if they wandered in and became lost? If they were to expire anyway, did it matter how the end came?

Her tension must have roused John, for he whispered, "Are you all right?"

"I heard a noise."

"Don't be afraid."

"It's hard not to be."

"I know."

She'd once read that victims in a catastrophe grew tremendously close, that class distinctions faded away. In light of their situation, the theory seemed to be true. They were intimately connected, their bond more powerful by the hour. His feelings for her had moved into an elevated realm she dared call *love*.

He loved her. She was sure of it.

If they died in each other's arms, she would perish convinced of his regard. But if they managed to emerge unscathed, what would it mean for them? Could they weather a return to society? Would his affection remain?

"Do you remember," she murmured, "when you caught me drinking those love potions?"

"You were trying to make Aiden Bramwell fall in love with you."

"No. Dudley told me to stare at the man I was destined to marry."

"You wound up staring at me instead."

She'd thought comprehension would sink in, that a more personal comment might follow—*Dudley's magic worked! If we get out of here, we'll be wed at once!*—but no declaration was forthcoming.

Apparently, even when facing death, he couldn't form so much as a verbal attachment to her. Would he ever grasp that she was important to him? Would he ever be able to ignore their disparate positions and recognize that they could be together?

The longer he was silent, the more she had to accept that he probably never would.

She felt foolish—as if she'd been begging for compliments.

"I've always been clumsy," she said, shooting for levity. "My swallowing those potions at the wrong moment was typical."

"Honestly, Lily. Bramwell? He's such a stuffed shirt. You could never have gotten him to really *see* you."

"I know, but I was humored by Mr. Dudley's stories. It was amusing to pretend I could change my fate."

Another noise sounded, and she jumped. "What was that?" she asked.

The ground shook, and he grabbed her and rolled them under the rock bench. They braced, expecting the worst, but it wasn't a second quake. There was a single loud *boom*, then all was quiet.

"Dammit," he muttered.

"What happened?"

"I hate to speculate."

"Tell me," she pressed. "Just say it."

"I think someone blew up the staircase."

"On purpose?"

"Yes."

"Why?"

"Well, there are several people who would benefit from my early demise."

"Are you accusing Edward . . . of . . . of . . . ?" She was too stunned to finish the allegation.

"Edward or Esther. Or maybe the twins."

"You're not serious."

"If I'm dead, Edward will be very rich. The twins can carry on however they please. Esther will be shed of my mother. There are numerous unsavory possibilities."

"So one of them is trying to ensure we can't get out?"

"Perhaps."

"But that's . . . that's barbaric."

"The rescue crews must have been close to breaking through."

"And now?"

"They will come back in the morning and discover there's been a further collapse. They'll decide the excavation is too dangerous and there's no reason to continue."

For the first time since the cave-in, she truly lost hope. She started to cry, and John drew her into his arms.

"I don't want to die down here," she wept.

"Neither do I."

"I can't bear to sit and wait for death to occur."

"My feelings exactly."

"What shall we do?"

"We'll give it a few hours—to see if we hear any digging again on the other side."

"If we don't?"

"We'll have to save ourselves."

Chapter 19

"THANK you for coming, thank you for coming . . ."

Esther shook yet another hand; she greeted another mourner, and she forced herself to keep smiling.

When they had sent word throughout the neighborhood that they would hold a memorial for John in the chapel in the village, she hadn't realized so many would attend.

And, of course, the servants—particularly those who'd expended such effort in digging—had all insisted on being present.

There wasn't enough room in the small church, and Esther was having to pick and choose who would sit inside and who would stand in the yard.

To her eternal disgust, vicious rumor was driving much of the interest in the proceedings. People were anxious to catch a glimpse of Esther and Edward, were anxious to congregate so they could blather over their suspicions, but Esther wasn't about to explain or defend her son's abrupt shower of good fortune.

They'd tried to save John, but they hadn't succeeded.

He was dead, and Edward was the earl. She wasn't sorry, and she wouldn't apologize. Not to anyone.

Let the vultures hover! she fumed. *Let them stare!*

She had nothing to hide.

"What time is it?" Edward murmured, as eager as she to get things moving.

"A few minutes before two," Esther replied. "We can begin the service shortly."

Esther gaped at him, then glanced away, unable to abide his ravaged face. His cheek was swollen, his eye bruised and bloodshot from the thrashing Phillip Dudley had administered. Esther had begged Edward to have Dudley arrested, but with John's affairs so unsettled, Edward had declined to stir any extra controversy.

Later, Esther mused. She would deal with the brutal criminal herself, and he would feel her wrath in ways he'd never imagined.

Edward tugged at his collar. "I'll be glad when this is over."

"As will I."

They were in the receiving line on the chapel stairs. The twins and Violet were with them, and Violet looked especially tragic.

Miranda peeked at Edward, then she whispered to Melanie. Both girls snickered. Esther flashed a glare that could have melted lead, but they simply gazed back with their annoying, cool expressions.

Esther was delighted that Edward was guardian to the horrid pair. John had been too lenient with them, and Esther's first order of business would be to have Edward marry them off. Esther didn't care who he selected as their spouses.

They could be wed to fishermen or coal miners. It was all the same to her. She just wanted them gone from her home and life.

Suddenly, a carriage flew around the corner, scattering bystanders as it hurled through the milling crowd and stopped at the front steps.

The door was flung open, and Barbara leapt out. Esther wasn't surprised to see her. The woman had never had a lick of sense, had never possessed an ounce of decorum. It would never occur to her that she wasn't welcome at the sad event.

She stormed over and raced up to where the family—the legitimate family—was greeting their guests. While everyone was wearing black, she was attired in bright red, as if to deny their bereavement.

"You couldn't wait to bury him, could you?" she seethed at Edward.

"We tried our best, Barbara." Despite her fury, Edward was very calm. "I don't know what else you could have asked from us."

"He's not dead!" she railed. "I'm his mother! I would feel it in my heart!" She clasped a dramatic fist over her bosom.

Edward shrugged. "We understand that you're grieving, so I'll politely refrain from answering you."

She spun on Violet, looming up over the girl. "You have some gall to loiter here, feigning sorrow, you disloyal little harlot!"

"I say!" Edward muttered, grabbing for Barbara, but she shoved him away to continue her tirade at Violet.

"I suppose you're dancing in your bedchamber, counting the hours till you can marry Edward." There was a sharp intake of breath from the assembled company. "Did you help to kill him? Was that your ploy from the start?"

"I have no idea what you mean," Violet had the temerity to respond.

"Don't you?" Barbara sneered. "How convenient that my son has vanished, and now, you'll wed his brother whom you wanted all along! Does your father know of this charade? Does anyone?"

"You are insane," Violet tightly charged.

"I've posted a dozen letters to England, so news of your perfidy will spread far and wide. You'll never get away with it."

Esther blanched, determined to contain the scene, to be shed of Barbara before any further damage was perpetrated.

Gossip abounded that rescuers had been nearing the grotto, that John was about to be found, but there'd been an unexplained explosion in the tunnel. Excavation conditions had grown too dangerous, so efforts had been halted.

Some had accepted Edward's decision to end the salvage attempt, but others had been foolishly willing to keep on forever, regardless of the perils. Edward had done what he thought was right, what any rational person would have done, yet he was being vilified.

Gad! They'd dug for a whole week. What did people expect? Why couldn't they be satisfied with an honest endeavor? If John had managed to survive the initial disaster, who could presume that he was still alive after so much time had passed?

In hopes of quelling the uproar, Esther had spoken to a Scottish attorney. He'd stared down his pointed nose and told her there'd been calls to immediately convene the coroner's inquest. He claimed that—depending on the findings—Edward might have to wait seven years before John would be officially declared as deceased. It might be seven *years* before Edward would have full control of the money and property.

The possibility had Esther so angry that she could barely function, and Barbara's allegations were only fanning the flames of discontent.

Esther nodded at two footmen. They approached Barbara, ready to physically remove her, but she thwarted them by dashing past Edward and into the chapel.

The congregants turned in their pews and gaped at her.

"My son is not dead!" she raged at them. "How dare you mourn him! How dare you let Esther bury him! He is not dead!"

The footmen seized her, one on each arm, and though she scrapped and fought, they wrestled her out. The entire episode was distasteful, but Esther tarried through it, exhibiting a stoic demeanor.

With Barbara hurling epithets, the footmen stumbled toward the carriage, as Esther noticed that the violent fiend, Phillip Dudley, stood next to it.

He ignored Barbara, concentrating on Esther instead. He shot her such a virulent look that—if she'd been a more superstitious sort of woman—she'd have sworn he was giving her the evil eye.

She shuddered, and even though she wasn't a Papist, she made a furtive sign of the cross to ward off any malevolent spirits.

Barbara was running out of steam, her fury waning, as the footmen tossed her into the carriage and shut the door. But the vehicle didn't drive off and Dudley didn't move.

He glared at Esther, and the moment stretched out until the horde in the yard grew restive. Then he walked over so he was directly below where the family was huddled like a flock of black crows.

"There has been wicked business done here this day." His voice billowed out like an evangelical preacher's. "Beware!"

"Beware!" Esther huffed. "What nonsense are you spewing?"

"I curse you *and* your son."

"Don't be ridiculous. There are no such things as curses."

"Aren't there?" Dudley said. "None of your dreams for your dear Edward will ever come true. I guarantee it."

He motioned with his fingers as he mumbled several phrases in a language Esther didn't recognize. She flinched as if a dire destiny was winging toward her and she couldn't stave it off.

The Scots were an illogical lot, and it hadn't been too long since they'd burned witches at the stake. What would they think of Dudley's pagan behavior?

She glanced around at the crowd, but from their stony expressions, they seemed to share Dudley's opinion of her

and Edward. Nary a brow was raised by his remarks, so
Esther couldn't hope they would intercede on her behalf,
and she wasn't about to dawdle on the church steps, debating with a madman.

"I've had enough drama to last a lifetime." She whirled
away from Dudley, ignoring him so others would, too.
"Let's go inside so the service can begin."

Though she was trembling, she herded the family into
the vestibule.

"I'll be watching you, Esther Middleton," Dudley
threatened. "Be careful what you do."

"Get out of here," Edward barked, finally speaking up,
"or I'll set the law on you."

"Try it," Dudley taunted. "I dare you."

He spun and went to the carriage, and he leapt up into
the box. His driver clicked the reins, and with a lurch, they
raced away.

"FRIENDS and neighbors," the vicar started.

Violet relaxed in the front pew, with Edward on one
side and Esther on the other.

The twins were in the pew behind, and for some reason,
they were angrily studying Violet. She could feel their
cold stares on the back of her head. The sensation was so
eerie and so thorough that they might have actually been
touching her.

"At this terrible moment," the vicar intoned, "I know
all of you are asking the same question: How could this
calamity happen to someone as kind and good as Lord
Penworth?"

Violet struggled to focus, wondering what was wrong
with her.

She wasn't asking that question at all. In fact, since the
accident, she had rarely pondered John, except for when
she was fretting over how quickly she could marry Edward without creating a scandal.

She wanted to be a bride so she could be independent,

so she could commence her tenure as a mature, adult woman.

What she *didn't* want was to go back to London, to her father's house, where he might refuse the match with Edward, where he might launch marital negotiations all over again. She would end up with another John Middleton—another stuffy, imperious boor who was very old and an exact replica of her stuffy, imperious father.

She yearned to wed flirtatious, charming Edward, who'd always loved her, who'd been smitten enough to woo her even when it was sinful, even when it was impossible for them to be together.

As Edward had suggested, she'd conferred at length with Esther. Esther had assured her that they should have a fast wedding in Scotland before they returned to England. Violet had agreed it was for the best.

If she was a tad hesitant, it was only because there'd been such vicious gossip. She wouldn't do anything precipitous that might stir even more animosity.

"The Lord works in mysterious ways," the vicar droned.

He certainly does! Violet reflected. She'd wanted John gone from her life and—poof!—he'd vanished so she could proceed to claim her heart's desire.

A buzzing noise reverberated through the church, and at first, she assumed it was all in her mind. Her thoughts were careening so wildly that she couldn't keep track of them all. Frowning, she tried to shake the sound away, but it didn't help.

She peered up at the vicar, who continued to preach, but she could no longer hear him. His lips were moving, but he was being drowned out.

Someone outside was shouting, then another person, and another, and another. The pandemonium increased in volume and intensity until it was a frightening ruckus.

Was it that horrid Barbara again? Or the brutal Mr. Dudley, who'd had the audacity to assault Edward? Had they come back to disrupt the ceremony?

For goodness' sake, let John rest in peace!

The vicar halted and snapped his prayer book closed as a cacophony of voices began to swell.

"He's here!"

"He's alive!"

"I can't believe it!"

"If I hadn't seen it with my own eyes!"

"It's a miracle! A miracle, I tell you!"

Like a giant tidal wave, a mob loomed into the chapel, villagers and tenants rushing into the vestibule as if planning to crush the gentility inside the nave.

"What is the meaning of this?" Esther bellowed, but the din was so raucous that only Violet, who was seated right next to her, could hear what she said.

Esther and Edward rose, and Violet rose with them. They left the pew and stepped into the aisle. Instantly, Violet saw what those outside had already seen.

John entered the church and marched toward them. He was covered with dirt, his skin filthy, his clothes grimy and torn. Appearing battered and bruised, he had cuts on his hands, forehead, and cheek.

Miss Lambert hovered behind him, in the same wretched condition, but Violet ignored her. Who cared about a stupid servant?

"John!" Edward and Esther gasped in unison.

He stopped in front of them, his fists planted on his hips, as he gazed up at the vicar.

"Lord . . . Lord Penworth?" the minister wheezed. "Is it really you?"

"I'm told," John retorted, "that you're holding a memorial service for me, but I must inform you that the rumors of my demise have been greatly exaggerated."

Violet looked at him, at the vicar, and at Edward, who was no longer the earl and who would never be able to marry her now.

She fainted dead away.

Chapter 20

❦

"WHAT was it like, swiving the earl?"

"I beg your pardon?"

Lily was taken aback by the outrageous question, and she glowered at the housemaid who'd been rude enough to ask it. The idiotic female simply grinned, as if Lily would participate in such a shocking conversation.

"We women here at the castle," the maid explained, "have always thought him a fine specimen of a man, but he's a tad reticent with the ladies—if you get my drift."

"I'm sorry, but *no*, I don't get your drift."

"He's never lifted a skirt on a single servant. A right, proper gentleman, that one."

"He certainly is," Lily huffed.

"You're the first who's had a chance to find out."

"Find out what?"

"Does he know his way around the bedchamber? There's some what says he's too much of a stuffed shirt to be any fun, while others says he's a bundle of unbridled passion. Which is it? We've wondered for years."

Lily was aghast. "You're asking me if . . . you want me to discuss . . . you assume I would have . . ."

"Come now, you was down there with him for an eternity. There's no use pretending nothing happened. Everyone is talking about it."

"About me and . . . the earl?"

"Yes, and there's no harm in speaking the truth. We're all glad he's back, and we don't begrudge you your little tickle."

They were in Esther's boudoir, in her sitting room. Lily had been commanded to attend Esther, who hadn't shown herself yet. The maid dusted as Lily dawdled, but the insult and innuendo were too much.

People knew about her and John? People were speculating over what had transpired between them?

She'd become so notorious that this servant—a virtual stranger—felt it perfectly appropriate to interrogate Lily on John's sexual prowess!

Mortification colored her cheeks, and she rose to her feet, fury rocking through her as she seethed, "Of all the despicable, disloyal, uncivil—"

"What's this?" the housemaid sneered. "You spread your legs for him, and now you're putting on airs? I'm just a working girl like you. There's no need to get your drawers in a knot."

"I must return to my bedchamber." Lily pushed past her and headed for the door. "Tell Lady Penworth I'll confer with her later."

The maid snorted. "Oh, I see how it is. You're thinking you'll be allowed to stay on, that you've earned some bloody spot that will elevate you above the rest of us."

"I think no such thing," Lily lied. She was panicked, needing to believe that their time together had changed everything. John loved her, and he wouldn't abandon her over a bit of gossip.

"He'll marry his precious Violet Howard," the maid sniped. "Just see if he doesn't."

Lily was so irate that she could have slapped the woman. Instead, she kept on and had nearly made it to the hall when Esther appeared, preventing any escape.

"We have a meeting scheduled, Miss Lambert," Esther pointed out.

"I realize that, but I am exhausted and feeling unwell. We'll have to proceed when I'm more myself."

"No, we'll finish this now."

Esther was standing in the threshold, and Lily could have shoved by her and stormed out, but theatrics weren't in her nature. Besides, with the way Esther was glaring, she had something to get off her chest. Lily would have no peace until Esther said whatever it was she was intent on saying.

Lily wished she could send for John and have him intervene with Esther, but she was quite sure no request would be granted.

During their harrowing climb in the unexplored tunnels behind the grotto, they'd struggled and clawed their way to safety. They'd gotten confused in the twists and turns, stuck in narrow passageways, injured in scrapes and falls. Through it all, they'd continued to move, seeming to ascend from the bowels of the earth, but not certain if—at the end—they would escape or perish.

The shared experience of peril and fear had bonded them, had brought them closer than two people could ever be. Or so Lily had thought.

The trek had been lengthy and impossible, but a hint of daylight had spurred them on. Yet once they'd found an opening and pushed to the surface, once their feet had been on solid ground, she'd become superfluous. John had instantly assumed the mantle of power and authority he so easily wore, being swept into the role of earl with numerous imperative chores to attend.

Lily had assumed the mantle of . . . what? She couldn't describe precisely where she fit in the castle's hierarchy. From the moment the crowd in the village had espied them, she'd metamorphosed into his forgotten companion who—she was terrified to consider—might no longer be necessary or needed.

Ever since they'd burst into the chapel, she hadn't spoken to him. He'd been whisked away, like a conquering hero, while she'd been left to stagger back to the castle on her own. After all, she was a servant, and thus a person of no consequence. No one cared that she'd survived, too.

Once she'd stumbled into her bedchamber, it had been abundantly clear that the societal distinctions separating them were firmly in place. She couldn't skirt around them. Her room had been shuttered, the furniture covered with sheets, as if she'd never resided in it. No assistance had been provided to make it more habitable.

She'd bathed in a washbasin—no bath had been offered—then she'd wrapped herself in a blanket and huddled before the small fire she managed to build in the hearth.

Though she'd asked to see John, the footman she approached scoffed at her impudence. She'd tried to come down for supper, but a curt warning from the housekeeper had advised her that she wasn't welcome and should keep out of sight until further notice. A tray of bread and cheese had arrived at her door instead.

She'd waited through the night, presuming John would sneak in for a furtive visit, but he hadn't, and she wasn't certain what his absence indicated.

The first hint that her fate had been sealed—without her opinion being sought—was Esther's summons, and Lily wasn't stupid. Esther did not have Lily's best interests at heart, so what was happening?

Where was John? Why was he ignoring her?

"Fine," Lily fumed. "I will listen to you, but I am very weary, so let's make this brief."

Esther motioned to the maid to leave, and the woman grabbed her bucket of supplies. As she walked out, she leaned very close to Lily and muttered, "Good-bye, Miss Lambert, and good luck in your next endeavor."

The snide remark rattled Lily. Servants always heard gossip before anyone else. What did the maid know that she, Lily, did not?

Esther gestured to two chairs, and Lily went over and sat. Esther joined her.

"I won't beat around the bush, Miss Lambert," Esther began, "and I shall be extremely candid."

"I hope you will be."

"I'm sure my comments will be distressing to you, but it can't be helped."

"Get on with it. Please."

"We have decided that you will depart the property immediately."

"To go where?"

"Back to London."

"I don't wish to do that."

"It is not up to you." Esther stared at her, an awkward silence ensuing, as a thousand thoughts careened through Lily's head.

"Who has decided that I am to leave?" Lily ultimately asked.

Esther didn't answer, but said, "There is a carriage ready for you out in the stables. I will escort you down to it. You will see no one; you will speak to no one. You will be conveyed to Edinburgh, where a ticket will be purchased for you to take the public coach for the remainder of the journey."

"I want to talk to John."

At Lily's familiar and brazen use of John's Christian name, Esther inhaled sharply.

"Lord Penworth is unavailable."

"When will he be *available*?"

"To you? Never."

Lily's temper flared, and she stood and started out.

"Where are you going?" Esther inquired.

"To find him. I'm a grown woman. I am fully capable of locating him on my own and initiating the conversation I insist we have."

Lily yanked open the door, prepared to march out, but to her stunned dismay, two burly footmen blocked her way. Unless she planned to brawl with them, she couldn't exit.

She scowled, calculating the odds, wondering how fiercely they would carry out Esther's orders.

Or were they John's orders? Who had commanded that she be detained?

"Close the door, Miss Lambert," Esther said.

For a moment, Lily dithered, then she shut it and returned to her seat.

"What do you want?" she snapped.

"As I mentioned, we intend that you depart at once."

"I've done nothing wrong. Why must I?"

"Why? You have the audacity to ask *why*?"

"Yes."

"Let me be blunt: You were hired as companion to the earl's wards and fiancée. The countryside is agog with tales of your carnal antics."

"There was no dalliance between us," Lily lied.

"You may spew what falsehoods you like, but they will have no effect on me."

"There was no affair!"

Esther raised a dubious brow. "Even if you were chaste as a saint, the truth is irrelevant. Rumor has spread, and only salacious details will be believed."

Esther went to her writing desk and pulled out a piece of paper. She lifted a quill and pointed to the inkpot.

"Come here, Miss Lambert."

"Why?"

"You will pen a letter of resignation to the earl, then we shall be on our way."

"I won't resign."

"You won't? You think to stay on? As his what?"

It was an intriguing question for which Lily had no answer. Before the quake, she'd been relieved of her duties, and she'd arranged to sneak away because of it. What had changed?

Nothing, except that Lily had fallen in love with John Middleton, had spent a desperate, glorious week by his side. If she could have figured out how to survive down in the grotto, she'd have remained there with him forever.

Lily glared at Esther, and Esther glared back.

"You've been returned from the grave," Esther said, "for approximately eighteen hours."

"I won't apologize for it."

"How do you suppose Lady Violet feels about your being on the premises?" Lily didn't respond, and Esther added, "I'll tell you how she feels: She is aghast."

"For what reason?"

"Your torrid frolic with her betrothed has *shamed* her before the entire world."

Esther placed particular emphasis on the word *shamed*, and Lily couldn't hold her gaze. Glancing away, her mind whirled as she struggled to formulate a reply.

She'd asked to see John and had been denied. She'd tried to stomp out in a huff but had been physically prevented.

What to do? What to do?

Ever since the liaison had begun, from the instant John had first noticed her in an inappropriate way, she'd known he was promised to Lady Violet. Lily had fought her attraction, had attempted to deflect his interest, but it had all been for naught. Passion had erupted, and they'd acted on it.

She'd convinced herself that Violet Howard didn't matter, but Violet was still in the castle, and as Esther had stated, Lily had been back for eighteen hours. During that time, there had been no mention of John's engagement being severed. She'd anxiously told herself that he hadn't broken it off simply because he'd been too busy and would deal with it as soon as he could. She refused to accept any other possibility.

"I think, perhaps," Lily cautiously started, "you should speak with John about Lady Violet."

"I have spoken to him. Why would you imagine I am speaking with *you* now?"

"He asked you to?"

"Yes."

Lily's pulse pounded with dread. She studied Esther, searching her expression, but there was no hint of fabrication.

"Are you claiming," Lily demanded, "that he will proceed with his marriage?"

"Of course. Why would he do anything else?"

Esther's remark fell into the room like the kiss of death.

Lily felt lightheaded; she was dizzy with dismay. The earth seemed to have tipped off its axis, and she was positive if she stood and walked across the floor, it would be tilted.

Tears welled into her eyes, her tongue thick in her mouth. "I must talk to him," she mumbled.

"Why?"

"I need him to . . . to . . ."

What did she need him to do?

Considering Esther's confident, stoic manner, if Lily could locate John Middleton, what would she say?

Esther returned to her chair. "Let me explain something, Miss Lambert."

"What?"

"I don't mean to be deliberately cruel"—Lily snorted at this—"but there's no easy way to make you understand what's happened."

"What has happened?" Lily tersely inquired. "I'd appreciate it if you'd enlighten me."

"I know you'll find it hard to believe," Esther said, "but I was a young woman once. I learned—from bitter experience—how fickle a man's attention can be."

Lily started to tremble. Since their desperate underground escape, she'd been overwhelmed by sensation. Everything was moving too fast. Colors were brighter, noises louder. People bustled by at a speed she couldn't match.

At Esther's implication that John hadn't been genuinely fond of her, Lily's defenses crumbled. She could no longer assert that nothing had occurred between them. All pretense was abandoned.

"He loves me," she tried to insist.

"Does he?"

"Yes."

"Are you sure?"

"Absolutely."

"Has he ever told you he loved you?"

After a lengthy hesitation, Lily murmured, "No."

"In all the time you were trapped with him, did he ever tell you he would renounce Violet?"

"No," she said even more slowly.

"Has he ever—by the smallest word or sign—indicated that he would wed you instead of her?"

They both knew the answer, so there was no need to respond.

Lily peered at the rug, remembering her amazing interval with him. She forced herself to truly *see* what had transpired: not much of consequence. Even in the grotto, when their demise had seemed imminent, he hadn't declared himself.

"Men are like beasts in the field, Miss Lambert," Esther quietly stated. "They can be amorous, physical creatures, but it doesn't mean anything to them."

"No, you're wrong," Lily argued, but it was a feeble protest. "He cared about me."

The fact that she would use the past tense, that he had *cared* about her, said it all. If he might have once, he didn't now. It had been a fantasy.

"He might have been fond," Esther allowed, "but where does that leave you?"

"I don't know."

"Will you wallow here in Scotland on the fringe of his life? Will you have him rent you a house so he can drop by in the evenings? These Scottish villagers are very conservative. They wouldn't tolerate such immoral behavior. You'd be tarred and feathered and run out of town."

"I wouldn't want to live like that."

"Will you follow him to England? And then what, Miss Lambert?"

"I don't know," she muttered again.

"You seem like a good person to me."

"I am! I always have been."

"I'm positive you don't wish to hurt Violet."

"No, I don't."

"Can you imagine what your continued presence is doing to her?"

Lily could only say, "Yes, I can imagine."

"How long will you tarry? How long will you hurt her? When will the scandal become sufficiently hideous that you'll go away?"

Lily kept staring at the rug, feeling petty and horrid and very, very foolish.

From the beginning, she'd been aware that she didn't have a chance with a man like John Middleton, yet she'd stupidly succumbed to his seduction. She'd persuaded herself that it could work out, that he could actually look beyond convention and tradition and wed her rather than Violet Howard. But it had merely been a dream.

"He could have loved me," she contended, needing to hold on to the fantasy a bit longer. "He could have married me."

Esther scoffed. "Violet Howard is a duke's daughter. Her dowry contains tens of thousands of pounds. A plantation in Jamaica. A villa in Italy. Factories in Massachusetts. A shipping company in Portugal. What do you have that could compare with any of those?"

Just me, Lily pathetically thought. *Just me and all the love I carried in my heart for him.*

She didn't think anyone had ever loved John Middleton, but perhaps, from his perspective, it didn't matter. If you were rich, and you could have even more ships and money and property, how could a paltry emotion like *love* possibly count for anything?

"I will give you two choices, Miss Lambert." Esther

cut into Lily's miserable reverie. "You're a smart woman; you'll do what's right."

"What are they?"

"You know the first one. You stay on in Scotland as John's mistress, but then, you'll be renowned far and wide as the Earl of Penworth's whore." Lily flinched at the derogatory term, and Esther paused. "Is that the future you've envisioned for yourself, Miss Lambert?"

"No."

"Or you may pen the letter of resignation I've requested and depart for England. If you will, I'll pay you two month's wages as severance, and I'll send a glowing letter of recommendation to Mrs. Ford at the Ford Employment Agency. That way, you'll rapidly garner another post. What is your decision?"

Lily was drowning and had been thrown a rope. Still, she said, "May I talk to Lord Penworth?"

"He declines to meet with you, and he hopes you'll understand his position. He's embarrassed by his conduct and distressed at how it's leaked out as crude gossip. Violet is mortified, and he wants the issue resolved quickly and quietly and with a minimal amount of discomfort for her."

"Oh."

So . . . it was all about pretty, wealthy, aristocratic Violet Howard. Could Lily really have expected any other conclusion?

How ludicrous to believe that Lord Penworth would have sided with her after the affair was exposed. She'd always comprehended the precariousness of her situation, that the liaison would bring her nothing but trouble, and it had.

Now, she had to extricate herself from the mess she'd made.

She could pick the harlot's existence, could loiter on the edge of his world, praying he tossed her a few crumbs of attention. Or she could return to England and build a new life for herself.

From the day she'd initially interviewed with him, she'd recognized him as a man of duty and responsibility. He had obligations to his family and his title that didn't—and never would—include her.

She didn't belong with him, and even if by some absurd stroke of fate he'd agreed to marry her, she would never have wanted to be a countess. She wouldn't have had the slightest idea how to comport herself in such an elevated, bizarre realm.

Violet Howard would know. Violet Howard would fit right in.

Lily disliked Esther immensely, and Esther had no kindly intentions toward Lily, but she had stepped forward and offered Lily the means to move on. It was that fact, more than any other, convincing Lily of the truth: Esther was acting on Lord Penworth's behalf. Esther was passing on his instructions.

He was doing what was best for Lily. He was doing what he could to save her reputation, to salvage something from catastrophe. If the end result was much less than she'd anticipated, much less than she'd dreamed, what did it signify?

"Yes," Lily murmured, "I'll write the letter. What would you like me to say?"

Chapter 21

"EXPLAIN yourself to me."

"Well . . . uh . . ."

John stared at Edward, who—of course—could *not* explain himself, and the moment stretched to infinity.

They were in the castle library, with John seated behind a desk that no longer looked to be his own. His inkpots and pens had been removed, the desk drawers emptied or rearranged, as Edward made himself at home.

John lifted a stack of papers, copies of letters mailed to his lawyers and bankers, notifying them of his demise. He was an important man, his business affairs wide-ranging and complex, so it was only natural that associates be apprised.

It was the question of *when* they'd been apprised that particularly galled.

He waved the letters at Edward. "What have you to say about these?"

"People had to be informed."

"Before you started digging? Were you that certain I wouldn't return?"

Edward's cheeks flushed with chagrin. "Mother thought it wise to seize the reins quickly."

"You're blaming this on Esther?"

"No. I agreed with her. I felt a smooth transition was imperative."

"I'll just bet you did." John fumed. "You ordered a new coach, restocked the wine cellar, purchased a wardrobe, and authorized a remodel of my London bedchamber— and I wasn't cold in the ground. Much less *in* the ground."

"Sorry, old chap. Priorities, don't you know?"

"Edward?"

"Yes."

"Shut the hell up or I will come around this desk and beat you to a pulp."

Edward's features were still bruised from the pounding Dudley had administered, and John wouldn't mind imparting another.

They'd occasionally brawled when they were boys, but John hadn't given Edward a sound thrashing since he was fourteen. Whenever Edward had been reprimanded, Esther was always so upset that John had stopped making him pay for his petty crimes. But it might be a good time to begin again.

An enormous amount of satisfaction would be gleaned from feeling his fist smash into Edward's smug, unrepentant face.

"Aren't you curious," John inquired, "as to where I spent the morning?"

"You were out at the west tower."

"Can you imagine why?"

"I assume you went to see the scene of the calamity."

"Or perhaps I went to see the scene of the crime."

John was leveling a filthy allegation, one that would tear the family asunder and sever his relationship with his brother forever.

Did it matter? Did John care?

The sad answer was: not very much.

"What are you implying?" Edward hesitantly broached.

"I was accompanied by our neighbor, Phillip Dudley. He told me a very interesting story."

"What was it?"

"The rescue workers were almost into the grotto. He insists Miss Lambert and I would have been located the next day."

"How bloody prescient of him."

"Someone ignited a charge in the tunnel, to destroy it so I couldn't be saved."

"Dudley has proved himself a violent fiend. I didn't realize he was a geologist, as well."

"The whole neighborhood felt the explosion."

"Really? We didn't feel it here in the castle." Edward sipped his whiskey, exhibiting what was—for him—an abnormal calm.

"Why would Dudley spin such a wild tale?"

"He's a madman. He assaulted me—for no reason— and threatened to have his sister poison me. Then he showed up at the memorial service and put a curse on my mother. If you hadn't come back, I'd have had him hanged by now."

"Lucky for him, then, that I'm alive."

"Yes, it is."

Fratricide was an ugly term, and John hated to have it popping up, but history was replete with accounts of brother killing brother in order to inherit title or land or money. Could Edward have behaved so despicably? Was he truly that greedy?

"Where is Barbara, Edward?"

"I heard that she's staying with the Dudleys."

"How did that happen?"

"She and my mother had a bit of a tiff, and Barbara decided to leave."

John scowled until Edward fidgeted.

"Has it ever occurred to you, Edward, that I talk to my servants? Has it ever occurred to you that they might have told me what actually transpired?"

Edward scoffed with derision. "You'd take a servant's word over mine?"

John raised a brow, but didn't answer, which was answer enough.

A lengthy interval ensued, where they angrily glared, but Edward never could best John. Not in games as a boy. Not in their school lessons. Not in their adolescent sporting contests. Not in their business associations or societal status.

In every way, John had always been the superior brother—bigger, stronger, smarter. It was why John had inherited everything from their father, and why Edward had been given a small trust fund that was dispersed by John. Their father had had no illusions about either of them.

"It has recently dawned on me," John said, "that when you are on the premises, I should fear for my personal safety."

Edward's temper flared. "What are you saying?"

"Did you try to kill me, Edward? Did you blow up the staircase so I couldn't get out?"

"How dare you hurl such a contemptible accusation!"

"I notice you haven't denied it."

Edward vehemently shook his head. "I may be many things, but I'm not a murderer."

There was a significant pause, where John could have accepted the declaration, where John could have forgiven him and smoothed over the impasse.

Ultimately, he said, "I don't believe you."

"I didn't try to harm you!" Edward asserted. "I don't know what caused the collapse, but it was none of my doing. I swear it."

John stood. "You're going back to London in the morning. The maids are already in your room packing your bags. I suggest you go up and supervise their preparations."

Edward stood, too, and he held out a hand, as if in supplication, but at the moment, John was beyond courtesy or absolution. There might come a time in the future when they could reconcile, but it was far in the distance.

"It is my intent," John explained, "that you and I will never again occupy the same lodgings. When I arrive in London in a few weeks, I expect that you will be happily ensconced in your bachelor's apartment and out of my sight."

"John, don't be like this."

"Unless I specifically send for you, you will absent yourself from my surroundings. Should you need something from me, deliver a written request to my London clerk. You have his address."

Edward's cheeks reddened further, and John couldn't decide what was fueling his heightened emotion. Embarrassment? Rage? Fury at being banned from John's presence?

Edward garnered many boons from being John's brother, from attending his parties and eating at his suppers. Most likely, his upset was driven by the fact that he would no longer be able to help himself to the wine stock when he stopped by for a free meal.

John nodded toward the door. Livid, Edward spun and marched out, and John was relieved to have him go.

Esther would leave in the morning, too, as would the twins and Violet. John would be alone with Lily while he figured out how to proceed with her.

He hadn't seen her since they'd burst into the chapel during the memorial service. They'd been separated by the crowd, and his reappearance had created such a stir that he hadn't had a chance to slip away and be with her.

No doubt she was confused by his conduct, but he'd been busy with many pressing issues that—in light of Edward's shenanigans—couldn't be ignored.

First, he'd wasted hours being doctored for injuries he'd sustained in their dark and treacherous escape. Next, he'd spent a good portion of the afternoon and evening with his land agent, drafting letters to revoke the power Edward had seized.

By the time John had fallen into bed, it had been very late, and he'd been too exhausted to visit Lily.

Then, shortly after dawn, Dudley had shown up, demanding that John accompany him to the old dungeon to review Dudley's evidence of perfidy. Upon John's investigation, his entire life was suddenly in flux.

His betrothal was up in the air. His brother and stepmother couldn't be trusted not to murder him, and he'd ceased to care about the twins or his obligation to them.

His experience with Lily had altered him, had forced him to understand that he needed to make different choices and consider other options. She would be front and center in any new situation, and he was excited to tell her.

He left the library and climbed the rear stairs to her bedchamber.

There had been terrible gossip about her—he'd heard some of it—and he'd sent word through the housekeeper that she should stay out of sight to avoid any discomfort.

In the meantime, he'd arranged for the family's exodus so he and Lily could have the castle all to themselves. He couldn't wait to see the look on her face when he told her of the changes he'd instituted. Just for her. Just to make her happy.

He rapped on the door, then walked in, but he was befuddled by the scene he encountered. Her possessions had been removed, and the furniture was covered with sheets.

She isn't here . . . she isn't here . . .

He couldn't shift his thoughts beyond that point.

Hurrying out, he stopped a maid to ask about Lily, only to learn that she'd departed early that morning.

"Departed?" he gasped.

"Yes."

"To where?"

"I don't know, milord. Your stepmother would have more information."

Esther! He should have guessed.

While he'd been putting out the fires Edward had ignited, Esther had been perpetrating further mischief. She hadn't yet realized that the pendulum of authority had briefly swung in one direction, but it had swung back swiftly enough. If she'd behaved horridly to Lily, John would wring her scrawny neck.

He stormed to her boudoir and entered without knocking. He was about to unleash a blistering tirade of questions and commands, when he noticed Esther wasn't alone.

Violet was with her. They were seated together on the sofa, watching the door, expecting him to arrive. He was momentarily confounded, and his bluster waned.

Since his return, he hadn't spoken to Violet, and he wasn't about to speak with her now. What was he to say?

I've been having an affair with your companion, and I'm not sorry.

"John, there you are," Esther said. "Please join us."

She gestured to a chair across from them, but if he sat in it, he'd have to stare at them while they chatted. He couldn't bear the notion.

"Violet, would you excuse us? I need to confer with Esther."

Violet bristled, but she couldn't refuse him. Grudgingly, she stood, her lips pursed with fury.

"I will go," she replied, "but I must know one thing before I do."

"What is it?"

"Are you still planning to marry me? If so, I would hear your affirmation at once."

"Wait outside," was his response.

"Should I take that to mean that your answer is *no*?"

"You should take it to *mean* that I would like to speak with Esther—without you being present."

"Why is it so difficult for you to verify your promise to me? Is it because you have decided to break it?"

This was not a conversation he was ready to have. Nor was it the setting in which he would have it. He was anxious over Lily's whereabouts, and he merely wanted to talk to Esther about her. Was it too much to ask that he could have some privacy while he did so?

"Go down to the library," he insisted. "I will meet you there shortly."

He forced himself to calm, forced himself to remember that it had been a traumatic week for everyone. They had all been operating under extreme stress, and she was only eighteen.

"I won't go to your library," she retorted with unusual temerity. "I won't waste another second wondering what you are about to do."

He sighed. "What would you have me say?"

"You have made me a laughingstock throughout the kingdom. Will you jilt me, too?"

"Wait for me in the hall."

He took her arm to escort her out, but she yanked away.

"I will tarry for fifteen minutes," she snapped. "If you do not emerge to inform me that your commitment is firm and unshakable, then we shall have nothing more to discuss."

She stomped out and slammed the door, leaving him with Esther. Esther studied him with a stony expression, and his own wasn't any better.

He was aggrieved over the power she'd usurped, over her treatment of Barbara. While his feelings for Barbara were conflicted and complicated, he would never have cast her out without a penny.

"Where is Miss Lambert?" he started.

"Why on earth would you feel it appropriate to mention her?"

There was a tea tray on the table in front of her, and as if she hadn't a care in the world, she leaned over and poured herself a cup.

"Where is she?" he demanded more sharply.

"Honestly, John, Violet is standing just outside. Lower your voice or she'll hear you shouting your paramour's name."

"I don't give a damn about Violet."

"Really? With how you've embarrassed her, you're lucky she's willing to proceed with the marriage."

He marched over, grabbed teacup and saucer away from her, and banged them down so hard that the saucer cracked in half.

"Tell me where she is, or I swear to God, I will take a switch to you."

She rose to her feet, looking regal and offended.

"If you must know, she has left."

"Left!"

"Yes."

He felt as if she'd delivered a body blow, and he doubled over and sank into the chair Violet had vacated.

"Where did she go?"

"She didn't confide her destination to me. I assume it was England."

Esther walked over to her writing desk, retrieved a piece of paper, and waved it under his nose. "Here is her letter of resignation."

"Why would she quit?"

"The more pertinent question is: Why would she stay? What is wrong with you? Have the past few days addled your wits?"

He scanned the words Lily had penned, trying to glean her motives, trying to ascertain some clue as to where she might be.

The last paragraph stuck in his craw: *I'm sorry for the scandal I've brought to Lady Violet. It was never my intent. I hope you'll offer her my sincerest apologies, just as I hope the two of you will be desperately happy together in the years to come.*

She'd addressed him as Lord Penworth, and she'd signed it as *Miss Lambert*. Not Lily. The note was cool and to the point, providing no hint of the remarkable ardor that had flourished between them in the grotto.

How could she just pick up and go? He couldn't accept that she'd done it of her own volition. She fancied him, and he might even be so bold as to say she loved him. She wouldn't sneak away.

"What did you do to her?" he seethed.

"Me! I did nothing. A housemaid was inquiring into your sexual prowess—if you were any *good* in the bedchamber—and Miss Lambert was aghast at realizing the damage to her reputation."

"You're claiming she asked to go?" he sneered, dubious.

"No. She came to me and begged to go. Why would I have prevented her?"

"Why? How about because I love her? How about because I can't live without her?" His heart pounded with elation. Why was it that he could declare himself to Esther when—in all the time he'd known Lily—he hadn't been able to tell her?

He'd frequently wondered if he was in love, and their underground nightmare had galvanized his emotions. He loved her. He loved her!

"You . . . *love* her?" Esther laughed coldly. "Oh, that's rich."

"I do! I love her!"

"So what? How can it matter?"

John ignored her, his anxious mind awhirl. Where was she? Was she all right? She was in a foreign country, with no funds. He had to locate her and fetch her home before she landed herself in a jam.

"I have to find her," he mumbled, and he started to stand.

"What?"

"I have to find her. I have to get her back."

"For what reason?" Esther placed a hand on his shoulder and shoved him down into his chair, and he was so discombobulated that he didn't fight her.

He tried to rise again, and she barked, "Don't you dare leave this room."

Her sharp tone halted him. She went to her cupboard and poured him a brandy. She brought it over, urging him to drink it, and he did. She poured him another, and he drank it, too. The alcohol quickly eased his disordered mental state.

"Listen to me, John, and listen well."

"No . . . no . . . I have to get going," he insisted, but with less vigor.

"John! You're scaring me. I truly believe your ordeal has left you deranged."

"Because I want to find Lily? It's the only sane thing I've ever done."

"John, listen to yourself! Hear how you're talking. Miss Lambert was a servant to this family. Yes, she was pretty and amiable and competent, but she was a *servant*. You hired her to work for us. Think, John. Think of what you're saying. Think of how you're acting."

"I'm afraid that she—"

"She wanted to quit, John. She was more rational about this than you, and she understood that she couldn't remain. It was impossible. She *knew* that. And you know it, too." She poured him a third brandy. "Cease your theatrics."

"Why couldn't she remain? Why is it impossible?"

He could list the excuses Esther would give, but he asked for them anyway, refusing to relinquish the dream he'd had that he and Lily could end up together.

"What would have been her role?" Esther nagged. "Your mistress? It is the only position she could have held. She had too much respect for herself to settle for such a demeaning situation, and she had too much respect for *you* to let you enter into such a sordid arrangement."

He stared at Esther, shocked to realize how he loathed her. It was a revelation. Deep down, he burned with a subconscious, abiding animosity.

She'd always been brittle and detached, but despite the distance she'd imposed, he'd usually followed her advice. What about now? Would he allow her to take Lily from him? Would he heed her?

She was absolutely correct in her statements, but he hated for her to be. He didn't want to be Earl of Penworth, engaged to Violet Howard. He wanted to be John Middleton, a single man, an ordinary man who could betroth himself to Lily Lambert.

"Where is she?" he queried a final time, defeat washing through him.

"I told you: I don't know. She requested a month's severance, and I gave her six. She's thrifty and prudent. She'll be fine. You needn't worry about her. You need to worry about yourself and how you'll proceed from here on out."

"I didn't have a chance to say good-bye."

"A clean break is for the best."

"But a simple good-bye! How could that have been wrong?"

"It would merely have prolonged the inevitable."

"She deserved more from me."

"Of course she did, but she recognized that she was in desperate trouble. She was drowning—because of you."

"So she had to save herself?"

"No. She had to save *you*. She loved you, and she saved you from yourself."

"I just want to be happy," he muttered to himself, his dream floating away. "I could have been happy with her."

Esther clucked her tongue. "You will be happy. With Violet. At the moment, you're still suffering the effects of your recent tribulations. Your faculties are rattled. You're not yourself, but you will be."

"I don't wish to marry Violet."

"Don't be ridiculous. If anything, you should smooth over the scandal by moving up the wedding date. As soon as we're back in London, you should apply for a Special License and hold the ceremony right away."

A knock sounded on the door. He glanced at the clock on the mantel and saw that they'd been conversing for exactly fifteen minutes. Apparently, Violet had decided his time was up.

"If you rebuff her, John," Esther said, "I'll never forgive you."

"What if I don't care?"

She threw up her hands in disgust. "Go ahead, then.

Ruin your life! Ruin your future! If you toss her over—to chase after your paramour—there's not a father in London who will let you within a hundred yards of his daughter. You'll die a bachelor—without issue. You'll have failed in your sole responsibility to your father and your family. Is that your plan? If so, why not simply abdicate to Edward so he can start his nursery? Put us all out of our misery."

They were harsh, cruel words, but they were spot on.

Lily had fled without a good-bye. She'd done it for altruistic reasons, but she'd left him—as his mother had left him all those decades ago. When he wasn't looking. When he least expected it.

He was alone and always would be. No one would ever love him. His bride would be Violet, but his spouse would be obligation to his heritage and line. Duty would be his poor bedfellow on cold winter nights.

He staggered to his feet, feeling as if he'd aged a hundred years.

"Edward and the twins are departing in the morning," he informed her. "You will go with them."

"You're being absurd. I'm your hostess. I'll stay at the castle as long as you're in residence."

"No, you're going, and when I return to England, I will make other arrangements for you. I don't trust you, and I don't intend to share a household with you or your son ever again."

He whipped away and went to the door. He yanked it open, coming face-to-face with Violet.

"Well?" she asked.

"The engagement is on."

"And your little . . . *friend*. What of her?"

"She's gone."

"Forever?"

"Yes."

"Swear to me that she will never be back to darken our lives."

"She will never be back," he said with a grim finality.

"Fine," she tersely retorted.

"Now pack your bags."

"Why?"

"You're traveling to London tomorrow with Esther." He pushed by her. "Go to England—and leave me the hell alone."

"Is the earl at home, Angus?"

"Yes, Lady Barbara."

Barbara untied her cloak and handed it to him. "Will he see me?"

"Probably not."

"Why?"

Angus leaned in and whispered, "He's in a peculiar mood. He's receiving no guests."

"That won't do. The entire country is atwitter over his rise from the dead."

"Quite so, milady."

"He should be throwing a grand ball every night to celebrate."

"Perhaps—if you were to mention as much—he might heed you."

She sauntered down the hall. "Where is he?"

"Eating his supper."

"By himself?"

"He sent everyone else to London."

"What about Miss Lambert? I thought he was enamored of her."

"Gone with the rest of them."

"Really?"

"Yes."

"Esther, too?"

"Yes."

"He needs a hostess," Barbara murmured.

"One who could breathe some life into this dreary place. It's been so gloomy."

"Well, I'm here to liven it up."

She swept into the dining room, and the sight that

greeted her would have been humorous if it hadn't been so sad.

John was at the end of a long table that could easily seat fifty, but he was the only one present. Two rigid footmen hovered like statues behind him.

She was extremely nervous over her reception, more so than she'd been when he'd initially come to Scotland. Then, she'd taken him by surprise. He hadn't known what to do with her, but he'd let her remain.

How would he act? He'd driven the others away. Even Miss Lambert. His isolation was complete, so might he be kinder to Barbara?

Although he pretended not to be, he was a compassionate person. He wouldn't toss her out. He wouldn't!

"I'll have what he's having," she blustered as she pulled up a chair.

Neither footman moved, and she waved an impatient hand.

"I'm famished!" She flashed her most flirtatious grin. "Please hurry."

The two men glanced at each other, then at John for instructions, but he didn't offer any. Ultimately, one of them shrugged, and they tiptoed out to ask others what they should do.

"If it isn't my mother," John snidely mused.

"Hello, darling. You appear tremendously hale. Dudley said you were, but I decided I should check for myself."

"Why are you always turning up—like a bad penny?"

She bent nearer and pushed his hair off his forehead. During his escape from the grotto, he'd taken a painful blow on the noggin, and fortunately, it was healing with no infection.

He didn't appreciate the maternal gesture, and he batted her away.

"What do you want?" he grouched.

"I hear my old bedchamber is empty, so I'm reclaiming it."

"Lucky me."

"Yes, lucky you."

A tense silence developed, and John continued to eat as if she wasn't sitting three feet away. She held her breath. If he was going to kick her out, this was the moment it would occur, but he said nothing, and she exhaled slowly.

Crisis averted!

Angus came in with her requested plate and silverware. He winked at her as he set them down.

"Where is Miss Lambert?" she queried to John as she began to eat, too.

"I have no idea."

"I assumed you sent the family away so you could consort with her in private."

"She did not see fit to stay on in her position. She resigned and left."

"The rude little minx! Didn't she realize you loved her? Didn't you tell her? My goodness, all those days down in the grotto, what did the two of you talk about?"

"Barbara?"

"Yes?"

"Shut up." He threw down his napkin and rose so rapidly that his chair fell over. Then he marched out without another word.

As his strides faded, she peered at Angus, and they exchanged a significant look.

"I'm convinced he loved that girl," Barbara said.

"Is his heart broken? Is that the problem?"

"I believe it is." She frowned, then smiled. "Do you know what I think, Angus?"

"What, milady?"

"I think we should locate Miss Lambert and bring her back. In the interim, let's plan a party. If he's surrounded by a castle full of guests, he won't have time to mope."

"IF your son finds me in here, he'll torture me on the rack down in the dungeon."

"He won't find you."

Barbara tugged on Phillip's wrist and pulled him into her boudoir. He went willingly enough, but still, he didn't like the situation.

When Esther had evicted Barbara, it had been a blessing in disguise. With Barbara living in his house, he'd been able to simply walk to the next room and climb into her bed. It had been the easiest affair he'd ever pursued, but he didn't like gamboling in the earl's territory. If they were caught, an uproar would surely ensue.

The previous week, Edward Middleton had threatened to have Phillip hanged. If John Middleton found out that Phillip was swiving his mother, Edward's threat would pale in comparison.

"What if he comes to check on you?" Phillip pressed.

"It's after midnight. He retired hours ago."

"That doesn't mean he isn't suffering insomnia and wandering the halls."

"He can't stand me, and he doesn't want me here. Why would he visit?"

"Stranger things have happened."

"Not to me."

She dragged him to her, his body crushed to hers so he could feel her all the way down. She'd already shed her clothes and was attired in a negligee and robe. The fabric was nearly transparent, giving him tantalizing glimpses of several naughty spots.

"Do you want to have sex with me?" she asked. "Or would you rather scurry home like a frightened rabbit?"

She was saucy and decadent and wild, and he chuckled.

"I'd rather stay and have sex."

He clasped her hand and ran into the bedchamber. Like a randy adolescent, he tumbled onto the bed and drew her down with him. They were merry, giggling like children who'd stolen cookies from the pantry.

She rolled on top of him and pinned him down.

"Tell me how much you lust after me," she demanded.

"Constantly."

"Tell me I'm not too old, and I'm still beautiful."

"You're the most beautiful woman I've ever met."

"And the *old* part? Tell me I could be a girl fresh out of the schoolroom."

"Sixteen, if you're a day."

She raised a wicked brow. "For that divine compliment, you get a special prize."

She stripped off her robe and negligee, and she hovered over his lap, her back arched, her glorious breasts on full display.

Yes, she was older than he. Yes, she was debauched and shameless and too indecent for her own good. Yes, she'd never bring a fellow anything but trouble.

But she was magnificent all the same.

He liked to imagine her, twenty years younger, waltzing in the courts of Europe, flirting and vamping, all the men falling at her feet. She must have been a sight.

"You, Mr. Dudley, are wearing too many clothes."

"Perhaps you should divest me of them."

"Let's start with your trousers."

She was unbuttoning them, when suddenly, a man cleared his throat. The sound was so unexpected that—initially—Phillip couldn't make sense of it.

Barbara halted and scowled. Together, they glanced over at the door.

John Middleton, Earl of Penworth, her only son, was glaring at them.

His coat and cravat were off, the sleeves of his shirt rolled up to reveal his forearms. His hair was mussed, as if he'd been running his fingers through it. He appeared vulnerable and weary. The imperious aristocrat had been replaced by the exhausted, overwhelmed, very mortal man.

A mortal man who'd just stumbled on his mother—whom he didn't like very much—having sex with the neighbor.

"Mr. Dudley, I presume?" Penworth's voice was tight with rage.

"John!" Barbara squealed. "Oh no!" She leapt off Phillip as if he was on fire and snuggled herself to his back, trying to conceal her nakedness. But she was quite a bit too late.

Phillip thought he should comment, but he couldn't fathom the topic. No explanation was necessary, and excuses were pointless. What remark could render the incident any less hideous?

He sat up and stood, grabbing the edge of the quilt and tossing it over Barbara. She clutched at it like a lifeline, holding it to her bosom, but she couldn't obscure the fact that she resembled a French courtesan. She was simply a very carnal creature, and there was no hiding it.

Penworth approached Phillip until they were toe-to-toe.

"You're fucking my mother?" Penworth crudely seethed.

"Yes," Phillip admitted, and he braced.

The blow—when it came—was powerful and hard, and it knocked him to his knees. He didn't attempt to block or deflect the punch. He figured Penworth was entitled to his fury.

"John!" Barbara bellowed. "Stop it this instant."

She scooted off the mattress, struggling to keep the blanket wrapped around her.

"Stay out of this," Penworth warned her.

"For pity's sake," she scolded, "I'm a forty-six-year-old divorcée. I won't have you brawling over me as if I was some virginal debutante."

Penworth stared and stared, as if really seeing her for the first time, and Phillip waited on tenterhooks to learn what would happen next.

Finally, Penworth staggered away from her.

"Get out of my house," he hissed. "Be gone when I awake in the morning."

"You can't mean it," she pleaded.

"Get out!" he shouted, and he stormed away.

Chapter 22

❦

"WELCOME home, milord."

"Thank you. It's good to be back."

"I trust your journey from Scotland was uneventful?"

"Completely dull, with nary a bump in the road."

John handed his gloves to the butler in his London house. Footmen traipsed in behind him with his luggage.

"We heard you had a spot of trouble up north," the butler said.

"A small incident, of minor import."

"So . . . all is well?"

"Yes."

The butler's inquiry—though casually posed—wasn't an idle one. A master's demise was always a time of great upheaval for his staff. John's servants were probably still worried that he wasn't hale or that he was suffering lingering effects.

In all actuality, so much had occurred since the cave-in at the grotto that it almost seemed as if it had never transpired. Considering the other catastrophes he'd endured in the interim, his near-death episode was downright blasé.

Lily had left him. He'd disavowed his mother. He'd split with Edward and had to make arrangements for Esther. He had to . . . marry Violet.

He wrinkled his nose with distaste. Perhaps Esther was correct, and he should wed immediately. If he forged ahead, the deed would be done, and he wouldn't spend the next ten months fretting over it.

As he peered around the vestibule, he thought it looked different, as if he was in someone else's residence. There was very little in the furnishings or décor to indicate the place was his.

"Who is at home this evening?" he asked.

"Your stepmother and Lady Violet. They're planning to dine in about an hour. Will you join them?"

Would he?

He was exhausted and had no desire to socialize. Yet he had no excuse to skip the meal. When he'd just arrived in London after such a lengthy absence, fraternization would be expected.

"Yes, I'll join them."

"I'll advise the chef."

"How about the twins? Are they here?"

"Yes."

They were another thorn in his side, another problem he had to solve.

"And my brother, I need to get word to him that I—"

"Your brother is here, too."

"In the house?"

"Yes."

"Where?"

"Up in his suite."

"Is he living here?"

"Well . . . yes."

The butler was perplexed. Without his having received instructions to the contrary, he would have assumed Edward could remain, but John had been perfectly clear with

Edward: He was to take himself off to his bachelor apartment and stay there.

Was Edward deaf? Or had he convinced himself that John wasn't serious?

At Edward's disobeying John's specific order, John was angrier than he'd ever been, and he relished the surge of fury.

Since Lily had departed, he hadn't been able to feel much of anything. No joy. No sadness. No irritation. No exasperation. He was dead inside, as if a vital organ had shut down and he couldn't get it to function.

"My brother is no longer allowed in this house," John curtly said.

The butler's brows raised to his hairline. "I apologize, milord. I hadn't been informed."

"No, you hadn't, but now you know. Please notify the staff. Should he show his face on my stoop ever again, you may call the law—if that is what is required to keep him out."

John started up the stairs, ready to physically evict Edward, when Esther peeked out from a parlor down the hall. Violet stood behind her.

"John, is that you?" Esther asked. "We didn't realize you were back."

He ignored her and spoke to the butler. "Send two footmen to attend me. Edward is leaving, and I will need them to escort him out."

"Very good, sir."

"What is happening?" Esther demanded, and she hurried to the vestibule.

From the steps above her, John said, "Your son is not permitted on the premises. He's been apprised of my opinion, yet he has defied me anyway."

"Don't be absurd. This is his home."

"No. This is *my* home. And he is not welcome in it."

"He will not leave!" She stamped her foot for emphasis.

"He tried to kill me!" John bellowed, which elicited a shocked gasp from Violet and the butler.

"That is a filthy lie!" Esther wheezed. "How dare you accuse him of malice!"

"How dare I? *How dare I?*"

John was so irate, it was lucky she was some distance away. If she'd been closer, he might have slapped her. He was that enraged.

"He will not go!" Esther insisted.

"He will not stay!" John shouted in reply.

He continued on, with Esther running after him, Violet dogging her heels. Esther grabbed at his coat, but she couldn't stop him.

He marched to Edward's door and entered without knocking, and the scene that greeted him was so astonishing—and so bizarre—that it took many seconds for it to register.

Stumbling to a halt, he muttered, "Oh, my Lord!"

He turned and shoved Violet away, but he wasn't as fortunate with Esther. She was in the room before he could keep her out.

Frantically, she studied the disturbing spectacle, her eyes wide with horror. Then she screamed at the top of her lungs and fell to the floor in a stunned heap.

"WHO do you prefer, Edward?"

He was seated in the chair in his bedchamber, Melanie and Miranda posed for him like a pair of nubile slaves. One was nude, the other nearly so, and he was so titillated that he could barely breathe.

They'd caught him unawares, sneaking in as he was dressing for supper.

For weeks, he'd put them off with deceit and fabrication, but apparently, they were tired of waiting for his answer. His mind was awhirl with what he should tell them, but it would never be the truth.

He had begun marital negotiations with a wealthy American he'd met while gambling. The man was eager to be shed of his ugly, fat, but very rich daughter, and

Edward was eager to have her. The contracts would be finalized in a few days, the wedding held a few days after that.

He just needed to fool the twins a bit longer, then he'd be rid of them and their constant badgering. In the meantime, if he could wrangle another erotic encounter out of them, so much the better.

"Miranda, stand behind your sister," he ordered. "Fondle her breasts."

Miranda didn't move, and he was unnerved by her reticence. With these two, he had to keep the upper hand. He enjoyed their brand of punishment too much, and it was easy to get distracted.

"We won't do anything else," Miranda complained, "until you tell us which one you've selected."

Drat it! He'd have to say something. If he refused, they'd stomp out, and he was too ready to fornicate. He had to stick his prick in one of them very soon, or his testicles might explode.

What was a small lie among friends?

"I pick"—he glanced back and forth, back and forth, the moment stretching to infinity—"Melanie."

They didn't remark, but continued to observe him with an eerie expression.

Ultimately, Miranda asked, "When will you speak to John?"

"The instant he returns from Scotland."

John wasn't due back for several weeks, and by then, Edward would be wed to his American.

"Why can't you write to him?" Miranda nagged.

"This isn't the sort of subject I would discuss in a letter."

"Why not?"

"The protocol is to do it in person."

"All right." Miranda nodded at her sister. "Melanie, what would you like to say to your betrothed?"

"I'm very happy, Edward."

"It was a difficult decision," he fibbed.

"It certainly seemed to be," Melanie concurred. "Would you like to copulate with me? In celebration? Or would you like me to dally with Miranda while you watch?"

"Ooh . . . a luscious choice." He mulled it over, then said, "I should like to see you and Miranda together. Then, after I'm sufficiently aroused, I shall join you."

Intent on having a good view of the festivities, he waved them toward the bed.

Melanie held out her hand, and he took it and was helping her up, when suddenly, he was brutally struck on the back of the head. He staggered to his knees, and before he could regain his balance, he was struck again.

Dazed and befuddled, he clutched at the blankets, but his limbs weren't working properly. He could feel himself being dragged onto the mattress, his wrists and ankles fettered, a stocking stuffed in his mouth. They cut away his clothes, and shortly, he was naked and fully trussed. He yanked at the bindings, but couldn't loosen them.

Miranda loomed over him, wielding her riding crop. She prodded his face with it so he would focus on her.

"We know about your American," she hissed.

He shouted, *No, no, you're wrong,* but with the gag firmly in place, he couldn't voice the denial aloud.

"We know what you planned," she charged. "You were lying to us; you were never going to marry Melanie."

No! Of course I'm going to wed Melanie. There is no American.

"Should I tell you about our father and the night *he* lied to us?" she asked.

Real fear danced in his eyes. *What happened to him? Tell me!*

"What do you suppose happened? He's not alive anymore, is he?"

She slid to the floor, and she raised her whip and brought it down across his genitals. It was no playful lover's pat, no erotic tap to spur arousal.

It was rage and pain, meant to wound, meant to terrify.

Edward yelped in agony, bracing as she hit him again and again.

The outer door slammed open. Angry strides pounded in.

Help me! Help me! Edward cried in his mind, not caring about discovery, but anxious for someone to come and cart the violent vixen off to Hell.

"Oh, my Lord," a man muttered.

The twins froze, Miranda pausing in mid-strike.

Edward glanced over to see John swooping in like an underworld god, bent on destruction. Esther followed, then Violet, but John shoved her out. Esther screamed and fainted, as Miranda grinned and tossed the crop onto the bed.

"Hello, John," she casually greeted. "Sorry to cause such a ruckus. We weren't informed that you were home."

John marched over, his curious, disturbed gaze moving from Edward, to the shackles, to the naked twins, to the shackles.

"Untie him," John ordered.

"Certainly," Miranda said.

She was all smiles and compliance, as Melanie began to fuss with the knots.

John glared at Edward, no pity or compassion in his expression as he seethed, "I will speak with you down in my library in fifteen minutes."

Miranda tugged the stocking from Edward's mouth.

"John, please," Edward gasped, "listen to me: I can explain."

"Fifteen minutes, Edward. Were I you, I wouldn't be late."

"WHAT have you to say for yourself?"

"They are the most vicious, dangerous girls who ever lived."

"That's it?"

"No, that's not it. They shouldn't be allowed out around decent people."

John gaped at his brother, wondering how they could possibly be related. They'd had the same father, so half the blood flowing in their veins came from him. Their mother's blood was from different sources, and in comparing Barbara and Esther, who would imagine that Esther would be the one to pass on any taint? Perhaps there was insanity hidden in her family tree.

"Edward, how old are you?"

"What a stupid question. You're well aware that I'm twenty-seven."

"How old are the twins?"

"Eighteen, but they're monsters. Don't let their big blue eyes fool you."

They were in John's library—again—with John haranguing at Edward—again. Sometimes, he felt it was all he'd done in his life, and he was tired of it.

Edward had always been a buffoon, but what type of man initiated the depravity John had just witnessed? And with two much younger women!

What was John to do with him?

He had to decide the best course of action, and he went to the sideboard and poured himself a whiskey. He sat at his desk and sipped it, using the liquor as a delaying tactic while he pondered his options.

"Why are you still in my home?" he inquired. "I instructed you to retire to your bachelor apartment. Was I not clear? Did you not understand me?"

"I didn't believe you were serious. We're brothers, John! You were angry, and you'd been through a horrendous ordeal. You weren't being rational."

"So you presumed you could flaunt me with impunity?"

"I . . . uh . . . uh . . ."

"When did you start the affair?"

"I started nothing. They seduced *me*."

"Really?"

"Before we even left for Scotland."

"This was their idea? The bondage, the whips, the nudity? They thought it all up and encouraged you to participate?"

"Yes, yes! They're devils, I tell you. Satan himself doesn't have anything on those two."

"Which one do you like better?"

"I don't like either. They're both fiends."

"You need to pick one—or I shall pick one for you."

Edward frowned. "What are you saying?"

"You're going to wed one of them."

"No, no. I won't. I can't." Edward put out his hands as if warding off evil. "I'm pursuing an engagement with an American heiress."

"Not any longer, you're not."

Edward studied John, taking in his resolute demeanor, and he began to tremble.

"I won't do it. You can't make me."

"You don't think so?"

"My mother would never let you. She has huge plans for me, and they don't include those two paltry girls, with their teeny-tiny dowries."

"I'm picking Miranda," John said, not missing a beat. "She's the eldest. It seems only fair."

"I won't do it!" Edward repeated, his voice rising in volume and intensity.

"If you don't, I'll have you jailed for ruining them. It's illicit fornication, and it's against the law—in case you've forgotten. Since they're my wards, you've damaged me. I'll sue you and seize the amount remaining in your trust fund." John sipped his drink. "Can you suppose your American heiress will want you after all that?"

"You can't raid my trust fund."

"I can if I get a judgment against you."

Edward scowled, and John could practically see the wheels spinning in his head. He was struggling to figure out how he could garner the conclusion he sought—as he always had in the past—but this time, there would be no changing John's mind.

Edward's behavior was too egregious. There was no way to fix this mess—except for him to marry one of the twins. Even then, where was the justice for the other sister?

"John," he begged, "you have to listen to me: They murdered their father."

"You're being absurd. He committed suicide in a drunken stupor."

"No, no, they bragged about it. They threatened me with the same bad end if I didn't do what they said."

John scoffed, "You're only making it worse for yourself."

"Please!" Edward beseeched. He came off his chair and knelt, his fingers linked as if in prayer. "I'll do whatever you ask, just don't shackle me to Miranda."

John stoically watched him, knowing he wasn't sincere. He'd never been sincere his entire life, and John was sick of his antics.

"We'll have the wedding on Saturday."

"I'll . . . I'll run away. I'll hide."

"I'll find you and drag you back. You can be married to her in chains if that is your choice. But married to her is what you shall be."

ESTHER raced to the library. She pounded on the door, then rushed in without waiting for a summons.

Edward was on his knees, pleading with John, who sat in his chair, calmly drinking a whiskey, completely unfazed by Edward's emotional appeal.

"Mother!" Edward leapt up and whipped around. "He insists I wed Miranda. Tell him I won't!"

"Of course you won't. Don't be ridiculous."

Esther had never been so shaken, and she fought to appear in charge and in control. Her stern manner had always cowed John into doing what she wanted. Hadn't she been able to sway him with regard to Miss Lambert?

In light of his fondness for Miss Lambert, if Esther

could get him to forsake her, she could convince him to do anything.

John had escaped peril in Scotland, but he could still perish unexpectedly. If he did, Edward had to have a suitable wife befitting an earl. It couldn't be a nobody like Miranda.

"There will be no wedding to Miranda," Esther declared. "Honestly, John, what are you thinking?"

"He *will* marry Miranda," John said. "On Saturday. You'd best make the arrangements."

"No, he will not!"

"It is not up to you, Esther." John rose, a signal that the meeting was over. "Edward understands my feelings in the matter, and he's aware of the consequences if he refuses me. Aren't you, Edward?"

"What consequences?" Esther fumed. "How has he coerced you, Edward?"

"I . . . I . . ." Edward stammered, so John explained for him.

"He will wed her, or he will be prosecuted and beggared. By me."

Had she been holding a gun, she'd have shot him. "You will *not* do this."

"You can't stop me."

"I'll see you dead before it ever transpires."

"You can certainly try to kill me, but you shouldn't count on succeeding. I intend to live a long, long time— just to spite you."

He walked to the door and flung it open, hollering for the butler. When he hurried up, John instructed, "My stepmother is moving out. Until further notice, she'll be staying at the Carlyle Hotel. Have the maids pack her bags."

"This is my home," Esther raged. "I won't go."

Her protest went unheeded as John continued speaking to the butler. "My brother is leaving, too, to return to his bachelor's lodging. Have the carriage brought 'round, so they may depart together."

The butler dashed off to implement John's commands,

and a dangerous silence ensued, the three of them frozen in place. John cocked a brow, indicating they should exit, but Esther didn't budge.

Grimly, she comprehended that if she vacated the premises, she might never be allowed back inside.

Edward took her arm, smoothing over the tense moment. "Come, Mother. Tempers are running high. I'll talk to him tomorrow, when cooler heads have prevailed."

"It won't do you any good," John asserted. "One way or another, you'll pay for your transgression."

As if they were an unwanted pile of rubbish, John pushed them into the hall and closed the door.

"How dare you!"

"What?"

Violet raised a hand and slapped Edward as hard as she could.

"Violet!" Esther gasped as Edward rubbed his reddening cheek.

"You little witch!" he seethed.

"You said you loved me," Violet accused. "You said you'd marry me."

"I said *that*?" Edward hedged. "How could I have? You're engaged to John. You have been for months."

They were in the vestibule, Esther and Edward with their coats on as they prepared to leave. Violet had just managed to catch them.

"I believed you!" she shouted. "I believed every word that spewed from your lying, deceitful mouth!"

"Mother"—Edward rolled his eyes in feigned amusement—"this residence has become a madhouse. Let's go."

He tried to escort Esther out, but Violet lurched into the threshold, blocking their way.

"I spoke to the twins," she told him. "You were having an affair with them the entire time we were in Scotland."

"The twins are renowned liars," he claimed. "Everybody knows it."

"You were carrying on with them, while making love to me! You despicable cad! I trusted you! I thought you were sincere!"

"Sorry," he simpered, "but I really have no idea what bee has gotten into your bonnet. Now then, if you'll excuse us? We've been hideously insulted, and we'd like to be off."

"You proposed to me! The instant we learned of John's accident, you proposed and I accepted. I loved you, when I never loved John, and this is how you repay me?"

Edward leaned in and hissed, "My dear, may I suggest that you shut the hell up? No one cares about you or your paltry romance. Shut your mouth and save yourself."

From down the hall, a man cleared his throat, and she, Edward, and Esther whirled around.

"What an interesting tableau," John commented. "Apparently, I missed a few details of what occurred in Scotland."

Violet blanched. "John! How long have you been standing there?"

"Long enough," he replied.

"She always loved me," Edward boasted. "I worked incessantly to steal her away from you."

"It appears you succeeded."

"I played her like a master at his violin. She was my greatest symphony." Edward shoved Violet out of the way. "Mother, let's flee this house, where we've never been welcome."

They stomped out, and Violet had to face John all alone. He frowned until she began to squirm with alarm.

"Whatever you heard," she maintained, "it wasn't true. I'm simply overwrought by what I witnessed upstairs."

He studied her, her future hanging in the balance. "Answer one question for me," he finally said. "Did you betroth yourself to him while I was buried down in the grotto?"

"Well . . . not *betrothed* precisely."

"What would you call it then?"

"We were just . . . just talking about what could happen."

"Before you knew whether I was dead or not?"

"It seemed likely that you were deceased. We didn't mean any harm."

"No, Edward never does." The butler was marching toward them, and John glanced over at him. "Esther and Edward have left. Summon another carriage, would you? Lady Violet is leaving, too."

The butler nodded and kept on.

"Please, John, can't we discuss this?"

"I believe we already have. Go home, Violet. Go home, and tell your father that I will visit him tomorrow."

Panic flared in her breast. "Why?"

"Why would you suppose? I'm once again a bachelor, and I must inform you that the feeling has me greatly relieved."

"ARE they gone?" Miranda asked.

Melanie stared out the window as Edward's coach pulled away.

"Yes."

"I listened to the maids gossiping. John has demanded that Edward wed me."

"You'll have your money very soon." Melanie peered over her shoulder. "What about mine?"

"John will have to find a husband for you, too. We'll select somebody on our own and have him tender an offer. I don't imagine John will fuss about it."

"Let's make it a clerk or secretary—an ordinary fellow who will deem my dowry to be huge. I don't want anyone too high in the in-step."

"No, that wouldn't do at all."

"And we'll need a man with no family, so if he passes on, no one will notice."

"Yes."

"I'll have my money very soon, too."

"Very soon."

They held hands and grinned.

"Has John departed for England?"

"Yes."

"Who told you?"

"I spoke to Angus personally."

Phillip watched as Barbara went over to the wardrobe, retrieved a satchel, and began tossing clothes into it.

"What are you doing?" he asked.

"What do you think? I'm going to London. If that's where John is, then that is where I must be."

For a few minutes, he observed her frantic packing, but he couldn't bear it. He walked over and stopped her, yanking the satchel away and pitching it on the floor.

She glared up at him, her gaze angry and hurt.

"Don't chase after him," Phillip insisted. "Let him go."

"Let him . . . go? No. I never will."

"He loathes you! He's been very clear!"

"He doesn't know what he wants. Esther has blinded him to what matters."

After Penworth had kicked her out of the castle, she'd spent weeks trying to worm her way back into his life, but to no avail. She'd always been able to wrangle the best ending for herself, so she'd been stunned to learn that she couldn't soften her son's heart.

Ultimately, he'd left for England without a good-bye or penny of support. What was she to do? And where did Phillip fit in to the entire scenario?

He couldn't decide, but one thing was certain: She shouldn't throw herself at the arrogant oaf. She had an enormous amount of pride. Why didn't she draw on it?

"Don't humiliate yourself over him," he seethed.

"If I don't follow him to London, what will become of me? It's not as if I have a carriage-load of options."

"Stay here with me."

"As your what?"

"As my wife. Marry me."

It was the proposal he should have tendered when Penworth caught them in bed together. It was the appropriate remedy, but the words felt like ashes in his mouth.

While he loved her very much, it was in the detached, general way he loved all women. He never wanted to be bound to any female. He was too independent, too accustomed to being on his own.

"Marry you?" She was extremely shocked.

"Yes."

She started to laugh.

"What's so funny?" he grouched.

"You. My Lord, but you are such a sweet boy."

She reached out and cradled his cheek in her palm. "No, my darling, Phillip. I will not marry you."

"Why the hell not?"

"Because I don't ever plan to wed again, and I don't love you." At seeing his scowl, she said, "Surely, you knew that. You couldn't have hoped that I . . ." She laughed again. "I was using you, Phillip. For sex."

He was a man with a substantial ego, so her remark was incredibly aggravating.

He was the great lover and user of women. He made a habit of it; he'd developed it into a fine art.

"Now you tell me," he grumbled.

"Oh, don't pout. You don't want to marry anyone. Especially me. Admit it. You're glad I said no."

"Perhaps a tad."

A grin tugged at his lips. Relief washed through him. She was correct: He didn't want to wed her, but had felt obliged to ask. Lucky for him, she'd saved him from himself.

Whew! He'd dodged a bullet.

"I have to get to England as fast as I can," she explained.

"He won't let you in the door."

"His London servants won't be expecting me. He won't

have warned them to keep me out. I'll be ensconced in his parlor before he realizes I've arrived."

He scoffed, "You're mad."

"Yes, I am. Will you help me?"

"How?"

"Will you take me to London? I don't wish to travel so far on my own."

He only considered for a few seconds.

He was weary of Scotland, weary of Odell's house, and the stuffy socializing that went along with it. Clarinda had thrived, but he was suffocating.

"Why not?" He shrugged. "What else do I have to do?"

"BARBARA refused you?"

"Yes."

"Thank God," Clarinda mumbled.

"Yes, thank God," Phillip agreed.

"I can't believe you asked her."

"I thought—if she wed me—it might smooth over the rift with her son."

"Who cares about her son? You'd have been shackled to her until you took your dying breath."

"My worst nightmare"—he gave a mock shudder—"is to ever be the sacrificial lamb on the matrimonial altar."

Clarinda chuckled, then she quieted.

They were in Odell's cozy drawing room. A cheery fire crackled in the grate. Supper was over, Barbara in bed, and he and Clarinda were sitting, like an old married couple, enjoying a whiskey.

In the firelight, she looked so beautiful, so much like their mother. Clarinda didn't remember her, but Phillip did. She had passed away when he was seven and Clarinda two. Since then, he and Clarinda had never been separated. They were two peas in a pod, the best of friends, the closest siblings ever.

How would he get on without her?

"You're about to tell me something I won't like." She was astute as ever, able to read his mind. "What is it?"

"I'm going to England."

"I guessed as much. With Barbara?"

"Merely to escort her."

"You won't stay with her there?"

"No. I'll convey her to Penworth's London residence in one piece. Then? I don't know."

"Will you come back to Scotland?"

For a lengthy interval, he stared, committing her face to memory, then he shook his head.

"No, I'm not ever coming back."

"But we're a team. You always said so."

"We are a team. Will you join me in my adventure? We could pull the wagon out of storage and take off again."

"Just like old times?"

"Yes, just like old times. I have some new scams I'd like to run, and I've conjured up some new potions we could try."

It was her turn to stare. Finally, she admitted, "I wouldn't like to go out on the road again. Is that your plan?"

"I'm debating."

He peered around at the furnishings and drapes, at the paintings and rugs. It was a fine house—as far as houses went. Odell was a man's man, and whoever had decorated it for him understood that fact.

There were no frilly objects or fussy fabrics. There was no feminine touch. It was a comfortable abode where a fellow could relax after a hard day's labor, but Phillip was bored to death and itching to escape.

"I have to go, Clarinda."

"I know. I'm surprised you remained as long as you have."

"Will you miss me?"

"No," she churlishly retorted, which they both knew was a lie.

She'd miss him every minute, and he hated to imagine her on her own, having to carry on without him. She was smart and tough and as independent as he was, but she was a female, and she wouldn't have him nearby if trouble brewed.

He asked, "What will you do with yourself once I'm gone?"

"I'll tarry here through the winter, but I have some money put aside. Come the spring, I might buy myself a cottage."

"You've always wanted that."

"Yes."

"You could grow a garden and sell herbs and tonics."

He could practically see her, puttering over her plants, mixing her medicines and delivering them to the neighbors. She'd be satisfied with that life. She'd be content.

Would he ever be?

"If you need to come home," she said, "I'll be here. Waiting for you."

"Watching my back?"

"As you have watched mine all these years."

He smiled and nodded, then hurried to the sideboard and poured himself a whiskey, anxious to hide his expression so she wouldn't note the tears in his eyes.

Chapter 23

❧

"I'M sorry, Miss Lambert, but further attempts are futile."

"You must have a position for me, Mrs. Ford. I've always been a model employee. I've always worked hard for you."

"That was . . . before."

Before . . .

Before the Earl of Penworth's roving eye had fallen on her. Before she'd stupidly leapt into their destructive affair. Before Violet Howard had written to Mrs. Ford at the Ford Employment Agency to inform her of Lily's disgrace.

Violet had also corresponded with her extensive coven of acquaintances, which comprised practically every woman in the kingdom. Her revenge had been personal and pernicious.

Lily—who had so furiously guarded her reputation—had no reputation remaining to speak of. She was completely compromised so all respectable avenues of service were lost to her.

"What should I do?" she asked Mrs. Ford.

They were in Mrs. Ford's office, facing each other across her tidy desk.

"You could try to find a post out of the country."

"Where?"

"Perhaps India."

"India!"

"It's a far distance, but then, you carry the stigma of *home-wrecker.* You need to move to a location where no wife has ever heard of you."

"I did nothing wrong," Lily lied. "I don't care what Lady Violet alleged."

Mrs. Ford simply raised a brow. Lily wasn't the first female to be seduced by a great lord, but she was definitely the first to have her good name so thoroughly besmirched.

There seemed no way to counter the swath of devastation Violet Howard had leveled. Lily had assumed—foolishly, it turned out—that no one in England would have learned about the cave-in at the grotto, about Penworth's brush with death, about Lily's being trapped with him.

How mistaken she'd been!

People were agog over the tale, so gossip hadn't waned. Men, in particular, were titillated by the notion of a single woman and a hot springs pool. The entire story was too salacious, and Violet Howard's angry missives hadn't helped.

For two months, Lily had traipsed about London, searching for a job, but to no avail.

Mrs. Ford had tried her best, had sent Lily's resumé for dozens of potential situations, but no interviews had been granted.

The severance Esther Middleton had promised was never paid. Esther had given Lily an envelope, supposedly containing the money, but Lily hadn't peeked in it until she was on the public coach whisking her to London. The envelope had been empty.

Using her meager savings, she'd been staying at a boardinghouse that provided one meal a day. But the rent was due, and she didn't have it.

Her worst nightmare had come to pass: She was alone and broke and about to be tossed out on the streets.

It she wasn't so afraid, she'd have been livid.

Lord Penworth had wreaked such havoc. Did he ever think of her? Did he ever—for the tiniest instant—wonder what had become of her?

She scoffed.

He'd coerced her into leaving so his dearest Violet Howard wasn't discomfited, but he'd been too much of a coward to tell Lily himself. He'd had his wicked stepmother do his dirty work. Why would he ever think of her?

He had to be glad she'd resigned without a fuss, that she had meekly acceded to his request she vacate the premises. Despite all they had shared, he'd gone on with his life as if Lily had never existed, and she'd been left to deal with the aftermath.

"Would you loan me some money?" she humiliated herself by asking. "Just until I receive wages at my next job?"

Mrs. Ford snorted. "I'm cautious with my finances, Miss Lambert. In light of your troubles, you're rather a bad bet."

"I'll pay you back."

"How? There is no post on your horizon—and probably never will be—so how would you reimburse me?"

Mrs. Ford stood, indicating that the appointment was over. She went to the door and held it open.

Lily didn't rise. She stared at the woman, wanting to say something pertinent, but not knowing what it should be.

There was such a sense of injustice about what had transpired. Lily shouldn't have dallied with Penworth, but she hadn't blithely ruined herself. She'd been madly in love. Why was that so egregious? And she'd certainly been penalized for her misconduct. How long would she be punished? Forever? Why was that fair?

Finally, she stood, too.

"You needn't come back," Mrs. Ford stated with great solemnity. "I've done all I can for you. Don't waste your time. Or mine."

She shoved Lily out, and in a matter of seconds, Lily was on the front walk. Crowds of pedestrians milled by, jostling her, but she dawdled, paralyzed by indecision.

Since her departure from Penworth Castle, she'd been plagued with doubts as to how she should proceed. She'd convinced herself that future employment through Mrs. Ford's agency was the answer, but she'd failed in her efforts, and that was without her having confessed the worst aspect of her predicament: Lily suspected she was pregnant.

With each passing day, she was more sure of it. She knew the symptoms and couldn't ignore them, especially the fact that—after she'd returned from Scotland—there had been no sign of her monthly courses. She prayed it wasn't so, that her flux would begin soon, but if it didn't, she would likely commit murder.

Somehow, she would find the means to buy a gun, then she'd go to Penworth's house and shoot him dead. She wouldn't suffer an ounce of remorse over her crime, either. She would march to the gallows with a smile on her face!

How could he behave so despicably? How could he abandon her to such a terrible fate? Who would treat a dog as he'd treated her? She'd once believed he was fond of her. Had it all been a sham? Had he possessed no genuine sentiment?

Off in the distance, a clap of thunder sounded, and it rolled across the sky. The clouds were very low, and they seemed to press down on her.

A raindrop fell, then another and another, a deluge commencing. She didn't have a penny to hire a hackney, so she'd have to walk to her room in the torrent. When she arrived, she'd be soaked to the bone. She might contract an ague and perish. If she did, who would care?

She started to cry. Not that anyone would notice. She was invisible, a ghost that couldn't be seen.

"Miss Lambert?"

She was so lost in her morbid rumination, that at first, she didn't realize her name had been spoken.

"Miss Lambert, is it you?"

Glancing up, she was stunned to discover Edward Middleton bearing down on her.

"Mr. Middleton? Hello."

"Why are you standing in the rain, you silly girl?"

"I just . . . just . . ."

She was too dejected to form a coherent thought.

He reached out and took her hand, which was very cold. "You're frozen," he kindly said. "And what's this? Tears?"

She swiped at her cheeks, hating to have him witness her despair.

"I've been looking for work," she admitted, "but I haven't had any luck. I apologize. I'm a tad overwhelmed."

"I can see that you are. I was wondering what had become of you. You fled Scotland in such a hurry."

"Yes, well . . ." She peered at her feet, mortified to have him mention the scandal.

"Have you talked to my brother?" he inquired. "Have you sought his help?"

"No." The notion had never occurred to her.

Approach Penworth? Beg his assistance? Remind him of his obligation to her? Tell him that he might have sired a child?

The pompous fiend was engaged to marry Violet Howard, a union he intended to pursue at all costs. Lily would slit her own throat before she asked him for a single farthing.

"May I be frank, Miss Lambert?"

"I suppose."

"I felt John treated you very badly. *Very* badly," he added for emphasis.

Lily did, too, but she didn't respond, and he continued.

"If you've suffered a fiscal hardship because of him, it's only fair that he rectify your situation. Wouldn't you agree?"

"Perhaps," she equivocated.

"I have an idea," Edward said. "You must come with me."

"To where?"

"I want you to discuss your dilemma with my mother."

"With . . . your mother?" Lily couldn't imagine anyone less likely to aid her.

"Yes. You need a powerful advocate to plead your case to John, and she's had her own troubles with him recently. She'd be more than happy to put his nose out of joint on your behalf."

"I don't know," she muttered, disconcerted by his offer.

"I insist, Miss Lambert. I really can't take no for an answer."

JOHN entered his quiet, empty foyer, but his arrival went unnoticed. He removed his coat and hat, threw them on a chair, then proceeded to his library.

To ward off the chill, he poured himself a whiskey, then ambled over to gaze out the window at the small garden in the back. It was a cold, dreary afternoon, and the gray colors matched his mood.

"Hello," he shouted, merely to see if he could generate a reply, if a servant would appear to attend him, but no one did.

Having pushed everybody out of his life, he was all alone. He cut a pathetic figure, but the solitude was his own fault.

He'd rebuffed his mother, had let Lily go without lifting a finger to learn what had happened to her. He'd broken off his betrothal to Violet. Esther and Edward had been tossed out. In light of events, no other ending had been possible, but still, he was saddened by the loss.

Only the twins remained, which he deemed a sorry statement on his condition.

They were confined to their bedchamber, and he'd ordered them not to come downstairs until Miranda's wedding on Saturday.

He refused to see or speak with them, and he would be vastly relieved when they were gone. Melanie wanted to live with Edward and Miranda, and she'd suggested that she might pick her own husband. John was happy to let her.

There was no reason to pretend he'd been any sort of guardian to them. He'd failed them miserably and would repair the damage by forcing Edward to marry Miranda. Melanie would soon be wed, too, then John's duty to them would conclude.

He would be left to putter around his sprawling mansion with just the servants for company.

Out in the garden, rain pelted the earth, and he watched it fall, his palm on the cool glass of the window. He wondered where Lily was, and he hoped she was warm and dry and safe.

Go find her! a voice in his head urged. *Bring her home!*

He wished he could, but pitifully, he had no idea where to start looking. In all the time he'd spent with her, he'd never inquired as to her background or friends. She was an orphan, but he'd gleaned no other information.

Who might know where she was? Who might assist him in any search?

He hadn't a clue.

Their sole common acquaintance was Mrs. Ford at the employment agency. John had bumped into her one morning, and he'd asked about Lily—where she was working, how she was faring—but Mrs. Ford claimed to have had no contact with Lily after she'd traveled to Scotland as part of his entourage.

Apparently, she hadn't returned to London, or if she had, she hadn't sought a job with Mrs. Ford.

Footsteps sounded in the hall, winging toward him, and he glanced over at the door, curious as to who was hurrying about. Old habits died hard, and he half expected

Esther to bustle in, but when he saw who it was instead, he had to blink and blink to clear his vision.

Was he hallucinating?

"Barbara?"

"Hello, darling," she said.

"Barbara?" he repeated more stridently. "What are you doing here?"

"I'm preparing the guest list for your party on Thursday night."

"I'm not having a party on Thursday night."

"Of course you are. You have to let everyone know you're back in Town—especially now that you've jilted that odious Violet Howard."

She was clutching a lengthy piece of paper, scratching names on it. It was crisscrossed with so many lines and arrows that it resembled an army general's convoluted war plan.

"I don't intend to announce that I'm back," he insisted, "and I have no desire to entertain."

"Don't be ridiculous. After your ordeal in Scotland, rumors of your deteriorated condition are running rampant. You must quell them, and a very public party is the best way."

"Let people talk. I don't care what they say about me."

She blanched with surprise. "*You* don't care? Are you ill?"

"Not that I'm aware."

"You have to show you're hale and healthy—and that Violet is but a distant memory." She grinned. "Did you know that stupid child fancied herself in love with Edward?"

"So I've heard."

"That fact alone should tell you how unqualified she was to be your countess. You're not pining away, are you? She was a spoiled idiot. You're lucky to be shed of her."

"No, Barbara, I'm not pining away."

"I'm so relieved. Now then, you need me, and I have everything under control."

"You do?"

"Yes." She studied her list of names again. "You're still friends with Jordan Winthrop, aren't you?"

"Yes."

"I'm told he's married a commoner, but you're such a stickler for proprieties. May I invite him and his new bride or not? I wouldn't want you to collapse from an apoplexy if she strolled in on his arm."

He thought about all the effort he'd wasted, focusing on status and rank. How could any of it have mattered so much?

Esther was a countess, but it wasn't too much of a stretch to say she could thrive in an insane asylum. His brother, an earl's son, was an irresponsible wastrel and not worth knowing. Violet, a duke's daughter, was an immature flirt who was fickle in her loyalties and easily led astray by inappropriate influences.

He was left with Barbara—his loose, notorious, unfaithful mother. But she'd returned and, despite his disregard, his insults, his ignoring her, she was determined to befriend him.

Why keep pushing her away? What purpose was served by remaining aloof?

Yes, she'd erred. She'd shamed the family and disgraced his father, but she'd been little more than a girl when she'd run off, just a year or two older than Violet. The impetuousness of youth had to have played a part in her rash conduct.

She seemed filled with regret, and she'd gone to such lengths to reestablish their bond. Hadn't she earned a second chance? If he tossed her out again, if he rebuffed this latest attempt, what did it say about him as a man? As a son? As a Christian?

He believed in redemption. He believed in miracles, and it dawned on him that he was absurdly glad she'd arrived.

"Yes, you may invite Jordan to the party," he said, "and please enclose a personal message from me, telling him how much I look forward to meeting his wife."

"Marvelous."

"While you're at it, I need you to arrange a small, quick wedding."

"A wedding?"

"Saturday morning."

"Here at the house?"

"Yes."

"Who are the bride and groom. Anyone I know?"

"Edward is marrying Miranda—if I have to hog-tie him and drag him before the vicar."

"Edward and Miranda?"

"We had an *incident*," was all he supplied by way of explanation.

"Ah . . ."

She scribbled some furious notes, then gradually, her quill drew to a halt. She glanced up and frowned.

"What is it?" she inquired. "Why are you staring?"

"You didn't bring that oaf Dudley to London with you, did you?"

"No. He dropped me off, then kept on going."

"Good. It was unnerving, seeing him and my mother . . . well . . ." He blushed from the roots of his hair to the tips of his toes.

"He proposed marriage to me afterward—if it makes you feel any better."

"It doesn't."

"But I refused him."

"Really? Why?"

"Why would I wed again? I was awful at it the first time, and I didn't suppose I'd improve with practice." She winked at him. "You throw a mean right hook."

"I belonged to a boxing club when I was at university."

"He had a black eye for two weeks."

"The cad."

"Yes, he was, but I liked him anyway." She sighed like a young maiden who'd had her heart broken.

A silence ensued, where they gazed at each other, and

he was astonished to realize that he had her exact same smile. He hadn't noticed before.

"What shall I do with you, Barbara?" he asked.

"Don't do anything. Just let me watch over you for a while. I want to. It will make me happy."

I wouldn't mind a bit of mothering, he mused.

What could it hurt to have her stay? If he wasn't careful, he might even grow to like her. Why not?

"Would you join me in a whiskey?" He tipped his glass toward her, offering to pour her one.

"Why, John Middleton! It's three o'clock in the afternoon, and you're drinking. What's come over you?"

"I guess you're rubbing off on me."

"About damn time."

BARBARA was walking past the front door, when the knocker was banged. She peeked out to see a man on the stoop, holding a sealed letter.

"May I help you?" she asked.

"I'm to deliver this to Lord Penworth. Is he at home?"

"Yes."

She extended her hand to accept it, and he hesitated.

"My orders are to give it to him personally."

"Sorry, but he's extremely busy. May I inquire as to what it's about?"

"I'm to say it's a private matter," he mysteriously said.

"Ooh, that sounds intriguing."

She went to the table in the hall, grabbed some pin money, and stuffed it into his coat. Instantly, he relinquished the letter.

"Will you wait for his answer?" she queried.

"No. If he chooses to act, the instructions are all written down, neat and proper."

He spun and dashed off, and she hastened to the library where John was buried in correspondence.

She entered the room, picking at the wax seal, trying to

peer inside at the clandestine message. She wasn't yet brazen enough to snoop through his mail, but if she managed to stumble on a fascinating detail, she wouldn't feel guilty.

"Are you having an affair?" she asked as he looked up.

"Not that I know of."

"Are you being blackmailed?"

"Not that I know of," he said again. "Why?"

"You've received a secret letter, meant for your eyes only." She dropped it on the desk.

"Is the courier waiting for a reply?"

"No. He claimed—once you read the contents—your instructions will be clear."

"Hmm. Interesting."

He sat back in his chair and opened it, and as he perused the words, he froze. The strangest expression crossed his face, and he muttered, "Well, I'll be damned."

"What is it? Not bad news, I hope?"

"No, no. It's from . . . Lily."

"Miss Lambert?"

"Yes. She left Scotland without a good-bye and without providing any information as to where she went. I would have tried to find her, but I had no idea how."

Barbara thought it a peculiar comment. Angus had told her the family sent Miss Lambert away to contain the scandal. By *family*, Barbara had assumed Angus referred to John, but if John hadn't arranged Miss Lambert's departure, how had it come about?

"I was just thinking about her," John admitted.

"What does she say?"

"She's had some trouble. She wants to see me, and she needs my . . . my help!"

He smiled, as if Miss Lambert's seeking his assistance was the most spectacular thing that had ever happened to him.

As if he'd forgotten Barbara was present, he shut his eyes and pressed the letter to his chest, directly over his heart. He held it there as she watched—agog and amazed—at how the missive had riveted him.

Suddenly, he rose and raced out.

"John!" she called after him. "Where are you going?"

"I'm going to get her, to beg her forgiveness, and bring her home where she belongs."

He continued on, and to the empty room, Barbara murmured, "Good for you, my wonderful lad. Good for you."

Chapter 24

❦

"HE won't come," Lily insisted.

"Won't he?" Esther replied. "I wouldn't be too sure of that if I were you."

"He doesn't care about me!"

"Ha! That's what you think."

"You said so yourself back in Scotland. He threw me out so Lady Violet wasn't discomfited."

"I lied. He and I never discussed you. *I* wanted you gone, and I tricked you into leaving."

"What?"

"I was still foolish enough to suppose that Edward had a chance with Violet, and I was able to tell her that I'd gotten rid of you."

"Well, your scheme certainly worked."

"John was livid when he found out that you'd sneaked away."

"Really?"

"He was determined to chase after you, but I talked him out of it by reminding him of his duty to Violet. He was always a stickler for doing his *duty*. It was easy to persuade him to forget you."

A flush of happiness swept through Lily. She'd presumed that Penworth tossed her over with nary a ripple in his conscience. It was heartening to hear that he'd at least realized she'd left.

Fat lot of good it did her at the moment.

She was tied to a chair in the decrepit room she'd rented, and Esther was standing behind her, a loaded pistol in her hand. They were waiting for Penworth to arrive, and bizarre as it sounded, Esther was planning to shoot him when he walked in.

Obviously, desperation had driven Lily mad. Why had she trusted Esther? Lunacy was the sole explanation for her folly.

Edward had delivered Lily to Esther's suite at the Carlyle Hotel, and Lily had followed along like a sheep to the slaughter.

Under Esther's meticulous prodding, Lily had revealed her dire plight—all but her possible pregnancy—yet Esther seemed to have deduced Lily's condition. She kept staring at Lily's stomach when she thought Lily wasn't looking.

Esther had confessed her own fury with Penworth over his demand that Edward marry Miranda. When Esther had offered to plead Lily's case to Penworth, when she'd offered to obtain some financial assistance from him, Lily had agreed to let her try.

She'd been swayed by Esther's wily argument: Lily had been grievously used by Penworth. Shouldn't he fork over some money in reparation?

It's only fair, Esther had crooned, and the longer she'd continued, the more Lily had concurred.

She'd written the letter Esther suggested, begging him to meet her at her dreary, dilapidated boardinghouse.

He should see the depths to which you've descended, Esther had urged. She had claimed that if he witnessed Lily's true situation, he'd feel guilty and more inclined to be generous.

Lily had swallowed Esther's nonsense, and now she was frantic with worry over what Esther had set in motion.

Esther didn't seem to be insane. If anything, she seemed completely rational, and her calm certitude was frightening. She hated John with a burning passion, and she would stop Edward's marriage by any means necessary.

Lily had to prevent an assault, but what could she do?

"I asked him to be here at two o'clock," Lily said, hoping to distract Esther with conversation. "It's almost three. He's not coming."

"He's coming. Don't you fret about it."

"You don't even know if he's in London. He might have been out when the message was delivered."

"He's home." At Lily's dubious scowl, Esther snarled, "What? You think I don't have spies in my own house? You think none of the servants are loyal to me? He's home, and that whore, Barbara, is there, too. I'll even the score with both of them in one fell swoop."

"Has it occurred to you that you're acting a bit odd? Are you positive you should do this? Maybe you should talk to your son. He likes Lord Penworth; he wouldn't approve of your harming him."

"What Edward doesn't know won't hurt him."

"But to shoot Lord Penworth," Lily pressed. "You can't imagine you'll get away with it."

"Of course I can."

"How?"

"I'll make it look like *you* shot him. You loved him, but he ruined then jilted you. I'm guessing you're pregnant, too, so I'll spread a rumor that you are. I'll say you confided in me."

"I'm not increasing," Lily contended.

"It doesn't matter. You have plenty of reasons for wanting revenge."

"Your story is too outlandish," Lily protested, even though the tale was extremely plausible.

The whole world was aware of Lily's affair with Penworth, and Mrs. Ford would be able to testify as to Lily's fiscal crisis. She'd be branded a murderer, would be prosecuted and hanged. Was there no end to the damage she'd suffer due to her allying herself with Penworth?

For a woman who was so levelheaded, how had she wound up in such a jam?

"Poor Miss Lambert," Esther mused. "You should have behaved better."

Lily couldn't argue the point.

"It was all Penworth's fault," Lily fibbed.

"I'm sure it was. He's a man, after all. They rut like beasts in the field. Even John—for all his puritanical ways—is not immune to pleasures of the flesh."

"You're correct. He was like a stallion with a mare."

Lily wasn't serious; she was simply eager to divert Esther while she watched for an opportunity to save herself—and Penworth.

"I don't know where I went wrong with that boy," Esther muttered. "I tried so hard to raise him right. His mother's wicked blood must be stronger than I suspected."

"He's actually quite a brazen individual, but he hides it well."

"I was afraid he'd turn out just like Barbara. Why anyone would—"

Suddenly, footsteps pounded up the stairs. They were heavy; a man's stride.

"Ah," Esther beamed, "here he is. And you said he wouldn't come for you."

"What is it you expect him to do? It's not as if he—"

"Hush!" Esther hissed, the pistol digging into Lily's throat. "When he knocks, you are to calmly bid him enter."

Lily was too scared to reply, so Esther leaned nearer and whispered, "Do you understand?"

"Yes."

Lily was trembling and couldn't catch her breath. Would Esther shoot her? Would she shoot Penworth? The prospect was so improbable that Lily felt as if she was trapped in the middle of a strange dream.

He rapped three times, and Esther nudged Lily with the barrel of the gun.

"Yes?" Lily said. "Who is it?"

"It's John."

"Come . . . come in," Lily stammered.

As he spun the knob, and the door began to open, she panicked.

"John!" she shouted to warn him, but Esther clasped a palm over Lily's mouth, cutting off most of the sound.

He strolled in, looking handsome and windblown and larger than life, and a rush of gladness swept over her.

He's here! He came for me! a voice chanted inside her head.

Her outburst had kept both of Esther's hands occupied, so she hadn't fired immediately. She was positioned behind Lily, using her as a shield, and Lily imagined they were a peculiar sight and not anywhere close to what he'd anticipated finding.

"Lily," he casually greeted, "hello."

She couldn't speak, but simply widened her eyes, yearning to communicate the terror she was feeling. He peered back with a bland expression, providing no hint of emotion or concern.

"Esther," he then said, "I'm surprised to see you here."

"Sit down."

She waved the pistol toward the table in the corner, but he didn't move.

"You seem upset," he mentioned.

"Sit down!" she barked. "If you don't do as I say—at once!—I'll shoot her before you can blink."

"Oh, all right. Whatever you think is best is fine with me."

Lily gasped with offense. If she hadn't been bound to the chair, she'd have marched over and slugged him.

"I'll shoot her!" Esther threatened. "I mean it."

"You can if you wish. She never brought me anything but trouble. Why would I care what happens to her?"

"You loved her," Esther fumed. "Don't deny it."

He scoffed. "I lusted after her. Maybe. I wouldn't ascribe a higher motive."

Esther started to shake. He wasn't behaving as she'd hoped, and her temper flared.

"You loved her! Admit it!"

"You have mistaken my physical conduct for a sentimental connection. You know me, Esther. I would never involve myself with someone like her."

Lily's blood boiled.

She'd been about to forgive him, having convinced herself that he'd raced to her side because he couldn't bear for them to be apart.

She was such an idiot! Why did she allow him to overwhelm her better sense? He hadn't been genuinely fond of her, and his affection had been a ruse to persuade her to lift her skirt. Would she ever learn?

"Will that be all?" Penworth asked. "If you lured me here merely to watch as you murder her, I'd really rather go. I'm busy this afternoon."

He turned to walk out, and Esther shrieked, "Get over to that table and sit down! You must compose a letter to Edward."

"I *must*? How will you make me?"

"I told you: I will kill her if you don't."

"And I told *you* to have at it. Be my guest."

Esther's arm was quaking wildly, the weight of the gun exhausting her, and Lily was worried that—in her distress—Esther might accidentally pull the trigger.

Couldn't the oaf lower himself to humor Esther? Couldn't he take this seriously and help Lily before she was murdered by the deranged woman?

"Lord Penworth," Lily snapped, "could you do as she's requested? Just for a minute?"

"I suppose," he grumbled.

The room was tiny, and he scooted by them, having to pass so close to Lily that his leg brushed her knee. She braced, assuming he would utilize his nearness to attack Esther, but he didn't, and Lily wanted to scream at him.

How could he be so unaffected? Esther might be threatening to slay Lily, but afterward, she wouldn't let Penworth waltz out. Didn't he realize they were both in danger?

He sat as Esther had demanded. Esther had brought paper, ink jar, and pen, and she'd previously laid them out for him. He picked up the ink jar, nonchalantly twirling it in his hand, but he didn't dip the quill.

"By any chance, Esther," he said, "were you responsible for the explosion in Scotland that ended the rescue effort?"

"What makes you ask?" Esther sneered.

Penworth gestured to the pistol. "It's recently occurred to me that *you*—rather than Edward—might have been the culprit."

"You always had it out for him."

"Should I take that as a yes? Did you blow up the tunnel so I would perish?"

"What if I did? If not for your mother, Edward would have been earl. Not you. I'm entitled to some revenge."

"I never would have guessed it was you," Penworth said. "Now then, what would you like me to write? Could we please get on with it? I had my driver wait, and he's blocking the street. I need to be going."

"Don't tarry on my account," Lily tightly retorted.

"I won't." He flashed a supercilious smile.

"Begin with this salutation," Esther instructed. "'My dearest brother.'"

Penworth dunked the quill and penned what she'd ordered.

"Then what?" he inquired.

"Add this: 'I've finally heard from Miss Lambert. It's as I suspected. She advises me she's pregnant, and—'"

"What?"

Penworth whipped around and glared at Lily. His arrogant gaze went to her stomach, and he smirked.

"It's not possible, Esther. She and I may have had intimate relations, but she's a bit of a doxy. A man must empty himself in a woman's womb to plant a seed. I had a few other options with her."

Lily sputtered with outrage.

He was denying her? He was denying the child he might have sired? Why not simply call her a harlot and be done with it?

"Of all the dirty, rotten, low-down, despicable—"

Lily struggled against the bindings, trying to loosen them so she could escape and beat him to a pulp.

"Finish the sentence," Esther commanded over Lily's litany of invectives. "Put this down: 'She advises me she's pregnant, and she's blackmailing me.'"

He fussed with the quill, but didn't write the words. Instead, he held up the jar and peered into the opening.

"What now?" Esther seethed.

"The ink is dried out."

"For pity's sake!" Esther angrily brandished the gun so it was pointed away from Lily's neck. "Why can't anything go as I planned? Can't you—"

Esther hadn't fully aired her complaint when he hurled the jar at her. The ink wasn't dried out, after all. It was runny and very, very wet. The black liquid splashed across her eyes, the jar itself thumping on her forehead.

She screeched and ducked, but not swiftly enough. Temporarily blinded, she staggered back.

Quick as a snake, Penworth leapt to his feet. With one hand, he snatched the pistol from her. With the other, he punched her, and she crumpled to the floor in an unconscious heap.

He stood, frowning down at her, rubbing his knuckles, his breathing barely elevated.

"I've never hit a woman before," he muttered.

"It seemed like a good time to start," Lily replied.

"It certainly did." He wrenched his focus from Esther to Lily. "Are you all right?"

"Yes."

After checking that Esther hadn't stirred, he laid the gun on the table and untied Lily's bindings. The final one fell away, and she jumped from the chair as if it was on fire.

"I won't ask," he scolded, "how you landed yourself in this mess."

"You wouldn't believe me if I told you."

"Yes, I would. It's dawned on me that trouble follows you like a magnet to metal."

"Only since I met you. I used to have a very ordinary, very dull life."

He grinned and extended his hand. "Let's go."

"Where?"

"Home."

"What?"

He'd insulted her, had practically claimed she was a whore, had just broken her heart all over again, and he assumed she'd go home with him? He thought she'd blithely agree?

The man was insane.

"I don't want to go anywhere with you."

"Don't be ridiculous. Of course you're coming."

"No."

"Yes."

He stepped in until they were toe-to-toe, and he loomed over her.

"I've had enough of your antics," he said.

"*My* antics! I was kidnapped by a crazy woman. How is that my fault?"

"You left Scotland without a good-bye. You never wrote to me. You never gave me the slightest hint of where you might be or how I could find you."

"It never occurred to me that you would be concerned. Weren't you the one who made me leave?"

"I was not!"

Esther had bragged that it was all her doing, that John had played no part in Lily's abrupt departure from the castle. Had Esther been telling the truth?

"You didn't want my presence upsetting Lady Violet."

"Who told you that?"

He looked furious over her accusation, and Lily hesitated, scowling over at Esther.

"Ah . . . her?"

"You believed her?"

"She was so convincing."

He snorted with disgust. "Have you any idea of how worried I've been?"

"I just heard you talking to Esther. You didn't sound very worried."

"Lily"—his exasperation was clear—"we will walk down to my carriage and head for home. You may accompany me of your own volition, or I will toss you over my shoulder and haul you out like a sack of flour." He raised a haughty brow. "Which is it to be?"

She knew him well. He didn't make idle threats, and he wouldn't take no for an answer. She could refuse and quarrel, or she could do as he bid her.

If she declined his offer, what was her alternative? She wasn't about to stay in the room until Esther awakened. The rent was only paid for two more days, and then, she'd be out on the streets.

He might not care for her. He might have simply dallied with her for carnal purposes. He might have proved himself to be a callous cad, but at the moment, a week spent at his London town house would be like a gift from Heaven.

"I'll go," she grouched, "but when we arrive, you and I have a few matters to discuss."

"Yes, we do, but let's get out of here first."

He grabbed the gun, then led her to the door. At the last second, she glanced back at Esther who was still out cold.

"What about her?" Lily asked. "Shouldn't we do something?"

"I'll send her son to fetch her. Let him deal with her for once; I'm tired of it."

Lily chuckled, and they hurried out together.

Chapter 25

&

"WILL you marry me?"

"What did you say?"

"Will you marry me?"

John smiled at Lily. They were in a downstairs parlor, having recently returned from the boardinghouse where he'd knocked Esther senseless. Lily had been unusually quiet on the ride. She'd sat on the opposite seat in the carriage and stared out the window, but his proposal would cheer her up in a hurry.

He'd retrieved from the safe a ring that would serve as an engagement ring until he could have one specially designed for her. He took her hand, ready to slip it on the moment she said yes. He was excited to see it on her finger, excited to have the whole world know she was his.

"No," she suddenly blurted out, "I most certainly won't." She yanked away and walked across the room.

"What?" he gasped.

"I won't marry you. Don't be ridiculous. It's out of the question."

"Out of the question," he muttered like an imbecile. "May I ask why?"

"Because you're John Middleton, Earl of Penworth, and I'm Lily Lambert."

"What has that to do with anything?"

She gaped with shock. "Are you mad?"

"No."

"Then in the months since I last saw you, you must have had your wits addled."

"Why would you think that?"

"You're babbling like a lunatic." She started for the door.

"Where are you going?" he demanded.

"I need to locate the housekeeper and find out what bedchamber has been assigned to me. I'm exhausted, and I'd like to lie down."

He leapt into the threshold, blocking her way so she couldn't step into the hall.

"You don't have my permission to leave."

"Oh, for pity's sake," she grumbled. "I'm too fatigued to put up with your high-handed manner, and I won't beg as if I'm a peasant currying your favor."

Completely perplexed, he frowned. It had never occurred to him that she might not wish to wed him.

Every female in the kingdom would give her right arm to be in Lily's shoes. Didn't she comprehend how lucky she was? She ought to be glad! She ought to be down on her knees and thanking him!

His temper sparked. "You will not refuse me. Cease your theatrics."

"What *theatrics* would those be?"

"As you mentioned, I am Earl of Penworth. I have presented you with a marvelous opportunity. I've proposed, and you will accept."

"Aren't you the same man who always lectures about status and rank?"

"Well, yes, but I've changed."

"Really?" Her incredulity was blatant and annoying.

"Yes."

"You're telling me that—practically overnight—your opinions have been altered. You're totally unconcerned about background or heritage. It doesn't matter to you in the slightest."

"No."

She studied him, her gaze intense and bewildering. "I don't believe you," she said.

"You . . . you don't what?"

At being confronted by her obstinacy, he couldn't muster a coherent thought.

He had changed. He had!

After his experiences with Esther and Edward, with Violet and Barbara, his focus had been transformed. Rank was an idiotic measure by which to judge a person, and his arrogance on the subject was at an end.

He'd been on pins and needles, eager to share his new insights with her. He felt reborn, as if a terrible weight had been lifted from his shoulders. She knew him better than anyone. How could she not see the difference?

"I love you," he declared.

"You do not."

"I do!"

"You're embarrassing me. Please stop."

She pushed by him, and he was so stunned that he let her go. He assumed she'd realize she was being foolish, that she'd halt and give him the answer he sought, but she didn't.

"Lily!" he snapped, aggravated in the extreme.

She whipped around. "What?"

"We are not finished discussing this."

"Yes, we are. I've told you before that I plan to wed a husband who loves me, who's proud to have me."

"I love you!" he shouted. "And I'll always be proud of you."

"Was I—or was I not—just with you when you denied me over and over to your stepmother?"

"I was toying with her, trying to get her to let her guard down so she didn't murder you. I didn't mean what I said."

"You claim that now, but if I relent and marry you, I can predict exactly how I'll end up."

"How is that?"

"I know your kind. I've worked for you people all my life."

"My *kind*?" He'd never been so thoroughly insulted.

"You're snobs. Currently, you're suffering from some ludicrous bohemian notion about lowering yourself through matrimony. I haven't a clue as to why. Perhaps you're wracked with guilt over ruining me. Or perhaps it's simply a cavalier whim. Whatever is driving you, you'll get over it."

"You don't think I'm sincere?"

"I'm sure you're not. If I accept, it will soon dawn on you that you made a mistake, and then where will I be? I won't place myself in such an untenable position."

She stormed off, and he loitered in the hall, feeling as if she'd ripped out his heart and stomped on it.

Footsteps sounded behind him, and he glanced over to see Barbara approaching.

On noting his baffled expression, she asked, "What's wrong?"

"I proposed to Lily, and she said no."

"She refused you?"

"Yes."

"Did she inform you as to why?"

"She wants to marry for love, and she insists I'm a snob who would never genuinely care for her."

"She said that to you?"

"Yes."

Barbara laughed. "Ooh, I like this girl. I really, really like her." She gave him a commiserating pat on the shoulder and walked on.

"Do you, Edward, take Miranda to be your lawfully wedded wife?"

Edward didn't reply, and Miranda peeked up at him, an evil grin on her rosebud lips.

John whacked him on the back, the force of the clout hard enough that he stumbled forward and jostled the vicar. Since it was a man Edward didn't know and had never previously met, he didn't apologize.

The fellow was drunk anyway, and John had bribed him. Edward wasn't even certain he was actually a minister.

"Say, 'I do,'" John commanded.

Edward whirled to face him. "Can we talk about this?"

"We already have."

"Please?"

"No."

"Don't go through with it," Esther barked from behind them. "This isn't the Middle Ages. Even this stupid oaf"— she rudely gestured at the vicar—"wouldn't dare coerce you into it."

"Mother, be silent!" Edward growled.

"Yes, Esther," John concurred, "be silent or I'll gag you, too."

Her hands were tied, courtesy of John, who'd declined to come within a hundred yards of her unless she was fettered.

Edward was twenty-seven years old, and he'd always been a dutiful son. He had respected and honored his mother, only to learn that she was mad as a hatter. It was a terrible blow, and he still wasn't sure how to deal with her.

Captain Bramwell butted in. "Could we finish this? The tide's about to turn, and we'll need to make way."

They were on Bramwell's ship, anchored out on the Thames. Edward and Esther were bound for Boston, but they might have been flitting off to the moon. The locale was that remote and exotic.

John had given him a choice: marry Miranda and sail off to a new land, or stay in England to be beggared while watching his mother hang for the attempted murder of a peer of the realm.

"I won't be quiet!" Esther fumed.

To Edward's stunned surprise, John grabbed a kerchief from his coat and stuffed it in Esther's mouth. The twins giggled. The assembled sailors looked the other way, pretending to see nothing.

"I've had about all of you I can stand," John told her. She choked and sputtered with rage, but he ignored her and spoke to Edward. "What's it to be, dearest brother? Will you say *I do*? Or shall we go back to shore so I can file legal proceedings against you and your mother?"

"You're being cruel," Edward seethed.

"Yes. Deliberately so."

"You always hated me."

"I never did. I merely wanted you to grow up and take responsibility for your actions."

"At least let Mother remain in England. She doesn't wish to go."

"She's a menace, and she's proven herself to be dangerous. I won't have her in the same country as me."

Esther was stamping her foot, malice in her gaze, as she tried to get John's attention. When that didn't work, she lunged toward him. Not that he had to fear her.

He had brought two burly footmen as bodyguards. They'd wrestled her—manacled—into the longboat, then hauled her up onto the ship like a bucket of potatoes. The brawny pair kept themselves between her and John, and they easily held her at bay.

Edward frowned at her, at the twins who were both traveling with him, at his mother again.

What a pitiful group! The voyage would be lengthy and tedious, and after they arrived in Boston, life would be no better.

How could John be so callous? How could Edward sway him?

"Give me another chance, John."

"I'm counting to ten," John replied. "If I haven't heard the words *I do* come out of your mouth, I will assume you refuse to continue, and I will proceed accordingly."

John paused, then began. "One, two, three . . ."

Edward was boxed in, out of options. He wasn't about to dawdle in London as John humiliated him to the entire world. Nor could he allow Esther to be prosecuted. Edward wasn't particularly fond of her, but he wasn't such an ingrate that he'd throw her to the wolves, either.

"The twins plan to kill me," he hissed at John, "once they have their dowry. I'm convinced of it. Don't you care?"

"They won't kill you," John scoffed.

"They will!"

"If anything ever happens to you, I'll hunt them down and make them pay. Do you understand me, Miranda?"

He and Miranda shared a charged look, then Miranda clutched Edward's arm and simpered, "I have no idea what Edward is talking about."

"Your concerns are unfounded, Edward," John said. "Now, what is your decision?"

There was no hope for it. Edward had no friends or allies. He was shackling himself to a girl he detested and being forced out of England—with his crazed mother in tow.

Had any man in all of history ever suffered so hideously? Had any man in all of history ever been so despicably treated?

He spun to the vicar.

"I do."

With his capitulation voiced, the vicar raced through the vows, and Edward's fate was sealed.

Bramwell had mentioned that they would be sailing south, taking advantage of the prevailing winds and balmy temperatures. They would stop at some of the West Indian islands prior to heading up the American coast.

Perhaps Edward would be able to sneak away. He would flee the twins and his mother, would vanish into thin air and leave the three of them to their own devices. It would serve them right if they wound up together. Esther had displayed bloodthirsty tendencies, and the twins would meet their match in her.

"Good-bye, Edward," John said. "I'm sorry it had to end like this."

Unaffected by events, John shook hands all around, then he and his bodyguards started for the rail, eager to climb down to the longboat that would row them to shore.

"John!" Edward called, terrified by his departure. "Would you like me to write?"

"Wait a year or two, would you? Let my temper calm before I have to hear how you've settled in."

"You don't want to hear how I'm faring?"

"Not really."

It was the saddest remark ever, and Edward was on the verge of tears. Had John no feelings? Wouldn't he miss Edward? After all they'd meant to each other, how could he be so heartless?

John gave a jaunty salute, aimed at Bramwell, who returned it. Then, without another word, he clambered over the rail and disappeared.

Miranda leaned in and whispered, "Let's go below to our cabin and consummate the union." She glanced over at her sister. "You can come, too, to help me."

"Did you pack the riding crop?" Melanie asked. "He needs to be punished for being disrespectful to you."

Edward gulped with dismay as Miranda led him toward the hatch.

"I don't want to be here," Lily muttered.

"But I insist," Barbara responded. "If you are to be my social secretary, you must learn the names and faces of those with whom you'll be dealing."

"I'm not comfortable in this sort of company."

"Honestly, Lily, you sound as if I'm torturing you at the rack when I've simply requested that you join me at my supper party. Stop complaining. If I didn't know better, I'd imagine you were distressed at being in such close proximity to John."

"I won't deny it. I hate having to associate with him,

and in light of our lurid past, everyone is staring at me. I loathe being the center of attention."

"You'll get used to it."

"I doubt it."

"Why does John's presence upset you so much? If you're as indifferent as you claim, why would it matter that he's standing across the room? Just ignore him."

"I can't. He keeps looking at me."

"Don't look back." Barbara handed her a glass of wine, and oddly, she stirred the red liquid with her finger, as if mixing something into it. "Drink this," she ordered. "You're entirely too nervous. These people are John's friends and peers. I won't have them thinking I've hired a ninny."

Lily sipped the wine, finding it a tad sour, but she didn't protest. Barbara was watching her like a hawk, ready to pounce if Lily didn't down the contents, and Lily had to admit that a bit of alcohol would work wonders for her disposition.

Since she'd spurned Penworth's marriage proposal, she'd been prepared to vacate the premises, without having any idea where she intended to go. Barbara had intervened and given her a job.

Barbara was extremely busy with managing Penworth's affairs and serving as his hostess, and she'd needed a competent assistant. Lily probably should have refused the post, but Barbara had offered an exorbitant salary, plus a fine bedroom suite facing out over the rear garden.

The opportunity was too good to pass up, but when she'd accepted, she hadn't understood that Barbara would throw her into social situations with Penworth. Or that she would require Lily to dress as if she was a member of the exalted group.

Without her being informed, a wardrobe had been purchased. Her bedchamber was filled to overflowing with clothes and accessories. She'd attempted to decline the generous gift, but Barbara had scoffed at her reluctance.

Do you suppose, Barbara had scolded, *that you can be employed by me, the earl's mother, and gad about like a pauper? I won't have you embarrassing John in those old rags.*

So Lily was in the front drawing room, awaiting the butler's summons to supper, and she was so fashionably attired that she might have been a duke's daughter. Violet Howard could hardly have had a gown that would compete with Lily's, and she felt conspicuous and out of place, as if she was putting on airs.

Vividly, she recollected the consequences in Scotland when she'd tried to rise above her station, and she wouldn't behave so foolishly ever again.

She gazed about, assessing the dignitaries who were Penworth's acquaintances. His school chum, Jordan Winthrop, Viscount Redvers, was there, with his bride, Mary. Penworth's neighbor, Michael Seymour, Earl of Hastings, was there, too, with his bride, Jane. They were chatting with Jane's sister, Helen, who had just wed Captain Odell, the notorious mariner in whose Scottish house the Dudleys were living.

It was an illustrious crowd to which Lily didn't and could never belong, and she wanted to slink to her bedchamber and hide.

She'd been so wrapped up in her miserable rumination that she didn't notice she'd emptied her glass. Barbara provided a second, stirring it as she had the first.

"How was your wine?" she asked.

"Sour."

"Try this vintage. You'll like the taste a bit more."

"Is it hot in here?"

"No."

For some reason, Lily was very warm, and her senses were enlivened. Her pulse was elevated, her cheeks flushed. Colors were very bright; noises magnified. She could hear what everyone was saying, and they were talking about her and Penworth, as if they knew a secret she didn't.

"Lily, are you all right?" Barbara's grin was full of mischief.

"I'm dizzy. It must be the alcohol; I don't drink that much."

"Have some more."

Barbara tipped the glass to Lily's mouth, urging her to finish.

Gradually, she noted that people were going into the dining room. Had the butler called for them to enter? She couldn't remember.

Barbara clutched her arm and led her in. When they stepped inside, Penworth was seated at the head of the table. The other spots were taken, except for the one at the opposite end, where his countess would have sat—had he already wed his countess.

A footman pulled out the chair as if it was meant for Lily. Barbara shoved her into it before Lily could point out that there had been a mistake in the seating chart.

She stared past the bejeweled, beautiful women and the handsome, dynamic men to where Penworth was studying her with an inscrutable smile. He lifted his brandy, tipping it toward her as if making a private toast, then he downed the contents.

Lily frowned and furtively glanced at the guests, worried that they'd observed his inappropriate gesture, but no one had.

She was shaking, so she drank more of her wine. As she did, the strangest thing happened. The world faded away so she was peering down a tunnel at Penworth. There was no sound, no activity. Time had ceased its ticking.

"Look at what Mr. Dudley has arranged for us to see," he told her, but his lips didn't move.

Her frown increased. Had she heard his comment in her mind?

Slowly, her view shifted, and a myriad of occasions drifted by. She recognized that they were moments in her future with John. There was her wedding day, the birth of their first child, a son. A second son followed, then two girls.

The decades surged by, their children growing, having children of their own. She and John were elderly, still together and blissfully happy.

"It's exactly what you've always wanted." He spoke in her mind again. "Say you love me, and you can have your heart's desire."

"I love you," she mumbled.

At her voicing the declaration, the peculiar episode abruptly concluded, and she felt as if she was being sucked from the tunnel. She was falling and falling, and she landed—with no gracefulness at all—in a rumpled heap in her chair.

The guests gaped at her, and her cheeks heated with horror. She must have spouted aloud her improper affection for the earl. Ah! How humiliating!

The gossip about them had to stop, but if she insisted on making a public spectacle of herself, how would the scandal ever abate?

Penworth stood, and he tapped a spoon on a plate to get the crowd's attention. All eyes whipped from her to him.

"Most of you have known me since I was a boy"— there was a general nod of agreement around the table— "so you're aware of the changes I've weathered lately. I was engaged—then I wasn't." His friends laughed. "I finally had enough of Esther and Edward and sent them away." A smattering of applause rang out, evidence that the pair hadn't been liked. "My mother came back, which has been a huge pain in the rear."

"You're delighted I'm here," Barbara chided. "Don't you dare deny it."

"Yes, I'm delighted. Who could ever have imagined I would be?"

"Anyone who knows me could imagine it, you oaf."

"I've always been a stuffed shirt. I was the one in school who demanded we play by the rules. I was the one who wouldn't cheat at exams."

"You were an absolute boor about it," Lord Redvers teased.

"Yes, I was, because I was terrified that if I misbehaved, I might enjoy it too much. Esther often warned me that I carried too much of my mother's blood, and if I wasn't careful, I'd turn out just like her."

"Perish the thought." Barbara gave a mock shudder that produced hoots of glee.

"I never rocked a boat," Penworth continued, "or flouted a convention, and I was the biggest snob who ever lived. It was drilled into me that I was elevated above others simply because of who my father had been, but recently, I learned an interesting lesson."

"What is that?" Lady Hastings asked.

"I possess all of my mother's worst traits, and I'm sick of being cautious and doing the right thing. I'm ready to do a few things that are reckless and unexpected."

"Like what?" Mrs. Odell inquired.

"Just watch me."

He left his perch at the head of the table, and he started down the side, marching directly toward Lily. His gaze was locked on hers.

She blanched. What was he thinking? What was his intent?

She pushed back her chair, prepared to jump up and flee, but Barbara put a hand on her arm, halting her.

"Last summer," Penworth said, "I met Miss Lily Lambert. I hired her to work for me, and I quickly found that I couldn't resist her. I was determined to commence an affair, and I chased her till she caught me."

"I never had anything to do with him," Lily vehemently asserted.

"She's lying." He was practically preening over the illicit liaison. "She's pretty and smart and funny. And sexy as hell."

"Would you be silent?" she fumed.

He was getting closer and closer.

"We spent a delicious week trapped underground in the hot springs at Penworth Castle. Every bit of the salacious story is true."

"It is not!"

"The interval was extremely decadent. Let your imagination run wild, and our carnal encounter was somewhere far beyond that."

"Ssh! You're embarrassing me!"

"I haven't begun to embarrass you, my darling Lily."

He skirted the end of the table, and he swooped in and fell to his knees in front of her. She didn't like to have him so near. When she was around him, she couldn't control herself. He overwhelmed her good sense so that she made stupid decisions.

She leaned away, needing to have more space between them, but she couldn't escape.

"I am madly, passionately in love with her," he announced.

The men smirked, while the ladies sighed with romantic pleasure.

"No, he's not," Lily scoffed.

"Can you believe it? I tell her I love her, and she says I'm a lunatic. I propose marriage, and she tells me no."

"I bet she's the first woman who's ever refused you," Lord Redvers guffawed.

"I've told her that I changed, that I no longer care about lineage or heritage, so her status doesn't matter to me. I want her to be my bride, so I had to do something drastic, something so out of character she would see my words are sincere."

He reached into the pocket of his coat and withdrew the engagement ring he'd previously shown her. It was a beautiful piece of jewelry, with a huge emerald in the center, surrounded by tiny diamonds. The candles in the chandelier enhanced the color so it glowed. It was like a talisman, luring her in, tempting her to grab for it.

She started to tremble.

"This silly, silly female—" he began.

"Is there any other kind?" Captain Odell inquired, and his wife elbowed him in the ribs.

"This silly female thinks I don't love her, that if she weds me, I will grow weary with regret."

He'd been staring at the guests, and he turned to face her. He was smiling, warm affection shining in his eyes.

"So I have created a spectacle. I have stirred gossip and fomented rumor, for she knows me well and can affirm that there is nothing I detest more. Before all of you, my lifelong companions, I make a fool of myself. For her."

"Don't do this," she begged. "You don't want this. You *can't* want this."

"I am Earl of Penworth, Lily. How many times must I tell you that I can do whatever I wish?"

He slid the ring onto her finger, and the odd sensation swept over her again. The room faded until there was only him. Her heart swelled inside her chest till it seemed too large, as if it might burst out of her skin.

A hundred scenes flashed through her mind: their first meeting, their first kiss, their first carnal tryst. She remembered the splendid autumn she'd passed with him, how happy she'd been, how alive she'd felt.

Why had she let such strident sentiment slip away? Could she get it back?

"Lily," he murmured, yanking her from her riveting reverie, "I have a confession to make."

"What is it?"

"I bought a love potion from Mr. Dudley."

"You did?"

"My mother mixed it into your wine for me."

"No."

"Yes."

No wonder Lily felt so strange. One of Dudley's potions was raging in her veins.

"I bought one for myself, too," he claimed. "It was in the brandy I just finished."

"You're joking."

"No, I'm not," he said. "There are a few people here who have had their own experience with Dudley and his magic." He peered down the table. "How many of you ladies drank his Spinster's Cure?"

Lady Redvers and Mrs. Odell raised their hands, and they were grinning.

"Lily drank it, too—while staring at me. She actually did it twice. What are her chances of evading its power?"

"None," they agreed.

"What are *my* chances of evading the fate it set in motion for me?"

"None," they replied even louder, chuckling.

"Lily, on bended knee, before my mother and all of my friends, I ask you to marry me."

"Oh . . . oh . . ."

"I swear to you that I will always love you, that I will always keep and protect you, that I will be faithful and kind and loyal till my dying day." He took a deep breath, then swallowed. "Will you have me?"

"You mean it. You're serious." She was shaking so violently that she could hardly stay seated in her chair.

"Of course I'm serious. Do you think I go around proposing to women at the drop of a hat?"

"Well, you were betrothed to someone else just last month."

The room exploded with peals of laughter.

"A minor mistake on my part."

"It certainly was."

"Say yes, Lily," he urged. "Make our dreams come true."

She gazed at him, then at Barbara, then down the table, settling on each person, one by one. These were the people who knew him best. They were nodding encouragement, as if they had specifically joined with him, a phalanx of family and friends standing as witnesses to his promise and guarantors to his pledge.

How could she refuse to believe him? How could she rebuff him again?

"I . . . I love you," she shyly divulged, embarrassed to have so many others listening in.

"You finally admit it, you scamp!" He leaned in and stole a wild, torrid kiss that had the onlookers clapping and exclaiming. "Don't be afraid. Say yes."

"I'm not afraid." Tears flooded her eyes.

"Trust me, Lily. Take a chance. Do it for me. Do it for yourself."

The weight of the ring felt heavy on her finger, and after they had watched him put it on, she could never remove it.

"I want it all," she murmured. "I want it so badly."

"And you shall have it."

"I've always been alone."

"I know you have."

"I've had to work and struggle and toil."

"Never again."

"I want to belong somewhere. It's all I've ever wanted. I want a home of my own and children to mother. Will you give them to me?"

"Yes, Lily, I will give them to you." He rested a palm on her stomach, his quiet confirmation that he suspected they'd already started the family she craved.

"Then yes, John Middleton, I will marry you."

There was a shocked pause.

"Do you mean it?"

"Yes, I mean it."

"With me it's forever. If you can't abide your life with me, I won't allow you to flit off like my mother did."

Barbara snorted, as Lily smiled and said, "Why would I ever go? I have everything I need right here with you."

Epilogue

❧

"WHERE will you go?"

"I haven't decided."

Phillip gazed at Miss Lambert, then stopped to correct himself. She was now Countess of Penworth, but he was having trouble getting used to the appellation.

The hell with it, he mused. She'd always been Miss Lambert to him, and she always would be. It seemed wrong to stick such a fancy label on her.

"How about your sister?" she asked. "Will she stay in Scotland?"

"Yes, she's content to remain, and it doesn't appear as if Captain Odell will return anytime soon to kick her out of his house."

"Will you travel north to live with her again?"

He stared at the sky as if he could see Scotland, as if he could see Clarinda smiling and waving.

"No, I won't go back."

"How will you occupy yourself?"

"I have no idea."

"Why do I assume you'll find some mischief?"

"I have a knack for it, don't I?"

"You surely do."

He pointed to her wedding band.

"I believe," he smirked, "someone owes me an apology. That would be you. Did I, or did I not, tell you he would marry you in the end?"

"Yes, you did, and I was an absolute churl to have doubted you."

He chuckled. "I love to be proved right. Say thank you."

"Thank you."

"You're welcome."

She clucked her tongue in disgust. "You're a vain beast. Much like my husband, but I like you both anyway."

She rose on tiptoe and kissed him on the cheek, which made him feel absurdly glad.

They were by his peddler's wagon, the rear doors propped wide to display his bottles and jars. During his sojourn in Scotland, he'd stored it in a shed, and with his being back in England, he'd pulled it out and cleaned it up, but it didn't hold the thrill it previously had.

Perhaps, at age thirty, he was finally growing up and becoming interested in honest endeavors. Or perhaps—without Clarinda by his side—his chosen profession no longer appealed.

He had no desire to seek out new customers, to hawk his wares or mix batches of potion. He was restless, chomping at the bit to be on the road. But to where?

He had no home; he didn't belong anywhere and never had. Where would he go, and once he arrived, what would he do?

Penworth's carriage was parked down the street. The door opened, and he climbed out.

"Lily," Penworth said, "I'm sorry, but we need to depart."

"Duty calls," she told Phillip. "We're off to Penworth Hall, his family seat in the country, so I can be formally introduced to the servants and tenants."

"My little countess," Phillip teased. "How are you enjoying yourself?"

"I'm so happy, Dudley."

"And I am so delighted for you."

He escorted her over to her husband, and Penworth helped her into the carriage.

He and Penworth didn't like each other very much. It was difficult to move beyond the night when Penworth had caught Phillip and Barbara in bed together. But as a favor to Penworth's wife and mother—whom they both adored—they could manage not to bicker.

"Take care of her, Penworth," Phillip insisted. "If you don't, you'll answer to me."

"It will never be necessary, Dudley. Lily is my rock and my foundation. She always will be."

Penworth hoisted himself in, and a footman shut the door. Miss Lambert leaned out the window, and Phillip clasped her hand.

"I'll worry about you," she said.

"I'll be fine."

"Write to me when you can."

"I will."

He'd never had a person with whom to correspond, and he was pitifully flattered that she'd suggested it.

"I have to keep Barbara apprised of your antics," Miss Lambert explained. "She'll want to know where you are and what you're doing."

"Well then, I'll definitely be sure to stay in touch."

A silence ensued, and suddenly, they were both ridiculously maudlin.

"Let me hear your French accent," Miss Lambert said.

"Let me hear it one last time."

"*Au revoir, mon amie.*"

"Good-bye."

"Ah, *chérie,* have a grand life."

"I intend to."

Phillip kissed her knuckles, and the intimacy was too

much for Penworth. He rapped on the roof, and the carriage lurched away. Miss Lambert waved until they were far in the distance and Phillip could no longer see her.

He nodded his farewell, pleased with himself and the conclusion he'd wrought, and then he turned to his wagon.

The placard painted on the side made him snort with amusement. He claimed to sell a bit of everything: Love Potions! Invigorating Tonics! The Latest Therapies Known to Man & Science! The list went on and on.

People were so damned gullible, so lonely and easily swayed.

Don't forget the spinsters you've cured, he reflected to himself. *If you don't believe me, just ask Lily Lambert.*

He puttered around, fussing with the display, rearranging the jars, but his heart wasn't in it.

Ultimately, an acquaintance arrived, a fellow for whom he'd been waiting. After a brief discussion, they settled on a price for the wagon, the horse, and all the merchandise. Money was exchanged, and there was no reason to linger. He peered down the street. Where to go? What to do?

He picked a direction and started off, but at the last second, he went back. He grabbed a few vials of love potion, of his Spinster's Cure, and a bottle of his Woman's Daily Remedy.

"You never know when one of these might come in handy," he advised his friend.

He spun and walked on.